THE GODDESS WORLDWEAVER

Book Three of the Seven Circles Trilogy

Douglas Niles

ACE BOOKS, NEW YORK

If you purchased this book without a cover, you should be aware that this book is stolen property. It was reported as "unsold and destroyed" to the publisher, and neither the author nor the publisher has received any payment for this "stripped book."

This is a work of fiction. Names, characters, places, and incidents either are the product of the author's imagination or are used fictitiously, and any resemblance to actual persons, living or dead, business establishments, events, or locales is entirely coincidental.

THE GODDESS WORLDWEAVER

An Ace Book / published by arrangement with
the author

PRINTING HISTORY
Ace trade paperback edition / March 2003
Ace mass-market edition / February 2004

Copyright © 2003 by Douglas Niles.
Cover art by Jean Pierre Targete.
Cover design by Rita Frangie.

All rights reserved.
This book, or parts thereof, may not be reproduced in any form without permission. The scanning, uploading, and distribution of this book via the Internet or via any other means without the permission of the publisher is illegal and punishable by law. Please purchase only authorized electronic editions, and do not participate in or encourage electronic piracy of copyrighted materials. Your support of the author's rights is appreciated.

For information address: The Berkley Publishing Group,
a division of Penguin Group (USA) Inc.,
375 Hudson Street, New York, New York 10014.

ISBN: 0-441-01127-6

ACE®
Ace Books are published by The Berkley Publishing Group,
a division of Penguin Group (USA) Inc.,
375 Hudson Street, New York, New York 10014.
ACE and the "A" design
are trademarks belonging to Penguin Group (USA) Inc.

PRINTED IN THE UNITED STATES OF AMERICA
10 9 8 7 6 5 4 3 2 1

PRAISE FOR THE
SEVEN CIRCLES TRILOGY

Circle at Center

"Douglas Niles is a master at creating strange and unique fantasy realms that make readers believe in the unbelievable. *Circle at Center* is a special work with strong appeal to fantasy lovers."
                                        —*Midwest Book Review*

"Niles has again conceived a fantasy setting of great richness and scope . . . his fans are sure to enjoy this sprightly tale."
                                        —*Publishers Weekly*

World Fall

"In this second installment . . . Douglas Niles so eloquently describes each circle readers will have a vivid visual image of each land. Fans of Tolkien and Brooks will love this epic fantasy and eagerly await the next book in the series."
                                        —*Midwest Book Review*

"A fast-paced tale of epic adventure."   —*Library Journal*

PRAISE FOR THE
WATERSHED TRILOGY

"Douglas Niles and I worked on Dragonlance together. This book captures all the adventure and romance of Dragonlance."
                                        —*Margaret Weis*

"Absolutely nobody builds a more convincing fantasy realm than Doug Niles . . . The landscapes are sweeping and complete, and the various races are believable . . . new and exciting. The detailed pantheon of gods gives the readers a deeper and richer understanding and appreciation of the motivations of the characters. Any reader will come away from this book fully satisfied."
            — R. A. Salvatore, bestselling author of *The Demon Awakens*

"Douglas Niles . . . writes so well that his characters come to life after only a few lines . . . This middle book . . . keeps the trilogy moving."   —*Starlog*

To Christine, forever

Shout the names of God,
Hail the gods of fame;

Cry the yell of war,
And mute the call of blame.

Heed the ancient creed,
Scorn the one falls lame,

Raise the warrior's sword,
To slay begets the same.

FROM THE TAPESTRY OF THE WORLDWEAVER
Bloom of Entropy

Prologue

There was a thing he hated most, hated more than the machine guns and the gas and the stink and the death; that thing he hated was the mud. He felt as though he had become a being made of soft, wet dirt. At first the mud had been like a layer of skin, heavy and cloaking and smothering, but by now it had seemed to seep into the very center of himself, so that his heart was a muscle of clotted clay, his lungs and limbs and head mere shapes of thick, viscous soil.

For the first weeks he had kept track of the days, and for the first months he had made an effort to distinguish individual weeks. Now that the years stretched into the third hot, humid summer, the months had blended into an indistinguishable morass, vaguely broken into seasons: in winter, the mud was cold. In summer, it was not so cold.

Intermittently, when the generals ordered the colonels to order the sergeants to lead the men out of the trenches, life in the mud was enlivened by the opportunity to die. Of course he went forward with the rest of them: his own regiment, drawn from the dairy-greened countryside of the south; and all the rest, boys and young men from London and Liverpool, Glasgow and Bristol, from Wales and Ireland and the craggy Highlands of the north. They rose in a mass, cheering and charging, rifles held before them, metal helmets like inverted dinner plates on their heads.

These brave men sallied from their muddy holes in a great rush, like a tide sweeping across a beach. They slogged across sticky ground, pressing through coils of barbed wire. They ran into the streaming fire of machine guns, the water-cooled darlings of Maxim, guns that stitched the air with streams of whistling lead, weaving a pattern of deadly intricacy. The bullets were tiny and seemingly insignificant things when compared to the mass and complexity of a man, but they flew very fast, and when they encountered flesh they still flew very fast and left the flesh and the vessels and the bodies torn and bleeding from their passage.

He knew the ways of bullets. Over the course of 1914 and 1915 he had charged into that tapestry of death on many occasions, and he had seen many of the boys from Kent torn by the lethal weavers. Some of them had been his friends, and more than one had died in his arms. During those years he had looked upon fields of carnage such as he could never have imagined. He had smelled the deadly whiff of phosgene gas, heard the rumbling growl of engines as aircraft snarled over the battlefields. He made new friends to replace those who were slain, but he kept these at a distance, and when they died it was not so painful . . . for him, at least. He knew there would always be the tears, shed in the cottages of the verdant country-side. But on the dark battlefield he had moved beyond any awareness of grief.

There was only the mud.

He lost count of the dead comrades, just as he lost count of the days and weeks and months during which he had lived this nightmare. A part of him was conscious of the horror, but he always told himself that it would get better, that it would—it *must*—soon come to an end. The greatest nations in Europe had been bashing each other bloody for two years by now; surely they were running out of will, out of steel and powder. At least they must be exhausting their supplies of young men.

His regiment came into the lines along the Somme during a time when the mud was not so cold; his colonel would have told him that it was late June, in the Year of our Lord, 1916. His captain was fond of the Lord and never failed to take advantage of an opportunity to remind his men that He was with them, with them in the trenches, with them when they rose from the dirt to scramble again into the bloody loom of the machine-gunning-weavers, with them as their flesh was torn and their blood scattered across the field, wet and slick to make a very precious kind of mud.

And the colonel proclaimed with great certainty that the Lord was with them after that, as well.

A period of a week or so passed while he lay in the trenches at the Somme. Guns pounded incessantly, a massive bombardment that continued for a very long time. Any of the officers could have told him that the barrage lasted for seven days, but he was beyond caring about such details. He merely lay in the mud with his comrades and waited.

Finally the big guns fell silent, and the order came to the men along many miles of trenches, the men of the British Third and Fourth Armies. In unison and in bravery they rose from the mud, crawled from their trenches, and hurled themselves against the German weavers who waited with machine guns ready, prepared as ever to sew their deadly fabric.

Of course, the brave men of England never had a chance. Courage and fortitude and comradeship and resolve meant nothing to those little bits of lead hurtling just above the ground. The enemy gunners were patient and skilled, and the friendly generals had no concept of any other way to make war. They could only send their men, the future and the promise—the very lifeblood—of their country, forward to perish in the hail.

In that storm he saw his sergeant fall, legs torn from that stocky wrestler's body by the ripping scythe of a water-cooled machine gun. More bullets flew, a tempest as engulfing as any winter storm. Blood splashed his skin as the man beside him died, and then he stumbled on the sticky ground, feeling the weight of age and war and mud drag him down, not knowing that his burden was heightened by the bits of metal that had already ripped through his flesh. He tumbled onto his face, and still he did not know that he had been shot, that each pulse of his heart sent precious blood spurting from the great gash in his side.

He lifted his head, saw a vista of wire and smoke . . . and then his face again lay in the mud. It was soft, now . . . really, it had at last become a part of him . . . his flesh was this dirt and this dirt was his flesh. He thought of the Lord, that great friend of his colonel, and wondered if he would meet Him as his soul broke free to rise like smoke from the battlefield, borne in concert with the souls of twenty thousand Englishmen—twenty thousand on that day, in this place, alone.

But neither he nor any of the rest of them went to Heaven nor to Hell nor to any place that their captains or their mothers or their priests had described.

Instead, he found himself upon a death ship, sailing on the Worldsea, preparing for another war.

1

Armada

Tide of looming darkness,
Smoke and oil and blood,
Surging forth, engulfing,
Comes the lethal flood.

From *Days of Worldfall*
by Sirien Saramayd

The bastion loomed high on the culmination of a world. Three great mountain ranges, jagged ridgelines that dominated their realm of shadow and chill, encircled the fortress like walls on a cosmic scale.

Great plains that had once teemed with ghost armies were still now, the hordes long ago marched off to war. Cliffs loomed silent and forbidding, while ramparts and towers stood empty and dark. Even the stony gargoyle, the bestial giant poised atop one of the loftiest crests, guardian of the great citadel itself, seemed as lifeless as a statue, a mere image carved from rock.

Deep harbors, sheltered by wall and tower, guarded by lofty fortress and shallow boom, had once contained the hulls of countless warships. Those ships were gone, formed into a fleet that had sortied more than fifty years earlier, embarked on the invasion of an entirely different world.

But though the warriors were gone, their ruler Karlath-Fayd, called the Deathlord, remained. He sat in his great throne, the stone blasted from the very bedrock of his great mountain, and he remained as immobile as that stone.

His very self was invisible, his flesh a transparent veil. Only his eyes were there, glowing like embers, burning from the deep fire within.

Those mighty eyes remained open, the pupils fixed and staring from their perch at the far end of the cosmos. There were those upon the Fourth Circle, druids with their Tapestry and sages with their scrying globes and other magic, who looked upon the Deathlord, studied him for signs of movement and burgeoning danger. Those eyes, hellishly bright, were all that they could see. But still, they feared him.

For the Deathlord was waiting, and all knew that his patience was beyond measure.

THEY spread across the Worldsea in a legion of darkness, black ranks of sails and masts covering the ocean's surface to the far limits of the horizon. Shadows shifted and danced across the decks of the death ships, ghosts of past violence seething impatiently, anxious to reach the shore, to draw warmth and sustenance from a living, fertile world.

The cold hulls sliced the waters of the vast ocean, and wakes trailed behind each transom. These were not the frothy whitecaps that chased every normal ship, however. Instead, the track of a death ship was marked by a spreading V of toxic black, smeared like oil over the surface of the sea. Fish died in great numbers and floated to the surface, forming rafts of rotting, scaly flesh. Seabirds were emboldened by the plenty, but as they dipped and slashed at the wasting meat, they convulsed and fell from the sky, adding their own feathered carcasses to the vast swath of decay.

The ships seemed without number, viewed from the sky like blades of grass in a meadow. The vanguard was ten miles wide, a hundred ships with lofty sails and smoky pennants of shrouded black. Behind them came rank upon rank upon rank of additional fleets, each wider than the last, sweeping across the horizon in a seemingly endless progression.

They were watched from the sky by a pair of observers, one sitting astride and borne by the other. The mount was massive, scaly, and serpentine: a monstrous dragon with a wingspan long enough to encompass a playing field. The rider was a man perched at the base of the great wyrm's neck, his long black hair bound into a tail, his bronze skin smooth and stern. He wore a leather shirt and gloves, with a slender sword at his waist. Together they soared above the vast armada, looking at the long lines of ships, wondering at the assemblage of black-hulled vessels.

The dragon flew with relaxed grace, riding the sea winds with little effort of his mighty wings. The pair had made this reconnaissance countless times over the last five decades. At least once every interval, Natac and Regillix Avatar had flown forth to watch the ships of the armada in their seemingly endless progression around the world of Nayve. Their target seemed to be that realm at the center of the Worldsea, the nexus of all the Seven Circles, of everything, but for such a long time the ships had made no move toward shore.

So the watchers watched, and they waited. Long ago Natac had given up trying to count the ships. The pattern of lines was deceptively irregular, and even in the early years he had never been certain if his count was accurate. As time passed, and more and more black ships sailed from the Deathland to join the armada, he formed an impression only of numberless vastness. He carried this impression back to the Fourth Circle when his draconic steed, after a week or ten days of constant flight, was forced to return to land.

"As always, it seems there are more of them than ever before," said Regillix Avatar, turning his crocodilian head to regard his rider with one slitted, yellow green eye.

"Many more," Natac agreed. "Their numbers are swelling with fresh blood. . . . Miradel told me that twenty thousand men were slain in the first day of yet another great battle in the Seventh Circle."

"Surely they have enough strength to attack," the dragon snorted in exasperation. "Do they expect to bore us to death? Fifty-one years of waiting for a war!"

"I have a feeling we don't have much longer to wait," replied the man. "In fact, I've seen enough here. What do you say we get back and make our report?"

"I was going to suggest the same," said the dragon. "The course of the vanguard is still circular, but I detect a shift, as if they are moving toward shore."

Natac had noticed it, too, as if the fleet was preparing for a great change of course, the lines of the armada dressing themselves in preparation for a turn toward the coast of Nayve. They had waited for this maneuver for decades, but he knew that, when the death ships turned, the attack would follow swiftly.

"Let's go, then."

The dragon banked steeply, the man resting without fear in the deep niche between two of the serpent's neck plates. Long wing strokes bore them through the sky. Soon the air felt brighter, cleaner, as they passed beyond the fringe of the dark armada. A thin line of green marked landfall before them, and with a look at the sky, where the sun was just beginning to ascend toward Darken, they knew that they would reach the shoreline by full night.

Before them, the world of Nayve awaited.

Two figures slipped through the night, gliding past rocks that jutted like sentries from the mountainside. Steep, craggy summits rose on all sides, a fanged horizon clearly visible against the starlit sky. One of the shadowy forms dashed from a gully to crouch beside a looming boulder while the other remained still, watching and waiting. Fifty feet down the steep slope a stream washed through a rock-walled draw, silky and shimmering in the faint light.

Waiting for Juliay to join him, Jubal paused to watch a constellation move like a formation of geese, curling through the cosmos in the direction that was neither metal nor wood. The stars danced and hovered, then dropped from view behind the shoulder of a huge, pyramid-shaped mountain.

Even now, after five decades in the Fourth Circle, Jubal allowed himself to be surprised when he saw the stars moving around. More of the twinkling lights popped into view, a cluster rising in an equilateral triangle before speeding apart, evenly dispersed into the three directions. He was reminded of the fireworks that he had watched every Fourth of July when he was growing up in Virginia.

The memory was jarring and anachronistic. That world was gone . . . had been gone even before Jubal had fallen, pierced by Yankee bayonets above the banks of Appomattox Creek. Now, as a man who had spent sixty years in Nayve, time had passed with no failure of his joints, none of the withering of strength that inevitably accompanied mortal aging. He couldn't imagine what the world of short-lived humankind had come to.

Unlike Natac, who regularly examined every aspect of Earth's ongoing history and had been doing so for more than four hundred years, Jubal made little effort to remain familiar with the world of his birth. Of course, Juliay and the other druids saw the Seventh Circle with the Wool of Time, and they had told him of the great war that now raged, threatening to consume all of Europe. It irritated him that mankind seemed to have learned nothing from the monstrously destructive American war that had claimed Jubal's life—his *first* life, in any event—some fifty years ago.

The fact irritated him, but it didn't surprise him. From what Jubal had learned, it seemed that the British and French and German generals were making the same crude and unimaginative attempts at battle that had characterized so much of the conflict he had known as the War for Southern Independence. These obtuse leaders expended their men in fruitless charges, and the spirits of the dead only served to expand the enemy's fleet. At least Grant had learned his lesson at Cold Harbor. Would the same ever be said of the brutes who were methodically sending the young manhood of their respective nations into the meat grinder of trenches, machine guns, barbed wire?

It made him tired just thinking about it, and he couldn't afford fatigue. Now, here, he had important work to do.

Juliay joined him, moccasins silent as the shadow in which they both sought concealment. He felt her hand in his, and he was heartened again, ready for the task at hand.

"There is one Delver behind us, another pair across the river right here," she said, barely voicing the words, pointing to indicate location.

He nodded, saw the two dwarves, dark metal armor seeming to absorb the little starlight penetrating the narrow valley. Knowing the preternaturally keen hearing of his enemies, Jubal carefully shrugged the small crossbow from its sling across his shoulder, pointed to his quarry, and started to carefully move down the slope toward the stream. Juliay, in the meantime, backtracked toward the lone Delver on their side of the water.

Finding a boulder with a relatively flat top, Jubal stretched out on the crude platform and leveled his crossbow, the razor-edged dart of steel homed on the breastplate of the nearest dwarf. The water was near, no more than fifteen feet below, but still it slipped past with an eerie, nearly soundless rush. Over that faint hiss he heard a grunt, then a jarring clatter as of an armored body rolling down the hill; he knew that Juliay had done her job.

The two Delvers heard the noise, too, stiffening, then crouching in the shelter of a rocky outcrop. Julbal winced; he had lost his shot.

He remained steady, holding his bead on the place where the dwarves had vanished. In a few moments a light flared down the valley, Juliay setting off her coolfyre torch. Not wanting to impair his night vision, Jubal avoided even a glance at the source of the illumination, knowing that Juliay would likewise keep her eyes away from the night-bursting brilliance.

The diversion was enough to draw the two dwarves forward. Jubal could see the blank helmet plates, completely covering the cyeless faces as featureless as shadows. He was not fooled; bitter experience had proved that, since coming to Nayve, these dark-dwelling dwarves had somehow learned to see. How they did so remained a mystery. For this mission it was enough to know that they could be distracted and alarmed by a sudden light. Now, the duo of Delvers crept along the steep trail, each armed with a pair of multiple-bladed knives, attempting to sneak up on whoever was making this brightness.

Jubal aimed carefully and shot the first one, the dart

punching through the dwarf's side just below his upraised arm. The force of the missile knocked the stricken Delver to the side against the rising slope. The wounded dwarf kicked and tried to make a noise before he started to roll down toward the water.

The second spun around and dove for the shelter of the rocky outcrop. With a smooth gesture Jubal nocked in a second dart, brought up the weapon, then shot in a single, continuous motion. The dwarf was pierced in the guts and cried out pathetically as he, too, rolled down to the water. For a moment Jubal was reminded of Gettysburg, the dreadful stillness after he had joined Pickett's attack. One of his men had made a moan that sounded exactly like the cry of the dying dwarf. Mercifully, the noises ceased as the dwarf plunged beneath the surface of the stream.

Knowing he had no time to lose, Jubal jumped to his feet and hastened along the narrow valley, meeting Juliay as she descended to the water's edge, upstream of where all of the dead dwarves had fallen in. She kicked off her moccasins and buckskin leggings before wading into the waist-deep stream. In seconds Jubal had joined her.

They knew that Belynda Wysterian had chosen this spot with care, when the elfwoman had studied this valley in her Globe of Seeing. The water slowed and meandered here, the current's impetus diluted at a bulge in the channel. Since it did not form a natural eddy, it was not a perfect place for the imminent magic, but those imperfections explained why this locale was so lightly guarded. All of the true eddies, where the stream swirled of its own accord, were heavily guarded by Delvers and harpies. This mission was only possible because Jubal and Juliay had selected a poorly defended section of this unique and precious stream—the waters that Juliay herself had discovered fifty years ago.

Before the mission could be performed, they would

have to create a disruption in the flow, a curl in the river so that the water spun through a circle, forming a vortex to anchor the spell that the sage-enchantresses in Circle at Center were prepared to cast.

"How much time do we have?" whispered the man from Virginia.

"I reckon a half hour," Juliay replied. "We'd better get to work."

Jubal was already probing along the shore, where he found a bank of small boulders. Many of them were loose, and he hoisted one in both his hands, carrying it toward the middle of the meandering stream. He dropped it in place, and the druid added another to the pile.

Working quickly, the two humans pulled rocks from the shoreline and laid them on the streambed, raising a quasidam in a matter of a few minutes. They were gasping for breath and exhausted when they crawled from the water, but they could see that the flow, before continuing down the channel, now spun through a rapid, circular swirl.

Sitting down upon a flat-topped boulder, they watched, knowing they would not have long to wait. Jubal was not surprised to see faint illumination sparkle in the air—the aura of magic being cast at night. In the space of three or four heartbeats the brightness took on a humanlike, though overlarge, form. In the next instant the light was gone, replaced by the hulking shape of the giant, Rawknuckle Barefist.

Jubal was about to offer a greeting when the giant waved his hand and pointed up. "Harpies! Belynda spotted them in her Globe. They're diving at you right now!"

Instantly the man toppled onto his back, clacking another dart into the spring of his crossbow. Julay rolled behind the boulder, nocking an arrow and drawing back her bowstring. Rawknuckle, meanwhile, raised his massive battle axe and looked at the sky.

Jubal saw wings, huge and dirty gray, spread wide to slow the harpy's headlong dive. He fired at the darkness between those wings and heard the shriek of pain, proof that he had found his target. The filthy beast crashed into the water, vomiting oily bile that slicked the surface and hissed into flame when it contacted the air. More specks of fire appeared, spattering the ground around him, gobbets spat by flying harpies as two more swept past.

Rawknuckle cursed as one of the fiery globules thwacked onto his shoulder. He swung the axe, the attacker flying past just too high—but not beyond the reach of the crossbow. Jubal cracked off another shot, and the harpy fell with a crippled wing. The giant stalked over to the spitting, infuriated creature and whacked off the grotesque, vulturian head with one swift blow, while Juliay brought the last one down with a well-placed arrow.

"Any more?" asked the man, crossbow at the ready, eyes scanning the starlit sky.

"Belynda sent me ahead to tell you about those three," the giant replied, wiping his axe blade on the harpy's limp wing. "But there will be more on the way, you can bet, as soon as they know we're here."

"Let's move, then!" Juliay urged.

By then more lights swirled, a dancing pattern of sparkling brightness cycling around the whirling water. Tamarwind Trak appeared, the elf blinking slightly and shaking his head to get over the disorienting sensation of the teleport spell. Belynda came next, followed by the druids Cillia and Waranda. Last to arrive was the centaur, Galluper, who shook his mane of thick, dark hair and snorted anxiously. Six water casks were strapped, three on each side, across Galluper's sturdy, equine back.

The travelers went to work without any wasted motion,

each taking one of the casks and lowering it to the stream. The centaur paced on the bank above, a sturdy bow, with arrow ready, in his hands.

Jubal pulled the cork from his keg and held it in the stream, allowing the silky water to pour into the container. Around him the others were doing the same, maintaining the filling even as they cast anxious glances at the sky.

Juliay was the first to finish. She stood her cask up and slammed in the cork. Rawknuckle was there, and he picked up the heavy barrel as if it was nothing more than a full tankard of ale. Quickly he placed it against the centaur's flank, strapping it to the harness and then holding it while Jubal and Tamarwind lifted a second keg and suspended it on the opposite side of Galluper's pack.

The rest of the casks were filled by then and quickly strapped into place.

"Above!" cried the centaur suddenly. He leaned back and launched an arrow into the sky as several dirty white shapes winged from the darkness. More and more harpies swept downward, blocking out the stars as they wheeled overhead. "The rest'll dive any second now!" warned Galluper.

"There," said Jubal, smacking the last keg as Tamarwind lashed it into place.

"Here they come!" cried Rawknuckle, lifting his axe and snarling into the sky. Dozens of harpies, perhaps a hundred or more, plunged downward, shrieking hateful cries, gurgling as they prepared to spit their fiery sputum. Jubal took a shot, watched the dart disappear into the night as a haze of brightness, like a circle of fireflies, suddenly sparkled around them. This was magic at work, but it seemed to inspire the harpies to press home the attack with increased savagery and desperation.

Fire glared and spattered above as the harpies, sensing their prey's escape, spat their fireballs. But then Jubal felt the magic take hold, the powerful spell seeming to grab him by the guts and catapult him and his companions through space.

And then the harpies were gone, and he was staring up at the silver loom of the Goddess Worldweaver, rising gleaming and proud into the night above Circle at Center.

THEY called themselves by a bewildering array of names: regiments and legions, divisions and brigades, corps and armies, and impis and battalions. They were organized into columns and lines and companies, commanded by centurions and captains and consuls and colonels. For centuries they had marched to battle on foot or ridden horses and sailing vessels. More recently, on the Seventh Circle, they were borne by trains and trucks, by steamships, and even, occasionally, by frail, sputtering flying machines. They fought with swords, with muskets and carbines and machine guns and cannons. They laughed and cursed and shouted and cried.

But mostly, they died.

Miradel had been watching them die for a long time. For years she had spent much of her time in the temple at the Center of Everything, in this sacred chamber. Here she studied the Tapestry of the Worldweaver, observing the great saga of life and violence in all the worlds of the cosmos. Mostly, her studies had focused on the Seventh Circle, the world called Earth. Long ago, many hundreds of years ago, she had found the man she loved by studying the Tapestry, picking Natac's thread from the war-torn land that was now called Mexico.

More frequently, however, her research brought only a sense of dismay. She had watched the fate of Natac's homeland as Cortés and his conquistadores had brought those peoples to their knees. She had borne witness to other great wars, watched Napoleon march upon Moscow, then beheld the horrors of the American Civil War in excruciating detail. At the time she had thought that mankind's capacity for self-inflicted horror had reached its zenith. But now, in the muddy fields of Flanders and France, she saw an even greater holocaust taking place . . . and there was no end to the carnage in sight.

"A half a million men killed on the Somme . . . and the same number slain at Verdun, not a hundred miles away. This is a bloody year, indeed." The words, the familiar sense of the calm and detached observer, came from behind her.

Miradel sighed and looked up as the goddess herself came into the room. The immortal weaver brought a sense of lightness with her, such that the druid could see her even though the only source of illumination in the dark viewing chamber was a small candle.

"And they all go to the death ships, swelling the fleet of Karlath-Fayd," Miradel acknowledged. "But how long can it last? Will his numbers just continue to grow until they darken the seas?"

"I fear we shall soon learn the answer." The goddess frowned, lines of care etched into her cheeks and chin. She looked to be a stout human woman of unusual height, sturdy and square, with graying hair pulled back into a tight bun. She had a pair of wire-rimmed eyeglasses that she wore occasionally, and now she took these off and rubbed the bridge of her nose.

"I have selected more druids, another hundred, from the Seventh Circle. The Ceremony of Arrival will occur at tomorrow's Darken."

"All female?" Miradel didn't know why she asked the question—she knew the answer even before the goddess nodded serenely.

"With the waters that just arrived, we may be able to retrieve another sixty or seventy warriors."

Miradel was silent, feeling strangely melancholy, and the goddess concluded her thought. "We shall need them all, and very soon."

"How do you know . . . and what do you think we will learn?" The druid asked, frightened by the resigned acceptance she detected in this being of such great wisdom and power.

"You have only to look," replied the Worldweaver, gesturing to the candle, the tiny tufts of wool that were nearby, neatly arrayed on the table.

Hesitantly Miradel took up some of the threads, allowed them to drop into the flame. Her eyes were on the white-washed wall of the room, where now was displayed the image of the Deathlord's armada, hundreds upon hundreds of dark ships. She took a moment to scan the skies, seeking the familiar image of her lover and his proud, draconic steed, but there was no sign of him. Instead, the fleet drew all of her attention. The steaming and polluted wakes, the marks of tortured water left by each hull as it passed, were hooked now, unusually curved. Instantly the druid realized that the entire fleet was changing course, each ship making a wide, precise turn to port.

She drew back from the image. The goddess was proved right: the fleet, for the first time in sixty years, had made a dramatic change in course. The new bearing was shown as the shoreline came into view, the verdant fields and forests of Nayve.

The fleet of the Deathlord was making toward that shore. At last, after so many years of circling the Worldsea, the legions of the dead were advancing toward war, toward Nayve . . .

Toward the Center of Everything.

THE first thing Awfulbark did every morning when he woke up was to reach for his sword. Typically he did this as soon as first consciousness glimmered, before he was fully awake. Since he kept the blade razor sharp, this practice had resulted in numerous stabs and cuts to himself and his wife. On three occasions, in fact, he had cut his right foot off and then spent the next hour cursing as the limb painfully grew back.

But such was his pride in the gleaming steel weapon, a gift from General Natac himself, that the king of the trolls could not bear to have it out of his grasp. It was his most treasured possession.

Of course, it was his *only* possession as well. Really, it was the only possession among the whole tribe of forest trolls, the thousands of them living under Awfulbark's wise and beneficent leadership. They were exiled, in a fashion, for their ancestral home lay across Riven Deep. They had fled that home, an extensive forest of ancient oaks, when they had been attacked by harpies and dark dwarves from circles beyond Nayve. Their king had led them across Riven Deep on the bridge that once stood at Sharnhome, where they had joined humans and elves in the defense of the Fourth Circle. When the bridge had fallen, they had been stranded.

Though the humans and the elves maintained their diligence—the dark dwarves and harpies were still present and abundant across the gorge—the trolls had grown bored with the war within a few months after the battle at the bridge. Awfulbark had led them inland, and they had settled in another forest of ancient oaks interspersed with numerous apple and cherry groves. Many of the trolls spoke wistfully of happy times in their ancient capital city, Udderthud, but in truth Awfulbark understood that living in the New Forest was easier, offering better weather and much more abundant food, than existence in Udderthud had ever been.

So it was that the king of the trolls was a little bit fat and was feeling very lazy when he took up his sword and ambled through the tangled paths of his domain. He left his wife, Roodcleaver, snoozing under the widespread branches of the oak they had claimed as the royal abode. Her easy snores comforted him, for they reminded him that she was well fed and thus content.

He stopped to speak with several of his subjects and watched a few youngsters play vigorously at the timeless game called Squash the Raccoon. The object of the game's attention proved quite vigorous and would have escaped back to the wilds, but for the keen aim of a young troll's stone.

"Stones good," the king remarked, drawing a beaming smile to the youngster's toothy gash of a face. "But sword better. Remember that!" He flashed the blade and instantly—despite the fact that it had been years since he had amputated a child's limb—all the young trolls disappeared.

Shrugging, he continued on his way, failing to notice the shadow that crossed the sky, interrupting the beams of sunlight that spilled through the leafy canopy. Only when the troll king came to a clearing did he see the massive serpentine shape, the mighty wings pulsing down to send a gust of wind blasting between the trunks. Blinking the dust from his eyes, Awfulbark recognized Natac, the great general already dismounted from the dragon and striding toward him.

The king tried to think. He judged it unlikely that the man was coming to take back his sword; after all, Natac had bestowed it with great ceremony, in thanks for the troll's aid during the Battle of Sharnhome. There was a chance, a good chance, that he was returning now to ask

Awfulbark's assistance in some undoubtedly unpleasant and arduous task. This, thought the monarch of the New Forest, was a much more likely prospect. He considered fleeing, knowing that he had a very poor record of standing up to Natac's requests for assistance.

But there was a third possibility, and this kept him rooted in place: perhaps the man was coming to give him another gift. Of course, he couldn't see any likely-looking parcels, either on the man or his dragon, but hope was strong in the troll king, and so he clutched his sword and waited for Natac to reach the shade of the trees.

"Greetings, O King," said the man, making a formal bow. "I hope that life in the New Forest continues to suit you."

"Well, okay enough," said Awfulbark grudgingly. "Could wish for some good Udderthud caterpillars though, spice up these soft apples."

"Indeed. The foods we are raised with, those are the finest tastes," Natac acknowledged sympathetically. "How I longed for the taste of tart chocolate and chilis when I first arrived here."

The troll didn't know what the man was talking about but pretended to nod in understanding. It was then that Natac sprang his trap.

"I need your help," he said.

Awfulbark blinked and, with longing, thought of the winding forest trail, the route into shadow and obscurity that he had considered moments earlier, before it was too late. Now, there was no way he could refuse the man, not when the trolls were *needed*. It had never happened before he had met Natac and the other warrior, Jubal. Never had there been a time when the trolls were needed for something. The first time it had happened, Awfulbark had tried to resist. But now, there was no use.

"What we do now?" he asked.

"There is going to be another war," Natac said. "I need you to bring your trolls, everyone who is strong enough to fight, to the shore of the Blue Coral Sea."

2

The Order of the Druids

Yea, though I walk through the valley
Of the shadow of death,
I shall fear no evil,
For Thou art with me.

Psalm 23
Religious text of the Seventh Circle

Cholera came to Zanzibar in the spring, and by the middle of the sweltering summer Shandira had closed the eyes of countless babies, praying reverently over each shriveled little corpse. When she was not in the crowded sick house, she helped to burn the lifeless bodies of fever-parched adults, trying to stem the tide of the plague. She worked tirelessly, her strength an inspiration to everyone who saw her, but it was perhaps inevitable that at last the sickness would strike her, as well.

Even as the chills racked her long limbs and the sweat beaded upon her ebony skin, she continued her work, always wearing the stained robe that marked her as a Sister of Mercy. When at last she collapsed, she was given a pallet in her cell, and Father Ferdinand himself came to visit her. Solemnly he administered the last rites, and then he lingered for a moment, his hand, tender despite heavy calluses, gently holding her sticklike fingers.

"I remember when you first came to us," he said in his stilted Swahili, his eyes filling with tears. "A wide-eyed girl from the bush. You had the Holy Spirit in you then, my child, and your life has been a testament to that glory. I know that your reward shall be everlasting."

His words were a comfort to her in the days that followed, as she grew weaker. She could not eat, and water was little comfort. A fire seemed to burn within her, growing hotter with each passing night, until at last, inevitably, her very life was consumed.

It was then that Shandira's story began.

"My Holy Virgin Mother!" cried the woman, dropping to her knees before Miradel, pressing her forehead to the floor.

"I am not your mother, nor blessed," replied the druid, gently placing a hand on the smooth black shoulder. "But I hope you'll consider me a friend."

Shandira looked upward, her eyes wide as she stared past Miradel, into the verdancy of the garden. Fountains spumed softly, unseen but soothing, and pale sunlight filtered through the canopy of palm fronds as the sun descended toward Lighten. Slowly, the black woman lifted herself, kneeling proudly, then standing. Her cowl of tight, curly hair seemed immense to the druid, like the mane of a lion, and her naked physique of wiry muscle was a monument to physical perfection.

"Where am I?" she asked warily.

"You are in the garden of the Goddess Worldweaver," replied Miradel, extending a hand, gently leading Shandira to a nearby bench of carved marble. "You have been brought here by the goddess, as a reward for your hard work in the world you call Earth."

"But surely our Lord Jesus . . . ?" The woman who had spent a lifetime as a Christian nun hesitated, looking around further. "Is it delirium?" She said wonderingly. "I have seen that madness many times—but it is always a thing of fever and nightmares. Now I feel at peace, whole again."

She touched her flat, muscled stomach, felt the sinews of her thighs and the fullness of her breasts. "If this is delirium, may God forgive me—I welcome it!"

"It is not madness. It is real, and you have been brought here not only as reward but also because you are needed. Our world is in danger, and you . . . you and all the other women who come to the Fourth Circle now . . . you must help us."

"What do you ask of me?" Shandira asked, her dark eyes level and shrewd as she met the druid's gaze.

Miradel knew that the answer to this question would shock, even appall, the newcomer who, in her previous life, had steadfastly adhered to her vow of chastity. The druid demurred. "Let me show you the Grove," she said. "There you will learn the truth."

"THERE'S the bay," Natac said, slapping the great wyrm on the shoulder. Regillix Avatar had already spotted the crowded harbor, and now he tucked his wings slightly to drop them through a shallow dive. Wind howled past Natac's face, streaming his black hair behind him and bringing tears to his eyes until he ducked his face behind one of the dragon's bony neck plates.

Sheltered from the buffeting air as the great serpent picked up speed, the man looked past the chestnut scales of the mighty shoulder. Though his narrow vantage revealed only a fraction of the druid boats below, he could not help but take heart from the extent of the fleet that had gathered to meet the armada of Karlath-Fayd. More than a hundred slender hulls clustered on the placid water just within his narrow frame of view—and that was only a small fraction of Roland Boatwright's flotilla.

A few minutes later the dragon pulled up, then bounced to a landing on the grassy bluff that overlooked this natural, deep-water inlet on the wilds of the metal coast. Natac slid from his perch and walked to the edge of the steep slope. Fifty feet below, a strand of beach encircled a stretch of placid water protected by a range of rugged hills to the woodward side, and a rocky breakwater, constructed by druids, that arched out to close off the sea swells that surged in steadily from the direction of metal.

The harbor, which was nearly two miles long and half that in width, was crowded with small, sturdy sailboats. Natac knew from his earlier counts that there were well over a thousand vessels here, but the reality of the fleet was still enough to bring him up short. The watercraft were small by comparison to the looming bulk of the death ships, single-masted, opposed to the triple masts on each vessel of the invaders' fleet, but they were fast and nimble, with sleek, weighted keels. Each bore a shining steel spike jutting from the bow, a ram capable of tearing the planking out of a much larger ship.

A metallic battery glinted coldly above the ram on each boat, well forward of the single mast. Looking like an oversized crossbow mounted on a metal pivot, the weapon was based on a design invented by the dwarf Karkald. It could launch a spray of incendiary spheres at a nearby target or fire a single, heavy missile—a steel arrow dubbed a fire-bolt by the crews—that could fly for a thousand meters and still punch through a hull of thick planks. The sailboats, each of which was crewed by anywhere from four to eight sailors, had small cabins, protected by thin steel plate, and an armored cockpit where the druid who captained each vessel could windcast in some safety, while still getting a good view of the surroundings. Many employed human warriors, men drawn from earth in the spell of summoning, to man the batteries and otherwise fight.

"I don't know if we can stop them, but we can make them know they've been in a fight." Roland Boatwright had come up to Natac while he looked at the fleet, and now the druid—and master sailor—voiced the speculation that all the defenders of Nayve had trained themselves to believe. "Any new word from the sky?"

"If they hold course, they'll make shore about a hundred miles up the coast, metalward, from here," Natac replied. "You'll have to leave today, if you have any hope of intercepting them."

"We're ready," Roland declared. "My wing captains rowed in to the beach when we saw you coming. Do you want to give them a quick briefing?"

"Sure." Natac followed the druid down the narrow footpath that switched back and forth across the steep, grassy bluff. Sunlight sparkled on the waters, and the boats were gleaming, clean and freshly painted. He grimaced at a momentary image of marred perfection, the destruction and death that would decimate this picture by the time the battle was done. But there was no point in that worry. He reminded himself that this fleet had been gathered, this band of druids and warriors trained, with one purpose, and that purpose, that need, now came to fruition.

Many of the boats, he saw, were already hoisting anchor, each sail filling with its local, druid-cast gust of wind. A few of the craft were closer to shore, still idle, and a group of men and a few women were clustered around some small dinghies that had been pulled up onto the beach.

"Greetings, General Natac," said one, a hawk-faced man of medium height with an impressive nose and red bronze skin that was similar to Natac's in tone. "Have you the latest word on the enemy fleet dispositions?"

"We flew over them this morning, Crazy Horse," replied the Tlaxcalan. He embraced the Indian, former chief of the Sioux tribe, who had been brought to Nayve nearly forty years earlier. He felt the tension in the great leader and leaned back to look at him in the face.

"Once I thought my days of war were over," the Sioux warrior said grimly. "But now I stand ready to shed blood in a new cause. Once my men rode ponies and whipped Custer. . . ." He gestured to the boats. "Now we ride a different kind of steed, make a new kind of war," he declared.

"I am glad to have you leading a wing of the fleet," Natac said sincerely. "In all my studies of the Seventh Circle, I never observed a bolder warrior."

Next Natac turned to Richard Rudolph, a squat and dark-haired Englishman of unfailing strength and cheery disposition. He had been a sergeant-major in the British Army, an Earthly victim of the inept officers who had commanded him during the Zulu war of 1898. With his keen eye for enemy weakness and his affable and courageous disposition, he was much admired by his warriors and one of Nayve's most trusted commanders.

"We'll be sailing soon, I'm thinking," he remarked.

"Before Darken, if you can," Natac confirmed.

Richard clapped Natac's arm, an expression preferred to the more formal salute among the army of Nayve, then stepped aside to let Fritzi Koeppler join the circle.

Natac shook hands with the Prussian, the man he had known the longest of these three captains. In 1879 Fritzi had led a cavalry regiment into France, until, at Sedan, the men on horseback encountered the repeating fire of modern weaponry. As with Crazy Horse and Richard Rudolph, Fritzi had been brought to Nayve by the magic of a druid's seduction: the Spell of Summoning that lifted and bore the soul of a warrior to Nayve. Fritzi was an enormously capable soldier with a keen eye for detail. Like his fellow commanders from England and America, he had learned to fight on land, but in the decades of preparation since then he had become a master of nautical tactics. Though Roland Boatwright was in overall command of the druid fleet, Natac was immensely glad to have these three veteran warriors to oversee the three individual wings of the sailboat force.

"The death ships are spread out across a frontage of twenty miles, maybe more; they seemed to be dispersing as they moved toward shore," he explained.

"Does it look like they will land this side of Argentian?" asked Richard, who had extensively surveyed this section of coast over the last fifteen years.

"I'm guessing they'll make for the Blue Coral Arc," Natac replied, referring to a smooth shoreline about a hundred miles away. "There's lots of good beaches where they can come ashore, and the reefs will protect them from the worst of the ocean waves."

"Good guess," Richard concurred. "There's rougher land, rocky bluff and the like, beyond. Closer by there's a whole mess of swamp and sea marsh."

"Then we need to get there first, to stand in their way," declared the Prussian. "Perhaps we can hold them back from the shore." He didn't sound as if he believed the last part of his statement, but neither did he sound at all reluctant about making the attempt.

"Our best hope is to destroy a great part of their fleet and insure that the rest of them land in confusion," Natac confirmed. "Tamarwind's elves, ten thousand strong, are already arrayed along the shore, and Rawknuckle Barefist is making a forced march with almost as many giants. They have a full regiment of rolling batteries in support, nearly a thousand centaurs hauling them. The whole force will fall upon the first wave to land . . . or try to hold the line if too many of them reach shore."

"You really think they'll make it to the beaches?" Richard asked. "This is a mighty fleet we send against them!"

Natac nodded. "As mighty as any fleet on any of the seas of Earth, I agree. But you have not seen these death ships from the air, the way they cover the seas for miles in every direction. No matter how much damage you inflict—and I know that all of you will do brave deeds—you must be prepared to fall back before you can be enveloped."

The normally jovial Englishman looked at him seriously, his expression grim. "Aye, then, General, we'll do as you ask. What are your orders?"

"Fritzi, your wing is closest to the mouth of the harbor?"

"Already on the way, yes," replied the Prussian. He indicated a strapping druid, wrapped in the traditional turban of Earth's Persia. "Reza will have to cast a gale just so that I can catch up to them."

"He can do that, I know." Natac smiled at the dour windcaster, who had spent nearly a thousand years in Nayve. "So you will go first. Get in front of the death ships, use your weapons to hit from a distance, to scatter as many as you can. Stand and fight while you can, but then pull back. Richard, you bring your wing right behind. Engage as you close in, but also keep an escape route open for Fritzi's ships—I don't want them trapped against the shore."

"Aye, General . . . we'll char a few of those black hulls, you can bet."

"Crazy Horse," Natac continued, turning to the Sioux. "You'll come behind, in reserve. Give the battle time to develop. Regillix and I will be overhead, keeping an eye on things. When we give you the sign, you should sweep around their left with all of your strength."

"It shall be my honor, General Natac, to strike a blow for Nayve," replied the valiant warrior with a stiff bow.

Minutes later they were all headed back to the boats. Natac, from the top of the low bluff, watched the procession of sails exiting the harbor and allowed himself a glimmer of hope—hope that was quickly quashed by the memory of the numberless enemy they faced. Even so, he could only admire the bravery and dedication of these warriors, each of whom had been brought to Nayve for just this purpose, and who had accepted the grim task with a sense of honor and duty.

Nevertheless, the reality lingered in his mind as he mounted the dragon, and Regillix Avatar's broad wings carried them both into the air: honor and duty, bravery and dedication, these were great things.

But they would not be enough.

JANITHA reined in her pony at the brink of Riven Deep and looked across the wide canyon. She was just metalward of Sharnhome, where once the great bridge had stood. This was one of the narrowest places in the chasm that stretched for most of the way across Nayve, and she could just barely make out the monolithic shapes of the golems, the giants of iron that accompanied the Delver invasion of her homeland. Countless thousands of the eyeless dwarves were over there, too, she knew, even though they were too small to see at this distance.

The rest of her riders, the fierce cavalry of the Hyaccan elves, were nearby but remained out of sight behind a low rise just back from the rim of the canyon. She knew several were lying on the ground atop the elevation, worriedly watching their leader as she stood in mute challenge at the edge of Riven Deep. All of the elves were armed, and many would be mounted.

A dozen or so of the Hyac busied themselves making final adjustments to the intricate device that was the reason for Janitha's bold posing. That mechanism had been prepared by Karkald, Seer dwarf and master engineer; if all went well, it would be put to its first test, here today. Janitha knew that Karkald, exiled from his native First Circle for the last fifty years, was a renowned weapon smith. Even so, she would not have termed his most recent invention a weapon. More of a trap, she mused . . . one that would allow the elves to wield their existing weapons with greater lethality than ever before.

At least, that was the idea. Growing impatient, she prodded her pony into a prancing trot along the precipitous rim of Riven Deep. The vast gulf of space was purpled by mist and shadow, fading into a featureless murk that, as always, gave no indication of a bottom. On the other side of the canyon, her enemy waited and watched. She raised her feathered lance high, waving it back and forth in a rhythmic taunt, a gesture that would be visible for miles.

At last she was rewarded by the keening shrieks, outrage building among the keen-eyed harpies who spotted her impertinent promenade. Some of the winged creatures were circling over the deep, but she soon discerned a great cloud of them rising like angry smoke above the opposite edge of the canyon. Like the mist in the chasm, they were visible as a background shade—in this case murky gray.

But she knew the cloud was made up of thousands of individual and savage creatures.

"Good," she murmured, her hand tightening around the smooth horn she wore at her side. "Come to me . . . and die!"

She tugged the reins, and her pony halted, alert and quivering, anticipating the next command. After half a century of battling harpies, however, Janitha had come to know their ways, particularly the reckless impatience that propelled them when their quarry was in sight and apparently helpless. She watched and waited as they swarmed closer, and gradually the cloud of darkness resolved itself into individual, dark-winged flyers. The outraged cawing grew to a cacophony, like a field full of insanely chattering cicadas, and she brandished her lance and cried her own challenge, a shout that somehow carried into the mass of noise.

The harpies dived close, black and gray feathered wings shiny in the full sunlight. Janitha waited until she could discern the grotesque expression upon the skeletal, leering face of the leader. Talons reached toward the elf-woman, while a few of the flyers—impatient in the extreme—spat their fiery bile, only to have the smoldering gobbets tumble into the deep, trailing plumes of black smoke.

Only then did Janitha move, nudging her pony with her knees. The animal spun about and immediately burst into a full gallop toward the notched boulders atop the ridge that she had earlier marked as her destination. The elf-woman ducked low on her mount's neck, lance leveled beside her. She did not look back: she had planned her escape well, or she had waited too long; in either case, a glimpse of her approaching enemy was not going to affect her success one way or the other.

The ridge sloped upward, and the pony lowered his

head, surging with steady acceleration up the hill, then bursting through the narrow gap between the two rocks. Janitha smelled the stench of bile and smoke as the ringing of harpy cries seemed to compress her ears, and she silently urged the steed into a last burst of speed, the shouts of her warriors a welcome embrace. Arrows sliced through the air as a score of archers shot down the closest of her pursuers. She saw the flare of torches, then the brighter flash of light as Karkald's invention came into play.

Four rockets, their launchers evenly spaced along a line three hundred feet long, exploded upward, trailing plumes of fire and smoke, tugging the slender lines of a vast net behind. Arching high, crackling overhead with explosive speed as they dragged their webbed cargo across the sky, they tilted toward Riven Deep in unison. The net leaped upward and curled like some filmy, cosmic embrace. Finally the four fiery engines flamed out and the still-smoking rockets tumbled through the flock of harpies as they bore the end of the net downward.

Hundreds of the shrieking flyers thrashed and twisted as their momentum bore them into the mesh of silk. As the weight of the dead rockets plunged into Riven Deep, the net pulled countless harpies out of the air. The whole mass crashed to the ground in a flailing mass of wings, talons, and spitting, hateful faces. Some of the great flock of harpies were too high or too slow to get caught in the trap. Spooked by the sudden attack, many of them scattered. Others dived lower to attack and fell to the arrows of alert Hyaccan archers. Those caught in the net were already incinerating each other, so blind was their fury. They kicked and raised a furious cacophony, but they couldn't get free nor could they raise their heads enough to direct their fiery sputum at the grimly advancing elves.

Janitha dismounted and advanced, sword in her hand,

beside the closing ring of Hyac. Five minutes later, the last of the harpies had ceased its screaming.

"You want me to do that which I have never done—in the service of a goddess who profanes everything my life has meant? Surely you see that this is blasphemy, a desecration of my church and my Savior!"

Shandira glared at Miradel. The newly reborn druid was clad in a gown of white, now, and stood in the shade of the great Grove. She was tall, even statuesque, possessed of a dignity and pride that struck the elder druid as almost superhuman.

Miradel drew a breath and shook her head. "No one will make you do anything you do not wish to do. But you must understand that so much of what you learned during your life in the Seventh Circle is untrue. Mankind does not understand the reality of the cosmos or even guess at the existence of the first six Circles. You have been brought here as a reward for your labors and suffering upon Earth. You are a very special person; the goddess recognized that and bade me to bring you here. Think of Nayve as a place not so very different as the Christian heaven of which you were taught."

"How dare you make such a comparison! You bring me here so that I can seduce a warrior from that world and bring him here as well? Why did you not just bring the warrior, then, and allow me to go on to a mortal death? Perhaps you are wrong. How do you know that I wouldn't have gone to heaven, to a blessed rest with my immortal God?"

"Do you remember what I told you?" Miradel said, allowing her own tone to grow sharp. "I was born seven times on the Seventh Circle, each time to grow old and perish—sometimes violently, often suffering from hunger or great pain. There was neither heaven nor hell awaiting me, merely another birth, another chapter of life so that I could watch the extermination of my people. All that ended when the goddess brought me back to Nayve, in the year that much of your Earth numbers as 1864. *This* is real—this is your destiny, Shandira!"

"I, too, know about the extermination of people," retorted the black woman. "I have watched the Arabs and the English, the Portuguese and Belgians and Germans and French overrun Africa and divide it into their private fiefdoms. My grandfather was carried into slavery when my mother was but an infant. She had to sell herself to gain enough money to feed her children. She sent me to the convent on Zanzibar before my thirteenth birthday so that I would not share her fate. The priests were kind to me, and the church gave me a home and a promise that became my life. And I was devoted to that life."

"That devotion is part of your power! Think of your life as the good, the virtuous tale that it is!" Miradel pressed. "And know that not all acts done in the name of your god have been so benign. I have seen damage done by your church—I will tell you what was done to the Mayan people of Mexico, sometime, in the name of your pope and your god—but I also know that your faith is capable of goodness. It gave you a home and a purpose, and you did good works." Her tone grew soft again. "I watched you, in the Tapestry, as you tended to the inhabitants of your city, when the plague swept through every street and alley. You eased the suffering of countless people, even saved lives against unthinkable dangers. Now you are called upon to do new works—but believe me, they are works of good and can result in benefits to very many people!"

"Explain to me how an act of fornication—*three* acts of

fornication, as you describe it—can result in benefits to anyone!"

"The Spell of Summoning is a cherished, sacred rite; it is not fornication!" snapped Miradel. "It is a rite that is blessed by the Goddess Worldweaver, and it is necessary to the bringing of humans to Nayve. It calls upon your beauty, your caring, your love—you must arouse your warrior and bring him to release three times in the night of the casting—but by so doing you bring him the chance of immortal life on Nayve."

"Immortal life, if he isn't killed, you mean. Tell me, how is this world, this Fourth Circle, heavenly?"

"Nayve is a world of peace, and yet we find ourselves beset by war—by a war greater even than those that convulse the world of our birth," the druid explained patiently. "The Lord of Null, Karlath-Fayd, is sending a fleet against our world that numbers thousands of ships and a million warriors—warriors whose souls he has drawn from Earth since before the age of Caesar. Nearly every man killed in war has come to him, unwilling yet compelled. In the last hundred years the carnage wrought by Napoleon and his enemies, by the American Civil War, and now this Great War that threatens to consume all of Europe, have swelled his ranks to an unthinkable degree. Even now, his ships have turned toward land; the battle will be joined in a matter of days."

"But you summon warriors from Earth yourself, you and your fellow druids?" Shandira challenged. "To fight and die in this campaign?"

"Yes. We select men of great skill and bravery and honor and goodness. We bring them here at the moment of death, through the Spell of Summoning . . . the carnal magic that you have called fornication."

"Why do you need me? I have seen many women here, in the temple and in the Grove. Some of them are clearly wanton. Can they not summon warrior after warrior, one every night perhaps?"

Miradel flushed, unease and guilt wrestling within her. "It is not that simple. When first the spell was cast, it was a sentence of death upon the druid who worked the summons. I used it to bring Natac here, more than five hundred years ago, because I sensed his greatness, and I knew that Nayve, that the goddess, would need his help. In the course of that casting I became an old woman in one night, commencing an inevitable slide toward mortal death.

"It was not until one of our order, Juliay, cast this spell to bring a warrior from America, at the end of their civil war, that we made a discovery: there is a stream in the Mountains of Moonscape, and a druid who drinks the water of that stream may cast the spell—*once*—without suffering the ravages of age. Juliay's discovery has given us the means to resist. Just two days ago a party of heroes journeyed, magically, to that river and returned with six casks of the precious liquid. In the years since Juliay's discovery, we have brought nearly a thousand valiant warriors from Earth, all of whom have been enlisted in the defense of Nayve. But no druid can cast the spell a second time without facing the future of aging and death. So each new warrior requires a new druid."

"You make it sound very clinical," Shandira said coldly. "Have you selected the man I am to give myself to?"

"No! You will undergo training, and you will study the Tapestry of the Worldweaver. The selection of a warrior is yours alone to make. And you should know that it is not uncommon for the druid to love her warrior . . . for the lovers to remain faithful to each other over decades, even centuries. It is that way with Natac and myself." Miradel was surprised by how defensive she felt; never before had she considered her spell worked upon the warrior as anything other than a pure and sacred rite. How was Shandira able to twist everything around?

"And if I choose no one?"

"That is your decision to make. You will still have work to do here, and you will certainly hope that our world survives the onslaught of the Deathlord. If not, it will be the end . . . not just of Nayve, but of everything."

Shandira drew a deep breath and turned away, stepping to the side of a massive oak trunk and placing her hand upon the bark, as if she would draw strength from the forest giant. She bowed her head, and Miradel wondered if she was praying, extending a plea for guidance—or succor—to the God in whom, perhaps, she still believed. At last, the black woman raised her head and looked over her shoulder.

"I will start this training," Shandira declared. "I make no promises that I will do your bidding. But at least, I shall try to learn."

"I could ask for nothing more," Miradel said sincerely. She extended a hand to the taller woman, who accepted the gesture with her own strong fingers. "Come this way," the elder druid declared. "You can start by observing the Hour of Darken."

3

The Goblin Ghetto

One Spark: Dumb!
Two Sparks: Bum!
Three sparks burns 'im,
Run, Gob, Run

Seer Dwarf Nursery Rhyme

Darann was used to the stares and insults of the guards, but she couldn't help bristling when one of them, a gap-toothed dwarf she knew as Blackie, suggested he'd have to subject her to a physical search.

"You lay a hand on me," the dwarfwoman snapped, "and you'll be pulling back a bloody stump!"

Blackie hooted in amusement as his cronies, the six guards at the Metal Gate of the ghetto, chuckled appreciatively. "Does that mean you *are* trying to smuggle a knife in to those cruds?" he asked, his eyes roaming freely down the outline of her tunic where it swelled over her breasts.

She ignored him, pushing past until she stood before the iron door. The black wall rose high above her, soaring nearly a hundred feet into the yawning cavern that was the Underworld. Water trickled through the sewers beside the street, gurgling through rusty grates as it passed into the ghetto, which was located in the lowest, soggiest quarter of the city of Axial. For most of her life this had been merely the quarter of the Seer capital that was home to its most benighted denizens, but for ten years now, since this wall had been erected by the king's order, it had become a virtual prison.

Her heart pounded, and for a moment she wondered if the guards would call her bluff insisting that she be searched. But apparently she still had some status left in this city; none of the men-at-arms dared to lay a hand upon her. Finally, the metal barrier began to rumble upward, and she could again draw a breath.

A *careful* breath, she reminded herself, as the stench of the ghetto spilled through the opening and quickly surrounded her with its cloying miasma, a mixture of feces, disease, and death. She quickly stepped through, conscious of the ironic truth that she actually felt safer here, in the brackish hole of the goblins, than she did among the duly appointed guardians of her ancestral home. As usual, there was no one in sight of the opening gate. The goblins had learned through bitter experience that the portal was far more likely to reveal a thuggish band of young Seers looking for a little blood sport than any visitor engaged on a mission of mercy.

Darann advanced, displaying a confidence she did not feel. She felt the eyes of the guards on her back and held her shoulders straight, her chin high. It took all of her will not to hurry as she strode into the lightless street that gave access to the ghetto. As the metal plate rumbled downward behind her, cloaking the narrow street in murky shadow, she finally became aware of movement, scuttling figures creeping forward, wide nostrils gaping, sniffing loudly, confirming her identity.

"It's the Lady," one whispered in a gurgling voice that carried far along the darkened byway.

"The Lady!" others repeated, the sound washing like waves through the alleys and tenements of the ghetto.

She felt a gentle touch on her arm, others against her shoulder. One, probably a youngster, brushed light fingers along her knee. When she had first started coming here, these contacts had startled, even frightened her, but now she recognized them for the affectionate greetings they were. It had surprised her to discover that goblins were such tactile people, in many ways more empathetic and caring than her own race.

Her own people. How sad that she couldn't even consider them, anymore, without the familiar flush of shame rising like a itch from her neck through the full-fleshed roundness of her face. It had been her own people, the Seer dwarves, lords of the First Circle, who had grown so fearful and afraid that they had locked these people away, behind the walls of this stinking ghetto, merely because they were different. Of course, there were good people among the Seers—her own father came immediately to mind—but there were too many who were afraid, who allowed themselves to become trapped in a mire of isolation and paranoia.

"Lady? It is I." She heard the familiar voice, sensed the flat-footed goblin who had emerged to shuffle at her side as she moved down the narrow street.

"Hiyram? Hello, my friend." She touched him on the shoulder and felt the shocking frailty of his body; he seemed to be nothing but papery skin draped loosely over ill-fitting bones.

"You are so welcome. But is it safe for you to keep coming here? I beg you, Lady Darann, think of yourself in this. My people are ever used to seeing to their own needs, and I would grieve beyond words if your caring for us was cause to bring you hurt."

"You are kind to think of me, Hiyram, but there is much I can do to help. And I can't ignore the guilt, to think that my people—mine and Karkald's—have brought you to this! Please allow me to atone as best I can."

"Ah, yes . . . good Karkald." As the goblin spoke her husband's name Darann's eyes, even after all these years, watered. She saw her grief reflected in the goblin's wide, shining eyes. "He would be very proud of you."

"If he was alive, and here, none of this would be happening!" the dwarfwoman said passionately. "He wouldn't let the king lock you away like this, take away your houses and shops and goods—none of it!"

Hiyram sighed loudly. "It is too bad, tragical bad, that it was the Marshal Nayfal and not the Captain Karkald who escaped the disaster in the Arkan Pass."

"Nayfal?" Darann bristled. "He's a coward and a liar. I don't believe his story for one minute, I *never* believed him! Karkald wouldn't turn his back on his men, even if he knew the battle was lost. I know he was there, fighting to the last!"

"Shhh, Lady," the goblin urged, staring wide-eyed at the listening slits high up on the ghetto wall. "I cannot let you say such things! You know how the times are . . . what might happen, if you are overheard!"

"Bah!" snorted the dwarfwoman. She turned to look at the slits, where the king's—and Nayfal's—spies were certainly paying attention to her visit. Angry words rose to her tongue, but she bit them back, knowing the truth of the goblin's warnings. Dwarves had disappeared for less insulting remarks than she had contemplated. Her reputation, as one of the two dwarves who had opened passage to Nayve more than four hundred years ago, would not protect her forever.

Not that she had much to lose, herself. Once she had had great cause for living, for hope of a bright future. She and Karkald . . .

But her husband had been gone for fifty years now, slain along with the entire Army of Axial during a vicious battle with the Delvers at Arkan Pass. Only a few battered foot soldiers and Marshal Nayfal had survived that debacle, bringing the tale of the historic catastrophe back to the city. He had reported that the Delvers were massed in a huge army, greater numbers than the Unmirrored had ever previously mustered. With the bulk of the Seer army annihilated, the knowledge of the teeming enemy lurking in the lightless fringes of the First Circle had become Axial's overriding reality. Everyone knew they were simply biding their time, waiting for the perfect time to attack.

Since then, the Seer dwarves of this great city had gone into a state of perpetual siege, waiting for the Blind Ones to attack in force. Though that attack had never come, the leaders of her city had seemed to succumb more and more to fear and paranoia. Even the goblins, once welcomed among the dwarves as reliable, if lower-class, workers, had been shunned. Nayfal had reported that a great company of the wretched creatures had abandoned their positions during the great battle, and since nearly every family in the city had lost at least one member in that doomed campaign, public opinion had been harsh and unforgiving.

This situation with the lower race had been exacerbated ten years after Arkan Pass, when a band of goblins had attempted to assassinate King Lightbringer. Only the actions of a heroic palace guard, a veteran sergeant named Cubic Mandrill, had thwarted the plot, though the brave guard had lost his life in the attempt. Lord Nayfal himself had exposed the plot and put the treacherous goblins to death.

Despite the fact that only a few rogue males had been

involved in the attempt on his life, the king had ordered all of the wretched creatures then living in Axial into this cramped and unsanitary quarter of the city. Eventually he had ordered the wall built, so that the goblins were confined until such time as the king and his marshal decreed them no longer to be a threat.

In her despair, Darann had to remind herself that there were reasons to take precautions, to remain free. Her father, Rufus Houseguard, depended on her more than ever. And she had two brave brothers, Aurand and Borand, who still served in the Royal Army. They would be heartbroken if anything happened to her. Finally, there were these goblins, many of whom had been loyal soldiers of King Lightbringer until, in the years following Arkan Pass, they become the targets of increasing harassment and suffering.

Her mind turned to practical concerns. She shrugged out of her heavy backpack and quickly undid the flap at the top. "Here . . . I've brought you forty pounds of citrishroom, all I could trade for at the market. And the rest is salt."

"I hope you know the depths of our gratitude," Hiyram said quietly. "The citrus alone will keep a hundred of our youngsters alive for another year. And the salt . . . well, it is more precious than gold or flamestone."

The goblin lowered his voice. "Have you been to see the king? Is there any word on his condition?"

She shook her head. "Nayfal controls the audience list, and he doesn't want me in there. He's even trying to keep my father out, though I know Rufus is still seeking an audience. I will see my father tonight, but I can't think of any reason to be optimistic about changes happening, not in the near future anyway."

"I understand." The goblin's eyes were downcast.

Darann had one more piece of business. She took the

goblin's arm, and they stepped around a sharp corner, where they were concealed from the observation slits in the outer wall. She reached into her tunic and pulled out a narrow dagger from the sheath she had concealed between her breasts. The keen steel glinted faintly in the dim light. "Here is another one," she said, as Hiyram took the forbidden weapon without a word, slipping it through his belt so that it vanished into his grimy trousers. "Only, please . . ."

"I understand," the goblin whispered. "And you have my pledge; we shall not use these weapons, save only if we need to fight for our very lives."

"I hope it never comes to that," she said fervently.

"Aye, Lady," Hiyram whispered as she started away. His words barely reached her through the darkness. "So do I."

KARKALD wandered away from the company while the Hyac piled the bodies of the slain harpies. The smoke from the fire rose like a pillar of blackness into the sky, and though he intentionally walked upwind from the pyre the air still seemed to reek of bile and char. His stocky legs bore him along the ridge, with the vast yawning gap of Riven Deep beginning a few hundred yards to his right.

Out of old habit, his hands went to various parts of his body, where he had his tools strapped to belts, slings, and harness. "Hammer, chisel, hatchet, file. Knife, pick, rope, spear."

He sought the calmness those words had once brought him, but it seemed that sense of placidity was gone forever, had been gone since he and his company of dwarves had been magically transported here, to the world of Nayve, following the disastrous battle at Arkan Pass. True, he had managed to keep those survivors, several hundred strong, together here in the Fourth Circle. And they had friends here, good and loyal people such as Natac and Janitha, Belynda and Roland Boatwright.

But how he missed Darann! At times like this, when he had created a new invention—a device that had worked perfectly, bringing more than a thousand harpies to sudden doom—he should have felt some sense of elation. Instead, he only wanted to tell her about it, and it seemed the only pleasure he would ever gain would be if his wife, herself, could again tell him that she was proud of him.

Janitha came up to him as he was sitting on a flat-topped rock, looking without seeing as the Darken shadows thickened along Riven Deep. "Our best count was more than fourteen hundred of them brought down by your net," she said cheerfully. "It was hard to get an exact count—lots of them got pretty well chopped up or burned before we had the time to count heads."

Karkald snorted, making the effort to be civil. "That's something, anyway. With the Delvers and golems stuck on the other side of the Deep, it's nice to know we have something that might give the harpies pause."

"Yes . . . it begins to seem that the decisive battle will not be fought here after all," the Hyaccan chieftain replied.

"Have you heard anything from Circle at Center?" asked the dwarf.

"The landing of the death ships appears to be imminent," Janitha said. "One of the faeries brought a missive just now. They are making for shore, to the metalward of Argentian."

Karkald nodded. "Good beaches there, the smoothest coast on all of Nayve, I should think." He felt strangely unmoved, though this was the development the whole world had been dreadfully anticipating for so many years. Was it because this was not his world, that he was a

stranger here? He knew it was much more than that. With
Darann gone from his life, nothing that happened to him
on any circle would seem to be terribly important.

She looked at him sharply, and he sensed that she had
more to say. He waited, and after a few heartbeats she
continued.

"There was word from the last group of miners, too,"
she said quietly. "The gnomes and goblins, and some of
your dwarves as well, that started their excavation four
years ago. They worked their way down for more than
three miles, following caves where they could, digging
when they had to . . . trying to find a link to the Underworld."

"And they were stopped, again, by the barrier of blue
magic?" guessed Karkald. "No way through, no way
down to the First Circle."

The elfwoman shook her head. "It's as you suggested
decades ago. There has been a shift in the barrier between
our circles, as if the Worldfall has forged an impermeable
boundary between the First and Fourth Circles. We are cut
off from the Underworld, no closer to getting through than
we were before this attempt. The wall of blue magic is
found in every place that we try to dig."

"I've been thinking about that some more," the dwarf
said. "The Worldfall might play a role, but there's more to
it than that."

"What do you mean?" asked Janitha.

"You know some of the story, I'm sure. When we came
here fifty years ago, after the battle at Arkan Pass, there
was powerful magic at work—and that force field was
blue, just like the barrier between the worlds. The magic
worked not just to bring my own company of Seers, of
course—there were sixty thousand Delvers, the army of
the arcane, Zystyl, that were transported at the same time.
I think that the same magic is what now forms a barrier

between our worlds—why every one of the dozen passages down to the Underworld has been closed off at once. That's why this last group, like all the rest, never had a chance."

"Well, they made the effort anyway," Janitha said. "It was a bold expedition, the best planned, best supplied yet."

"Did they all make it back?" Karkald asked.

"Two goblins were killed in a cave-in. The rest are back in Nayve. They came up just this side of the Lodespikes, I understand."

"I hope that we've finally learned to accept the truth," the dwarf said, the bitterness in his voice surprising himself. "We're cut off from Axial, from my homeland, and there is no point risking lives—*costing* lives—just to try to restore a link that is lost forever!"

"Don't sit here and whine about it!" Janitha said sharply. "I know how it feels. Remember, my homeland is the one that is gone forever— torn by the dragon into the depths of Riven Deep. But I have to believe that if there was any chance that Shahkamon still existed, I would not rest until I had found a way to get there! Especially if I had a spouse, one I truly loved, there!"

Karkald spun around to face her, too infuriated to articulate anything beyond an enraged sputter. It was that garbled noise that brought him back to some sense of proportion, with an accompanying flash of guilt.

"You're right," he said, hanging his head. "There are others who have suffered worse than I. And I can't, I *won't* give up! Only, by the goddess, I need some new ideas, some glimmer of hope!"

"And you shall have that," Janitha said gently. "Until then, you have more work in front of you."

"Work? Yes, that's what I need," said the dwarf, standing up, bowing stiffly. "You sound as though you know some specifics."

"Yes. The request comes from Natac himself. We are to set up a whirlpool so that you can be drawn through the teleport spell. They'll want you on the beaches, I'm sure, before the death ships land."

BORAND pulled on the rope, two short tugs, and felt the answering yank of Konnor's reassuring presence. He knew the belay was set, and there was nothing for it now, but to try to inch his way above the yawning gap in the subterranean chimney. He felt that peculiar excitement that only came from life-threatening danger, forced himself to draw a deep breath, and made ready to proceed with the climb.

With a flash of irritation he noticed that his hands were trembling. "Come on, you old graybeard," he whispered soundlessly, addressing himself in the vast silence of the Midrock. "You've done maneuvers like this a hundred times before!"

Though not exactly like this, he was forced to admit. For one thing, he would have to make his way along a wall that leaned out precariously, and gravity would work to pull him off the face. The rock was not exactly seamless, but none of the cracks offered more than a very tenuous grip. Finally, Konnor's belay was too far away. If Borand fell, he would plunge fifty feet downward and then swing, hard, against the near wall of the chimney before coming to a halt.

The contemplation of these real conditions proved calming, however, and in moments the dwarf was ready to attempt the crossing. He checked his carabiners, made sure that the rope moved smoothly through the metal loops, and reached out for his first handhold. Wedging his fist into the opening, he swung into space, his short climber's pick ready in his left hand. With a careful strike he thrust the tool into the same gap, farther from the ledge.

His feet came free, and he was hanging, by pick blade and fist, from the ceiling of the First Circle. Borand thought of the great space yawning below, thousands of feet above the ground of his world, the First Circle. His brother, Aurand, the third member of their scouting party, was much lower on the cliff, but even he was high above the ground. Still, to the experienced climber there was no unusual terror in the vast, world-spanning gap. After all, there wasn't much difference in result when a climber fell more than a mile or merely a hundred feet. He glanced back, reassured by the sight of his rope trailing easily through the piton he had hammered home.

Now he relaxed his fist, feeling the hand drop free of the crack as his body, supported only by the wedged pick, swung forward. On the upswing he extended his long arm, slipped his hand into the continuation of the crack, and once again clenched his fingers. Without pause he freed the pick and swung forward again, through four or five repetitions. Here he halted with one last axe wedge, as the gap began to grow wider.

This was the trickiest part of the move. The bottom of the chimney entrance gaped dark with shadow, ten feet across, just beyond his line of sight. He allowed himself to hope: this could be the place, the route up to the Fourth Circle! With renewed fervor he lifted himself up with the sheer strength of his arms, kicking one leg into the widening crack. Wrenching his knee so that it held his full weight, he extended his other foot, turning his stiff-soled boot sideways. In one smooth drop he was hanging upside down, supported only by that foot. An instant later he had completed the flip, reaching up with pick and fingers, pushing apart and lifting upward until his head entered the crack and both shoulders wedged into the tight rock walls.

He got one, short glimpse: a heartbreak; the chimney narrowed and then ended in flat stone just a short distance above. Then the rock moved, very slowly. He heard a grumbling, distant kind of noise and felt the unmistakable pinch as the great slabs to either side of him began to grind slowly together. His shoulders tensed and he twisted as he felt the pressure continue.

To stay was to die, crushed like a bug between massive rocks, so he slipped downward, trying to support himself with just his hands. But the gap continued to narrow, so he had no choice but to let go, falling free into space with a sickening sense of weightlessness. Borand shouted an inarticulate word to warn his companion of the fall, then tried to brace himself for the shock of the rope's pull.

Konnor was an experienced climber, and his belay was strong and quick, tightening as the falling dwarf plunged past. Borand felt the line clamp around him, a gut-crushing force, and then he swung like a pendulum, hurtling toward the sheer rock wall. He twisted, trying to get his feet up, but there wasn't time. The rock seemed to lunge at him, striking a glancing blow against the side of his foot, then bashing his knee.

Borand grunted, clamping his jaws over the scream of agony that strained for release. His vision was shrouded by a film of raw pain, yet even through that filter he saw that the edge of the world cracked and strained under the force of monstrous pressure.

He gasped, sobbing uncontrollably, as the whole cliff face across from him—the very wall of the First Circle—crumbled and fell away. The rope girdle cinched tighter across his belly, restricting his breathing, choking him until, mercifully, the world went black.

———

THE great stone house sprawled above a tiny bay, a rocky niche in the shore of the Undersea on Axial's wood coast. Two great watch beacons, bright with eternal coolfyre, blazed from the promontories at either side of the bay's mouth, lighting the placid waters with white reflection, casting a gentle wash of light across the columned portico, the balconies leaning outward from each of the manor's three broad wings.

Darann had always found this view soothing, and even now, when her heart was still heavy with the reality of the goblin suffering, she felt a lightness in her step, a girlish sense of anticipation as she climbed the smooth path toward the great front door.

That portal was open, and Rufus Houseguard stood there, outlined by the spill of brightness from within. He threw out his long arms as his daughter came closer, and Darann relished the strength of his hug, the familiar musk as she buried her face in his long, soft whiskers.

"I'm glad you could come," he said. "It gives me an excuse to get out the nice dishes, to have something beside dried shroom for dinner."

She patted his gut, bulging slightly as ever, and laughed as she passed him into the entry hall. "You don't seem like you're in any danger of starving."

His expression grew grave as he followed and carefully shut the door. "Not from lack of food, in any event," he said guardedly.

Darann understood; any more pointed discussion would have to wait until later.

"I picked up a bottle of Toad's Head Malt," she said, producing a flask of the dark brew from her pouch. "Bermie was just rolling a fresh keg into the market square as I started on my way out here. This is the first gallon he drew."

"Ahh, now that looks to be a treat," exclaimed Rufus,

taking the bottle, holding it up to the full brightness of the coolfyre chandelier. Brown bubbles meandered through the syrupy fluid, and a foam of chocolate-colored lather formed at the top. "I think I have a main course worthy of this: grilled blackfish, taken with my own spear from the bay not three hours ago. Are you hungry?"

"I can't wait."

As usual, Rufus took great pride in laying the table and presenting the dishes. Since his wife had died, some thirty years earlier, he had become something of a gourmand. In addition to the serenity she felt in his company, Darann was always delighted by his culinary accomplishments, and tonight proved to be no exception.

"The spiderweb fungus came from my own mold house," he proclaimed as she sampled the flaky filet on its bed of netlike mushroom strands. "I bought the citrishroom, of course. It came from the warrens on the Basalt Islands. Tart, don't you think?"

"Unbelievable!" the dwarfwoman agreed, speaking around a savory mouthful before reaching for her brimming flagon. The mead was the perfect complement to the delicate food, for the drink was thick and sweet and potent enough to put a nice burn into her belly.

"Any word from my brothers?" Darann asked, as they meandered through dessert: a sweet roll made from moon wheat and caveberries, two crops that had been cultivated to grow under the illumination of coolfyre.

"Yes," Rufus said, "I had a letter two cycles ago. It seems they've found another niche in the Midrock, a tiny gap on the edge of Null." He frowned. "Don't like to think about them runnin' around in that lightless void," he admitted. "Wherever the Delvers are collecting themselves, that seems to be a likely place."

"At least they have Konnor to look after them," Darann said, trying to mask her own alarm. "And who knows—

maybe they'll find the opening, the route that will lead us back to Nayve!"

"I still think our best hope lies with the Worldlift," Rufus said. "I was talking to Donnwell Earnwise, last week—you know, the engineer who's in charge of the project."

"Of course I know, father. I've only called him Uncle Donnwell since I was a little girl!"

"Er, yes," Rufus said, reddening. He huffed. "Guess I'm not as sharp as I used to be, and that's the truth. But that's beside the point. Donnwell said that his rocket experiments have been remarkably successful. He thinks that's the way to break through the barrier, to reach Nayve again."

"If he finds someone foolish enough to ride a rocket!" Darann said scornfully. "If I ever get back to Nayve, it'll be the old-fashioned way, step by step!"

"Well, that worked for you four hundred years ago . . . and for your brothers, when they went to see what trouble you'd got yourself into. But this is a new and modern age, girl, and things like rocket lifts are going to be a part of it."

"I'm glad you think so," she said, growing serious. "As for me, I don't know . . ."

Her father looked at her, his expression morose, and she was unable to maintain the hopeful façade. "I know," she said quietly. "I've admitted it: the Worldfall closed us off for good. I don't think any dwarf will ever go back there."

"Makes it all the more important that we manage our own affairs. Come, humor me while I smoke a cheroot. I'll show you my fountain—I've installed a few new valves, and a flute that plays a tune when the water flows across it."

She followed him onto the wide portico overlooking

the bay. Rufus pulled a lever down, activating the water
flowing from an uphill tank, then fiddled with an array of
circular valves. Soon Darann heard the trilling of water,
and moments later a curtain of white spray erupted from
several nozzles flush with the paving stones. A circular
bowl rose from the middle of the ring of spray, catching
the spumes, then channeling the water through an intricate
series of chutes. As it splashed downward, a simple tune
emerged, deep musical notes that sighed through a mournful, minor key.

"It's ingenious," Darann declared in wonder. "That's
the *'Dirge for Cubic Mandrill,'* isn't it?"

Rufus nodded. "It's one of my favorites. And what a
story: a hero who died protecting his liege, serving in
good faith. But it has come to my attention that there
might be more to the story."

"What do you mean?" Darann asked, very curious.

His eyes were narrowed as he looked around, casually
inspecting the balconies of the house, the slopes of the
surrounding hillside. Instead of answering, he asked a
question of his own, somehow mouthing the question
without visibly moving his lips.

"Did you see Hiyram?"

"Yes," Darann replied in the same discreet fashion. "I
gave him another knife and some provisions. I think his
people will be patient for a little longer. I don't know how
long it will be before they revolt. But tell me: what makes
you think that there might be more to the story?"

"There is a dwarfwoman in the city who knows much
of that assassination. She has written me a letter and
makes some intriguing speculation. There will come a
time, my daughter, when I shall tell you about it."

"But not now?" pressed the dwarfmaid, knowing that
her stubborn father had made up his mind.

"I have to see the king," Rufus said, glowering in spite

of himself. "A few minutes, a real conversation—that's all it would take for him to see the wrong he is perpetrating, or that is being perpetrated in his name!"

"I wish I shared your optimism," the daughter answered. "But I cannot believe he doesn't know exactly what is going on in the ghetto. The guards—there were six of them at the Metal Gate today! He's getting ready to put down a rebellion."

"A bad sign," Rufus agreed. "But we can't know they were sent there under King Lightbringer's orders. You know that Nayfal has complete command of the garrison."

"Nayfal!" Darann all but spat the name. She drew a breath, conscious that her emotions might be visible on her face. And there was no way to know who was watching the house, lurking in the darkness beyond the beacons. At least she consoled herself that the fountain's noise made it impossible for them to be overheard.

"Have faith, daughter," Rufus said gently. "I have some indication that I might be invited to the throne room, perhaps within the next ten cycles. We have survived travails before. You should know that this, too, shall pass."

Later, as she walked backed to her apartment in one of the city's Six Towers, she reflected on her father's words. Try as she might, she found his sentiment impossible to believe.

4

The Prussian

Shrouded sunset,
On long horizon;
Canvas clouds approach.

Crimson rain,
Yields only crop
Of carnage.

From *The Ballad of Seafall*
by Sirien Saramayd

Though his death had occurred more than forty years ago, Fritzi Koeppler stood on his command deck and remembered the moment as if it had been just last week. Circumstances could not have been more different: then, he fought on a horse; now on a boat. Then he had joined a great army battle, part of a clash between two prideful and nationalist leaders; now he raced toward a sea fight, battling for the destiny of all creation.

Nevertheless, as he led his flotilla of more than three hundred druid boats, his mind inevitably turned to that other fight, his last battle—indeed, his last experience of any kind—upon the world of his birth.

He had been a minor leader in the hierarchy of a mighty army, his command a battalion of crack Prussian cavalry troops. Together with hundreds of thousands of men and hundreds of lethal cannons, he had gone to make war upon France.

He had enjoyed heady success during the start of the campaign, in the summer of 1870. Under the command of King Wilhelm I and the able leadership of General Moltke and his modern, efficient general staff, the Prussians and their Germanic allies chased the hapless French back from the border with dazzling attacks through Strasbourg, Nancy, and Metz. Finally the invaders trapped the enemy force, more than 200,000 strong, within a bend of the river Meuse, at Sedan. There would be no escape for the army of Napoleon III: even a humiliating crossing into neutral Belgium would be the equivalent of unconditional surrender. So the French would stand; the Germans, attack.

The heavy Krupp guns pounded relentlessly, lethal shells plunging into packed ranks. Fritzi could still feel, smell, hear his own mare, the big horse prancing and snorting under the noise of the bombardment, eager to charge. She was a powerful creature, black and sleek and vibrant, and he longed to unleash that power. He watched shells whistle overhead, witnessed the obliteration of breastworks, fortifications, and men.

The French fought with courage, the thumping cadence of their heavy, primitive machine guns, called mitrailleuses, chattering in the background of the barrage. These innovative devices were mounted upon two-wheeled frames, like light artillery pieces, and fired a rapid fusillade of bullets through a series of rotating barrels. Many Prussians had fallen to the deadly fire, but the weapons were mostly useful for harassing skirmishers; they seemed to have little place on the field of an epic battle. Truly, the new weapons were no match for crunching, well-organized artillery.

But guns alone would not decide this battle, and so the cavalry moved up in the time-honored fashion. The French formations were badly battered, clearly weakened and ready to break. Closing his fist around the hilt of his saber, Fritzi looked at the ragged lines, the infantry battalions torn and gashed by the fire, and his heart pounded with excitement. The horses would cut through those ranks, the enemy army would break, and the war could be won—all with one epic charge. After a lifetime in the saddle, he knew there could be no better way to decide the affair.

His mare shared his excitement, snorting and kicking, restless in the close formation. All along the battalion's lines equine nostrils flared, hooves stomped, and manes blew in the wind. Then came the signals: pennants up, horns braying, the huge animals advancing at a walk, a trot, surging into a canter. The ground itself seemed to tremble under the impact of many thousands of hooves. Finally the steeds broke into a gallop, thundering across the field, the surge of attack drowning out all other sensations. French cannons fired sporadically, shells that screamed past or, occasionally, exploded among the lines of men and steeds. The bloody gaps in the cavalry ranks quickly filled, elite troops merging to tighten ranks, still maintaining the frenzied momentum of the charge. Already some of the enemy troops fled, panicking in the face of death; Fritzi's lip curled in disdain of this shameful cowardice.

Now the French troops stood visible before them, in line formation—they had not even formed the squares that were the traditional defense against such a charge. Fritzi leaned low, murmuring words of encouragement into the mare's laid-back ear. A few small guns stuttered here and there, the squat and toylike mitrailleuses opening up as the charging cavalry came closer.

And then a strange thing happened. Those little chattering guns began to sweep their fire—streams of mere bullets, not the explosive shells of true artillery—across the front of the Prussian horsemen. Men and mounts fell in gory tangles, bodies forming an instant breastwork, breaking the tight ranks. Some of the trailing horses leaped the fleshy rampart, only to perish in the continuing volleys; others tripped and stumbled through the chaos of suffering, thrashing flesh. Still those pesky little guns fired, barrels smoking as they spun through their rotating cylinders. Everywhere horses were rearing and kicking, men were falling, and both mounts and riders were dying.

The charge was not merely broken but utterly shattered. The realization came to Fritzi as he lay on the ground, his broken leg pinned by the weight of his dead horse: warfare had changed, changed fundamentally and forever. He was saddened and ashamed, for it seemed that all glory had been taken from this most glorious of pursuits. It was not long before the French infantry came forward, bayonets glittering, and Fritzi lacked the strength or the will to reach to his belt and draw his side arm. Everything was sad and wasted, and for what kind of world?

At the last, when a razor-sharp bayonet plunged through his throat, he was ready to die.

"You were thinking of that day again, Sedan? Were you not?" Reza asked the question directly, his brow furrowed with concern. The big Persian sat at the tiller, the wooden bowl in his lap as he effortlessly rotated the windspoon with his free hand. The gust he cast swirled upward, filled the sail, propelled the boat with all the power—and none of the noise or smoke or heat—of a good-sized steam engine.

"Yes," Fritzi answered, shaking his head as if to physically break free from the reverie. He could see the white sails, the blue sky, the sun-dappled water. Ahead, on the horizon, the darkness of the armada lay like a stormy murk. With that glance, and the smell of the fresh, salty air, he returned to all the truths of this place and this day. "You know, that was my last battle . . . until now. When Gretchen summoned me to Nayve, I allowed myself to believe that my days of war were over. But now . . ." He gestured vaguely in the direction of the dark, stormy fleet.

Reza nodded, his dark skin growing smooth as his expression became more peaceful. "Today looks to be a battle that will make them all, from Salamnis to Traflagar, seem but skirmishes."

Fritzi clapped the druid on the shoulder, feeling the familiar camaraderie of the warriors' brotherhood. It made little difference that now his comrades were sailors, not horseman, that they came from all over Earth and Nayve instead of just the Germanic states . . . and that he in fact counted very many sisters among that brotherhood. He looked over the gunwale, across the span of white sails fluffed with wind, and he thought of the brave druids, sailors, and soldiers on the small vessels. Every one of them was ready to fight, and he realized with a sense of surprise that he, himself, was ready to die again, if it came to that. In this place, for this cause, he would allow himself no regrets.

"You will need to spin me a tornado, my friend, in order to catch up to my boats," he remarked dryly.

"And I am ready for that, warrior," said Reza. "Shall we go after them, a mother hen chasing her chicks?"

"Aye. And no need to strain either your arm or our canvas. I think that the armada will be waiting for us, whenever we arrive."

THE sea was shrouded in darkness, though full daylight reigned over the world of Nayve. The armada extended in all directions, individual sails blending into smoky cloud at the farthest distance. They spanned the breadth of an entire sea, sweeping toward the shore, darkening the waters and sky with a murk half real and half imagined. The ebony sails were smoky clouds wafting above polluted wave crests, and a stench of carrion was borne by the breeze, creeping toward the shore.

If there was any sense of formation to the mass of ships, it was not made clear by observation. Instead, they came as a swarm, neither in rank nor file, simply dark-timbered hulls churning through waters that seemed to recoil from the planks as if in revulsion. The fleet was at least as wide as it was deep, with a few sleek vessels drawing away from the vanguard in an undeniable hurry to reach the virgin shore.

The armada was propelled by a storm that seemed to swell in fury as the vessels moved closer to the trembling shores of Nayve. Imagined clouds grew real, and illusory darkness fell like a cloak of twilight as the sun, even in the midst of day, failed to penetrate the escorting vapor of murk. Harpies flew out from the land in great, shrieking clouds, to swirl and cavort through the plumes of smoky befoulment.

In contrast to the shapeless, natural force of the armada, the Metalfleet of Nayve sallied forth in three distinct wings. Each numbered more than three hundred vessels and advanced under full sail in a series of squadrons, twenty or thirty vessels strong. They made a great force in their own right but seemed impossibly small when measured against the vastness of the armada.

The first wing of Nayve's boats, commanded by the Prussian Fritzi Koeppler, took the lead and stayed the closest to shore. The second, under the Englishman Rudolph, trailed the first by only a short distance, forming up within sight of Koeppler's sails off the port quarter, somewhat farther out to sea. The third wing was commanded by the Sioux warrior Crazy Horse, and it held farther back and took a course that carried it beyond the sight of land.

Natac could see them all as he once again rode the natural saddle on the back of the great dragon. He could see the Worldfall, more than a hundred miles away in the direction of null, still plunging downward, and he couldn't help but fear the many vast forces arrayed against his small, green world. From high above they watched the deadly dance of war. They would not remain observers: Regillix Avatar had already consumed the incendiary pellet of saltpeter and limestone that would allow him to belch forth great gouts of fire. Natac was cloaked in a suit of supple leather, including gauntlets over his hands and a mask that concealed most of his face. The material had been imbued with a magical protection by the sage-enchantress Quilene, so that it would protect his flesh from the fiery assaults of the harpies, whose recent arrival over the armada had not come as a complete surprise.

But neither would the lofty pair commit themselves in the first skirmish. Instead, they would watch and wait and strike where they could do the greatest good. For fifty years they had been patient, planning and learning and preparing for this. Natac reflected on that time, on the evolution of this plan, and he still wished they had more time—that the armada had never turned toward Nayve at all.

For decades, the Fourth Circle's reconnaissance of the enemy fleet had been remote, conducted by sage-enchantresses using Globes of Seeing to watch the black ships. Eventually Regillix Avatar had flown forth, without a rider, for a direct look. The great serpent had swept close above the ghostly ships, learning that the vessels were made of timbers that could snap and buckle just like normal wood. The decks were crowded with ghost warriors who had fired arrows that proved to be real enough to prick skin and pierce flesh. The crewmen were garbed as legionnaires or Vikings, Zulu warriors or veterans of the American Civil War; lately their numbers had been swelled by great corps of Germans, French, Russians, British, and others slain in the Great War that racked the European continent.

As the armada moved closer to the Nayvian coast in later years, Natac—protected as now by a suit of enhanced leather—flew with the giant dragon, observing firsthand the armada he was determined to defeat. They swept close past the ships, enduring volleys of arrows shot from bows and crossbows. They also saw ranks of pikes, swords, and shields, but, thankfully, encountered no firearms among the invaders, nor even any spring-powered weapons comparable to the designs invented by the dwarf, Karkald. Nevertheless, the sheer number of the black ships and the utter lack of fear displayed by the ghost crewmen, were proof enough that the campaign, when it began, would be a desperate affair.

On land, that numberless horde would be like a tide, and Natac doubted that any army in the history of the Seven Circles would be able to effectively resist the attack. Therefore, the greatest hope of success meant that they would have to destroy much of the attacking force while it was still at sea. Violent experiments had shown that the ghost warriors could be wounded, could burn, and could drown just as mortal men. For decades that fleet had remained far from Nayve's shores, out of reach of the land's defenders. But for all that time, Natac had known beyond any doubt that this attack was inevitable; he had only lacked knowledge of the place and the time of the onslaught. Now, with the great turn toward land, the Deathlord at last had revealed his hand.

It took all of Natac's patience to hold his position, leaning outward to peer past the great, scaly shoulder, observing the closing of the mighty fleets. The waiting was over, and he knew that he watched the commencement of the greatest naval battle the Seven Circles had ever known.

IVAN Dzrystyn was born a Cossack, raised to ride across the steppes of the Ukraine. Only two years earlier he had led a band of howling warriors against the Germanic barbarians who had invaded his homeland. Loyal to his czar and courageous beyond all reason, he had led a charge against entrenched machine guns. His shock, when he had found himself in Nayve, subjected to the sensual ministrations of a beautiful, brown-skinned druid named Sari, had quickly been replaced by a fervent enthusiasm to wage war for this new cause—a cause that rendered all of Earth's wars, by comparison, into trivial squabbles.

Sari was with him now, spinning a powerful wind in the cockpit of their sleek sailboat, the *Kiev* pulling them slightly forward of the rest of Fritzi Koeppler's wing, leading all the vessels of Nayve as the immense battle was joined. The Cossack smiled, a fierce grin splitting his flowing black beard as he realized that he would have the honor of striking the first blow in the defense of his new homeland. He crouched in the bow behind the weapon that looked like a large, primitive crossbow, but it was not at all primitive, as Ivan had discovered in mock combat.

"Faster, Sari!" he shouted. "Don't let the bastards get in front of us!"

Wind exploded past as she heeded his call, and the *Kiev* leapt forward, a flying fish seeking to gain purchase in the air. They coursed past the bows of the first death ships, with those black sails looming high, still a mile away to port. Black clouds rose above those ships like tactical thunderheads, while a froth of brown water churned ahead of the enemy vanguard, a small tsunami surging in escort of the befoulment. In the opposite direction, just a fringe on the starboard horizon, the coastline of Nayve lay in wait.

"That one," muttered Ivan, seeing one of the black-hulled ships surging into the lead, marking a course that would take it across his bow. Turbulence frothed in a wide V from the prow, and the small sailboat rose up as it struck the foaming crest. Ivan felt the boat rock up and over the wave, then lurch violently in the rough waters beyond. A thick miasma choked his nostrils, like the stink of a charnel house, but he fought the instinct to gag as he held on to the weapon and tried to draw a bead. He crouched behind the steel battery, hand on the trigger as he aimed at the enemy vessel's broadside.

The Cossack glanced at the missile in the slot of his weapon, the metal shaft shining with a silvery glint, though Ivan's reflection looked dark and murky in the strange twilight. The steel head was sharp and barbed, like a monstrous harpoon, while the tail of the shaft was feathered with bright plumes to insure the accuracy of its flight. Most unusual of all were the four vanes, thin triggers of aluminum, which jutted perpendicularly from different locations on the shaft. These were the burners—at least, that's what the dwarf had called them—and when they were bent by impact, the shaft of the missile would supposedly ignite into a dramatic fireball. It had been tested on targets with satisfying results but never before used in war.

It pleased Ivan that he would be the first to discover if the device really worked.

The death ship before him was tall and wide in his sights, perhaps a half mile away now. He noted that the craft had three masts, each with three or four black sails aloft; in shape, it was not very different from the largest sailing vessels that he had seen on the Black Sea or making way up the Bug toward the city that was his sailboat's namesake.

His introspection quickly gave way to the need for action, as the target seemed to grow to vast proportions before him. He pulled the trigger, felt the metallic *twang* as the powerful spring sent the steely arrow hurtling forward. The missile flew gracefully, and it seemed as though time slowed enough for him to enjoy every detail: the bristling vanes, sparkling wickedly in the pale sunlight, rotated smoothly as the feathered tail kept it on a true course. Climbing slightly—he had aimed high to adjust for the long range—the steel shaft curved gently through the top of an arc and angled downward, striking the death ship exactly in the center of the hull.

The arrow disappeared through the planks, and Ivan blinked in astonishment, unable to discern whether or not it had even made a hole in the black surface. Had it failed? In the next instant, he was rewarded by a flash, white light outlining the middle of the ship. Smoke puffed upward, followed by a blossom of orange flame roiling outward, followed by pieces of hull and deck erupting into the air, propelled by the violence of the explosion. There was a moment of eerie silence, and then Ivan flinched under the guttural impact of a loud boom. Crackling flames engulfed the entire center of the death ship, and the mainmast toppled away, dragging rigging and sails to the water in a tangle.

Ivan heard Sari's triumphant shout mingling with his own hoarse cry, but there was no time for celebration. Immediately he set about reloading the mighty bow. Choppy seas made the task difficult, but he was aided by a small crane as he lifted another shaft from the hold and finally laid it in the firing track. Before him the stricken death ship careened to the side, fire spreading rapidly until the entire deck was alight, sails still aloft going up like crackling torches. By the time the *Kiev* swept past, the burning ship was listing, and black shapes, some of them afire, were spilling off the deck, dropping to the water, where they disappeared into the depths.

"It's true what the Mexican said: even ghosts can drown," the Cossack observed with satisfaction and a certain amount of surprise. A look behind showed him that the rest of the First Wing came on in full sail. Many other druid ships were launching their missiles, and other vessels in the armada erupted into flame before him and to port. Ivan picked out another target, closer this time, and fired a lethal shot into the belly of the black hull. Arrows darted toward him, hissing through the air and thumping into *Kiev*'s deck. The smell of carrion was even thicker now, making it very difficult to breathe.

Seeing three or four death ships surging before and aft, Ivan loaded his next shot as a canister, two dozen spheres filled with incendiary explosives nestling in the breech. With smooth gestures he cranked back the spring and launched the spray of metal balls, many of the weapons striking along the side of a hull looming barely a hundred yards away. As Sari steered him past, that ship reeled and groaned under the onset of six or eight small fires, blazes that quickly spread to engulf the entire hull.

But now they were in the midst of the enemy fleet. The

druid steered with consummate skill, spinning her wind and guiding the tiller at the same time, pushing *Kiev* through a narrow gap between two looming black ships. More arrows whistled toward Ivan, and he grunted in pain as one of the missiles bit into his shoulder. There was a third death ship beyond, and they could not get past; instead, the little sailboat bumped hard into the ebony hull. Sari fell, pierced by a dozen barbed arrows as she cried out his name.

Hit by another black shaft, Ivan stumbled but still managed to draw his sword as he saw the ghosts coming down at him, mouths gaping but silent. One, in the garb of a Roman legionnaire, fell to the deck following a single slashing blow, Ivan's blade cutting ghostly substance just as it would have carved into human flesh. But he could not recover in time to block the next attack, delivered by a bayonet on the end of a long, rifled musket by a shrouded warrior who wore a tattered uniform of an American army of the 1860s. The shadowy blade pierced the Cossack's guts, and he fell, grunting in agony. The last sound he heard was Sari's scream as a pair of swarthy Mongols set upon her with smoking, lethal blades.

"THE First Wing is meeting with some success," said Regillix Avatar, curling his neck around to cast a glance at Natac.

"Yes," the warrior agreed, looking down in awe. The murk over the armada was darkened further by plumes of thick smoke spewing up from spots of bright orange flames. A hundred or more of the sinister ships had been wrecked in the first clash. "Better success than I could ever have hoped. Look at those black hulls burn!"

"It is time for us to attack, as well," the dragon murmured, and Natac could only slap the hard scales in agreement.

"Be careful," he whispered, as Regillix tucked his wings. The great body plummeted through the air, angling toward the front of the armada, beyond the leading boats of Fritzi's wing. Natac saw one of the white-sailed boats smash into a death ship's hull, wincing as tiny ghost warriors scrambled across the doomed Nayvian vessel. How many would die today? He couldn't even try to imagine.

The clouds were thick and swelling to all sides, obscuring Natac's view of the sky. The dragon leaned forward, sweeping under the thick smear of smoke. Then the air was filled with shrieks, and harpies by the dozens swarmed out of the murk above the armada. The dragon belched a great fireball, incinerating a score of the hateful flyers, but many more swept past, spitting gobs of oily fire that spattered on Natac's leather armor and seared the dragon's tender wings.

"Look out—to the right!" called the man, as a hundred or more of the haglike attackers dived from the concealment of a neighboring cloud. Still more of the creatures were swarming ahead of them, swirling through tight spirals, waiting for the proper time to attack.

The dragon twisted in the air, and Natac held on with both hands. He felt the heat as another great fireball erupted from the crocodilian jaws. Then the serpent banked away, veering around to leave the harpies behind, pulling for altitude and the clean air beyond the armada.

Their attack would have to wait.

FRITZI Koeppler stood upon the observation deck, a narrow platform raised ten or twelve feet over the deck of his sailboat, the *Kaiser*. He had admired the Cossack's attack and noted the effectiveness of the fire weapons against the death ships. Now his responsibilities afforded him no time to grieve for the warrior or his druid as their impetuous rush carried them to doom within the armada.

"Raise the flag for a line formation—we'll give them a volley!" he shouted down to the deck. His signaler, an elf-maid from Barantha named Faerwind, swiftly ran the appropriate banner, a long, slender pennant of silver and blue, up the post.

As the commander's flagship, *Kaiser* was a bit larger than the standard druid boat. For one thing, she bore two batteries, one facing off either quarter of the bow, and in addition to Reza, who so resolutely spun the wind in the cockpit, she was crewed by a dozen elves to aid with communication as well as man the batteries.

Now the druids throughout the First Wing took note of the formation. The ranks of the sailboats changed shape smoothly, the squadrons merging line abreast to cut across the front of the shoreward-bound armada. The *Kaiser*, as well as a few dozen straggler vessels, sailed behind the line, but more than 250 batteries were arrayed in a row, each sighted upon one of the dark, looming death ships.

"Send up the order for a volley!" cried Fritzi. Faerwind was ready with the prearranged signal, and with a touch of a torch sent a sputtering rocket shooting straight up into the sky. Red smoke spumed from the tail, and throughout the wing the warriors took note of the order.

The sailboats lurched all along the line, recoiling as they launched their steely bolts into the black ships. One of the dark vessels veered as its masts were clipped off, while another turned to evade the shot and collided with its neighbor. Fires started instantly, a few smoldering hulls quickly consumed, more and more of the ships smoking and burning as the incendiary missiles exploded and began to burn within their bowels.

Within half a minute the entire front of the armada was

a mass of flaming wreckage. Some of the black ships, borne by momentum and the strong ocean wind, collided with the burning hulls, and hungry flames leapt from deck to hull to sail with crackling eagerness. Here and there a dark prow burst through the line, shaking off the scraps of burning debris, until a dozen death ships forged ahead toward the sailboats arrayed in such a tenuous line. The rest of the armada's vessels roiled and came about behind the line of fire, resulting in dozens of collisions, hundreds of ghost warriors toppling from their decks, vanishing under the wave-tossed waters.

Overhead, black clouds seethed and churned, thundering loudly, sparking with bright flashes of lightning. Monstrous thunderheads billowed magically, rising into the sky, then erupting. Rain pounded downward, drumming on the decks of many of the burning ships, dousing some of the fires but steaming away from the worst of the blazes.

Like a great charge! Fritzi couldn't help but make the comparison, even fleetingly wishing he had a bugle. "Go, my warriors!" he shouted. "Take the battle to them!"

Now the druids sighted on individual targets, the ships that had pushed their way through the wrecked vanguard. Several of these advancing vessels burst into flames, one struck by a half dozen of the fire-bolts at once, exploding violently in a cascade of burning timbers, sails, and crewmen.

Fritzi looked along the line, three or four miles long, and took heart from the damage the enemy had suffered. Many ships were sinking, while others burned to the waterline or spumed black smoke from unseen blazes deep within the hulls. Beyond the druid fleet, however, hundreds of dark ships surged around the fires, strong winds bearing them toward shore.

The Prussian looked back, knew that the enemy had

much more strength in this armada, thousands of ships that could eventually work around the other side of the firewall to trap his wing against the shore. He remembered his last day on Earth, the great charge on the Meuse—and that was nothing compared to this fight for the future of the cosmos.

The targets were clear before him now, and he didn't hesitate. He had lived in Nayve for forty-five years, and he understood that the stakes of this war were far higher than any battle waged in Flanders, Europe, or anywhere upon the Seventh Circle.

"Faerwind," he called down from the tower, his voice calm. "Send up the flag for a general attack."

5

Masters of Axial

Whisper in the dark,
Deadlier than assassin's
Poison'd blade

From *Lords of the First Circle*
Traditional Seer Dwarf Legend

Darann awakened from a dream, a dream wherein she was rubbing her nose and her cheeks into the soft bristles of Karkald's beard. She could hear the hairs rasping around her ears, a *scritch . . . scritch . . . scritch* of pleasant memory—until she found herself alone, again, in her large, cold bed. The apartment that she had shared with Karkald for so long yawned like a tomb around her, lightless and lifeless.

But the scratching sound, she was startled to perceive, was very real. The noise seemed urgent yet strangely gentle at the same time, as if someone wanted to attract the attention of one, and only one, person.

In an instant Darann was out of bed, her bare feet soundless on the cool slate floor. Wrapping a blackfur robe around herself, she made her way through the hallway into the anteroom, listening for a moment at the front door, but all was silent beyond. She waited, and then the sound was repeated, coming from somewhere near her kitchen.

For a moment she considered picking up some kind of weapon—one of Karkald's hatchets hung near the door—but she immediately discarded the notion. She was unable to imagine this sound as some kind of threat. Quickly passing into the kitchen, she heard the scratching again, louder and closer, and she understood: someone was scratching at the delivery door, the iron hatch that led to the pillar's central stairwell. The apartments all faced outward, overlooking the city with their high balconies, while the interior of the pillar was hollow, a dark stairwell.

Instantly she crossed to the portal and lifted the latch on the iron barrier. She heard a hiss of indrawn breath as she pulled it open, then recognized the stooped figure crouched in the shadowed alcove beyond.

"Hiyram!" she whispered. "How did you get out of the ghetto? And tell me, what do you want? Here, come in, quickly."

The goblin scuttled past, ducking into a corner as she pulled the door shut as quietly as possible. "You here alone by yerself?" he asked, his voice rasping urgently.

"Yes," she said with a nod. "Here, let me get you a cold drink—then tell me what's the matter."

Her hands trembled as she pulled the cork from a bottle and filled a mug with creamy ale. She handed the glass to the goblin and then, with sudden fear, took a long drink from the bottle herself. Hiyram noisily drained his mug and then looked at her with his wide, moist eyes shining in the nearly total darkness.

"D'you know dwarfmaid, Greta . . . she's a pailslopper, for master of the palace."

A pailslopper, Darann knew, was a scullery worker of

the lowest class. They worked in inns and of course at the palace and for some of the loftier nobles. She couldn't think of one that she knew by name. "This Greta . . . she works for the king, then?"

Hiyram shook his head. "*Master* of palace," he repeated with a snort. "Not king . . ."

"Nayfal!" Darann guessed. "She works for Nayfal?"

The goblin shrugged, his ears flopping with the exaggerated gesture. "Hates Nayfal, but sees him lots. She nice person . . . like Lady Darann."

The dwarfmaid reflected on the irony: she was flattered to be compared to the pailslopper who hated the esteemed Lord Nayfal. At the same time, her stomach tightened, and she began to fear Hiyram's news.

"Greta comes to ghetto—told me secret, told to tell you."

"What is it?" Darann's voice was a taut hiss.

"Nayfal has plan . . . a trap . . . a trap for Lord Houseguard. He must change to Nayfal's side, or bad thing will happen."

"My father!" Darann felt a stab of fear. "When is this . . . this *trap*, to happen?"

"Must be soon," the goblin said. "Greta said I had to tell you right away."

The dwarfmaid felt a rush of gratitude followed by an ache of fear. "Rufus is going to see the king today. I have to stop him!"

"Good lady, do that—please!" urged the goblin.

But Darann barely heard; she was already racing to get dressed, trying to stem the trembling of her hands, and wondering if she would possibly be in time.

KARKALD kicked his feet into the sand, tromping up the steep slope of the dune. He resented the wasted effort of his climbing as the loose grains collapsed under his weight. He estimated that, for each foot that he gained up-hill, he slipped down three or four inches. Working as hard as he could, he was still frustrated by the amount of time it took him to reach his destination at the top of the sand pile.

Furthermore, he was still disoriented by the teleporta-tion spell that had brought him here from Riven Deep. He avoided that magic whenever possible, but occasionally—such as now—it was required for haste. It always left him grumpy and irritable, with a sensation of prickling that lingered along his belly and chest for the better part of a day. Still, it had snatched him across a hundred miles in a moment of time, bringing him from the great canyon to this verdant coast. He wanted to rest, to sleep, but instead he was to be confronted by yet another vista of war.

When he finally arrived at the battery position, he leaned forward and braced his hands on his knees while he caught his breath. Even so, he was already inspecting the position out of the corner of his eye, and by the time he straightened and walked onward, he was mostly pleased with the disposition of the weapons.

"Karkald's here, General Galluper!" called one of the elven gunners, and the big centaur turned from the for-ward lip of the dune to greet the dwarf.

"Ah, my good engineer," said the horse-man. "I trust you will approve of my placements."

"You know better than I how to shoot these things," Karkald said, gesturing to the wheeled weapons, four in number, that had been dug into the soft sand. Each com-manded a view and a field of fire over a great swath of the beach below.

That smooth strand was still clean, washed by waves of emerald seawater and trimmed with white foam, but it was impossible to look across that view and not see the menacing presence of the armada, a cloud darkening the sea to the limits of the horizon. Karkald was taken aback. Now that he was this close, the black ships seemed limitless in number and terrifyingly real in proximity. The bows were angled toward the shore, and the first wave—perhaps five miles out, certainly closing fast—advanced in a line that spanned the view from right to left.

He corrected himself: far to the left, in the direction of metal, he saw an array of white sails, triangular sheets of canvas marking the placement of some of Roland Boatwright's fleet. There were precious few of them by comparison to the ships of the armada, but the dwarf was heartened by the sight of the flames and smoke that marked that end of the enemy line.

"The batteries on the boats are inflicting great damage on the death ships," Gallupper said, as if reading his mind. "Many hundreds of the enemy have been destroyed this morning alone—and the killing yesterday, they said, amounted to nearly a thousand ships."

"A thousand ships . . ." Karkald could hardly conceive of such numbers, especially when it was merely a fraction of the massive fleet that was still deployed before him. He looked along the crest of the dunes, where this battery was but one of a hundred or so, deployed with killing zones along a twenty-mile stretch of the shore. In that realization, he knew that the batteries, and the brave elves entrenched below the crests of the dunes, the giants and gnomes deployed in reserve . . . they would not be enough.

When he looked to the rear, he saw that his concern had been anticipated by Gallupper. The batteries could be pulled out of line quickly, each hauled by a couple of powerful centaurs, and a rough pathway had been cleared, leading down the dunes and into a patch of scrubby pines beyond. Still farther away, two or three miles from the beach, rose a range of rugged, rock-crested hills.

"If we lose the shoreline, we will fall back to the hills," Gallupper was explaining, following the direction of Karkald's gaze. "There are narrow ravines leading through them, and we will deploy to block them, to bottle up the Deathlord's army for as long as we can."

"Aye," Karkald said, relieved that the plan had been made, disappointed that it was not just advisable but essential. He looked seaward again and could have sworn that the armada was another mile closer to landing.

"Just beware, old friend," he said, clapping Gallupper on his equine shoulder. "And do not wait too long to pull out."

DARANN took only the time to don her sandals and a light robe, the soft deerskin a hallmark of an earlier time, when trade between Axial and Nayve had been commonplace and profitable for the merchants of both circles. Now, the warmth of the soft fur gave her just a suggestion of the life and the security she had once taken for granted.

She hurried to the lift station, leaving Hiyram to make his way to the stairway. Coolfyre lights blazed from each of the Six Towers, and she could see below the great city coming to life for another interval. Darkbulls pulled carts toward the marketplace, formations of royal guardsmen marched back and forth for the change of the duty, and the hammers of early rising forge men were already battering their irons.

The lift cage was quiet, however, lacking even the low hiss of steam that indicated pressure. Almost groaning in despair, she reached toward the test pipe, felt the cold metal.

Why now? She wanted to scream. The lift went

through a half interval's maintenance every cycle or so, but how could she have the accursed bad luck to find it shut down now, when she so desperately needed haste?

She wasted no time in turning around and racing back to her apartment, unlocking the door with haste and charging into the anteroom. "Hiyram?" she asked, louder than she intended, hoping to catch the goblin before he departed.

There was no answering sound. She charged through the kitchen and found the delivery door closed and latched. Pulling it open, she ducked through the narrow passage beyond and found herself at the edge of the deep, central pit that ran the full length of the pillar's center. There was a metal handrail before her, and she seized it, swaying to a sudden onset of vertigo.

It was not just the long drop that made her dizzy. As she drew a breath she nearly gagged from the foul stench, a mixture of garbage and other, unidentifiable odors that clogged the air with a greasy, penetrating miasma. Somewhere near the bottom a coolfyre beacon flickered, and another illuminated the landings near the top of the tower. Darann was near the middle, five hundred feet from each of the feeble lights, perched on a brink of a well of impenetrable shadow.

She was trying to decide if she dared call for the goblin, knowing her voice would echo up and down the vast shaft, when she saw a shadowy figure advancing up the stairway. Recognizing Hiyram just before she gasped out an alarm, she allowed herself to slump back against the wall and waited for her loyal friend to join her.

"Lady? What you here? Take lift—make haste!" he hissed, his mouth close to her ear. Even then, the sounds he made sounded disastrously loud in the close space.

"I can't," she whispered back, quickly explaining

about the maintenance shutdown. "I have to go down this way, or wait."

Hiyram looked alarmed, his eyes growing wide, glowing dimly even in the faint light. "No dwarf ladies here!" he insisted. "Goblins, pailsloppers, wretches, and rats . . . not for you! But no wait, neither . . . not to give warn to Honored Fatherbeard!"

"I have no choice," the dwarfmaid replied, oddly taking some comfort in the fact that Hiyram obviously knew this place. He was right: she had never been in here before, had never climbed by foot all the way up or down from her lofty apartment. "Show me the way, won't you?"

Reluctantly, he agreed, pointing out the steps that seemed shockingly narrow, with a long drop from one to the next. The stairway spiraled around the inside of the great shaft, which was otherwise lined with a web of cables and landings that, she assumed, were used by the freight lift that carried supplies up to the many apartments that lined the outer face of this lofty pillar. There was a metal rail, slick with moisture but, fortunately, pocked with enough rust that it seemed to give a good grip to the hand that she clasped, very tightly, around it. The wall to her right was cold and slick with fungus, while the drop to her left was . . . she didn't want to think about what it was.

Urgency overcame her fear, and she descended as quickly as possible behind Hiyram as the goblin padded down the stairway. His broad feet slapped slightly with each step, but otherwise he remained silent, looking around constantly, pausing every minute or so to give Darann time to catch up. The spiral was a dizzying descent, and even going as fast as she could they had only gone a quarter of the way before they had to stop so that she could catch her breath.

She grimaced and despaired, as each inhalation sounded like a bellows to her ears. The goblin, apparently unfatigued, simply waited until she was ready to move, then started onward again. Her hand was cramped from clutching the railing, but she dared not let go; the drop to her left was dizzying and certainly lethal, and in places the steps were crumbled or slicked with oil, water, or some combination of treacherous slipperiness.

Hiyram let out a hiss and suddenly sprang forward, leaving Darann to cling to the rail and try to see and hear. Angry screeches filled the air, claws scratching at the stones as small bodies climbed and jumped away; she realized with revulsion that the goblin had scattered a pack of rats that were clustering on a nearby landing, feasting upon a pile of rotting garbage. Holding her breath, she inched past, then hurried on, ignoring the sounds behind her as the angry rodents returned to reclaim their prize.

The light grew more intense as they neared the bottom of the shaft. They heard a door open down below, a beam of bright coolfyre spilling in as dwarven workers hauled in several crates and stacked them on the platform of one of the freight lifts. Darann and Hiyram froze, crouched against the wall a hundred feet above, and the dwarfmaid felt new despair at this evidence that the city was coming to life around them.

Finally the workers departed, and they all but flew around the last few spirals to the bottom of the shaft, arriving out of breath and weak-kneed from the long descent.

"You go on now, Lady," Hiyram said, pointing to the door the workmen had closed. "Not be seen with me . . . I come out later."

"Thank you, my friend," she said, giving the goblin a firm embrace.

She stepped toward the portal when she was startled by a stern bark. A dwarf was there, standing hitherto unseen

in the shadows beyond the lift. The beacon reflected off
his silver helm, marking him as one of the Royal Guard.

"Halt there!" he cried, then raised his voice in a pitch
of excitement. "Goblin! Goblin in the tower!" He rushed
forward, drawing a short, fat-bladed sword.

Hiyram yelped and bounded back up the stairs as
Darann bolted for the door, sensing freedom. She pushed
the portal open and rushed forth, only to have her arm
seized by another guard, this one apparently posted outside the door.

"Keep that bitch right there!" shouted the first guard
over his shoulder as he clattered up the stairs. "She's a
goblin friend, I warrant. Lord Nayfal will want some
words with her! I'm after the gob!"

By that time he was out of sight, but two more guards
advanced to surround Darann, pressing her against the
wall at the base of the pillar. She fought back an urge to
sob, seeing that the city was fully awake now, knowing
that Hiyram was in terrible trouble, and that her father was
going, all unwitting, into Lord Nayfal's trap.

BORAND awakened to a sensation of suffocating pain, as
though his ribs were on fire and a giant vise had been
clamped around his chest. Dimly he remembered the fall,
and the temblor that had shaken the First Circle with such
brutal violence. There was a pale light coming from somewhere outside of his line of sight, and hot pain jabbed
through his neck when he tried to turn his head. Still, he
was able to ascertain that he was in some sort of niche or
cave. Beyond the mouth, the ceiling of the Underworld reflected the light barely a hundred feet above, so he knew
that he was still high up on the barrier wall.

Moments later the light grew bright, and he saw that
Konnor and Aurand joined him. Both dwarves looked pale

and shaken, but they brightened as Borand looked at them and tried to contort his face into a smile—though he was sure the expression became more of a grimace than anything else.

"A relief to see you move, brother," said Aurand, squatting next to the injured climber. "You took a nasty hit, broke some ribs at least. We wondered about your neck, tell the truth."

"Sprained but not broken," Borand replied, ignoring the pain enough to wiggle his head back and forth. He looked at Konnor. "Thanks for the belay, my friend."

"A good save it was," Aurand noted. "The whole world started coming apart while you were falling. It's a miracle you didn't go all the way to the bottom."

"What, and spare you louts the pleasure of carrying me down?" snorted the elder dwarf, drawing reluctant smiles from his two companions. "That is, if we can still find our way down. How much of the cliff fell away?"

"More than you'll believe," Konnor replied. "We were just having a look. Care to sit up and see for yourself?"

With great effort, and assistance from both of his fellows, Borand pulled himself into a sitting position. His back was against the rock face, and he looked out of the niche—it was too shallow to be a cave—and into the great gulf of the First Circle. Vast blackness yawned beyond.

"Funny . . . I thought we could see the wall from here," he grunted, ignoring the pain that flared through his ribs. "Or did you move me farther along the cliff?"

"No, this is where you ended up on the rope," Aurand explained. "And your memory is good. Before you fell, you *could* see the whole face of the circle from here."

"What happened—did the quake knock it down?" Borand found it hard to imagine that such a vast section of the world's edge could have fallen away, leaving the space he now observed.

"It fell in the quake, but it wasn't solid. The wall we were looking at was only a shell, and when it went, we got a look into the space beyond."

Something in the way Konnor said "space beyond" gave Borand a chill of discovery and dread. Grunting against the effort, he pushed himself farther outward, expanding his view. His companions obliged by turning their coolfyre beacons out, the light spilling far, not quite vanishing into the distance.

There, at the limits of his sight, he saw a façade of rock, and he quickly realized this was not a face of natural cliff. Instead, he saw lofty balconies, grand parapets, a score of stairways crossing back and forth and up and down, the surface newly revealed. Below, in the nearly lightless depths, he got a sense of broad, shadowy courtyards, and at least one place that looked like a vast, circular coliseum.

"A city?" he whispered, wonder and fear softening his voice. "A *huge* city?"

Konnor nodded. "It can only be one place."

"Nightrock?" Now Borand felt the cold clamp of fear. The legendary capital of the Blind Ones had never been observed by Seer eyes. Now that they had come here, their lives were certainly forfeit. But at the same time, there was a sense of stillness and quietude to the place. Surely this was no hive of the Unmirrored!

"Indeed, it must be," his brother said. "We could see a thousand buildings just in range of our lights, and who knows how many more in the lightless hive within."

"But the Delvers? Surely they must have smelled us, or heard us . . . at the very least, one of their arcanes would sense us!"

"That's the thing," Konnor explained, maddeningly calm. "We have found the great city of our enemies, the threat that has kept our army bottled up in Axial for these last fifty years—"

"But—" Aurand couldn't help finishing the explanation. "There are no Delvers there. The whole place has been abandoned!"

"YOU may go in to see the king now, Lord Rufus," said the palace attendant, offering the grizzled dwarf only the barest suggestion of a bow. "But he has many appointments today; beware of wasting his time."

The elder dwarf stood straight and glared at the servant, who was a young fellow wearing armor of oiled leather with a short, double-bladed sword at his waist.

"Time was, a dwarf knew his place, and a king knew how to command his own schedule," Rufus Houseguard commented in a tone of elaborate calm, making no move to step forward. At the same time, he held his eyes steady, allowing the contempt and frustration to burn forth. The attendant tried to match his look for a moment, then flushed and turned to open the door.

"Ah, Rufus—please, come forward, my old friend!" King Lightbringer was seated on his throne, and he sounded genuinely pleased to see the patriach of clan Houseguard. "Too much business these days, not enough chance for a pleasant chat."

"I am at your service, sire," Rufus said, striding forward and offering a deep bow.

At the same time, he noticed more of the changes that had been taking place in the court of the Seer Dwarf king. For one thing, there were no longer courtiers here, nor the ladies that had once made this throne room such a lively and welcoming place. Now there were only guards, wearing the ubiquitous leather shirts and short swords. Marshall Nayfal, the monarch's senior adviser, stood to one side and made no attempt to conceal his displeasure at Lord Houseguard's arrival. Only as he stood straight again did Rufus notice that another dwarf had been in audience, a balding, earnest-looking fellow in fine silk robes who was peering through wire-rimmed glasses at a ledger he held in his hands. He cleared his throat, obviously impatient to continue whatever he had been talking about before Rufus's arrival.

The king, however, seemed to have different ideas. "How is your daughter?" he inquired. "Such a wonderful maid, she is. I would see her again, the next time you come."

"She is well, sire, and I know she would be honored to accompany me."

"Good. . . ." King Lightbringer leaned back in his throne and closed his eyes. Rufus was shocked at the pallor of the monarch's skin, the thin and stringy nature of his hair and beard. It was as if the ancient king, who had ruled Axial for centuries, was withering away before his eyes.

"Go ahead, Commisar Whitbeard," Marshal Nayfal declared, speaking to the bespectacled visitor. "Please continue."

That dwarf cleared his throat and cast Rufus a glance of no small annoyance before he again squinted at the page of numbers scrawled in his ledger. "I regret that the goblin demands remain as unreasonable as ever, Majesty," he said. "No matter the food and fresh water we provide them—without requiring any labor in return, I might add—they keep insisting that our care is insufficient, that hunger is rampant in the goblin quarter."

As the commissar continued his report, Rufus noticed a familiar face among the guards and nobles on the other side of the hall. Donnwell Earnwise, the royal engineer, gave Rufus a smile and a small wave, which the patriarch of clan Houseguard cheerfully returned. He wondered about subtly going over to say hello to his old friend when he noticed that Whitbeard seemed to have concluded his report.

The king sighed and winced; to Rufus it appeared that the news caused him physical pain. "The situation in our own granaries is still dire?" he said, making the remark a question.

"Indeed, Your Majesty." It was Nayfal who answered. "The good citizens of Axial are as hungry as the goblins, to be sure. We are merely more stoic and know to avoid the unseemly whining of the lower race."

"What do you think, Rufus?" said the king, suddenly sitting up, opening his eyes, and fixing the lord with a stern glare.

"I think, sire, that perhaps it may be time to expand our interests beyond this narrow margin around Axial," replied Rufus Houseguard, speaking impulsively, sensing he had to make his point before Nayfal found a way to divert the monarch's attention. "I note the presence of our esteemed Engineer Earnwise—and I recall there was some hope of using his device, the Worldlift, to penetrate the barrier that has arisen between our world and Nayve. I urge you to devote as many resources as possible to that task! If we can penetrate the barrier of blue magic, we already have the route to the Fourth Circle; the Rockshaft, as you know, extends from your palace here, through the Midrock, and all the way to Circle at Center."

"As a matter of fact, I had just heard some rather encouraging reports on that very matter," said the king, brightening visibly. "Isn't that right, Donnwell?"

"Absolutely, sire," proclaimed the famed scientist and inventor. He addressed Rufus. "I have been able to send a rocket projectile through the barrier. The key seems to be incredible velocity—enough to breach the magic shield that had rendered upward travel hitherto impossible. Of

course, we are some ways short of sending an actual
dwarf—the traveler's survival, at this juncture, is far from
assured. But nevertheless, it is progress."

"If anyone can solve that problem, it will be you,"
Rufus declared sincerely. "And if we can break through to
Nayve, our prospects for food, for trade—everything im-
proves!"

Nayfal chuckled, a dry sound devoid of amusement.
"You always were a dreamer, Lord Houseguard," he said.
"Fortunately, our monarch realizes that our dangers, and
our salvations, lie closer to home. We have a responsibility not just for the present but for the future of our people!"

Rufus pressed on with his argument. "It has been fifty
years since the loss at Arkan Pass, and we have discerned
no major Delver move toward our city. Admittedly, in the
aftermath of the battle, caution demanded that we pull
back from our more far-flung outposts, even though we
sacrificed much of our food supply."

"And the Blind Ones are still out there, waiting—"
Marshall Nayfal attempted to intercede, but Rufus trampled ahead as if he hadn't heard.

"There are the great fungus flats of the Metalreach,
food enough to feed the city for a year in a single harvest.
We could send an expedition, well protected of course, to
retrieve many barges full of those mushrooms. It is worth
the chance, sire. Consider: perhaps the Delvers suffered a
loss as great as ours at Arkan Pass! We need to venture
into our world again, explore, reconnoiter . . ."

"Perhaps seek to open the routes to Nayve, again? Is
that what you are getting at?" asked the king with a toler-
ant smile.

"Your Majesty!" declared Nayfal, his face growing
pale. "Remember the disastrous attempts of four decades

ago. Hundreds of brave miners buried, seeking a passage that no longer exists."

Rufus snorted, contempt getting the best of his judgment. "Indeed, sire, we suffered great losses—because the shafts were poorly shored, and we faced the barrier of magic—the force that we were barely beginning to understand. A tragic mistake, but one that can be rectified, especially if the Worldlift can be completed. And why not seek a return to Nayve? The peoples of the Fourth Circle would be happy to trade food for gold, iron, flamestone—resources we have in abundance."

"And you know where you would look for such a route?" the king asked, still smiling tolerantly. "In case the Worldlift does not prove to be the panacea?"

"I have ideas," admitted the dwarf lord. "My sons, Borand and Aurand, have explored some routes on their ferr'ells. They have found a promising gap in the direction that is neither metal nor wood. With reinforcements, they might be able to—"

"We have no troops for such expeditions!" snapped Nayfal. "We cannot risk the warriors, the precious few ferr'ells in our corrals, on such a mad quest!"

Rufus bit his tongue and watched the king, who once again seemed very old, very tired. Lightbringer settled into his throne, and his head leaned forward, his beard bristling across his chest almost as if he was falling asleep. Finally, he shook his head. "No, my good Rufus, I cannot sanction such an attempt, not when we still don't know the status of the Delver armies. They could strike at any time . . . any time at all. . . ."

"But we can be prepared for an attack, sire. There are many ways! We could man the watch stations again . . . even enlist the goblins to scout for us." Rufus heard Nayfal's gasp but forged ahead with his arguments. He sensed he was making his points too frantically, but he couldn't hold back. When would he get the king's ear again?

"Remember, the goblins have fought on *our* side in a dozen campaigns! Why, we could even venture out and seek the Delver army, take the battle to them, strike by surprise. . . ."

His voice trailed off as he noticed that the king was snoring. Rufus knew the audience was over. He was not surprised when Nayfal came over to him, the marshal solicitous, sympathetic, as he escorted Rufus through the door, toward the steam-powered lift beyond. "I understand your frustration, my lord. But we must be realistic. There are grave threats to the kingdom, and we dare not take the chance to weaken ourselves. Why, the goblins themselves present a real threat!"

"Bah! The goblins would be our allies again if we could but treat them with a modicum of dignity!"

"I know your feelings on this. It should not be a surprise to you that we are aware of your daughter's activities on their behalf. I admire her generosity, even if there are those who feel that she is rather unwise to be such a sympathizer with those miserable wretches in the ghetto."

"I am proud of my daughter and her work," Houseguard said stiffly. "Would that there were more with her courage and her insight in our once-bright city. Perhaps there would be some questions asked—investigations, even?"

"What do you mean?" the royal adviser asked, his eyes narrowing.

"I mean regarding the death of Cubic Mandrill. There are stories abroad, you know?" Rufus regarded the other dwarf carefully, saw the flush creeping up the ruddy cheeks, the cold fury in his eyes. With visible effort, Nayfal drew a deep breath and made a display of shrugging unconcernedly.

"Admirable sentiment," Nayfal said breezily. "Who knows—it may happen someday, though I suspect we already know the truth. Goblin treachery nearly claimed the life of our beloved king, and since then the goblins have met the fate that they deserved. Still, it does not hurt to ask. You are very influential in this city, perhaps more than you know."

The two dwarves arrived at the lift, where the metal cage rattled to a stop and the door of metal bars clanked open. "But . . . are you sure you won't reconsider your support of continued exploration of the Midrock? Can't you see the danger?"

"I see the danger in cowardice," Rufus Houseguard retorted. "In hiding behind our walls and shutting out the rest of our world, of all the worlds!"

"I am truly sorry you feel that way," replied the king's closest adviser. Rufus had the odd sensation that the marshal was, for once, speaking with true sincerity. He watched, puzzled, as Nayfal signaled the lift operator, the cage starting down.

And then the floor seemed to drop away. The dwarven lord slammed against the wall as the lift plummeted without any support, any brake on its shrieking, quarter mile descent. Rufus clung to a railing, stunned by the blow, feeling the strangest sensation . . . as if he was floating, utterly weightless.

The crash as the cage hit bottom was a monstrous noise, tearing metal and shattering rock exploding into lethal splinters. In the middle of the tangled wreckage, Rufus Houseguard, esteemed lord of Axial, was far beyond any sensation of pain.

6

Admiral of the Oglala Sioux

Images of light and color,
Sounds of nothing at all;
Violence binds the souls together,
Mortal flesh in chains will fall.

From the epic *Days of Worlds' End*
by Sirien Saramayd

How much had he learned in the past forty years, since the soldier's bayonet had sliced his guts and ended his brief and glorious life on the Seventh Circle? As the battle raged before him, Crazy Horse reflected on the question and knew that it was impossible to imagine the answer.

Beauty . . . he had learned so much about beauty. Certainly he had known for all of his first life the splendor of a sunrise above the Dunkapapa, the Black Hills. He had seen the wondrous grace of a fleet deer, the sleek musculature of a fast pony . . . and he had beheld the grace and tenderness of a splendid woman. But not until Cloud-walking Moon had revealed herself to him in the grotto of

Nayve's highlands, where stars drifted overhead and the scent of pine was sweet nectar in each breath, had he known the true depths of wonder that beauty could provoke. He had taken Moon at once, and again and again, and over the course of the night was spellbound beyond any previous measure.

And he had gained wisdom . . . he had conversed for hours, days, cycles with the druid Miradel, and his mind had grown broad with the knowledge of reality far surpassing anything the Sioux shamans had understood. The study of the Seven Circles, he had realized with no small amount of pleasure, even made mockeries of the truths accepted by the white men who had come to claim his lands, to drive his people from the hills and plains.

He had also learned of courage. Crazy Horse, of course, had always been a courageous man, and he had battled mighty foes without ever a thought of running away. It was he who had led the Sioux and Cheyenne warriors who had smashed the cavalry and taken the life of the ambitious general Custer on the hills above the Little Big Horn. And when his people had been starving, and the white soldiers were everywhere, he had gone bravely to meet the soldiers at Fort Laramie, there to face the steel cage of a cell and at last the steel blade of the bayonet.

When he came to Nayve and learned the truth, his bravery at first compelled him to cry out, to beg for a return to the Seventh Circle, a chance at vengeance and honor. He had fantasized, for a time, with his new knowledge, wishing he could return to the plains and unite the bickering tribes, leading them in a great war. But then the warrior Natac had shown him a different kind of bravery. Crazy Horse had learned the fate of Tlaxcalans and Aztecs, of Iroquois and Cherokee, and had seen the inevitability of change.

He had even begun to understand the cold reality of

such change as it was overtaking his world: it was not that one people was evil, the other good. It was, instead, that one side had far more people, as well as better weapons and better tactics of war, than the other. Most significantly, he had seen the effectiveness of troops who could be controlled by a commander, wielded as a weapon of one mind. His beloved Sioux were independent and impetuous warriors, each man doing as he sought fit, seeking individual glory over a coordinated objective. Because of that more than anything else, they were doomed, as were the Cheyenne and the Nez Percé and the Apaches and all the other tribes . . . doomed because the white men would follow orders, wielding their better weapons and better tactics in a pursuit of a common objective. And they had so many people, so many soldiers, that they would never be stopped.

Now, he looked down at the deck of his boat, and he felt a strong measure of hope: this time, *he* had the better weapon.

Dakota was a large sailboat, like *Kaiser*, the flagship of a fleet numbering hundreds of vessels, equipped with an observation tower, and a pair of powerful batteries. Crazy Horse took a look to the stern, where Cloudwalking Moon spun the wind in her great bowl, and he was rewarded by a smile from the woman he loved, loved more than he had ever loved anyone. A part of his mind, a very old part lingering from the Seventh Circle, felt a tremor of chagrin that she was here with him, going into such danger. He simply shrugged; he was a warrior of Nayve now, and so was she.

Turning his attention to the fore, he watched the dark ships of the armada surging against Fritzi's wing. He admired the Prussian's courage, the discipline of his sailors, and he thrilled to the sight of the smoke and flames blossoming among the death ships. His own wing, the middle of Roland's fleet, numbered some 350 boats and now waited in three great lines. The druids spun enough wind to keep them aligned forward, moving very slowly, but they would wait for their leader's command before they rushed ahead.

Crazy Horse narrowed his eyes as he saw large death ships, dozens of towering vessels, veering toward him, swerving around, blocking his view of Fritzi's line. He sensed the encirclement as it began, and with that realization he ordered the flag raised, the signal for a general advance.

Cloudwalking Moon spun a fast wind now, as did the other druids of his fleet, and the sailboats surged forward, slicing the waters, leaving white wakes behind. For the first time on Nayve, Crazy Horse thrilled to a martial charge, the boat pitching and speeding as vibrantly as any pony could run. He saw the tall shapes of his enemies, sensed the impetuous eagerness of the druids and warriors as they raced in to the attack

The first rank of boats, including his own, launched their steel bolts when they were still a half mile away from the enemy fleet. The metal spears ripped into the black hulls, exploding and burning and wreaking fearful havoc. The rest of the druid boats came on, spreading out, shooting at unscathed ships as soon as another dark vessel swerved into range.

Fighting raged all across the front, acrid smoke mixing with the miasma of the Deathlord's fleet to clog nostrils and sting eyes. In a chaos of movement the deadly dance evolved, sailboats darting between lumbering ships, spitting their deadly barbs, pressing forward with courage every bit the equal of a plains warrior trying to count coup.

But where were Fritzi's ships? Crazy Horse squinted through the murk, tried to catch a glimpse of white canvas—even a single sail!—but there was nothing to break that aura of darkness. A glance to the left showed him more ships, a hundred of them, sweeping out from the armada, attempting to encircle his own wing of boats just as the Prussian's had been devoured.

The truth was bitter gall, but it was apparent: if they held the charge they, too, would be swept into the insatiable belly of the deadly armada. There was no sign of any white sail, any surviving boat, in the tangled and smoky melee before them. The First Wing was gone, utterly destroyed, and if he held the current course, Crazy Horse would lead his own men and women to the same fate.

He raised the blue flag, the signal for a withdrawal, and like magic the druid boats responded, turning through tight half circles, running for the clean water along the metal coast, away from the armada. They were running, leaving many of the enemy intact. . . .

But they would be alive to fight again tomorrow.

THE pictures of war played out on the whitewashed wall of the Worldweaver's inner sanctum, but Miradel found her eyes drawn not to the waterborne carnage but to the face of the druid Shandira. She was surprised to see the African woman looking back at her when Miradel glanced over to gauge her reaction to the First Wing's destruction.

Many druids were gathered in the viewing room to witness the commencement of the long-dreaded war. Cillia herself, eldest druid of the order, fed the Wool of Time into the candle flame, though her fingers trembled slightly as the image of the armada darkened the whole, vast wall. The white sails of the druid boats seemed like tiny snowflakes wafting toward a great gulf of smoke, and Miradel heard murmurs of fear and horror as the two fleets mingled.

The pictures showed the view from high overhead, and for that she was grateful. They could make out the three separate wings of Roland Boatwright's fleet, and they marveled at the bravery of Fritzi Koeppler's wing as it rushed to intercept the advancing tide of darkness. Tiny sparks glowed every time a death ship exploded, and the druids collectively held their breath as the thin line of white sails stood firm before the onslaught.

But of course the armada was too huge, and as the arms of black reached around the boats of the First Wing, one by one the white sails broke or burned or sank. In a surprisingly short time, the entire wing was gone, engulfed by the darkness. They had endured no longer than the snowflakes they resembled, melting away in the furnace of battle. Miradel looked up as she heard a sob, saw Gretchen—the druid who had summoned Fritzi to Nayve—clasp her hands over her face and run from the room, sobbing.

Some unknown time later Miradel and Shandira walked into the garden, alone in the midst of a hundred somber druids who all emerged from the viewing chamber to cleanse themselves in the sunlight and try, for the most part unsuccessfully, to dispel the lingering nightmare of the sea battle.

"The black ships . . . they will reach the shore in a matter of hours, it seems," Shandira observed quietly. Her face was downcast, but she still carried that regal sense of pride in her tall frame. The white of her gown stood in stark contrast to the darkness of her limbs and her face. Her eyes were wet with tears as she looked at Miradel. "The carnage . . . it was horrible!"

"Beyond horror," the elder druid agreed. "I don't know if the armada will reach shore that quickly, though. There are still two more wings to Roland's fleet, and they were close." She glanced at the sky, where the sun was already receding upward, purple twilight closing in from all horizons. "I think they will wait until Lighten before attacking."

"All those ship masters, the warriors who fought with such courage . . . all of them were brought here by druids, performing the spell of summoning?"

"Yes . . . many of the same druids were spinning the winds for their warriors. The loss of each boat meant the loss of at least two lives."

Shandira nodded, and her eyes narrowed. "There was that serpent flying above—like the Beast of my church's nightmares, though you call it benign—and the man astride his back. He is your lover?"

Miradel drew a quick breath. "How did you know? I said nothing about Natac."

"I saw the way you clenched your fists, tightened your jaw, when the picture was upon him. Also the way many other druids looked in your direction, quickly and secretly, when the picture moved to him."

"You are right. I love him very much . . . have loved him for more than four hundred years."

"You brought him here, with your Spell of Summoning?"

"I did, though it cost me my youth. And I had no regrets. It was the mercy of the goddess that I returned to earth and lived through seven more lives there, before again returning to Nayve in this young woman's body."

"But if your goddess was to command you to give yourself to another, to work the magic to bring a warrior here, you would do so?"

Miradel stared at Shandira, astounded by the question—and by the rush of outrage that arose within her at the thought of giving herself to another man. "I told you . . . one druid can only summon one warrior. Natac is my warrior," she said, sensing the evasion even as she tried to sound decisive.

"That is no answer." The black woman's tone was not accusing, but blunt. "Anyway, I know the answer: you would not. Because you love this man, and the love you share is a treasure. Can you not know this about me: the love I hold for my Savior is as precious, or more, to me. I cannot betray it by performing this carnal act!"

"Even though you know that Savior, the promise of Heaven and the threat of Hell, are myths, created by humans to explain that which they did not know? Cannot you see that *this* is real, here . . . the truth lies with the Worldweaver, at the Center of Everything? Do you deny the existence of Nayve?"

Shandira shook her head sadly. "My faith has been shaken in so many ways, yet I feel that it is all I have left. Perhaps this is a test of that faith . . . a temptation to deny the real truth." She raised her head, looked at Miradel from beneath that great mane of hair, then extended a hand and placed it on the shorter woman's shoulder. "I believe that there is evil here, just as there was upon earth. And I will devote myself to fighting that evil. But I cannot do it in the way you ask. Is there not some other means with which I may wage my battle?"

Miradel felt those strong fingers squeeze her shoulder, and she was surprised by the comfort she derived from that touch. She placed her own hand over Shandira's and nodded, watching the druids in the garden start filing back into the viewing chamber. "There will be a way," she promised. "I don't know what it is, but we will find it."

THE coast of the Blue Coral Sea was obscured by smoke, a thick dark cloud that rolled from the water onto the land, stinging the eyes and nostrils of the elves arrayed above the beaches. Tamarwind Trak stood on the highest sand dune, a wet kerchief pulled across his face in an effort to alleviate the pain of each breath. One eye was closed, the other pressed to the viewpiece of a telescope.

"I can't see any more of our boats," he said grimly to Gallupper.

With an angry snort, the centaur pawed one of his fore-hooves through the sandy ground. "It was as brave an attack as I've ever seen or imagined," he said, his deep voice rumbling like distant thunder. "They deserved a better fate."

"Just because I can't see them doesn't mean that no one escaped," the elf demurred hopefully.

In truth, however, there was little hope. The two arms of the armada had simply been too large, hundreds of ships surging in front of Fritzi Koeppler's wing, blocking the advance even as the fire-bolts tore through their hulls. The valiant warriors and druids had found themselves trapped by fiery wreckage before them as well as off-shore, while land itself blocked flight toward the center. Thus, when the death ships had surged around behind the wing of druid boats, the Prussian's vessels had no route of escape.

For more than two hours Tam had watched the black ships closing in. He lost count of how many had burned, but even this had been a vain tactic: the flaming ships of the enemy had been blown right into the mass of sailboats as the defenders had been packed into tighter and tighter quarters. At last, the entire surface of the sea was obscured by smoke, broken only by bright plumes of crackling fire.

"I don't see how any of them could have survived," the elf said, his words hushed by awe.

"But they have managed to buy us some time," the centaur pointed out. He indicated behind them, where a long column of warriors—centaurs, giants, and elves—was marching into view, pouring out of the gap between two mountain ridges. "And that will allow us to give them a real pounding, once they try to land."

"I lost a hundred or more boats before pulling back," Crazy Horse announced grimly. "There were too many death ships; I could not break through to Fritzi's wing, though we charged four times. They have coordination and tactics, these ghost warriors, for they closed ranks to prevent our advance and paid no heed to the numbers they lost—five hundred ships ablaze, just in the last hour."

"They are well led, it seems," Natac noted, not surprised by the observation. Even so, it was a chilling realization, for he couldn't imagine the nature of the enemy general.

"But by the goddess, what a blow," the Sioux warrior continued, his eyes moist. "To hear that Fritzi's fleet perished to the last vessel! Even that Prussian—I thought he would live forever!"

"He fought and died as well as any man could," Natac replied. "I saw it from the sky. He had a death ship to either side, ghosts swarming onto his deck. Faerwind wielded a sword like a master, guarding his back while he launched volleys from his two batteries, canister blasts into the hulls rising up to either side of him. Only then did he fall, and the druid perished on top of him—but not before the black ship to each side was engulfed by flame."

Darken had come to the warriors gathered on the wide beach. A large bonfire, fueled by driftwood, illuminated a ring of grim-faced men and women. Dick Rudolph was here with his druid, Christina, who stood beside Cloud-walking Moon, the windcaster for the Sioux's boat. Tamarwind Trak had ridden Gallupper to the meeting on the beach, and now the lanky elf stood beside the grim-faced centaur. Roland Boatwright and Sirien Saramayd were also in the circle, while Regillix Avatar was coiled on the dunes above the beach, extending his long neck so that his crocodilian face loomed just above the conference.

"And the armada?" asked Roland. "Will they wait for Lighten to move in?"

"We saw a dozen death ships crash on the reefs," Natac reported, "and then the rest of them drew back. I think we have until morning."

"We have ten thousand elves of Argentian entrenched above the beaches," Tamarwind offered. "All the batteries in the centaur arsenal are there in support, and we have two regiments of giants held in reserve, ready to strike at the first sign of a breakthrough."

"Then we need to make another attack at first light," Rudolph said. "Follow up on Fritzi's blow, wreck as many of them as we can."

"I agree," Natac said, "though I will not order such an assault. Whatever gains are made must surely be offset by another day of grievous losses."

"We have a lot of strength on the beach," Tam reminded them. "You can let them land, and we'll try to stop them at the water's edge."

"We're here to fight," Cloudwalking Moon said. She was a plump, round-faced woman of bronze brown skin, like Crazy Horse, of Native American heritage. Her ancestors had dwelled among the Nez Percé tribe. "No point in standing back now, when the issue will be decided. If we perish, we know we give ourselves to a great cause."

"I think we are all agreed on that," Christina said, her head held high. "We are here, and we can hurt them. No matter the cost, we need to strike, and strike hard."

Natac had a hard time speaking, so tight was his throat.

He loved these warriors and druids, loved them all with a passion that he could not even begin to comprehend. It grieved him to know that, tomorrow, so many of them would die. But he also knew that Christina and Cloud-walking Moon were right: there was nothing for it but to continue the battle, no matter what the cost.

"You have the admiration and respect of all Nayve," he said thickly. "Try to get a good night's rest; then do what you have to do tomorrow.

THE druid boats came on in two waves, white sails aloft, magical winds propelling the sleek hulls through the coast waters. When the first rank drew close to the fringe of the armada they began to shoot, and once again the heavy steel fire-bolts wreaked havoc on the black ships of the Death-lord. One after another of the ghost-crewed ships burst into flame, breaking apart, sinking, or careening wildly as the small, nimble sailboats darted between them and drove deep into the crowded seas at the great fleet's heart.

Natac and Regillix flew overhead, knowing there could be no retreat, not anymore. This time they would have to press home the attack, inflict as much damage as they could. The serpent tightened his wings, arrowing toward the skies over the armada.

Again the harpies sallied forth, a great squawking formation in the sky. This time, the serpent had a new tactic ready—a maneuver he put to instant use. Climbing toward the flock, Regillix belched a great cloud of fire into the midst of the beasts, searing a hundred or more in the killing blast. Natac, meanwhile, fired shots from a specially modified crossbow. Each missile launched a spray of marble-sized canisters into the air, and when these flew out to several hundred feet, each of them exploded with a violent burst, knocking many more winged attackers right out of the sky.

The dragon immediately tucked his wings and dove away, as the warrior launched one more shot at the flock, which was not so much a cloud as a tattered sheet by now. They plummeted downward, wind stinging past as they plunged through the murk toward the black ships. This time Natac and Regillix Avatar wasted no time, displayed no caution. The dragon roared above the black decks, striking with his claws to knock down tall mainmasts, belching clouds of fire that quickly engulfed one death ship after another in roiling conflagration.

Natac was armed with two bags full of another of Karkald's inventions: metal canisters with fins on one end and a metal trigger on the other. He pulled one out as the dragon swerved over a death ship. Seeing that Regillix was still drawing a breath after his exhalation of fire, the warrior took this target as his own. He timed his throw carefully, tossing the bomb toward the middle of the deck. The fins stabilized the flight, angling the trigger downward, and the canister struck the vessel near the port railing.

As they swept past, flying fast, Natac saw the device break through the planks of the deck with a bright flash. He looked back as the serpent drove his wings downward and was rewarded by the sight of a fiery plume, oily flames mixed with timbers, rigging, and the shredded forms of numerous ghost warriors. The main and foremasts of the ship toppled into the water, carrying rigging and sails with them, and before his scaly mount swerved into another attack, the Tlaxcalan saw flames cracking along the length of the vessel's port side.

Impressed, he reached for another of the bombs, holding his throw as Regillix leaned down to belch a cloud of fire across another death ship. Once more they swept past their doomed victim, and Natac made another toss, cursing angrily as the speed of their flight carried the bomb too far; he saw it explode harmlessly in the sea.

But he had more of the bombs—ten slung from each side of the dragon's powerful neck—and so he readied for another throw as Regillix banked sharply and came around, winging toward the fringe of the armada where the death ships were heavily engaged with the advancing line of druid-steered sailboats. In places the invading vessels were packed so tightly that it seemed as though the ocean itself was afire. A dozen of the black ships had collided and were locked in a tangle, masts toppled across each other, flames leaping hungrily from one ship to the next.

Nimble boats sailed past the confused mass as more flames skyrocketed upward, turning the group of doomed ships into a waterborne pyre. Still more of the Deathlord's fleet closed in, however, and Natac grimaced in almost physical pain as he saw one of the black hulls bear down on a sailboat, crushing the smaller craft into kindling before the druid could steer out of the way.

"I want that one!" he snarled, and Regillix heard. The dragon dove past, and the man lobbed another of his bombs, grimly satisfied as this one shattered the stern of the black sailing ship and quickly brought the vessel to a curving halt. Flames erupted from the deck as the dragon dove low, reaching his talons down to strike the masts and rend the sails from another pair of boats. They heard the cheering of druids and warriors as they swept past, and more and more of Roland's ships soared into the great breach they were tearing in the armada's flank.

The individual plumes of smoke from burning death ships merged into a pall of darkness, a cloud that stung Natac's nose and brought tears to his eyes. The dragon swerved wildly, banking right and carving a tight turn; as he looked to that side, the warrior had the impression of a world turned on end, a great cliff of dark ocean marking the periphery of space. With another lurch the serpent leveled his flight, then curved the other way, and Natac closed his eyes as they sailed right through a thick spume of churning smoke. He felt the heat against his skin, then a rush of coolness as they emerged.

"Can we get above this murk?" he called. "See what's really happening down there?"

Obligingly, the mighty dragon sliced his great pinions through the air, pressing downward, lifting himself and his passenger as he flew a great circle above the entangled fleets. Regillix snorted, releasing a thin cloud of smoke, and Natac knew the wyrm was letting the magical blaze smolder in his belly, building pressure for a renewed series of fiery exhalations. A thousand feet above the sea they found cleaner air, and by the time Regillix had completed another full circle and gained hundreds more feet of altitude, Natac could get a good view of the entire battle.

Again the harpies rose toward them. This time Natac launched several blasts while they were still far below, and when the dragon turned his head as if to breathe, the cowardly creatures dove back down to harass the druid boats. Ignoring the flying pests, Regillix and his rider turned their attention back to the vanguard of the armada.

"There, to the left—all of Roland's boats are engaged," Natac observed. "Can you get us over there for a better look?"

"As you wish," the dragon replied. "Though I do not like to let these others advance unmolested."

"I share that reluctance, old friend," Natac said. "Get us a look up high, and then we will dive back to our work."

Willingly, the serpent flexed his wings and bore them

along, above the first rank of the death ships. Natac was appalled at the vast ranks of dark hulls, line after line of them, extending out to sea as far as his eye could discern. Brown wakes trailed behind the ships, and the smoky sails billowed with unnatural, fetid wind. They were already inside the reefs, and within the next hour or less the first of the invaders' vessels would reach the shore.

Only where the druid boats attacked was the armada in disarray. The flyers passed above a hundred ships that burned from stem to stern, sails ragged and masts toppling. Others had capsized, the dark hulls looking like long, slick whales as they bobbed and twisted in the swells. Everywhere the sea was a mass of smoke and debris, and there was no order to the enemy ranks; indeed, dozens of the death ships had become tangled together, masts and rigging fouled as frantic maneuvers forced them into collisions.

And still the little boats pressed on. Here and there they saw white sails draped across the water, and several of the narrow decks teemed with black specks, ghost warriors who had boarded and slaughtered the crews, but that had no effect on the tide as a whole. The silver batteries flashed, launching their arrowlike harpoons from a distance or firing barrages of the metal spheres that burst into flame as soon as they contacted the target. Each propelled by its private wind, the little vessels ducked and weaved and dodged among the leviathans of the death ships, and more and more of the latter burst into flame.

Natac could see that Crazy Horse was extending his flank along the front of the armada, trying to interpose his boats and crews between the invaders and the shore. But he was cautious enough to keep his line intact, preventing a massive envelopment such as had annihilated Fritzi's wing on the previous day. As a counterpart, however, the defenders were not numerous enough to block the front of the enemy fleet, and hundreds of black-hulled warships surged forward, their route to the beach unimpeded by Nayvian action.

"Let's break up that line," Natac suggested, and Regillix readily agreed.

The serpent tucked his wings, and the pair swept into a blistering dive, pulling up just as they passed the farthest extent of Crazy Horse's boats. The dragon roared and spat a boiling inferno of oily fire, a blast that encompassed three or four ships at once. As his great steed inhaled for another attack, Natac lobbed more of his bombs, dropping the incendiary missiles with lethal accuracy onto the decks of one after another of the leading death ships.

He paused only when Regillix spewed another fireball, rendering a pair of side-by-side vessels into an instant inferno. Immediately after, Natac started throwing again, not even taking the time to wonder at the spectacular eruptions following each of his tosses. They continued along the line, flying, roaring, bombing, making a wreckage of the entire first line of the armada, leaving sixty, eighty, even a hundred ships flaming and sinking and dying.

But still they hadn't reached the end of that massive fleet, and by then the warrior was out of bombs, and the dragon was laboring, wearily, just to stay aloft. When Natac cast a glance over his shoulder, he was not surprised but he was filled with despair for, as he had expected, the next rank of the armada had merely passed through the first, and a new set of hulls, keen and undamaged, made its way unimpeded toward the green shore. Already they crested the breakers, sliding into the shallows. A hundred yards beyond, the beach of Nayve lay white and smooth and inviting, for the first time in all existence awaiting the touch of an invader's boot.

7

Matriarch

Mother's grace,
Father's strength,
Clan's destiny,
Child's hope;
All virtues drawn
On daughter's brow

From the Tapestry of the Worldweaver
History of Time

Darann gave up resisting as soon as she figured out that the guards were taking her to the Royal Tower. Not that she could have escaped the strong hands grasping like clamps to each of her arms, but she found some little cause for optimism in the realization that her captors were marching her directly to the place that had been her original destination. She marched along in step with the royal guardsmen, having wrested her arms out of their grasp. As they neared the king's hail she looked for her father, hoping to intercept him on his way to his audience.

That hope was dashed as they approached the lift station in the base of the tower and found a scene of chaos and destruction. Dwarves in guardsmen's tunics were pulling desperately at the wreckage of steel bars that lay tangled at the base of the long chute. King Lightbringer himself had descended by a secondary lift to examine the scene, and he noticed Darann as soon as the guards brought her through the outer doors.

"A terrible accident!" he exclaimed, rushing forward with outstretched arms. In that instant Darann's heart turned to stone and her knees gave out; she would have collapsed if not for the two guards quickly grasping her arms again.

The dwarfmaid drew a ragged breath, burying her face in the king's embrace, vaguely aware of many others gathered around, silent and tentative. "He felt no pain, I can assure you," the king was saying. "It was all over in an instant. . . . The cable broke, and the lift came down. The brakes should have locked on, but they failed. . . . My dear, it is so tragic. Axial has lost a man who will be missed, sorely missed. . . ."

The words seemed vague and distant, as if they bore no relevancy to her life, to this strange situation. Through her shock she tried to make sense, and to make decisions. What should she do? The answer was beyond her right now . . . but there were things that she felt, that she understood on an instinctive level.

Slowly, determinedly, she broke from the monarch's embrace and looked into his eyes, then past to the many guards and Lord Nayfal, who were all gathered in the cavernous anteroom at the base of the vast pillar.

Her eyes were dry, though as she drew a breath it took all of her willpower to keep the tears from exploding. But instead she studied the ruler of her people, saw his ashen complexion, the redness that smeared his own eyes with grief. King Lightbringer choked back a sob but freed the dwarfmaid from his embrace as she took a slow step backward. His grief, she concluded, was real.

Next she looked at Nayfal. His face was a mask, and when her gaze fell on him he turned away, barked a few unnecessary orders at the guards who were still trying to untangle the wreckage of the lift.

"A terrible, unhappy coincidence . . . nothing like this has happened here, not in all my reign," the king was saying to nobody in particular. "To have the cable snapped— and the brakes fail at the same time! Why, it's unthinkable, tragic!"

It was *not* an accident. Darann wanted to bark the statement loudly, to throw it in Nayfal's face just to see his reaction. But a small voice, coming from a place below her grief and through her shock, counseled her that this would be madness. No, such an accusation—now, with no evidence, barely a moment after hearing the news— would only play into the lord's hands and make her look like a vengeful and irrational child. There would come a time for accusations and for vengeance, Darann vowed, but she would act with great care. And she would choose her moment, take advantage of careful planning and preparation. Oddly enough, it was her crystallizing fury that seemed to give her a measure of self-control.

"W-when did it happen?" she asked, allowing a tremor to creep into her voice. Her mind was in a tangle, silently crying even as it groped for a truth and for proof that she wondered if she could ever find.

"Not more than half an hour ago, my lady," volunteered one of the guards. "I was on duty at the outer doors there when it come down with a mighty screech—then a crash as loud as a pipe chorus!" He blanched as he absorbed the impact of his own words. "That is, er, beggin' your ladyship's pardon . . ."

She walked past him, up to the mangled steel, until another guard stepped in front of her. "Nothin' that can help you to see here, my lady," he said firmly. "We'll have the, er, body out of there before long, but it's too late to do anything to help."

Too late—Hiyram had risked his life to warn her, but she was too late! Now Rufus Houseguard was dead, and she was alone . . . so utterly alone. Karkald was dead, her brothers gone to the far edge of the First Circle . . . There was no one, no dwarf she could turn to.

So she would have to act, very carefully, on her own. Coolly, she looked around the anteroom. The two guards who had brought her here from her own tower were sidling to the door. Obviously, they were in no great hurry to press charges against this dwarfmaid who had just been hugged by the king himself. That was fine with Darann. She turned her attention back to the monarch as the two dwarves made a hasty exit.

"I thank you for your concern, Your Majesty. The death of my father has stunned me, and my wits are slow to gather. Did you say he was on his way to meet with you?"

King Lightbringer blinked, as if he had to think about the answer to the question. "No, well yes. Actually, he saw me—my first audience of the day—and was on his way back down. Lord Nayfal escorted him to the lift."

"How thoughtful," she said dryly, not wasting a glance in the lord's direction. "Sire, if you would direct your men to bring me his possessions, all that he carried with him when he came to see you, I should like to retire to the Houseguard manor. There will be matters requiring my attention, arrangements to make. . . ."

"Indeed," agreed the king, nodding almost eagerly. "You men, see that it is done, and quickly!"

Now she allowed herself a look at Nayfal, saw the lord watching through narrowed eyes as a burly guard captain unbuckled the belt from around the figure in the lift. He came forward with the object, and Darann recognized the golden buckle, in the shape of the square doorway, that was her family's ancient symbol.

For some reason this brought the truth of her father's fate into sharp focus, and she did sob softly as the man wiped off the blood Rufus had spilled and then gently handed the heavy belt to her. She was gratified by the weight, for it seemed that something of her father had been given to her, a solidity that she didn't know she had lacked. Carefully she lifted the belt and let it hang over her shoulder.

Nayfal was watching her now, she noticed from the corner of her eye. It suited her to let him think she was ignoring him, so she turned back to the king "I . . . I will send word, Your Majesty, when I have been able to make the necessary arrangements. Naturally, I will want to wait for my brothers' return before we proceed."

"Of course. And know this, my dear: Rufus Houseguard was a great man, and I intend to see that his legacy shall not be forgotten."

"Thank you, sire," she replied softly. To herself alone she added her own vow: and *I* intend to see that his death is avenged.

Politely declining the king's offer of an escort to her father's house, Darann, new matriarch of clan Houseguard, made her way out of the palace, through the streets of her city, toward the manor of her ancestral home.

BORAND listened for sounds made by Konnor and Aurand. He wanted to shout, just for the reassurance of a reply, but he dared not make a sound. For the hundredth or maybe the thousandth time, he silently cursed the injuries that forced him to remain here, sitting at the base of the great— but apparently abandoned—cliff city, while his two companions boldly explored.

They had been here for two intervals now and had yet to see sign of a living Delver. Even so, they all acknowledged that it would be worse than foolish to announce their presence by unnecessary sounds. So the two younger dwarves skulked about, seeking and searching to gather as much information as they could before returning to Axial, while Borand waited here and listened to the vast silence.

Slowly, painfully, the injured Seer walked around the circuit of the small room they had taken for their base. It was open at the ceiling, with the great vault of the First Circle yawning overhead, but the four ground-level exits were all barred with solid iron doors. A pool of fresh, cold water bubbled constantly from a small well, filling a raised bowl and then draining through a grate in the floor. Gold embrasures were built into every wall, while strips of the precious metal had been used to edge the frames of each door. The half-dozen sturdy chairs were made of pure loamstone, as comfortable as any in the First Circle. Following comparisons with some other apartments in the area, the three Seers had concluded that this had been the residence of a very wealthy Blind One.

They had immediately recognized a secondary advantage: the faint noise of the flowing water would provide some minimal masking for the inevitable noise made by their own existence—though they limited themselves to a few careful whispers, as well as the incidental sounds of respiration and simple movement. They had set their soundless coolfyre beacon a hundred feet away, strapped to the balcony of a tall building high enough overhead that it still cast generous light into the chamber.

They had found several crates of dried rations, of the virtually tasteless bread that was a staple of lower-class Delvers, and after carrying these here had established a camp where they could remain for an indefinite time. They had a good supply of flamestone, maintaining lights not only for the searchers but also the beacon that illuminated the floor and the four walls around Borand. Still, none of them felt comfortable enough in this city of the Blind Ones to want to remain here any longer than necessary.

Borand was already feeling as though he would be strong enough to make the long trip back to Axial. Though several of his ribs were clearly broken, he would endure the pain and still maintain a reasonable pace as they rode their ferr'ells back to the Seer capital. The fierce creatures had been turned loose several miles away, but the three explorers knew their mounts would return within a reasonable time when they whistled for them.

Ferr'ells were fast, but they were not easy to ride, requiring a lot of strength from the rider. It was to prepare for his saddle that Borand now paced around the room, working his muscles and lungs into some sense of readiness.

He froze suddenly, hearing a scuff of movement, hoping that it was his two companions returning. Turning slowly on his heel, he checked the four doors, ensuring by sight that each was locked and barred. He made his way toward the exit through which the others had departed, expecting them to return there. The sound was not repeated for several heartbeats.

Something raised the hackles on the back of the dwarfs neck, and he spun about. The door behind him was still shut, but a flash of movement attracted his attention up the wall, to the open top nearly twenty feet above.

A wyslet crouched there. Lips curled in a fang-baring grin, the wicked carnivore sniffed the air and stared with its dark, tiny eyes. Perched like a monstrous, scruffy weasel, it glared at him, appraising. Instinctive, animal hatred fueled Borand's reaction, and his sword was in his hand before he even thought about the weapon. Apparently that movement was enough to inflame the beast, for without further hesitation, it leaped into the air, a quick pounce shooting the slender body toward the dwarf like a spring-loaded spear.

The wyslet was long and slender, covered with sparse fur and armed with long, sharp fangs and hooked claws. It was a large specimen, outweighing the dwarf by a factor of two or three, but it moved with a lightning quickness that shocked Borand. He tried to duck away, slashing with his blade, but the creature smashed him in the shoulder. He grunted as claws raked his side, and the wyslet shrieked as the blade ripped through its flank.

But it did not seem to be seriously wounded, not when it pounced off the floor, twisted around on the wall, and came springing at the dwarf again with that shocking speed. Borand tumbled to the side, ducking behind one of the food crates as the monster again darted past. This time it coiled right behind him, low growls rumbling in its belly, a black tongue snaking along the sharp teeth. The drawf crouched, blade extended, hoping only to stab the beast to death as it leapt upon him.

Instead, the wyslet suddenly spun sideways, snapping loudly at its own flank. Belatedly, Borand heard the sound of a twanging crossbow, then another as a second shot flew from the now-open doorway. The wyselt flipped onto its back, kicking wildly, and Borand lunged forward to slice it through the throat. Air escaped with a gurgle of rushing blood, and with a final thrash the beast shuddered and lay still.

Shaking, Borand looked up to see Aurand and Konnor coming through the door, each slinging his crossbow onto his belt.

"Are you wounded?" his brother asked. "It tore your shirt . . . and the skin, too?"

He checked the skin, which was scraped but barely oozing blood. "Just a scratch," Borand said weakly.

"Good," Aurand said. "Doubly good, then, to find this thing here."

"Good?" groaned the elder brother, shaking his head. "How is that?"

"Once more we found no sign of Delvers—but we'll never be able to check this whole place. So what better proof can there be that the city is abandoned than to know the wyslets have moved in?"

THE pulse of the ground was like a living thing. He could feel it through his boots, thrumming up his legs, into the pit of his belly.

Not very far away, the vast chasm of Riven Deep opened in the fundament of the Fourth Circle, like a wound in the world.

Zystyl smiled. Like a wound in flesh, this one was a weakness, a gap that would allow entrance, a conduit for chaos and evil.

Soon, it would be time.

He turned his back to that chasm then and allowed his senses to wash over the glorious spectacle of his army, arrayed for his inspection. The front rank, a score of metallic giants, black-stained shells pocked and streaked with reddish rust now, after all this time under the frequently rainy skies of the Fourth Circle. But they were still powerful, capable of crushing any warrior—or company of warriors—daring to fight for Nayve.

Beyond the golems were arrayed more than fifty thousand Delvers, the Unmirrored dwarves standing in their crisp lines, helmets and breastplates polished to a reflective sheen. Fifty years ago, before they came to Nayve, the idea of reflection was unknown to this blind race of dwarves, but with the transport to the Fourth Circle had come the blessing of sight, a gift from the Deathlord himself.

Now Zystyl shuddered at the very notion of life without that gift. In his case, the supersensory nostrils of the Delver arcane gave sweet enhancement to all sensations . . . and the most delicious of all was the power of vision. The gleaming metal, marked by lines stretching more than a mile in length, gave him a physical thrill of pleasure as he looked upon them, a sense as intense as any pleasure given him by female or slave.

The impression was less sublime but still pleasing, as he looked beyond the Delvers to the harpies gathered in loose clumps upon the surrounding hilltops. Some of them wheeled through the air with typical undisciplined insolence, but most had come to land in response to Zystyl's command. The flyers formed a dirty arc around the rest of the army, fitting for their role as scouts and skirmishers.

How long would it be until he received the order, the command to attack. More than the command, in fact, but the *means* to attack. As to the intent, he was willing, had been more than willing but eager to launch an offensive for fifty years! But there remained the physical obstacle, this great canyon, yawning in his path.

Zystyl had no doubt but that his master, the Deathlord, would find a way to pass that obstacle. He was curious and eager, but he knew the time would come. And when it came, he and his army would be ready.

As always, when he pondered the future, Zystyl found his thoughts returning to the past . . . to a moment in time when his army had embarked on a great campaign. More than three centuries old now, was that campaign, but he remembered the smell and the touch as if it was yesterday.

He had held her in his hands, fingers clenched like iron brackets around her struggling arms. But it was the hair, trailing across his nostrils, fragrant and musty at the same time, an allure that tingled throughout his body. There was no instance, nothing with of the women he had taken before and after that day, of comparable ecstasy in all his experience.

Was she lost to him? Certainly she remained in the First Circle while he was trapped here, with the Delver army, in the Fourth. The power of the Deathlord, Karlath-Fayd, had summoned sixty thousand of the Unmirrored to this place, and Zystyl knew they wouldn't be going home again—unless such a journey somehow pleased the will of the Carrion-Eater.

So the Delver arcane instead turned his attention to the world beneath his feet, Nayve, the Fourth Circle. This chasm had blocked him, halted the advance of his inexorable army, for fifty years. Still it yawned there, beheld in the darkest corners of his mind, a perfect barrier. . . .

Perfect, perhaps, but not necessarily permanent.

NAYNE! Why did they obsess about that accursed, sun-scoured world so much? Lord Nayfal could not understand it: for all of creation dwarves had been creatures of the First Circle, and this was where they belonged! It should have been obvious to the most obtuse Seer, especially in this literally enlightened modern era, when the miracle of coolfyre guaranteed that his people would be the supreme masters of their circle.

Wasn't that *enough*?

The questions churned in the lord's mind often, but never more so than times like now, when he lay in his luxurious bed and sought the blessed release of sleep. Instead, he was cursed with memories.

Vividly he recalled the last moments outside of Arkan Pass, when the dwarf Karkald had taken his small company of dwarves, all those who had survived the battle, and followed the mighty army of Delvers onto the Underworld plain. Nayfal watched, spellbound and horrified, as a storm of magic, great sheets of blue, flickering light, had surrounded the Delvers, their iron golems, and the Seer survivors. The entire group, tens of thousands of them, rose from the First Circle and passed right into the Midrock overhead, vanishing from Nayfal's view.

He had returned to Axial and, not wanting to appear mad, simply reported that the army had been annihilated. Within a few cycles dwarven merchants had discovered the barrier, the same field of blue magic Nayfal had seen, and all commerce between the First and Fourth Circles had been abruptly terminated.

Nayfal could not know for certain what had occurred above that barrier, but he had a strong belief: Karkald was up there in Nayve . . . trapped up there for now, so long as the barrier of blue magic held. And if Karkald returned to the First Circle, then the truth about Arkan Pass would be revealed.

And Lord Nayfal would be finished.

IT seemed that Darann had never fully appreciated exactly how huge was the manor that was her family's ancestral home. There had always been life to be found in the big stone building. If nothing was happening nearby, she had known that she could walk down a hall or up a spiraling stairway, wander through some lofty corridor, and eventually come to a place where her mother was painting, or her father reading, or her brothers engaged in some trivial but fiercely contested argument.

Now, there was just the silence.

She had come here after learning of her father's death, under the initial sense that she did not want to return to her lonely apartment, the cold chambers she had shared with Karkald so many years ago. Yet it seemed that here, in the big house by the dark sea, there were even more memories. Certainly this was a place she associated with gatherings, with jokes and feasts and lively people. She walked the long halls by herself, listening, hoping to hear echoes of long-ago galas.

She spent much of her first several days in the home seeking the letter that her father had mentioned, the note that gave some indication of Nayfal's involvement in the death of Cubic Mandrill. Searches of her father's apartments, of his office and his library, had been unsuccessful, and she was forced to admit that there were literally thousands of places where a piece of paper could have been concealed in the great house. With tears in her eyes, she regretted not asking him for more details, even to see the letter, on their last night together.

Finally she gave up and sat in the chair—her father's chair—beside the great hearth. She was half afraid that she would start to hear those echoes, and that was a very scary thought, for down that road, she was certain, madness awaited.

Where were her brothers? She cursed them, halfheartedly, resenting their freedoms that were so easy to perceive as a lack of responsibility, knowing she was being irrational. They were probably safer out of the city than they would be if they were garrisoned here, she reasoned, for who was to say that Nayfal would not have looked to do them harm, as well as their father?

For that matter, how safe was Darann, herself? This was the question that had been dancing around the fringes of her awareness for the three intervals since her father was murdered. She had come up with no good answer.

Despite the chill in the large hall, she felt no desire to build a fire; that had always been her father's job, something he did with joy and with pride. It would have been blasphemous to his memory had she stooped to arrange the peat and coal in the grate, to touch spark to tinder and ignite a blaze. She started to laugh at a whimsical notion: perhaps she should just wait for Rufus to come in and start a jolly blaze. Her laughter dissolved into a sob, even as the thought drifted past.

Irritated, she rose and crossed to the base of the great stairway, climbing to the second story with a series of stomping steps, until she heard the echoes coming up from the cavernous main floor. Shivering, she moved silently into the upper hallway.

It was in that silence that she heard a single thud of sound, something forceful but vague, originating from one of the wings of the great house. Darann didn't wait for a repeat of the sound; instead, she jogged down the long hallway, passing the doors to her sleeping apartments and her father's rooms without hesitation. Only when she reached the end did she pause, carefully lifting the latch and quietly entering the anteroom of one of the guest apartments.

She had chosen these rooms with a purpose, for in one of the closets she knew Rufus had stored several of his weapons: keen and sturdy, each of them, though not ornate enough to deserve display in the family's great hall. Now she was grateful to find a silver short sword, the blade slick with preservative oil. Gingerly she girded on the scabbard, thankful that it was supple leather and thus soundless to manipulate.

Only then did she notice the tube, a golden cylinder about the size of a small knife. She picked it up, finding that it was surprisingly light; the gold must be a very thin sheet of metal. Curious, she noticed that one end of the tube screwed off; when she twisted this, she quickly discovered that the cylinder was hollow, and that it contained a single sheet of parchment. A quick look showed her a note written in a delicate, female hand. She knew this was the note that had aroused her father's curiosity, but before she could look further, she heard another scuffing sound from below.

Strangely enough, she never even paused to wonder about the origin of the sound; she was utterly convinced that intruders were here and that they came with violent intentions. That brought to mind the second advantage of this guest chamber: the private balcony, small and well concealed, extending from the metalward end of the house.

Carefully she slipped open the door to the balcony, crouching low as she emerged to peer over the railing. Her stomach tightened nervously as she saw dark shapes moving through the courtyard, four or five dwarves scurrying past to guard the rear exit where the balcony sprawled above the dark, placid water. She forced herself to breathe slowly and calmly, watching until the dwarves were out of sight. There would be others, she knew, guarding the front, and probably still more already in the house.

As if to confirm her fears, she heard footfalls in the upper hall, doors opening as searchers probed through the sleeping apartments. They were moving quickly, more concerned with surprise than stealth.

She wasted no time in lifting herself over the rail and hanging down to the limits of her arms. She notched one toe into a gap in the building stones, then found a grip for her fingers. As quickly as possible she eased her way down the wall, dropping the last six feet to land in a shadowy corner of the outer plaza. She was still concealed from the back door as she scuttled across the open area and slipped down the steps to the rocky yard.

This was her element; she had played tag and hide-seek with her brothers for many years among these very stones.

Darting from one to the next, she made her way down the slope until she reached the lakeshore.

The boat was where she had remembered it: a narrow fishing dory of metal, with light tin oars under the bench. With one last look up at the house—there were still no lights on, but she could see figures swarming across the upper balconies now—she pushed the boat away from shore, slipped over the gunwale, and silently paddled away from the house, the city, and the king, which had been constants for all of her life.

Two hours later, she judged that she was far enough from the manor to risk a light. She found a small box of matches near the lamp in the boat's bow and quickly ignited the wick. Then she sat down, opened the tube, and took out the letter.

She read the contents with a strange sense of sadness.

Dear Lord Houseguard,
I write to you, as I know that you are a goblin friend. You must know that these hapless people are innocent of the charges leveled against them, especially in the matter of the attempt to kill King Lightbringer forty years ago.

I know for a fact that Cubic Mandrill was Lord Nayfal's toady. The plot was Nayfal's, and it was intended to fail! I have proof of this, and would share it with you if you desire.

Though I am a dwarf, I am the lowest of the low among our people, and this is a fitting station for me. I will find you at the right time.

One of the lowest of us all

8

Invasion

By steel and by stealth,
By might and by wealth,
By valor and flesh
And by blood.

Elves bold in their mail,
With allies, still fail
To stem and to dam
Such a flood.

From *Days of Worldfall*
by Sirien Saramayd

Miradel watched, horrified, as the pictures played out in the Viewing Chamber. The sight of the armada struck like a cold blade into the pit of her stomach, and she choked back a sob as the tall, dark ships for the first time cast a shadow across Nayve's verdant shore. She was so appalled that she couldn't draw breath when she saw Natac, astride Regillix Avatar, vanish into the inky miasma. Orange flame blossomed in the murk, and she shuddered with each explosion, not knowing if her beloved had cast, or been struck, by fire.

Finally the great serpent emerged into view, wings striving for lift, a dozen harpies straining to catch the dragon from below. But those massive pinions were strong, and Miradel slowly drew in a breath of air as serpent and rider at last rose free. It was a little victory that meant all the world to her in that instant, yet what could it mean against the complete scope of the disaster?

The druids in the chamber, a hundred or more of them, were stunned into silence by the awful scene.

"It can't be real!" gasped one woman, a novice brought to Nayve by the goddess barely two years ago.

But it was real. Nayve was facing a threat beyond anything in her historical memory, and it seemed that every effort of resistance must be as futile as the last. If the thousand beautiful boats of the Metalfleet could be brushed aside by these ships, what hopes could they place in the army on land?

All the peoples of Circle at Center had been following the news of the invasion with growing terror, and none of them knew the answer to that question. Indeed, from beneath the Loom of the Goddess Worldweaver, it seemed as though the whole Fourth Circle, the nexus of the cosmos and the Center of Everything, could only tremble in dread. A multitude of earthquakes rippled across the land, crumbling mountains, clawing fissures through verdant plains, draining lakes and streams through cracks in the ground, leaving wastelands of mud, silt, and sand. In Argentian, tall towers of crystal and wood crashed to the ground, killing hundreds. In the Lodespikes, a prosperous gnomish town was buried under the rubble of a crushing landslide.

All these scenes were played on the wall of the Viewing Chamber, the elder druids taking turns sifting the wool through the flame. Of course, many of the order were gone from the Center now, playing an important role in the army and navy of the world. Not only were druids windcasters for Roland Boatwright's fleet, but they served as healers in the ranks of the foot soldiers. Too, the mightiest among them could wield goddess magic with devastating effects.

But others were needed here, in the temple and the city, and Miradel felt a flush of shame as she thought about her fear, relieved in a small measure that she was not in the front of the fight.

As to the actual scene, five hundred death ships simultaneously grounded themselves in the shallows at the edge of the Blue Coral Sea, and it was as though the strands of threads refused to draw close to complete the picture, to give a specific view. Instead, the druids saw a storm of darkness, like a cloud of black smoke lying low and heavy over the sea, drawing close to land. Here and there sparks blossomed as fires burst into sight, but mostly it was more like a single vast blanket than any individual collection of ships and warriors.

Yet when those first keels touched ground, the hundred druids in the chamber uttered a collective groan. They felt the pain in their feet, in their guts, in their souls. Several ran sobbing from the room, and Miradel caught a young woman next to her, who fell into a complete swoon. She noticed that Shandira was kneeling, helping several others who had fallen.

The black woman looked at her, and Miradel was shaken to see this tall, lithe woman trembling like a frightened deer.

"What happened?" Shandira asked, her voice a harsh whisper.

"You are one with Nayve, now," the elder druid replied. "And so you are suffering the pain of the world."

"Why, again? Tell me why this scourge strikes such a peaceful world."

Miradel went to the candle, still burning near the flat,

white wall; Most of the other druids had left, but there were several tufts of thread remaining near the single flame. She lifted them, stretched them gently with her fingers, fed them one at a time into the yellow tongue of fire.

"View the Fifth Circle . . . to the far distance in the direction that is neither metal nor wood," she intoned.

The world of Loamar was there, portrayed on the wall as it might have been viewed by a bird flying at impossible height with impeccable clarity of vision. The dark shore of the Worldsea fringed the circle, the coast separated by narrow channels, bays, and harbors. The terrain rose into the distance, each inland plateau of Loamar higher than the last, until the dark fortress of Karlath-Fayd himself rose like a mountain range at the far end of the world . . . the far end of all existence.

"I have heard tales of Hell," Shandira said in awe. "And they make it seem to be such a place. Only this is so cold, so dark . . . it is lifeless."

"Yes," Miradel said. "Lifeless, now that the armada has sailed forth. But look, see the gargoyle atop his highest precipice?" She gestured at the grotesque statue, a visage of fang and horn, leathered wings folded back as if poised for flight. "It will fly forth in rage to defend its lair, should any intruder approach."

"As horrible as any demon of fire," acknowledged Shandira. "But this prince of death . . . he dwells within?"

Miradel fed more threads into the flame, guiding the image through the deep canyons that formed the halls of the fortress. Finally the route emerged into a wide bowl. On the far side of the cavernous space was a throne carved from the very mountain itself. "It is hard to see very well, but look—there is his cloak, shimmering in the distance. And of course you can see his eyes."

Indeed, the monstrous presence was discernable in the gauzy screen, and the two fiery eyes—like the flames of infernal hell—glowed and flared from on high. "Does he never move?"

"Not in the half century since the death ships sailed," explained the elder druid. "It is as though he is a statue. But the goddess told me that his eyes can flash mighty destruction, and that any who beholds that gaze is immediately burned to ash. There is great power lurking within that stony shell!"

"Power enough to send an army against a world," Shandira murmured, as the picture of Loamar faded, and once again the green shore of Nayve trembled on the wall as the toxic cloud swept toward land.

HE had forgotten the Somme, forgotten the mud and the machine guns and the talk of the Lord. He didn't know how long he had been aboard the death ship, only that he had come here more recently than the pikemen who wore tattered uniforms reminiscent of Alpine heights, much more recently than the legionnaires who still wore the toga and kilt of Caesar's guard. But they were all brothers in arms now, a company of men ready to wage war. They knew and hated their captain, the black-bearded brute who ruthlessly ruled their ship and their lives. For a long time they had had only some vague notion of their enemy, unseen but also hated.

His existence was not so much a life as a vague passing of time, just as time had been passed by the ghost warriors in Loamar for the past several dozen centuries, and for those same warriors, embarked upon the death ships, over the course of the last fifty years.

But now that enemy had a face, had white sails and silver missiles that brought fire and death. He had seen many black ships burn, and he did not want to face the fate of those crews who had plunged, burning and suffering, into the water. When the dragon had flown overhead, breathing fire that incinerated ships to both sides of his own, he had felt an upswell of fury. He had no weapon to strike at a flying creature, but he opened his mouth and wailed an inarticulate groan of fury. His weapon, the familiar, heavy Enfield rifle, was in his hands, and he longed to plunge the bayonet into the guts of a living foe.

When the sturdy keel struck the shallows, and the vessel was grounded on the shores of Nayve, he moved to action as if he had trained all his life for this moment. In his hands he bore that thing shaped like his rifle, with a lethal bayonet affixed to the terminus. In some dim recess he knew that it was *not* a rifle, for he had no bullets, no way to shoot. It was the blade that was lethal, and he knew that on this green and verdant shore there were enemies to be slain with that keen point and sharp, serrated edge.

So he moved to the fore of the deck, with the legionaires and the pikemen, and he felt the planks begin to lower. The ship changed around him, the once-steep hulls bending, folding, flattening to form a smooth ramp. This ramp descended into the shallows, and the front of the vessel was open, facing the land. In a single mass the ghost warriors charged down and out, splashing into water that surged as high as their hips, slogging toward shore with rifles, pikes, spears all leveled toward the enemy lurking on the dunes.

From somewhere within him a cry gurgled up, a howl of battle that was no longer a human sound nor even the noise of any living thing. Instead, it was a plea for blood, a promise of violence . . . and as the death ships came to shore it erupted, simultaneously, from twenty thousand ghostly throats.

———

·

TAMARWIND'S knees went weak as he heard that awful
sound wail upward from the shore. Elves in his line, warriors who had trained for hundreds of years, clapped their
hands over their ears and fell, writhing, to the ground. A
whole rank of younger troops turned and started to flee,
only to pause before the roaring scorn of Rawknuckle
Barefist, who had blocked the inland paths in fear of just
such a rout.

The beach was black with charging troops, spears and
bayonets bristling all along the front. Against that tide
Tam's regiment of elves, a thousand strong and arrayed in
a two-rank line, seemed like a tissue paper dike attempting to hold back the tide. Even the knowledge of other
formations—more great regiments of elves, as well as legions of gnomes and an army of trolls—seemed like
merely potential casualties. All would fight bravely he
knew, but one of them would eventually be overwhelmed.
With the line breached, the rest of the defenders would be
imperiled; they would have to flee or die. At best, they
could hope to buy a little time, for a tremendous payment
in lives and in blood.

Yet he had trained and prepared too long to abandon
hope now. He shouted commands, inarticulate barks for
the most part that nevertheless served the purpose of stiffening the ranks, letting the elves know their captain was
with them. Most of these men had never been in a battle
before, but he knew they would serve bravely and well.
He had first learned this about himself nearly five hundred
years earlier: the elven heart had some kind of instinctive
war memory that proved unfailingly courageous in the
hour of need.

At the same time, he was overwhelmingly sad, thinking about these elves who could have looked forward to
hundreds more years of pastoral life. All that was put at

risk, for many would be lost, because of the necessity to fight.

Lastly, as the ships towered above the beach, still surging forward with teeming decks, Tamarwind allowed himself to think of Belynda. There were so many things he wished he had told her: for centuries he had planned to speak to her, to convince her of his love, and yet the time had never been right. He had waited, always hoping for a better opportunity, and now it occurred to him that his opportunities might have run out. That thought frightened him more than death or injury, violence or flame, and in that awareness he wanted very much to get away from here alive.

The death ships had spilled their cargo with appalling haste. Tam had watched in astonishment as each bow had folded into a ramp, dropping forward into shallow water to disgorge a tight rank of shadowy warriors. Already the first of these were scrambling out of the surf onto dry land. Water dripped from their tunics and legs just as it would drip from real flesh, and for the first time the elven veteran accepted the fact that these were real foes capable of inflicting genuine and lethal wounds.

He was heartened to see a few silver spheres fly through the air as Gallupper's guns, atop the nearby dune, opened up. The metallic shot skipped across the sand, rolling into the tightly packed ranks before exploding in a blaze of white heat. Again and again the batteries spoke, dozens of shots scattering into the files of ghost warriors, tearing great rips in those lines. There were more of them shooting from the dune to his left, and as the enemy masses tried to form ranks, they found themselves under resolute and fiery assault.

But still more of them were coming ashore, the numberless tide of death ships looming tall and black just beyond. Those already on land, meanwhile, ignored the lethal barrage, re-formed the ranks where they had been torn by the explosions, and started to march toward the elves. Either the batteries slowed their fire or, more likely, the numbers of the enemy simply dwarfed that responding barrage. In any event, it seemed to Tam that they came on without so much as awareness of the explosions flashing among them.

"Steady—raise those pikes. Hold your ranks, elves!" Tamarwind shouted, taking some comfort from the sound of his own voice. The front of the elven line bristled like a hedgehog as the steel-headed pikes were tilted forward. At the junctures where one company met the next, giants stood ready, fighting in trios armed with massive, long-handled axes.

"Giants—take up your halberds and move into position!" Tam called, as the ghost ranks advanced, approaching the markers that had earlier been placed. When the leading rank was a hundred yards away, the elf turned to the rear, signaled the company of longbowmen who had been waiting for his sign. "Fire away—volleys, one after the other!"

The deadly missiles arced overhead, flying in eerie silence, slashing through the sky and then plunging down into the dark rank of attackers. Many arrows plunged into the sand, but numerous others tore into flesh, puncturing heads and shoulders and chests among the grim legion. A hundred attackers fell in that first volley, and already the second barrage of arrows was rising into the sky, passing high over the elves to once more pepper the lethal horde.

Now that eerie wail was repeated, an ululating cry from a hundred thousand bloodless throats. Sand churned, and the air itself seemed to tremble as the Deathlord's legion advanced into a trot, then a ragged run. The tight discipline wavered as the faster runners broke ahead of the slower. A hundred tall, black spearmen, carrying leather shields and garbed as Zulu veterans, rushed toward the center of the elven line. They halted, casting their spears into the midst of Tam's troops, then came on in another rush. A few fell to well-aimed arrows, and the rest met a bloody end on the pikes that danced and bobbed before the defenders' faces.

But now the rest of the horde was close, and there was a great clattering of wood and steel as the pike butts were planted and the blades chimed together, then quivered under the impact of undead but very corporeal flesh.

Tamarwind drew his sword, the slender, double-edged blade forged a hundred years ago by a druid master. He stood with the First Company to his right, and a trio of halberd-armed giants at his left. In another instant the ground before him was swarming with dark, hateful faces. A spear thrust toward him, and he hacked the weapon in half with a single slash. Two muskets tipped with lethal bayonets jabbed, and he was forced to take a half step backward. But he lunged forward again, two quick stabs dropping the ghost warriors that might have been summoned here from Shiloh or Gettysburg.

A giant roared, and the mighty axe blade swept past, cleaving a centurion in two before plunging deep into the sand. The halberdier tried to wrest his weapon free as three swordsmen rushed in; Tam dropped one with a throat-cutting slash, then held the other two at bay until the giant raised the halberd and brought both attackers down with a single, haymaking swing.

Feeling the rhythm of his comrade, Tamarwind rushed forward in the wake of the halberd's swing, stabbing a charging Turk in the throat. The man, who might have fought in Saladin's army or even in the legions of Mohammed himself, fell to the sand and thrashed, choking and gasping as new death slowly claimed him. Tam had already found his next target and moved on from there.

His blade stayed eerily shiny, even as it ran through guts and lopped off limbs. The attackers pressed forward with that keening wail, a sound unlike anything raised from human voice, yet in its very strangeness it seemed a potent and demoralizing battle cry. He realized another strange thing as the battle wore on: the attackers he slew fell to the ground as corpses, yet as more and more of them died, the piles of corpses did not swell to the heights he would have expected. It was as if the flesh of these warriors gradually dissolved, even as additional ranks of ghost warriors kept rushing forward to replace the gaps left by the slain. As fresh bodies collapsed on top of the pile, those at the bottom slowly vanished into the dirt.

Tamarwind took a glimpse along the length of his line, heartened to see that most of the pikes were still in position. A few elves had fallen, but the attackers that pressed between the long shafts were quickly felled by swordsmen. All told, the line was holding well.

Indeed, so effective were the pikes that the attackers seemed to be focusing on the junctures where the giants—and Tamarwind—fought. One of the tall defenders groaned aloud and staggered backward, clutching his belly where it had been ripped open by a Viking's battle-axe. The other giants were bleeding from scores of cuts on their legs and hips, and the elf wondered how much longer they would be able to hold.

But for now, the attackers could make no progress, and at the cost of blood and pain and sweat, Tamarwind and his warriors battled on.

He marched up the beach in a file of ten thousand warriors, his Enfield heavy and lethal in his hands. A flash of light and heat erupted to his right, sending fiery bits of metal through the column. Warriors to both sides of him fell, keening their death wails, while a tongue of fire reached around to singe his arm. But he ignored the flash of pain, stepping over the bodies of the slain without a second thought. In a few minutes his ghost flesh had healed, leaving not so much as a sign of his wound.

The beach was littered with bodies, and more of the silvery fireballs were erupting to all sides. The warrior looked at the top of one of the high sand dunes just as another barrage came forth from that place. He watched as the spheres scattered through the air, falling along the file of warriors advancing to his left. It was a good shot: the entire line erupted into flame and death over a hundred feet of its length, warriors blazing, stumbling, and falling as the incendiary explosive seared undead flesh.

But there, too, the loss was ignored by the survivors, more and more warriors kicking through the smoldering sand, tightening up the column, marching inexorably inland.

The warrior wanted to charge up the dune, to strike with his bayonet against the purveyors of those fiery assaults, but that was not the direction he was ordered to go. Instead, he heard the words of his captain, the croaky and rasping sound that seemed to come from within his skull, urging him to tighten up the rank, to speed up into a trot.

The same command must have been delivered to the whole file, because now the column was moving at a lumbering run, feet in sandals and boots churning through the sand, bearing the attackers closer to the sounds of battle. He pushed along behind the warrior in front of him, a fellow Tommy from the fields of Flanders. Behind him came a pair of fierce-looking warriors in face paint and feathers, each bearing a stone-headed tomahawk.

The enemy came into view, a long front of short, bearded warriors protected by steel breastplates, helmets, and shields. They were squat and powerful looking, with feet spread wide, and short-bladed weapons—swords, daggers, axes—wielded opposite the round shields. All along the front the ghost warriors were attacking, and these creatures—*gnomes*, the warrior called up from some recess of knowledge—were holding their ground with courage and skill.

He opened his mouth and found himself making a strange noise, a boiling gurgle of sound that seemed to propel him forward with great fury. The Tommy before him went down, thigh hacked by a gnomish sword, and then he was into the line, thrusting the Enfield forward with a practiced stab, bypassing the small shield, penetrating the bristling beard to jab the bayonet into the gnome's throat, above his protective plate. Immediately the white whiskers were stained red, and the little fellow tumbled backward, dropping his blade from nerveless fingers.

And the warrior charged ahead, pushing through the gap in the gnomish line. Another diminutive warrior charged, then fell back, gagging through the blood of the awful thrust into his mouth. The two Iroquois came behind, one falling dead, the other bringing the stone tomahawk hard against a gnomish helm. The blow knocked the defender to the side, and the painted warrior snatched up a metal axe, pushing onward as the captain urged more of his troops through the breach.

Slogging ahead, his rifle light in his hands, the warrior looked in astonishment at the green, grassy field beyond the line. Never in his fighting in France had he beheld such a glorious sight; there, even a successful attack had only yielded another field of mud, another trench and fencing of barbed wire.

But here, the enemy line was broken! Ghost warriors poured through the breach, a hundred strong in the first

minute, a thousand more coming as the gnomes to either
side were butchered and driven away.

NATAC and Regillix Avatar had flown back and forth above
the front throughout the long day of fighting. Twice they
had landed, once to patch a breach in the elven lines, and
again to repel a sudden rush, warriors charging up a dune
to try to take one of Gallupper's battery positions. Each
time the dragon had breathed a fiery cloud of death, disrupting the attacks enough so that additional troops could
rush to the danger spot and hold the tide.

The Tlaxcalan was proud to the point of awe as he witnessed the doughty defense. There were four possible
routes off of the beach, each leading toward a wide valley
in the range of hills just beyond the coast. Each of these
routes was defended by an army of nearly ten thousand
Navyian fighters. To the right were two elven forces, the
troops of Barantha on the far right, with the forces of Argentian, commanded by Tamarwind Trak, just to the left
of that formation.

Third from the right was the rank of gnomes, a number
of forces mustered from Circle at Center, the Ringhills,
and the Lodespikes. These warriors were small but well
armored and tightly packed; for hours they had stood up
to the press of attackers without any sign of wavering. Finally, on the left, the trolls of King Awfulbark of Udderthud were waging deadly combat, tearing at the ghost
warriors with their great claws, lifting and rending with
brutal force. The trolls suffered grievous wounds, but the
injured simply fell back from the line until, a few minutes
later, their hurts were healed.

Between each of these armies, as well as posted on the
heights to the left and right of the entire force, emplace-
ments of batteries showered fiery barrages onto the

beaches. The attackers pushed right through the flaming onslaughts, but that didn't keep them from exacting a terrible toll.

Now, as the dragon took to the air once more, Natac strained to see into the distance, wanting to insure that the positions remained intact. He was disturbed to see a lot of activity behind the gnome position, and as Regillix flew him closer, his worst fears were realized.

"They have breached the line," he observed, the dragon nodding grimly in agreement.

"Shall we land and try to block that up?" asked the serpent skeptically.

"No, there are too many of them," Natac admitted, cursing the luck that had kept them away from this spot. A few minutes earlier they might have made a difference; now, the attackers had spilled through the line in a flood. The two wings of the shattered gnomish army were falling back, away from the breach, and the press of attackers surged inland unabated. Already thousands of them were turning right, to come at the flank of the trolls, or left, to push against the vulnerable end of the elven position.

Regillix dipped a wing, curling into an arc around the shattered position. Natac was tempted to go down and help the gnomes—they could insure escape for at least some of the nearly surrounded fighters—but he acknowledged a more important role for the sake of the whole army.

"Let's land behind Tamarwind and give him warning. With luck, the elves can pull away before they're surrounded, and we can be on our way to warn Awfulbark and his trolls."

"Aye," grunted the dragon unhappily. "A bitter choice, that, but the only one we can make."

Already he was veering downward, gliding to a patch of open ground behind the rank of Tamarwind Trak's elves. Natac took one glance back, saw a hundred gnomes vanish under the onslaught of the unholy attack. He thought of Nistel, of King Dimwoodie, and the other great gnomes he had known, and tears rose to his eyes.

"You will be avenged, my loyal warriors," he muttered, before turning to the task of saving the rest of his army to fight another day.

MIRADEL walked through the beech trees on the fringe of the Grove. A long reflecting pool stretched toward the College, the pillared ramparts and marble towers mirrored perfectly in utterly still water. The sun was climbing, the Hour of Darken well advanced, and the purple twilight seemed to add an ethereal luminescence to the view, brightening the alabaster stone beyond that of the midday sun.

Other druids wandered past, heads down, silently treading across the grassy floor, the smooth walkways leading between the trunks of the great oaks.

Miradel found Shandira at the edge of the pool. She looked like a statue, regal and tall and, even amid the gentle folds of her white robe, sleek and strong. Staring in the direction of the Center of Everything, the black woman was a miniature, vital version of the Worldweaver's Spire, rising high into the darkening sky at the same time as it pierced the infinite depths of the reflecting pool.

"I will speak to the goddess," Miradel said. "There can be no other answer."

9

Centerflight

Tangled threads
Tattered cloak
Fabric charred
Colors marred;
A tapestry ravaged
Lays waste
To infinite souls

From the Tapestry of the Worldweaver
Bloom of Entropy

Miradel entered the temple in the middle of Darken. A few candles brightened the alcoves along the entryway, though shadows carpeted the floor of the main hall. The druid walked soundlessly down the center of this lightless aisle, passing the bolted iron door where the Rockshaft, long ago, had connected this temple to the city of Axial on the First Circle, so far below. Once that had been a route for trade and travel, but since the barrier of blue magic had descended, the shaft had been impassable. Some time ago, the upper terminus had been permanently sealed behind these locked iron doors.

The druid moved on, unconsciously stealthy as she approached the chamber of the Tapestry, the heart of the Worldweaver's Loom. She thought of Shandira, the other woman waiting for these last moments on the plaza outside. Miradel had counseled her to watch the dancing stars, the reflections sparkling in the placid lake, and not to worry if she had to wait there for most of the night. Indeed, Miradel herself had no idea what would happen, how long or how short the discussion would be. She had questions, did the druid, but she was not certain that the answers she sought even existed, much less that they would be revealed to her.

The ivory doors to the inner sanctum, parted slightly to reveal a pale wash of light beyond, soon loomed, and Miradel drew a deep, slow breath. Then she reached forward, pushing the portals softly aside as she entered the large, circular chamber.

The goddess was at her loom, her long fingers supple on the threads, colors interweaving faster than the druid's eye could follow. The tapestry, a blur of colors and images—the blue of water and sky, green of forest, and teeming collage of lives—rose from the wheel to cover the wall. For ten thousand years it had been growing, encircling the vast chamber, rising on the walls that towered high overhead. The pedals of the great loom hummed and whirred under the Worldweaver's steady pressure, and the fabric, as shimmery as silk, continued to form and to rise from the machine.

"Ah, my faithful daughter, come in," she said. "What do you seek in the midst of this night?"

"I have been wondering about Karlath-Fayd," Miradel began—then halted in surprise as the goddess abruptly halted her weaving to regard the druid with narrowed, penetrating eyes.

"I would think you have more immediate concerns," the goddess said sarcastically.

Never had the Worldweaver looked quite so severe, Miradel thought: her eyes glittered coldly, like diamonds, and a frown of displeasure creased her high forehead with more than a usual complement of wrinkles. She presented a rather frightening visage, an aspect the druid had never seen before. She fought an impulse to quietly acquiesce, to lower her eyes and murmur a deferential apology before she fled. Instead, she met that sharp glare with her own expression of honest curiosity.

"I mean no disrespect, lady. But I am curious and, as ever, I work to serve the cause of Nayve. To that end I ask: Is Karlath-Fayd not at the root of *all* our important concerns?" She faced the glowering expression of the goddess and continued. "Perhaps we need to know more about him."

The goddess blinked and snorted, clearly offended by the question. "Why do you speak to me of this?" she demanded. "Do you now lack faith in my vision, in my knowledge of the Seven Circles. Know that I can see all in these threads!"

Miradel forged ahead. "I understand, lady. But because—I wonder if there is some cause for hope to be found in the Fifth Circle! Is it possible that we might strike at Karlath-Fayd himself, somehow destroy his power in his very lair? Perhaps that would be an effective tool—cutting the head off the snake in order to render the snake harmless, so to speak."

"The armies menacing my shores are more dangerous by far than any snake!" retorted the Worldweaver, stern and stiff, with a voice that was icy cold.

"But still, you understand what I mean! He has no troops in Loamar now; they are all embarked on the death ships! This would be the time to strike . . . or at least, to scrutinze and study that foul god in his lair, to seek a weakness!"

"He doesn't need troops! Have you not seen his gargoyle?" snorted the goddess. "It could destroy you, any of you, an entire army if it desired to do so. Regillix Avatar himself would be helpless against that giant! And even should one get past the gargoyle, why, the very sight of the Deathlord's gaze is enough to turn one to stone! Imagine that horrible fate: frozen as a statue, immobile but aware, for as long as he desired to keep you as his ornament."

"But . . ." Miradel was surprised and about to argue further, when she decided to hold her tongue. She needed to think, to understand what she was hearing. "Perhaps you are right," she said quietly. "Forgive my impertinence."

"Of course. But remember, the Deathlord is *my* concern," the goddess declared sternly. "You should concentrate on preparing the initiates for the Spell of Summoning. That casting will occur tomorrow, you recall?"

"Yes," Miradel acknowledged with a pang of guilt as she thought of Shandira. She considered raising further objections, but another look at that uncompromising visage caused her to hesitate. And the memory of a fresh question, newly growing in her mind, bade her to excuse herself as quickly as possible. "Very well, lady," she said with a bow. "I leave you to your weavings."

When she emerged from the temple, the night seemed to have grown much colder. She thought of her warm chamber in the Grove, longing for sleep, for blessed escape from the true world. But there was no time for that. Instead, she turned her steps toward the College, toward the apartments of her good friend.

She needed to talk to Belynda Wysterian.

———

THE dragon spread his wings, ready to take to the air, while Natac remained on the ground. The Tlaxcalan looked at his mighty companion—more than a steed, the serpent had become as true a friend as he had ever known.

"See if the trolls need help," said the general. "They have to get back from the shore as quickly as possible."

"I may be able to delay the pursuit for a bit," declared Regillix, snorting a sulfurous cloud that discolored the air over the man's head. "Once again I am ready to spit some fire!"

"Good. I will help Tamarwind hold the elves together. If the trolls can join up with us by the time we reach the Swansleep River, we'll have a chance to make another stand."

"But if the Deathlord's army stays between troll and elf, then there is no choice but to keep running," the dragon noted.

"Exactly—so haste is important. Good luck to you and to Awfulbark," Natac said, clapping the mighty neck affectionately.

"And to you. Stay well, my human," urged the wyrm.

Natac trotted backward, experience having taught him about the downdraft that would emerge from those massive wings. With an eager snort, Regillix extended his neck, crouched upon his massive legs, and hurled himself into the air. Even two dozen paces away, the man was nearly knocked down by the gust of air pushed by the liftoff, but he braced himself and watched as the dragon rose upward, a hundred, two hundred feet in the air within a few seconds of his initial leap.

Turning to look into the valley, Natac watched the fleeing file of Tamarwind's elves. They had fallen back from the shore in good order and were now marching inland at a good clip. Even so, when the man looked toward the coast, he saw the dark mass of the pursuing army. The

ghost warriors were in contact with the rear guard of the
elven march, and any slowdown in the pace of the retreat
would bring yet more of the enemy troops into the en-
gagement.

But how long could they keep marching?

Natac stood on the crest of an elevation that divided
two valleys. Now he looked nullward, trying to see some
sign of the Baranthian elves. He had spoken to their commander, Kelland Windreader, a few hours earlier, trying to
convey the importance of a hasty but well-ordered retreat.
At the time, Kelland's force had been holding the original
line at the beach, and the elven veteran objected to the
idea of retreating before his warriors had been defeated.
Patiently, Natac had explained about the gnome collapse,
and the Baranthian leader had seen the fate that lay in
store for his army if he didn't pull them back before they
were cut off. So he had started the withdrawal inland, like
Tamarwind, keeping an aggressive rear guard engaged
with the pursuing invaders. Jubal was with them. The
human general, veteran of the American Civil War, was
contributing his expertise, and Kelland Windreader had
proved more than willing to accept his help.

Now, from the ridge between the two armies, Natac
could barely see the advance elements of the Baranthian
column. At the same time, the rear guard of the Argentian
elves was drawing closer; it seemed obvious that the two
columns were in danger of being catastrophically separated. The roads through the hills were long, twisting, and
narrow, the next smooth ground some twenty miles away.
There, a scenic river—the Swansleep—meandered
through meadows and glades. The stream spilled from the
Lodespike Mountains and through this long valley, until it
ended in a waterfall, plunging from the edge of Riven
Deep.

After the beach had been lost, that river became

Natac's next and best hope. His plan had been formed years ago, when he had studied the Blue Coral Coast as one of a half dozen landing sites suitable for a force the size of the armada. In long conversations with the elder druids and especially their matriarch Cillia, he had settled upon a tactic, and now he was ready to put it into place. He leaned his head back and cupped his hands to his mouth.

"Runner!" he called. Then he sat on a flat boulder, taking a little while to breathe, to prepare his strength.

Less than five minutes later he heard the telltale buzzing of wings as a small faerie buzzed into sight. Quick as a hummingbird, he flew up to Natac and came to rest on the same rock. Even standing, the little fellow barely came to the man's shoulder. He bowed gracefully, then looked at the general.

"You require a courier, Lord Natac?"

"Please—take a message back to the Grove. Tell Cillia that we need a hundred druids experienced in windcasting at the Swansleep. She'll know what that means."

"Very well, my lord. And may I wish you the best of luck in your endeavors on behalf of the Fourth Circle," said the faerie with polite dignity.

"You may," Natac replied with a chuckle, the first levity he had experienced in what seemed like weeks. He enjoyed the company of the faeries, several hundred of which served his armies. He didn't recognize this one. "What's your name?"

The handsome, young-man-faced creature's eyes widened. "I am called Horas of Gallowglen," he said seriously.

"Then I bid you the best of luck as well, Horas of Gallowglen, in all *your* endeavors on behalf of the Fourth Circle."

"Thank you, my lord!" Beaming, the faerie hopped

into the sky and, with hum of speeding wings, darted to-ward the Center. In seconds distance rendered him invisible.

His mood lightened slightly, Natac of Tlaxcala, general of all the armies of Nayve, started jogging down the hill to try to make a workable plan. He concentrated on the ground as he ran, but another part of his mind was analyzing the battle, his concentration aided by the activity. Of course, he had learned how to ride—horses, as well as the dragon—but he came from a place on Earth where the horse had been unknown, and for all of his first life had gotten where he needed to go on the strength of his own legs and the endurance of his lungs. So he gave no thought now to the fact that he would have to cover nearly four miles to reach the vanguard of the Baranthian column; he simply started to run.

It was not even a half hour later that he reached the valley floor, loping along until he could climb onto a dramatic outcrop of rock rising thirty or forty feet above the trail. They moved in a long file, trudging with stooped shoulders and plodding footsteps. But they still bore their weapons, he was glad to see. As he watched, four centaurs came into view, pulling along a pair of the batteries, the silver carriages rolling through the muck in the midst of the retreating Baranthians.

"Hail General Natac!" cried an elf, as soon as he came into view. The warrior took heart from the cheers that rose from the troops—they didn't sound like an army that was running away—but he quickly raised his hands and brought about a silence.

"Brave elves of Baranthia!" he called. "The battle has not gone as we desired, but all is not lost. Your brothers from Argentian march in the neighboring valley, in position several miles ahead of you. So make haste, my elves; hurry down the vale and join with Argentian for another battle. We will find the place and bring this horde to a halt!"

He wished he could unequivocally believe his own words, but the elves certainly took him at face value. They shouted another hurrah, then started to jog, the column moving notably faster as it snaked along the gentle valley floor.

Natac stayed atop the rock for nearly an hour, exhorting each company of elves as they came within earshot. He was rewarded as they hurried along, and he felt certain that they would pass through the hills at nearly the same time as the Argentians.

Spotting Jubal in the file, Natac waved, and the Virginian quickly scrambled up to join him.

"I reckon we can pick up the pace a bit," he agreed, after Natac had explained his hopes for the retreat. "But what're we gonna do at the river?"

"I have sent for druids to help us," replied the general. "Juliay will be there, as a matter of fact."

"That's encouragin'," Jubal replied. "Wish we coulda had a few druids at Gettysburg—things mighta come out a little different."

With that, the human warrior was off. Natac stayed in place, and Kelland Windreader came along near his rear guard. Only then did the general scramble down from the rock to speak to the Baranthian commander.

"We're holding them back for now," the elf, his skin streaked with soot, sweat, and blood, explained. "But they come on tirelessly; it will be hard to outdistance them."

"Do your best, my friend," Natac counseled. "For if we can get to the Swansleep before them, there might be some hope there." He explained that he had already urged the bulk of the elven column into haste. "Jubal's with the vanguard, he will work on getting the troops in place."

Windreader nodded wearily. "We'll try to catch up," he offered.

"See you at the river, then," Natac said. He left the elf to his column and trotted back up the hillside until he was running along the crest of the ridge. Now he could look down and see an elven column to each side, and he was pleased by that symmetry. He looked into the distance, toward the next ridge, and thought about the brave gnomes that had fought beyond that crest. Had any of them made it out? Or was that vale even now churning with the soulless march of the ghost warriors? Would the advance render his whole plan useless?

He couldn't answer those questions now, not without a two-hour run that would take him miles out of his way. Instead, he turned toward the problem he might be able to solve. He ran faster now, moving toward the Center much more quickly than the marching elves. Night fell, and he kept going through the darkness and into the following Lighten. He still ran, finally emerging onto a low elevation, with a green valley opening before him. In another hour, he had completed the descent into the valley of the Swansleep River. That flowage, a shallow and meandering stream, marked a shiny ribbon in the center of this verdant lowland.

If he could reach that river, and if he found the druids there, they might just have a chance.

THE sailboats of the Metalfleet, those that survived the frenzied battle with the armada, had withdrawn into the harbor. Less than five hundred hulls gathered in the placid water, and nearly all of these were scorched from the fight, gashed and gouged, with torn sails and grimy, soot-stained surfaces.

But at least they were alive.

Roland Boatwright gathered with his captains on the shore. Crazy Horse was here, as well as Richard Rudolph and the elfmaid, Sirien Saramayd. The Sioux chief was despondent, reporting that his druid and lover, Cloud-walking Moon, had perished in the fight. "I killed the bastard who stabbed her, but there was naught I could do for her," he said, his eyes filled with tears. "Brendal was there in a moment, using her druid's healing magic, but even she was too late."

"I am sorry, my friend," said Roland. "All we can do now is to seek revenge, so that she has not died in vain."

"Aye," agreed Crazy Horse. His eyes were suddenly dry, and the boatbuilder sensed that desire for vengeance already burning there.

"The invaders have moved inland," Roland reported. "We can't affect them with our boats, but we have five hundred druids and more than a thousand warriors here. This is too valuable a force to waste."

"I agree," said Rudolph. "We gave them a jolly good rush, but it wasn't enough. So where do we go from here?"

"Let's march to Circle at Center," Crazy Horse said. "I think that's where the next fight will be."

"Aye," Roland agreed. "And if we lose that one, there will be no more."

THIS was already the worst war Awfulbark had ever seen, and it wasn't about to get any better. These horrible fighters were tearing his trolls to pieces, and every time the king's warriors killed one, it seemed that three or four lunged forward to take the place of the slain one. The battle had raged for more than a day, and still the black ships pulled up and disgorged more attackers.

"Come this way!" he shouted. "Get away!"

Every instinct of his being urged him to lead the way, to turn tail and run as fast as he could toward . . . well, it wouldn't be so much *toward* something as it was *away* from here. His sword arm was weary, and his body ached in a dozen places where his flesh had been pierced by spear or sword and was slow to knit itself under these frantic conditions.

But there were others, including Roodcleaver, who were far worse off than the king, so Awfulbark resolved to stay and fight long enough for the rest of his fellows to get away.

"Run!" he urged Roodcleaver, who was sinking her teeth into the throat of a squirming ghost warrior. Her right arm had grown back, but the king winced to see the red slash across her back, the deep cut still bleeding. "Take trolls away from here!"

He seized her shoulder and pulled her away, slashing his blade down onto the head of an attacking Hoplite who lunged after. She blinked at him, but then bobbed her head and took up his call. "Run! Come away!" she brayed.

One by one the trolls fell back from the line until they were streaming away from the beach. The attackers charged forward, rushing past him on both sides. Awfulbark was nearly surrounded, but he hacked his way through a dozen primitive spearmen, leaving all of them torn, bleeding their ghost blood into the ground. Only then did he lope after the rest of the trolls, hearing the ghastly wails rising from the horde behind him.

Fortunately, his own warriors were much faster than the attackers, and in a short time the mob of fleeing trolls had put more than a mile between themselves and their enemy. Furthermore, they were capable of great feats of endurance. Awfulbark knew they could run all night and through the next Lighten, if they needed to. He was grateful, for he guessed that it would take him at least that long to figure out what to do next.

He was spared this decision making as the shadows thickened and the sun was already well advanced on its nightly ascent into the heavens. He heard a buzz of wings and turned to see a small faerie flying along beside him and eyeing him warily.

"What you want?" he asked, loping along at the rear of his army.

"I bring word from General Natac," said the faerie. "Keep going toward the Center, away from the sea. He wants you to do your best to get to the Swansleep River."

"The Swansleep River?" snorted the troll, not having the faintest idea where this body of water could be found. "We try to make it to river—but first, we gotta make it through the night."

MIRADEL was in the temple when she heard the horn. She ran out onto the plaza, saw that Darken was well advanced, and discovered druids streaming from the Grove, from the gardens around the lake, and from the loom. They were coming to gather around Cillia, who stood in the circle of stones and once again sounded the horn.

"What does this mean?" Shandira made her way through the crowd and whispered the question into Miradel's ear.

"A general alarm," she replied. "Cillia will tell us more. But look—the enchantresses are coming from the College. This is something unusual."

As the throng of white-robed elven sages mingled with the druids in their colorful tunics, Miradel spotted Belynda and, with Shandira in tow, made her way to her friend.

"There must be word from Natac," the sage-ambassador

told the two druids. "Quilene warned us to be ready for this."

"What have you seen of him—in your Globe?" asked Miradel. "And of Tamarwind?"

"They are well," Belynda replied, "insofar as they have survived the battle on the beaches. But the attackers were too many; the elves have fallen back through the hills. The gnomes, I am sorry to say, were not so fortunate."

Miradel felt a rush of guilt for, in that moment of brutal honesty, the fate of the army meant much less to her than the safety of her lover. But in another instant she acknowledged the despair brought about by the dire situation. If the Deathlord's horde was unstoppable, how much longer could Natac, or anyone else on Nayve, hope to survive?

"Druids and sages," Cillia declared, commanding in her position in the center of the ring. Immediately the gathered throng fell silent. "Our efforts are needed in this new war, at the Swansleep River. General Natac has sent a messenger . . . a not-unexpected summons, to be sure. Sages, we will need you to generate the teleports. We will use the whirlpools in the garden. Druids, the hundred of you that I have spoken to about this plan: make yourselves ready for war. We depart with the first glimmer of Lighten."

Immediately there was murmuring among the gathered druids, knowing looks between the sages. Such a mass teleport was not unprecedented, but it was a very complicated undertaking, requiring careful coordination and a great concentration of magic. Everyone had much to do, and quickly the group broke up as individuals and pairs went about their tasks.

Miradel turned to Belynda. "You knew about this plan?" said the druid. "You are helping with the teleport spell?"

"Why, yes," replied the sage-ambassador. "We were told that it might be necessary. But you didn't know?"

"My work is here, in the temple; there was no need to inform me," Miradel said. She glanced at Shandira before turning back to Belynda. "But listen, I need you to do us a favor."

"Of course."

"You must send the two of us tonight, when the great teleport spell is cast."

"But your place is here, isn't it? Why do you want to go to the Swansleep River?"

"My place . . . I am still trying to find it," Miradel said. "As is Shandira. But I have concluded that place is not here. We can do good work elsewhere."

"But there are a hundred druids, all practiced in the art of water and wind magic, going to serve at the river. Why must you join them?"

"I never said I was joining them," Miradel answered, lowering her voice and meeting the elfwoman's eyes directly. "I want you to send us someplace else altogether."

"Where is that?" Belynda looked a little alarmed, which didn't surprise her old friend.

"Later," said the druid. "I will tell you when we come here for the spell casting."

10

Running in the Dark

Shadows whisper
Darkness breathes,
Pulses quicken,
Mem'ry grieves

Song of the Darkdweller

The dwarfmaid walked the street next to the ghetto wall because it was the shortest route between her workplace, the low city fish market where she earned enough in gold coins to keep herself alive. Long ago her walk had taken her through the goblin neighborhood; often she would stop in a tavern there or pick up some cookshrooms at the bustling market. Since the wall had gone up, forty years earlier, her walk had gotten longer and more dull.

But she did it because it was her job, and dwarves were nothing if not dedicated to their labor. Now she was just in a hurry, hungry and tired, anxious to return to her home.

She would never get there.

The liquid came from above, a sloshing spill that caught her ear just in time to cause her to raise her face. The oil struck her in the eyes first, searing away her flesh with the burning strength of its heat. She opened her mouth to scream, and it poured down her throat. Before she could make any sound, she was dead. Her body was cruelly burned, her passable beauty mutilated even beyond recognition, for she had been murdered in the foulest fashion that anyone could have devised.

"THE goblins seek to terrorize our population!" Nayfal insisted passionately, though he kept his tone low, as befitted a conversation with the king. "This latest attack is simply the most gruesome evidence of the fact that we need to act!"

King Lightbringer closed his eyes and leaned his head against the back of his throne, looking very old to the agitated lord. He spoke without looking at Nayfal. "They killed this poor woman by pouring hot oil over her?"

"Indeed, sire. It is clear that our people are no longer safe in the vicinity of the ghetto. We must take action—drastic action!"

"Are you sure it was goblins?"

"Who else would it be?" the marshal retorted. Then he added, "Of course, I interviewed witnesses. Several of your own guardsmen were in position to see. They even chased the wretches, though the gobs were quick to get off the wall. They vanished into the ghetto. Sire, we must strike those impudent wretches at once!"

"You are right, of course," replied the king. At last he opened his eyes and looked at Nayfal, his expression immeasurably sad. "Do what you must," he commanded.

THE ferr'ells came out of the darkness, slinking soundlessly around a massive pillar of rock. Long and low and sleekly furry, they looked like stronger, and much larger versions of the wyslet, to which they were vaguely related.

The three steeds crept toward the dwarves, round ears alert, seeking signs of danger or familiarity. For several moments tension was apparent in every aspect of their quivering whiskers, staring eyes, taut posture. But then, satisfied, the creatures relaxed and trotted quickly toward them. Even so, they snapped jaws and uttered deep-throated growls as proof of the resentment still aroused by their lifelong domestication.

"This was faster than I expected," Konnor acknowledged. An hour earlier he had blown upon his ultrahigh-pitched whistle. The three dwarves had waited with growing anxiety, hoping that the mounts they had turned out many intervals before had remained within audible distance.

The trio wasted no time in saddling the ferr'ells, which hissed and pranced restively. Immediately Borand's, perhaps sensing its rider's weakness, turned and snapped toothy jaws. The dwarf whacked the whiskered snout sharply with his leathered fist. Accepting his rider's mastery, the beast lowered its head and allowed the saddling to proceed without interruption. The dwarves slung several saddlebags and stowed their remaining food, climbing equipment, extra weapons, and flamestone. Then they mounted and started the long journey back to the city.

For a full cycle, forty intervals of sunless time that would have been two score days and nights on Nayve or Earth, they rode toward the center, toward the remembered lights of Axial. A quarter of the way into the trip they found the long-abandoned camp of a massive army, broken weapons and discarded equipment covering a plain four miles across. They explored the area, found the track leading toward Arkan Pass, and deduced that this had been the bivouac of the mighty army that had fought the Seers in that ill-fated battle fifty years before.

"This was one of their last camps," Borand guessed,

kicking through a cracked stewpot within which the remnants of food had long turned to dust. "They marched to Arkan Pass and to disaster, lost to Nightrock just as our army was lost to Axial."

"Which makes me think that the Delver city has been abandoned for that long, or nearly so," Aurand mused. "All those years we Seers have been cowering in the city, locking up goblins, pulling back from our ancestral food warrens—in fear of an enemy who no longer exists!"

From there they crossed the Salt Plain in a stretch of unbroken gallop, lashing their ferr'ells into a frenzy of speed so that they could reach the centerward heights before the nightbats could gather. By the time the great, shrieking flock winged in pursuit, the dwarves, on lathered mounts, were racing up the limestone bluffs of Escarpment. The bats, for reasons as mysterious as they were consistent, refused to fly among the crags of the broken bluff, and the Seer scouts continued toward their home city at a more leisurely pace.

The implication of their discovery occupied their thoughts, and their conversation revolved around numerous speculations, hypotheses to explain the fabled city's abandonment. They wondered if the Delvers had been destroyed at the same time as Axial's army, a conclusion that seemed too good to be true—and too dangerous to assume. But now signs they'd seen over past decades of scouting the Underworld, memories of abandoned boatyards and silent mines, withered warrens and untracked pathways, began to make sense in a larger pattern.

Borand was also thinking about other things, and he made these known as they rode toward the last interval of their long journey.

"I'd suggest we say naught of our discovery at first," he suggested to the younger dwarves. "Not till we've had a chance to speak to Rufus. So don't be spilling your tales over a cold ale in the first tavern we visit. We need to do this carefully. If we can convince people that the Delvers are gone, it will change a lot of things about Axial."

"For the better," Aurand agreed.

"Wise counsel," Konnor agreed. "The news will be embarrassing, at the least, to Lord Nayfal. It was he, after all, who gave impetus to so many of the measures taken since Arkan Pass."

"Aye," Aurand chimed in. "Measures to guard against the Delver menace he claimed was just beyond the next row of hills. I'd like to see the expression on his face when he learns the truth."

"As would we all," said Borand. "But again, let us be the ones who control when that lesson takes place. I'm sure Father will have some ideas. I have lots of questions about how we tell the king and make sure he believes us."

The questions remained unanswered as, at last, they came into view of Axial's lights. They were weary and saddle sore, and even the hardy ferr'ells were limping, hopping gingerly from foot to foot as they approached, in single file, the miles-long Null Causeway leading to the city.

Before they set foot on the crossing, however, Borand's steed reared back, startled. A shape, cloaked in dark clothes, emerged from the ditch and took the ferr'ell's bridle—an act of no small courage, especially as the animal started to rear and was pulled back down with a forceful yank. This was clearly someone who had worked with the fierce animals before.

Even so, Borand was startled to see that black veil pull away to reveal his sister's face. "Stop right here, big brother," she said grimly. "The city isn't a safe place for the Houseguard clan."

———

"Boss Hiyram—wake ups! Wake ups, now!"

The voice penetrated the goblin's sleep-fogged brain, and he blinked, sniffling a loud inhalation as he tried to understand where he was, what was happening. With the first touch of the air he recognized the ghetto, pungent and unmistakable . . . and then the other details of his circumstance came to him in a rush. He was hungry and lonely, utterly without hope. Even the Lady was gone, her father slain and Darann perhaps dead as well.

"Listen! Dwarves is comin'!" The voice, in breath sickly sour with malnutrition, hissed urgently at his ear, and he knew that things, bad as they were, could still get worse. He recognized the speaker as Spadrool, a courageous goblin who had been his friend since the Delver Wars.

"What? What you mean?" asked Hiyram, sitting up groggily.

Then he heard it: a deep thrumming that at first reminded him of a basso drumbeat, some kind of ceremonial cadence. But quickly he recognized, felt in his belly, the rhythmic rumble of an army on the march.

Instantly he sprang from his pallet, sniffing the air more carefully as his floppy ears pricked up. He analyzed the sound; it seemed to come from everywhere, but in fact arose in the direction of metal. He sought a trace of smoke scent, felt a moment of relief when he failed to detect that particular menace.

But then he heard the screams.

"They come against ghetto," Spadrool explained, confirming Hiyram's deduction. "Breakin' down gates in Metal Wall."

"Are the fighter gobs gathering?" Hiyram asked. He groped through the grimy straw of his pallet, clutched the hilt of the dagger, one of the precious weapons smuggled in to him by the Lady. "And the she-gobs and little ones running?"

"Best as can be," replied Spadrool. "Needs you to tells us."

"Come!" Hiyram was fully awake by then and raced out the door of his hovel with his comrade, who was armed with a stout pipe of iron, trailing right behind. They sprinted from the alley into the main thoroughfare of the ghetto, a narrow lane leading upward from the waterfront. Goblins were running in every direction, crying, calling, shouting.

"All you men-gobs!" Hiyram shouted as he ran into the middle of the street. "Go to metal way—bring you sticks, stones, bring you blades if you got! Right away!"

He turned and started up the hill, alarmed to realize that he *could* smell smoke now, that the stink seemed to be getting stronger with each step. At the same time, he was encouraged by the fact that dozens, quickly a hundred or more, goblins were following his lead. Many were unarmed, but some bore makeshift weapons like Spadrool's. Nowhere else but in his own hand did Hiyram see the gleam of a steel blade.

They came to the top of the hill and saw the wall rising before them. Orange flames were bright at the base, where the gate had once stood. Now dark, armored figures were tromping past that blaze, entering the ghetto in a long, undeniably military file. Another waft of smoke carried past, and Hiyram knew that other gates along this wall were under attack. In the stone maze of the ghetto's alleys, the fires could not spread into a conflagration, but they could be destructive and frightening where they were used.

"You there, halt! Drop those weapons!" shouted a burly and bearded Seer, lifting up the faceplate of his helm and striding imperiously forward. He was backed by a rank of armored dwarves. "You'll be coming with us, you lot!"

"Go away!" shouted Hiyram, the first thought that came to his mind. He lifted the knife and brandished it at the officer, who was twenty or thirty paces away.

"They're armed!" cried the dwarf. "It's a rebellion! To the attack, men!"

Hiyram had seen dwarven armies before, but he was still surprised at their precise discipline, the quickness with which they obeyed orders. As if they were of one mind, the dwarves tightened ranks and charged the goblins with swords raised and shiny steel shields held across their chests.

The motley group of ghetto denizens turned tail and fled at the first rush of the dwarves. Hiyram held a second, his knife pointed pathetically, but his ears told him that every one of his comrades had run away. Gulping, he spun about, strangely moved to see the redoubtable Spadrool, eyes wide and pipe clutched in trembling hand, had remained at his side.

"Go now!" he shouted, and his companion turned with him. Wide feet slapping on the wet stones, they dashed away from the dwarves, sprinting into the tangle of alleys and sewers that was the goblin ghetto.

DARANN knew that her brothers had innumerable questions, but she held them at bay as they dismounted and gathered around her. "Let's not talk here. Come with me, up the hill."

After they tethered their ferr'ells, she led them on foot, with their companion Konnor, up to the pinnacle of the seaside elevation. Here they sat on a stone bench, one of several which formed a ring on the hilltop.

The summit was a popular destination for dwarven

walkers because of the splendid view of Axial. Now, however, Darann paid no attention to the array of coolfyre beacons. The six pillars of stone stood outlined in sparkling brilliance, torches and lamps illuminating the skirts of balconies, the vertical stripes of the lift channels.

"What did you mean, when you said that the city is no longer safe for clan Houseguard?" Borand asked. "Your words send an uncanny chill down my spine."

"I am sorry to greet with you such news, but I meant just that. My brothers, our father is dead, slain—I am certain—upon the orders of Lord Nayfal."

"No!" cried Aurand, bouncing to his feet, clenching his short sword so hard his knuckles turned white. Tears came to his eyes, and his mouth worked frantically, though no sound emerged. Finally he choked out a thought: "I will not believe this!"

Borand, the elder brother, watched Darann carefully, finally stepping forward and taking her shoulders in his strong hands, still looking into her eyes. "I hear and sense your pain. It *is* true, my brother." He addressed Aurand while still looking at his sister. "And I am sorry, little one, that you were left to deal with that blow by yourself. . . . I wish that I could have been here."

"Father slain . . . by murder . . ." Aurand's voice was numb, as if he was trying to convince himself by stating the facts. He shook his head, blinked back his tears, and looked around fiercely. "I swear by all the ancestors of Axial—I will avenge him!"

Then his eyes fell upon his sister again, and he wept loudly, staggering to Darann, sweeping her into his arms. She sobbed, too, at last giving vent to her grief. "I am sorry that we were gone . . . that you were here alone to face such a crisis."

"Rufus Houseguard murdered?" Konnor said, horror muting his voice to a dull whisper. He looked at Darann, reached out to touch her hand. "And you have fled the city. Did you sense that you were in danger?"

"Yes . . . more than sensed, I *saw*." She told of her flight from the manor, of the dark intruders who broke in and searched the rooms with clear and menacing purpose.

"These are dark days upon us," Borand said grimly. "And to think, we returned to Axial with a message of hope."

"What hope can there be?" Darann asked.

Borand told her, patiently, about their discovery of the abandoned city, the indications that the Delvers might be gone from the First Circle entirely. "We were going to tell father, then go with him to see the king! We hoped to persuade him to open up some of the far warrens to food gathering again, even to let the goblins free to help with the work they have always done for us. But Father . . . I can't believe he's gone!"

"How did he die?" Aurand asked grimly, fingering his sword as he looked across the water at the lights of Axial.

Darann described the warning from Hiyram, her detainment by the guards, and the discovery of the shattered lift. "The king suspected nothing but an accident," she said quietly. "I looked into his eyes, and I believed him. But he told me that Nayfal himself walked Father to the lift, that he was standing right there when it happened. The cable snapped, and the brakes failed, the first time those two systems have ever malfunctioned together."

"Sabotage. He would have needed help, but that's a simple thing for a man of Nayfal's connections." Borand scratched his beard, his eyes narrowed. "You were wise to leave the city, my sister."

"It was not so much a decision—I was *chased* out!" She recounted the tale of the intruders into Manor Houseguard, of her harrowing escape, and her flight over water. "I knew you would return by the Null Causeway, so I waited here, camping beside the shore, until I saw your ferr'ells coming past the outer beacon."

"What do we do now?" Konnor asked. "Surely something, besides hiding out in the dark?"

"Yes. Now that you are here, we have to take action," Darann declared. "We must try to get to the king, tell him what you've learned about the Delvers, and what I suspect about Nayfal."

"You are right, I think," Borand said. "But I wish we had more to tell him than mere suspicions. Is there some way we can get proof?"

"You said someone helped him to sabotage the lift. We could try to find that person, force him to confess," said the dwarfmaid.

"Not an easy task, perhaps even impossible," said the elder brother, shaking his head. "But Hiyram gave you warning about the plot against Father. Do you have any idea how he learned?"

"He knows a dwarf, a pailslopper, who works in the Royal Tower, seems to know something about Nayfal's activities. But she's not loyal to him—she gave Hiyram the warning to bring to me. If we find Hiyram, perhaps he can lead us to her, and she might be able to provide us with proof?"

"A pailslopper?" Aurand said with a grimace. "Makes us seem pretty desperate."

"We *are* desperate!" snapped Darann, glaring at her younger brother. "In case you hadn't noticed, your life is probably in danger as well! If our best hopes lie with a goblin and a pailslopper, then what does that say about our countrymen?"

"I am sorry. Your point is taken," Aurand acknowledged. "And it says some very ugly things about our fellow Seers . . . very ugly indeed."

"I have been thinking of something else," Darann

noted, continuing as her brothers remained silent. "Father got a note from a dwarfmaid who claimed to be 'one of the lowest' or something like that. I am wondering if she is the same woman as Hiyram's pailslopper."

"It's possible," Borand concurred. "Certainly worth speaking to the wench."

"Your boat—is it nearby?" asked Konnor.

"At the foot of this hill," she replied. "And big enough for the four of us, but barely."

"We can get the supplies off the ferr'ells," volunteered Aurand, "and meet you at the shore. Let's get started right away."

"Do you think the king will see us?" Borand asked, staring at the city shining so brightly in the distance. The white coolfyre beacons reflected off the still water, amplifying their brightness against the backdrop of the sunless circle.

"We don't have any choice but to try!" Aurand said sharply. "Our father has been murdered! Do you not desire to avenge him?"

"I do," said the elder brother, nodding grimly. "I just wonder about our chances of success."

"That's a waste of time from over here," Konnor said. "Better to wonder while we're waiting in the throne room for our audience with the king. Until then, we've got other problems to solve."

"Agreed," said Borand. "Perhaps I am simply feeling my age. It is easier, certainly, to wonder than it is to act. But so, too, is such pensive reflection undeniably useless. So let's move."

The two brothers started to descend the back side of the hill toward the ferr'ells, while Darann led Konnor down the steeper side facing the city. They worked their way down the rocky slope for some distance before stopping to catch their breath, still a hundred feet above the shore.

"I . . . I feel terrible that you were here alone," the dwarf told Darann, clearing his throat awkwardly. "That is . . . since Karkald was lost, I have worried about you. . . . I mean, with concern, of course."

Darann sighed, touched and irritated at the same time. He had a point. Why did it seem as though she had to deal with so many problems by herself? But she clapped a hand on his shoulder. "Thank you," she said simply. "I am glad that the three of you are here now."

Konnor nodded, looking at her seriously, as if he had something important to say. But in the end he swallowed his words, nodded gruffly, cleared his throat again. "Yes, I'm glad that we're here, too," was all he said.

HIYRAM ran with terrible fear pounding in his heart, but he did not let that fear turn to panic. Spadrool was still at his side, and together they had been able to send many females and youngsters toward the lower end of the ghetto, while they raced into view of the Seer troops and led the invaders off the track.

Of course, despite his determination, there was plenty of panic to be found in the goblin ghetto. They found several bodies, goblins of all ages and both genders who had been cut down with violence. Sometimes other fleeing goblins were too distraught to listen to their advice; one elder fellow, half deaf and limping along with a cane, simply waved them off and hurried up the street, straight into the path of one of the Seer patrols. Hiyram groaned aloud as he saw the goblin flinch back from a blow, then fall to the ground to be kicked and stabbed by the dwarves. Crouching in the shadows, he waited until the dozen or so Seers had tromped past, then went to see if he could aid the old goblin. He was not surprised to find that the fellow was already dead.

"Why they do?" Spadrool asked pathetically, looking down at the frail-looking corpse. "What for they come?"

Hiyram shook his head, a low growl rumbling in his throat. He didn't know the answer. For a time, earlier in this very interval, he had wondered those questions himself, not coming close to an acceptable answer. Now, with violence and suffering all around him, he would no longer worry about the whys and the what fors. The knife had been almost forgotten in his hand, but he discovered his fingers clenched painfully around the hilt.

"Come. We got work," he said, starting off at a trot, the faithful Spadrool sprinting after until he caught up.

The two goblins came around another corner and found several females with a score of youngsters huddled, sobbing, in the niche between two buildings. The heavy footsteps of dwarven interlopers grew louder in the street, coming toward them.

"Follow him!" cried Hiyram, pointing at Spadrool. "Take them down to sewer flats—hurry!" he urged.

"But—you come, too!" declared his companion.

"Right after," Hiyram said. "But go!"

With an anxious glance back, Spadrool took off, the terrified goblins hurrying along behind. Hiyram trotted after, looking over his own shoulder, seeing the rank of dwarves turn into the street. One spotted the fleeing party and raised a shout; immediately, the tromp of marching boots broke into the clatter of a dead run.

One of the females screamed, and several children started crying. Their progress was too slow; the dwarves would catch them inside of a minute! Casting around for something to do, Hiyram spotted a stack of empty, rotting barrels stacked haphazardly beside the roadway. He ducked behind the stale-smelling kegs, looking anxiously as the fleeing goblins hurried up the street. From his hiding place he couldn't see the pursuers, but the sounds of clomped, nailed boots grew thunderous as they approached.

Judging his moment carefully, Hiyram pushed against the bottom barrel, nudging it over, toppling it into the street. Several casks atop that one fell outward, one shattering and the other tumbling over the stone roadway. Immediately he heard cursing and crashing, saw the rolling barrel bounce toward him as a heavy object—an armored dwarf—collided with it. Urgently he pushed at the stack, sending more barrels rolling across the street, scattering the pursuing guards like ninepins.

"There he is—get him!" The shout seemed to be right in Hiyram's ear, and he whirled in sudden fear. A dwarf, huge and strapping and fiercely bearded, thrust at him with a short sword. The goblin ducked under the blow, then dove headlong into the tumbling barrels, dodging a heavy boot that tried to stomp down on his head.

Bouncing to his feet, he darted behind another dwarf, thankfully observing that Spadrool and the fleeing goblins had disappeared down the street. But now the dwarves were focusing on him, circling menacingly. One hacked downward with an axe, shattering a barrel into kindling as Hiyram tumbled away. He ducked, crept past another barrel, then leaped to his feet. The road was open before him, and he put down his head and sprinted—

Right into the gut of a dwarf who somehow emerged into view, having been hidden by a rolling keg. This one had a sword, and as he gasped for breath, he raised the weapon, aiming a blow at Hiyram's head. Other dwarves closed in, the rest of them coming from behind, jeering and shouting.

The knife seemed heavy in the goblin's hand. He remembered Darann's entreaty that he never use it against a dwarf, not unless his life depended upon it. Every fiber of his conscience urged him to hold back his hand, resist the violence that was overwhelming him. But that dwarven blade was close now, quivering as the fellow lined it up for a killing blow.

"I'm sorry, Lady," Hiyram groaned.

And then he stabbed.

11

The Horde Undammed

Hard as ice,
Soft as steam,
Soothing mist,
Quiet stream;

Till surge and tide,
And typhoon's breath,
Give gentle brine
An edge of death.

From the Tapestry of the Worldweaver
History of Time

"You can't be serious!" Belynda declared, aghast.

"Lower your voice!" Miradel urged, her own tone a rasping whisper. "And yes, I have never been more serious in my life!"

"You want me to send you to the Fifth Circle, to the Deathlord's world?" the elven sage-ambassador shook her head. "That would be tantamount to murder!" She turned away, shaking her head, drawing a few glances from the other druids and sages gathered along the casting pools beside the lake. The Hour of Darken was imminent, and they had gathered here for the mass teleportation that Natac had requested.

But Miradel had a different idea and had just broached it to her elven friend. Now she continued her efforts at persuasion. "No—it is the best hope we have!"

Shandira had been watching the exchange in silence, but now she queried Belynda. "Why do you argue? Does not Miradel's plan make sense?"

"Make sense?" The sage-ambassador's elven serenity had already wavered, was in danger of cracking altogether. "That depends: if your goal is to waste your lives, throw them away to no effect, for no benefit, well, then Miradel's plan has distinct advantages."

"Please!" The druid was shocked and nonplussed at her friend's sarcasm. "You have to try to understand!"

"Explain it to me, then," Belynda demanded, her eyes narrowed.

"I think that the goddess may be wrong about the Deathlord, Karlath-Fayd. She seems to think there is nothing we can learn, nothing we can *do* against him! But I believe—at least, I hope—that by doing some reconnaissance, spying on him, we may find the weakness that allows us to defeat his army."

"What makes you think the Worldweaver is mistaken? Isn't the very idea rather blasphemous?" The elfwoman's eyes were narrowed, her expression stubborn, but at least she was listening.

Miradel shook her head. "I don't believe so. If I can bring her information, I am certain she will be grateful for the knowledge. As to why I think she is wrong, it is a little thing, but proof to me: long ago she told me that no one could survive in the presence of the Deathlord, because his very gaze would be enough to turn that person into ashes. Yet more recently, when I raised the issue again, she claimed that his gaze was enough to render a person into a stone statue. It is clear that she doesn't know *what* effects, if any, might be engendered by a journey into the Deathlord's presence. I intend to learn."

"By sacrificing yourself or this novice druid to his whim? Either stone or ash is a terrible enough fate!"

"But she is just guessing!" Miradel retorted.

"I am willing to try," Shandira said quickly. "Indeed, this is a sacrifice I prefer to the other task that has been explained to me."

Belynda shook her head. "That doesn't change the fact that you are almost certainly doomed if you go to Loamar. I cannot be a party to that fate!"

"But you must help us," Miradel pressed. "It is our best, not our only, chance. When the great teleporting is done at Darken, when the druids are sent to the Swansleep River, you can simply send us to a different location."

"Even if I consent to do this, and supposing that you do enter the citadel of Karlath-Fayd and learn something of use, how do you propose to return here with that knowledge?"

"There, too, I will need your help," said Miradel quietly. "You will need to seek me periodically in your Globe of Seeing—perhaps you could look twice each day, as the Hour of Darken commences and the Lighten Hour begins. Those times will be the same throughout the circles, though much colder and darker on Loamar than they are here. If we have learned what we seek and are ready to return here, we will await your sighting around some swirling current of water, so that you can bring us out with a teleport spell."

"I tell you, I don't like this," Belynda repeated, but there was a sense of resignation in her voice. "Though I begin to understand your glimmer of hope. You have thought about this carefully, I see." She looked at

Shandira. "You understand that you will probably perish in this quest?"

"I am prepared for whatever might happen. I have made peace with my Savior and within myself," the tall woman replied with great dignity.

"Very well," the sage-ambassador acquiesced, turning back to Miradel. "But what about Natac?"

For the first time she felt the tug of regret, but she pushed it out of her mind. "He risks his life every day in this war. He and I must both accept the same imperilment."

"Have you made your preparations? Provisions? Weapons?"

Miradel nodded, indicating the two backpacks they had brought with them. "Enough food for five or six days. Also, I have a knife, and Shandira her stave. Though I do not think weapons will decide the success or failure of this mission: we are going there to learn, not to fight."

The notes of a flute trilled along the lakeshore, and the druids started moving toward the pools, the ten circular wells of water that had been carved into the bedrock of the shore. The teleportation spell required a focus of swirling water, both at the beginning and the destination of the magical transport. A hundred miles away, on the banks of the Swansleep River, elven warriors had prepared an equal number of eddies to serve as destinations. The druids would be sent, ten at a time, until all hundred had made the journey.

"I presume you have spotted an appropriate destination?" Belynda said.

"Yes, I have viewed Loamar through the Tapestry. There is a great waterfall that spills from the front of the citadel, down a thousand feet of cliff. At the base it has hollowed out a great bowl in the rock, and the water swirls violently there before flowing onward. There is a flat shelf of rock nearby. All I ask is that you send us there and let us proceed on foot."

"Very well." Belynda's Globe, the crystal sphere that allowed her to view any place in the first Six Circles, rested on a pillow on one of the stone benches, covered with a velvet cloth. She pulled the cloth away and peered close at the glass. Miradel could see a vague glow, pearly light growing pleasantly bright within the ball, though she could make out no details. The image shifted and wavered, light fading and then growing to sudden sparkles, until it blinked out as quickly as if someone had shuttered a lamp.

"I see the place," the sage-ambassador said. "The water will work for the spell, though I beg you again to reconsider! What a barren, awful place it is!"

"I know," Miradel said. "But we have to go there."

"Then, my friend, I can only wish you the best of luck. I will check twice each day, seeking you, hoping to bring you back. But remember, you must stand close to a swirl of water for my spell to bring you out."

"I remember," the druid said. "I am grateful, too." She gestured to the shore, now etched in the growing swell of daylight. "Now, good women, it is time for us to go."

NATAC had walked the bank of the Swansleep River for more than ten miles and was dismayed at the low water level. Rocks poked from the bed where once-deep waters had flowed unbroken. The shores were muddy and flat, overgrown with cattails and reeds. The ground in both directions rose only gradually: toward the coastal hills in the direction of metal; while centerward the land opened on a long, open highway leading to the Ringhills and Circle at Center.

Nevertheless, if his army was going to make a stand, it would have to be here.

Late in the long day, nearly forty-eight hours after the army had fallen back from the beach, he met the vanguards of the two elven columns. He led the elves to the two good fords, where the smoothly graveled riverbed spanned the distance between dry, open approaches. He was relieved to discover that most of the batteries had escaped the battle at the shore, and he had the centaurs quickly haul them into position for a vigorous defense of the two fords. Nearly half the wheeled weapons were placed at these two junctures. The rest he scattered along the length of the river, counting on the centaurs' speed to bring them into position when the enemy, as he inevitably would, forced other crossings of the water.

"Go and find the trolls," he ordered Horas of Gallowglen, who had returned to the general with confirmation of the great teleportation spell from Circle at Center. The faerie was accompanied by several dozen of his fellows, and Natac was grateful for the extra couriers and scouts. "Tell them to get to the river as quickly as possible. Also, can you return here and tell me how far they are? When I should expect them?"

"As you wish, General Natac. It is my honor!" replied the bold courier. He flew off with five comrades, while Natac addressed the others. "I need some of you to find the gnomes—any that survived the battle on the beaches. Get them heading this way if they can, or tell them to hide out until the Deathlord's army has passed. The rest of you have to locate that army . . . get an idea of the strength and the locations of his columns."

Quickly the winged messengers darted away, and the general had already turned to his next problem.

He had set the elves to work in parties of a score of diggers, striving to create ten circular bowls beside the river.

These were to be filled with water and manually stirred to create the focal point for the teleportation. But though the elves found good spots to dig and quickly channeled trenches across the short distances between the riverbank and the circular waterholes, there was not enough water in the channel to carry more than a trickle into most of the crucial sites.

Natac found Tamarwind, worrying about that same problem. "There are lots of deep spots within a mile up- and downstream," the general explained. "One thing we have is numbers; let's send ten thousand elves out to fill their waterskins. We'll get our waterholes that way."

The elf agreed and set the troops to work. Hundreds of elves marched away, carrying empty water sacks, return- ing an hour later with those containers dripping full. Though the day was drawing to a close by the time the last of the holes was filled, the elves transported enough water for each of the ten pools to serve as a focus of the spell. As soon as the sun began to pull away, a dozen elves knelt at each basin and used makeshift paddles to start the water swirling.

Pacing along the length of the riverbank, trying to con- tain his agitation, Natac swung his eyes from one group to the next. It seemed as though he had been waiting forever, but it was only a couple of minutes before he saw the lights sparkling in the air, like miniwhirlwinds of fireflies that soon coalesced into druids, a pair of them arriving at each focus with the first casting.

Quickly, elves helped these new arrivals away, offering sips of water to help with the momentary disorientation that always followed the teleport. A few minutes later, the second group arrived, with subsequent castings—each performed by a new set of sages back in Circle at Cen- ter—bringing in the rest of the druids as the sun slowly rose toward full nightfall. Twenty druids arrived in each of the first four waves, but on the last group there were but eighteen; none materialized at the last waterhole along the line.

Juliay was one who arrived at the next basin. "What happened to Miradel and Shandira?" she asked, as Natac jogged up to investigate.

"Miradel was coming here?" he asked. "I thought she had work in the temple!"

Juliay shrugged. "So did I, but I saw her just before Darken. It seemed odd; Shandira is just a novice and wouldn't be able to help with your plan in any event."

Natac frowned, concerned.

"I presume she must have changed her mind at the last minute," Juliay suggested hopefully. "In any event, ninety-eight of us are here. We can do what you need."

"I know," the general agreed. He turned his attention to the local problem, though he remained concerned about Miradel. What had she intended? And where was she?

Those answers would have to wait. He found Cillia, the matriarch of the druids, critically inspecting the low level of water in the river. She was a tall woman, sturdy of frame, with black hair flowing freely down the length of her back.

"It would help if we had some rain," she said as soon as Natac came up to her. "This isn't much to work with."

"I know," he agreed. "They picked the driest year in two decades for their invasion."

The venerable druid leaned back to look at the sky. "There's some evening mist rising up and a few clouds blocking out the stars. Let us see if we can do something to help. Any idea how much time we have?"

"The scouts report that the ghost armies will be here by the middle of the night," Natac replied.

"Druids, gather to me!" shouted Cillia, and in ten minutes the members of her order had assembled from their focal basins along the riverbank. Natac went back to inspect the fords, so he didn't hear what she said or see what the druids did.

He was just relieved when, an hour after Darken, it started to rain.

IF there was one thing that made a dark night even more miserable, it was rain. Awfulbark reflected on this truth as he slogged through mud that seemed to clutch his feet with sucking mire every time he tried to take another step. He was following at the tail end of a long line of trolls, and it seemed that they were all doing their best to churn up the ground so as to make it virtually impassable for the king.

Cursing and muttering, Awfulbark simply kept going. Roodcleaver was right in front of him—for some inexplicable reason she had refused to leave his side during this inglorious retreat—and somewhere behind, not terribly far away, came the implacable legions of the ghost warriors.

Frequently he glanced behind him, certain they were closing the gap. It was impossible to see much of anything in the lightless night, further obscured by the rain spattering down in large drops. Aside from the eerie wails they had uttered in combat, the troll had heard no noise from the enemy, so he fully expected them to be moving in complete silence.

"Faster!" he shouted. "March faster!"

Awfulbark hoped that the faeries who had been guiding the front of the troll column were still there. They claimed to have come from Natac and were going to show them the way to the nearest ford across the Swansleep. The little flyers could be leading the trolls right off the edge of Riven Deep, for all he knew.

Lightning flashed, illuminating a hundred miserable

trolls, their rough, barklike skin slick with rainwater, and then a crash of thunder split the night. The king cringed, whipping his sword around so hard that he buried it four inches deep into the trunk of a willow tree. Angrily he pulled it out, yanking it free just as another flash brightened the night.

They were back there, the ghostly pursuers, a hundred paces away and coming on in a dense column. As the lightning faded he was left with the image of a thousand spear points, raised above the rank of marching warriors. Those in the lead bore swords, and even as the darkness closed in again, they raised that terrifying yowl that struck chills into Awfulbark's gut.

"Run!" he cried. "Run to the river!"

He lurched and lumbered along, pushing Roodcleaver impatiently, tripping over a troll who had sprawled in the trail. He cursed as he picked that fellow up and shoved him forward, carelessly piercing him with his sword in the process. The troll howled but found the strength to continue on.

Only then did Awfulbark think of the tree he had struck: a willow! Surely the river must be near!

In two more steps he was in the water, feeling the hard gravel of the ford under his feet. The rest of the trolls were crossing or scrambling out, gasping and panting, on the other side. He saw ghostly blue fires along the bank there and groaned at the knowledge that magic was being cast. Nevertheless, his terror of the pursuing horde was even more acute, and so he pushed through the last few steps, stumbled onto the riverbank, and threw his hands over his head as magic exploded behind him.

"WHY did Miradel plan to come out here to the Swansleep?" Natac asked Cillia, as they stood at the riverbank in the rainy night. "I thought she was busy in the temple."

"That's what I thought, too. In fact, I didn't know she was coming," the druid matriarch replied. "Where is she?"

"Well, I'm worried about that. Juliay said she was with Shandira, but they didn't arrive with the last group of teleports."

"Strange." Cillia looked at Natac in concern, her skin pale ivory against the dark background of her hair and the night. "Shandira certainly isn't ready to help with the water magic. Miradel was supposed to be training her to prepare for the Spell of Summoning. Perhaps Juliay was mistaken. There were lots of our order on the lakefront, many more than actually came out here to the river."

"I hope you're right." Natac was still concerned. The absence of two druids from the last group of twenty suggested that Miradel and Shandira had departed Circle at Center, but somehow did not make it to their destination.

His worry was overridden as Horas of Gallowglen buzzed up to him, then dropped wearily to the ground. "The trolls are here. The last one just crossed the river, and the ghost warriors are right behind."

"Thanks for the news," Natac said to the faerie before turning to the druid. "It's time!"

Cillia had overheard and was already raising her arms, stretching them like wings as she turned her face to the rainy skies. The warrior was stunned by the loud clap of thunder that seemed to emanate from the air right beside him. Lightning flashed from the druid's fingertips, searing to the right and left, bolts crackling parallel to the ground but over the heads of the warriors and druids gathered on the riverbank.

"My signal," the matriarch said with a wry smile. "I

hope it didn't startle you, but I had to let the rest of the druids know."

"No, fine," Natac said, patting down the hair that, even soaked, had stood stiff upon the back of his neck.

More lightning sparked along the course of the Swansleep, and he could see that the water level had risen dramatically after the half night of rain. Here and there the current swept along with visible force, and even where the water was placid he knew that it was deep; the rocks and tree trunks that had jutted into sight on the previous day had all disappeared.

Additional, sinister images came into view in the sporadic flashes. He could see the Deathlord's horde advancing through the grassy marsh on the other side of the river. They looked so very much like living men, he thought; they slogged across the muddy ground, sometimes tripping or falling over obstacles. He noted that the ghastly invaders were more likely to trample a fallen comrade than to help him up. Water was slick on their skin, soaking through their tunics, plastering hair to heads, and trickling from bushy beards.

But none of them, apparently, had dropped their weapons during the long night march: there was still a wide array of spearheads and bayonets visible above the ranks, and those in front carried their weapons at the ready. They had followed through the hills in broad columns, but now, in the river valley, they seemed to have spread into a massive front—at least, the enemy rank was solid for as far as Natac could see to the right or the left.

The first of the ghost warriors slowed as they approached the opposite riverbank. A few of them probed through the grassy shore, poking the butts of their spears into the water, apparently seeking solid footing. More lightning flashed, brightly etching the image in Natac's mind: the ghost warriors inspecting the river and then slowly venturing in, starting to wade.

On the near bank the elves, formed in a double line at the water's edge, lifted their weapons and prepared for the onslaught. Far to the left the trolls made ready, too, growling, snapping, and barking at the relentless invaders. Whether it was fearlessness or simply the pressure of the horde advancing behind them, Natac couldn't tell; in any event, the first ghost warriors pressed on toward the middle of the stream, while more and more of them marched down the bank and followed the leaders into the water.

Beside Natac, unnoticed by the general, Cillia had taken up her windcasting bowl and spoon. A sudden gust of air swirled outward, driving the raindrops horizontally, right into the faces of the attackers. Miniature cyclones burst into being all along the riverbank, and in moments the steady rain had been transformed into a driving storm, the sheer force of which knocked many of the attackers backward.

More wind swirled, driving waves now as well as rain, a gushing current of river water that swelled into frothy crests and pounded like ocean surf into the chests and faces of the ghost warriors who were now neck deep in the Swansleep. In the force of that surge the first rank of the attackers simply vanished, overwhelmed and knocked off their feet by the power of angry water. Waves lashed harder, attacking with physical violence, pounding and smashing against the enemy horde.

The storm only seemed to enrage the following troops, for they lowered their spears and bayonets and charged headlong into the streambed, slashing and pushing through the floundering bodies that were tangled in the far shallows. The force of the wind relaxed momentarily, giving Natac a jolt of fear. But he looked at Cillia, saw her concentrating, and realized the druids were simply timing their gusts for maximum effect.

Indeed, as water that had been whipped against the far bank flowed back to a more normal level across the entire river, the rush of current pulled the warriors along with it, unbalancing many of them and drawing still more into the channel. Some thrashed and fought while others, apparently drowned, floated lifelessly downstream. This time the attackers pressed through the dead and came more than halfway across before the wind blasted outward again, churning the water into a compact hurricane of force, once against blasting into the faces of the attacking ranks.

Those ranks were shattered again, leaving the far side of the river choked with bodies. Survivors straggled and clawed their way out of the water, while others fought to proceed. In several places violent skirmishes erupted between the ghost warriors, and Natac saw several cut down by their own comrades. This time the blast of water actually carried onto the far bank and through the marsh, breaking up the attackers arrayed in their neat ranks at the edge of the river, playing havoc with the legions extending into the darkness beyond.

Natac heard the clash of steel, cries of alarm and fury, and saw that some of the ghost warriors had struggled through the torrent and were trying to scramble up onto the near bank. The elves moved forward with lethal precision, two or three of Tamarwind's warriors meeting each of these survivors, cutting them down and pushing the corpses back into the flowage. Thus far, the few attackers who fought their way across, or, in some cases, had been carried across by the water that inevitably flowed back against the wind after too much of the liquid collected against the far bank, were no threat to break through the line of doughty defenders.

"Take a rest for a few minutes," the general suggested to the druid matriarch. "You've wrecked their formation for the time being. Let's see if they try to come up with a new tactic."

"Very well," Cillia agreed. She set down her bowl and once again raised her hands, lancing the lightning over the heads of her druids. This time the bolt was an eerie green in color, and Natac guessed that was the matriarch's pre-arranged signal, for the gale faded away along the entire river.

For the first time he noticed gray light seeping through the rain, and he knew that the Lighten Hour was near. It gave him a sense of some relief to be able to see his attackers more clearly, and it was further encouragement to witness their disarray. Though the far side of the river still teemed with ghostly warriors, their once-neat ranks were a shambles, and a great many corpses lay scattered in the shallows and through the muddy grass of the opposite bank.

He turned around and was not surprised to see Horas of Gallowglen standing there, watching and waiting. The faerie's wings were soaked and drooping, but when the general looked at him, he buzzed them quickly, casting off a spray of drops and, in seconds, drying the delicate membranes enough for flight.

"Can you go down the line and see if we've had any casualties?" Natac asked. "Let me know if there's anyplace where they nearly made it across."

"Right away, Lord Natac!" replied the fleet scout, saluting and then vanishing into the misty dawn with a loud hum of his wings. A short time later he was back, reporting that a few elves had been injured by the attackers who made it across the river. But nowhere was there any danger of a breach, at least not from the first assault. Natac thanked the brave faerie and turned his attention toward the enemy, which was clearly gathering for a second push.

Daylight was growing brighter, though the thick clouds muted everything into a drab gray. Rain still fell, though it was more of a drizzle now than the downpour that had drenched the armies and filled up the riverbed through so much of the night. Across the river the attackers were getting themselves sorted out, ranks tightening, weapons poised. A thousand ghost warriors stood shoulder to shoulder within Natac's field of view, while the number of spearheads and bayonets in view behind them was far beyond his ability to count.

"It won't be long," he predicted quietly. Cillia, who was watching, too, and waiting for his command, nodded as he held up a hand. He knew that windcasting required a lot of energy, and the druids' ability to sustain the storm was limited, so he was anxious to conserve their power for as long as possible.

But within a few more minutes it became obvious that the lull was over. The rank of attackers was arrayed across the entire length of the river. Spears lowered, the first of them stepped forward, down the bank and into the water. Others followed closely, tightly packed ranks extending as far backward as Natac could see.

"Now!" he said, and in almost the same instant the druid matriarch sent her lightning signal blasting in both directions along the line. Once more the winds howled and the waters surged, and the ghost warriors marched headlong into the teeth of the gale.

"SURELY we have been sent to Hell itself!" Shandira exclaimed, as soon as the flickering lights of the teleport spell had faded. She was shouting to make herself heard. Her ebony skin had paled to an ashen gray as she looked up at their looming surroundings, black stone cliffs rising like colossal walls to the right and the left.

Miradel found it hard to argue, but she tried. "Do you think there is such a waterfall in Hell?" she asked, more to hear the comforting sound of her own voice than from any real desire for an answer.

In fact, her words were all but drowned in the thunder of the lofty spume, the source of the whirling maelstrom in the stone-walled channel that had given focus to Belynda's teleport spell. Never had she been in such a forbidding place, and her immediate thought was that she was a fool, had made a disastrous decision that would inevitably cost two lives for no good purpose.

The two women were standing on a flat-topped boulder no larger than a typical dining table. The base of the waterfall was up the channel a hundred yards or so, but the air was cold and penetratingly wet. The water, a white inferno of rapids and foam, churned past them, ten feet below the rock. On the other side of their precarious platform was a small eddy, where the stream spilled into a natural bowl in the rocky bed, spun through a rapid circle, then poured itself back into the main current. It was that minivortex that had caused her to select this location for their arrival.

When she had made that selection, she had identified what looked like a negotiable trail leading up a ravine and out of the gorge. Now that route seemed more like a narrow chute of loose scree, an invitation to a fatal fall. She had brought a rope, of course, but it suddenly occurred to her that at least one of them would have to be able to reach the top on her own before that rope would be any use to the other.

"It's cold in here!" Shandira said, shouting again. There was a little light from the stars circling overhead, but the temperature was lower than anything one could experience on Nayve.

"We need our cloaks!" replied Miradel, shrugging out of her pack as Shandira nodded in agreement. Moments later they had pulled their woolen shawls around themselves, hoods pulled up and cinched around their faces.

"Now we have to get away from the river. We're getting soaked, just by being in this air!" The African woman took the lead, lifting her pack onto her shoulders again, then hopping from the rock to the steeply sloping ground at the base of the ravine. A cascade of loose stones tumbled down, and she lurched forward, landing on her hands and knees. "Careful!" she shouted back.

Miradel didn't need the warning. She was trembling, frightened to move, but Shandira's decisiveness gave her the strength to follow. She, too, donned her backpack, then stepped after her companion, taking a strong black hand to keep her balance as she made the long step to the ravine.

Slowly the two women made their way up the steep, narrow passage. Miradel was grateful as the river fell farther and farther away below them, but she was acutely conscious of her scraped hands and knees, of the aches and cramps that were growing in muscles kept taut to prevent a fall. Again it was Shandira who served as a tireless example, pressing ahead with sure steps, then pausing to encourage Miradel, often to extend that helping hand.

Whether it was an hour or three hours later she could not tell, but at last they crawled from the top of the ravine to collapse on a flat and barren wasteland of dark rock. It was still cold, though the air was drier. Stars whirled and danced overhead, providing a minimal spray of light. For a long time the two druids simply lay still and rested, catching their breath, easing their sore limbs.

Finally Miradel sat up and looked around. She was facing the direction of center, and saw a vast sprawl of descending terrain, a series of shelflike terraces of stone dropping eventually to a dark, flat lowland. She could not see the Worldsea, a hundred or so miles away.

Only then did she look behind her, in the direction that was neither metal nor wood. She could barely suppress a gasp of horror as she saw the citadel rising there, like a grim and black-faced mountain of sheer cliff, vaulted parapet, and impossibly lofty summit. Black space yawned beyond, like an infinity of bleak hopelessness or an eternity of suffering.

"I told you," Shandira said, sitting beside Miradel and following the direction of her gaze. "Nothing less than Hell itself."

12

Deathscape

In the Third Direction rises
The End of all Beginnings,
The Proof of all Lies,
And the Virtue of every Sin.

From The Tapestry of the Worldweaver
Bloom of Entropy

The forces of the cosmos marshaled, summoned by the immortal will of a proud deity, deepened by the forces of frustration, boredom, and immortal anger. These powerful forces had been contained for a very long time, but as events on the Fourth Circle settled into a stasis of war, the need for change exploded, and the effects rippled outward, upward, downward, tearing through the fabric of six circles.

The storm was fierce near its epicenter, so that it wracked the very bedrock of creation. In the distant corners of the cosmos it was naturally less potent, but even there it was felt as much more than a ripple of distant thunder.

Waves of destructive energy concentrated at the source of the immortal one's power, emanating outward in a great explosion, mighty and violent, though at first it made no sound, emitted no visual indication of its presence. Instead, it flowed as an invisible river of energy, palpable proof of the diety's power as it crossed the middle of a world and took hold of the landscape in a physical grasp.

For there *was* a god, and she desired entertainment.

THE pony pranced anxiously, hooves skipping across the rocky ground. A loose pebble bounced away, tumbling over the rim of the canyon. Janitha Khandaughter heard it bounce several times, tumbling against the cliff wall as it vanished into Riven Deep.

"Easy, big boy. What's got you so nervous today?" asked the elven rider, patting the stallion on his shoulder.

In fact, she felt the same agitation that seemed to be bothering her normally steady horse, as though the air itself was charged, ready to release some unimagined force. She scrutinized the dark mass gathered across the canyon, knowing that the Delvers had been arrayed there with their iron golems for an unusually long time now . . . not moving, just formed up as if for march or battle, but with no place to go.

It was not far past the Lighten Hour, and her elves were still in their bivouacs for the most part, though the usual scouts were posted. The Hyac patrolled the edge of Riven Deep for a distance of more than fifty miles, as far as the Swansleep Waterfall in the direction of metal. There, where the river of the same name plunged from the precipice into the misty well of the Deep, her elves had linked with the regiments from Barantha, who held the river line against the ghost warriors. Even with all the clans gathered here, the mounted Hyac were far too few to garrison that entire length of canyon. Instead, they maintained fast-moving patrols, riding ceaselessly back and forth along their entire position.

In fact it had been her stallion, Khanwind, that had awakened her this morning. All the horses had been restive in the late-night hours, but he had been the loudest, most demanding. At the first signs of pale daylight he had whinnied and kicked in the corral, and as the Lighten Hour advanced, his agitation had correspondingly increased. Though she herself had been up till well past midnight, Janitha found herself unable to ignore the agitated animal. She had risen and saddled him, allowed him to canter along the rim of the canyon for several miles, finally turned back toward her encampment. They had just made their only stop, for both of them to drink from a shallow stream, but as the elfwoman regained her saddle, the pony once again began to dance and whicker in agitation.

Everything seemed normal on this side of the canyon, she thought. There were crows and ducks flying nearby, good indications that the harpies had not made a recent aerial foray. Of course, there was that oddity across Riven Deep, the formation that had lasted for a surprisingly long time, now. She could see them from here: the Delvers standing in those precise ranks that they had maintained without wavering for ten days. But they were miles away, across an unbridged gulf of space. They remained still, arrayed in blocklike formation, making no move to march, nor did they display any visible preparations for some kind of battle.

Even so, she was concerned. She knew that the great invasion had come ashore. Faeries continued to bring her twice-daily reports on the progress of that battle. Janitha had known the despair of the retreat from the shore and the encouragement of the stand at the river. Even though Natac's army had held the ghost warriors up at the

Swansleep—a stand that had lasted four days now, without a single breach in the position—she knew that Nayve was threatened in a new and lethal fashion. But there was nothing for her to do about that except to stay vigilant and keep the Hyac focused on guarding the Deep, the task they had maintained for fifty years.

Abruptly Khanwind whinnied and reared, surprise almost dropping Janitha from the saddle. She held on and whispered soothingly—until she, too, felt a stab of irrational terror. Some force was moving through . . . through *everything*. She could feel it in the ground, in the air, in her belly; a rumble of invisible strength had made her seem smaller than the most insignificant bug.

Next she heard a sound, a rumbling of the deepest basso, growing louder and louder as she worked to control her panicked, bucking pony. Khanwind staggered, went down to his knees, and Janitha flew from the saddle, smashing to the ground with a force that drove the breath from her lungs. The sturdy horse quickly stood again but staggered like a drunkard. Only then did the elfwoman realize that the ground itself was rippling and surging in the throes of a major quake.

She looked across Riven Deep, sensing that, as violent as it was here, the disturbance was actually focused over there. The first crack appeared quickly, as if a blade of cosmic proportions had torn through the fabric of the precipice, rapidly widening the breach. It looked to Janitha as though the opposite face of Riven Deep had been slashed in two, the gap growing wider and extending downward until it vanished into the misty depths.

Then other cracks appeared, great chunks of the landscape breaking away. The movement, miles away, was clearly visible to her. She stared in awe, waiting for the huge pieces of ground to tumble, even allowed herself a flash of dizzying hope: the Delver army was arrayed on those great platforms of rock; surely the hated invaders would be carried to their doom in Riven Deep! There, another piece broke free, and another. The whole shelf over there was obviously crumbling, broken apart by this quake that was affecting all the ground under the enemy army!

The rocky terrain cracked into great slabs of rock that teetered and wobbled precariously. Below, the face of the vast cliff broke and fell way, carrying downward the cliff that supported the far rim of the canyon. Now, the Delvers had to fall!

Janitha held her breath, waiting . . . and waiting. Finally she exhaled in slow, dull realization. The pieces of ground that had broken away from the opposite precipice were not going to fall, not going to carry the enemy army to its doom. Instead, those huge slabs began, very slowly, to rise into the air.

MIRADEL looked at the sun, low in the sky, faint of brightness, and impossibly far away. It was hard to imagine that it was full daylight on the world of Nayve, but she knew that the Lighten Hour had passed some time ago, that the sun was suspended above the world, directly in line with the loom rising from the temple of the Goddess Worldweaver. She could remember the power of that orb of warmth and heat, imagine the rays soaking into her skin.

But from here, in the remote recesses of the Fifth Circle, that distant light was a mere flicker, low on the horizon, struggling vainly to penetrate the gulf of space, to cast some semblance of life-giving heat toward the two druids in their lonely place. The black massif rose to the high horizon, a wall across the very path they needed to follow. It stood as if a barrier at the edge of the cosmos, the perfect refuge for a god who sought the dead of other worlds and turned them into his own pawns.

Against that backdrop Miradel felt like less than a tiny speck, a mere mote of vitality in a panorama of death—or not death, so much, as a lack of life. There was no grass to be seen on this whole vast mountainside of stone, not a tree or bush sprouting from the lands spreading out behind and below them. Even the course of the mighty river, as it emerged from its gorge, looked more like a crisp line carved into the ground than any naturally eroded waterway. There were other canyons and chasms cutting through this vast mountainside, but wherever she saw them, they reminded her of vast graves, full of shadow, yawning, and silent. Finally, there was that sun, so very far away, so faint.

"It's like early dawn's light on an autumn day, back on Earth," Miradel mused, as she and Shandira paused to rest and eat a little of the trail bread, followed by a few sips of water. "Only the sun will never rise over us here."

"And perhaps we'll never be warm again," Shandira said. "At least, we won't if we don't keep moving."

"You're right," Miradel agreed, suppressing a shiver. Fortunately there was no wind, and their cloaks had dried since they had emerged from the misty gorge, yet the chill in the air remained a palpable if insidious enemy, constantly trying to penetrate through skin and flesh into the very substance of her bones. She pushed herself to her feet, noticing for the hundredth time how cruelly the straps of her heavy pack dug into her shoulders. She shifted the load around, but each bit of her upper back seemed to be bruised.

"I miss the river—at least it made some noise," Shandira said. She lifted her pack easily and slung it onto her shoulders, standing tall, moving with easy grace as she turned.

Miradel felt small and weak by comparison, desperately dependent upon her companion. She felt the same about the river, feeling the vast and lifeless silence of this world as an oppressive force. "I think your notion of Hell is beginning to seem apt," she admitted.

Shandira smiled wryly, then turned toward the ground rising before them and said, "Let's go."

As they started to walk, Miradel limped against the pain of a blister that was forming on her right foot. For a dozen steps she analyzed the pressure against her heel, trying with some success to shift the way she placed her foot. Satisfied, she noticed that they had climbed another steep section of trail while she worried about the sore on her foot. She chuckled aloud as she rationalized that at least one source of her pain—the blister—was bad enough to distract her from the nagging ache of her contusions.

"Do you see something funny up there?" Shandira asked.

"Just the opposite," Miradel admitted, turning her attention to the vast and precipitous citadel rising before them. It was as big as a whole range of mountains and climbed toward the twilit sky in a series of massive cliffs and crenellated towers. They could pick a path freely along the relatively open slope, but every route toward the Deathlord's citadel had one thing in common: it led steeply upward, an ascent greater than any mountain to be found upon Nayve.

Carefully they made their way around a shoulder of mountainside, a craggy knob of natural rock into which had been carved numerous platforms and ramparts. All of these seemed vacant now, at least to their visual inspection from below, but the elevation nevertheless presented a dour and forbidding aspect. Passing the foot of that height, they started moving upward again on an open slope that was crisscrossed by a wide road that cut back and forth through dozens of switchbacks.

"The armies marched down that road," Miradel explained, "After they appeared in the hall of Karlath-Fayd."

"So that is the way to his citadel?" asked Shandira.

Miradel nodded, her gaze rising toward the summit of the long slope. Abruptly she gasped and seized the African by her arm.

"What is it?"

"I see the gargoyle up there!"

"The statue you told me about—the winged guardian carved into the mountaintop?" The African woman looked upward and grimaced as she, too, spotted the stony image. She squinted, and they both examined the frightening visage, the monstrous shape perched on the edge of the upper ramparts of the mountain. They could see it well from where they stood. The gargoyle overlooked a pass that was also flanked by two castellated fortresses. That gap in the cliff seemed to be the only way through the palisade and into the citadel. The two humans were at the foot of a long, steep climb leading up toward that pass, while the gargoyle was two miles or more overhead.

"It's terribly realistic, as if a living being frozen in stone."

"I have studied it for many years in the Tapestry and never seen it move," Miradel declared. "But the Goddess Worldweaver told me that it is a living guardian—at least, that it will spring to life to defend the citadel against intrusion. She claims that, thousands of years ago—before the first ghost warriors came—the gargoyle flew above Loamar as a living monster, a sentinel patrolling the Fifth Circle. Only when the Deathlord started to bring his warriors here, some three or four thousand years ago, did it come to rest on that summit. It has been there since, but it may take flight again."

"Then I think we should do our best to make sure it doesn't see us."

"Yes, I agree. For the lower part of the climb I think we can stay out of sight by keeping off the road. It will be harder going on the mountainside, but if we stay just below those walls, I think we can zigzag our way close to the top without coming into view."

"Very well," Shandira agreed.

They made their way sideways across the slope until they came up against the wall of the roadway, rising some ten or twelve feet up to the paved surface. It served well to block the line of sight, so they continued upward, with the barrier at first rising to their left.

Now the real agony began, Miradel soon realized. The ascent out of the gorge had been child's play compared to the long, steep climb up this massive incline. The ground was rough with sharp-edged rocks and loose scree. Often they needed to use their hands to help keep their balance on the steeply pitched slope. Though the great roadway that ascended here took a sprawling approach through dozens of switchbacks, the druids followed a more direct route. They were able to use outcrops of rocks and sometimes the fortress walls themselves to keep out of view of the gargoyle.

Even though they stopped frequently to rest, Miradel had reached the point of utter exhaustion by the time they had climbed no more than a third of the way up the massive slope. Furthermore, the climb had grown more hazardous as, far away, the distant sun had started to recede upward, away from Nayve and even farther from the Fifth Circle of Loamar.

"We'll have to stop soon and get some sleep," she said, whispering in the midst of the eerily silent world. Again she felt the absence of wind, of birds and bugs and rodents that gave a background of vitality to Nayve and to Earth. "Can you spot a flat place where we might be able to stretch out?"

"Not too far away," Shandira said, pointing obliquely up the slope, toward the right. "The road curves back below a steep shoulder of the mountain. We can stop right there and be well out of sight of anything above."

They moved away from the road, following the rough ground to remain screened from the gargoyle. A large rock jutted from the slope, and they skirted its base, then crawled upward across a face of cracked stone. A few minutes later, the black woman paused at a steep crossing, a slide of small rocks and gravel no more than ten feet in length. Just beyond was a wide ledge, nestled hard against the wall that bordered the roadway running past two dozen feet overhead. The spot was sheltered from above by an overhang and protected by a steep slope that curled around to cover three sides.

"Looks like a perfect place to rest. Just be careful here," said Shandira, leaning against the rock, bracing her hands as she slid her booted feet across the loose, steep surface. She went another step, and a third, making it halfway across.

And then her traction gave way. With a gasp of surprise, the druid skidded downward, reaching for handholds but failing to find purchase. Miradel saw her slide twenty or thirty feet, balancing on her hip and left hand, then bounce sideways off an outcrop of rock. Shandira fell on her back, her head sharply striking the hard stone of the ground where she came to rest against a boulder, utterly still.

"Oh, by the goddess—no!" whispered Miradel, stunned and despairing. She froze for an instant, and then shucked out of her pack, dropping it, paying no attention as it tumbled away down the steep slope. Sitting, she slid toward her companion, using her hands to control her speed, ignoring the cuts and scrapes inflicted on her by the rough surface. She stopped by bracing her feet against the same jutting rock that had knocked Shandira to the side. Carefully, Miradel worked her way around the boulder, then slid the last few feet to her companion.

She found Shandira facedown on the steep slope, braced against another solid boulder, the tangle of black hair shiny with the thick sheen of fresh blood. Gingerly, Miradel probed through the wiry coils to touch the back of the injured woman's skull. She felt torn skin and sticky wetness but was relieved that the bone seemed to be intact.

Next she rolled her friend onto her back, using Shandira's pack to cushion her head. Miradel bowed for a moment of silent prayer, then reached forward to touch her hands to her companion's temples, to invoke the healing power of her goddess to knit the torn flesh and restore the lost blood.

"Goddess Worldweaver, I beseech you to grant thy tender touch, to repair this woman's hurts." She said the prayer humbly, with all of the faith that she had always felt, anticipating without doubt the imminent tingle of magic, the generous spirit of her goddess flowing through Miradel's flesh, in order to do good.

But this time there was no tingle, no healing, no magic. It was as if the Goddess Worldweaver was too far away to hear her plea.

Miradel felt a new stab of fear. Was the goddess in fact too far away, or was there a more dire explanation? Was the Worldweaver displeased by the impertinence of her druid, and in her displeasure did she choose to turn her back?

In any event, there was no help to be found there. She

remembered her pack now with renewed despair. Though she scanned the slope below, she could not spot it. She guessed that it had tumbled beyond the ground visible for a hundred yards below her. Further view was blocked by a clump of jagged boulders.

"Shandira? Can you hear me?" There was no response, not even a flicker of eyelids. "I have to get my pack, but I'll be right back," Miradel promised.

She turned to pick the best route down to the pack, then glanced at her companion once more. Shandira simply lay there, still except for the slow rhythm of her breathing. Against that faint backdrop, the vast silence of Loamar seemed to press in even harder, terrifying in its scope, smothering in its omnipotent extent.

ZYSTYL had heard the command of his distant master, the immortal will carried to him by virtue of the dakali, the stone that he wore under his tunic, against the skin of his chest over his heart. That was the talisman of the Deathlord, he knew, and it had provided the power that brought his army from the First Circle to the Fourth Circle. Once they were here, it had bestowed upon the formerly blind dwarves the limited ability to see. It was a mighty tool, and it had helped him to do great things.

When the directions had come to him ten days earlier, they had been in his mind as he awakened, and he had acted immediately. The tens of thousands of Delvers had been arrayed along the edge of Riven Deep in their vast camps—camps that had become virtual cities in the five decades since the army had been here. He ordered them all to deploy, formed in ranks, armed and armored for battle. Their golems stood with them, one metal giant for each dwarf regiment of approximately four thousand warriors.

They had taken these positions within a couple of hours of receiving the order, and for all the next ten days they had stayed here. Food and water had been circulated through the ranks, and eventually the Delvers had even slept while they stood in place. None, of course, had questioned the commands of their arcane lord—it was well known that to question Zystyl was to die—but surely they had wondered about the purpose of this apparently irrational deployment.

Actually, Zystyl himself had done his share of wondering. The harpies had been keeping him informed of developments along the coast. He knew that the Deathlord's invasion had come ashore, that the ghost warriors had seized the beach and won a great battle. Then they had advanced inland as far as the river that emptied into the gorge on the opposite rim, some twenty miles to Zystyl's right. Ahead of him were the Hyaccan elves, numbering several thousand riders. How often he had fantasized about striking them with his compact, powerful army. Their only hope would be to mount their ponies and flee, since they would never be able to stand up to his offensive.

For fifty years, of course, the yawning gulf of Riven Deep had prevented that fantasy from even approaching fruition. But now there was a sense, carried through his dakali and also growing within his own mind, that the gulf might, somehow, cease to be an impassable obstacle. So he had stood with his dwarves and waited.

As the first tremors rumbled through the rock, he heard the panicked cries, sensed the fear of his dwarves. The ground shifted and pitched underfoot. He felt the rumbling in his belly, a terrifying sensation of disturbance. But he clenched his jaw and planted his feet a little bit farther apart, determined not to flinch.

"The world falls away! We are doomed!" All around

him the troops were murmuring or shouting, but then they seemed to draw strength from their leader's example. As the arcane remained still and aloof, the cries of distress lessened, until the troops were standing firm as well.

Zystyl remained silent as he felt the ground, solid bedrock, heave with the convulsion of a major quake. Indeed, the effect was quite unsettling, but he was determined to display no fear. He had faith in his god . . . faith in his dakali. He would stand still and show naught but courage.

More convulsions rocked the ground, and a slab at the edge of the Deep broke free and tumbled away, carrying twoscore dwarves to their doom. More discouraging, one of the beautiful iron giants was caught at the brink; the golem turned awkwardly, trying to take a step onto solid ground, but it, too, vanished.

Yet the mass of ground, despite the crumbling base, did not seem inclined to fall. Great fissures ripped through the ground, scoring more or less between the gathered regiments, though these gaps, too, were imprecise, and hundreds more Delvers plunged, screaming, into these seemingly bottomless crevasses. He could see daylight through the nearest gap, knew for certain that the ground supporting this bedrock was gone. It was as though the stone under his feet was a platform floating freely in the air.

But still he felt no fear, did not imagine that they would fall. He grinned, then laughed aloud as he felt the slab of stone begin to rise. The effect was gradual—it was easier to see than to feel—but when they moved out from the edge, drifting over the yawning space of the chasm, he knew that his god's power had been made real and that his enemies were being delivered into his hands.

———————

"PLEASE, Shandira . . . wake up! Can you hear me?"

Miradel was close to utter despair. There was no healing magic in her touch, and nothing but cold fear in her heart. Her companion, this strong, proud woman who had come here at Miradel's own suggestion, had not regained consciousness since her hard fall nearly an hour before.

The best Miradel had been able to do was to roll her companion onto a reasonably flat patch of ground, no larger than a small bed, that happened to be right next to where she had landed. She had folded the extra cloak from the other druid's pack to serve as a pillow, replacing the bulky pack. Then she placed her cloak over the woolen garment Shandira was already wearing in the hopes of keeping the unconscious woman warm.

But there was no wood with which to build a fire, even if she would have dared to attract such attention; no way to give her hot broth or warm bread, anything but the dried trail rations they had brought with them. She had trickled a little water through Shandira's lips, but the woman had not swallowed. The only encouraging sign, and it was a small one, was that she continued to draw long, deep breaths.

Finally Miradel returned her attention to her own pack, which had tumbled quite a ways down the slope when she had dropped it in the moments after Shandira's fall. Her muscles rebelled at the thought of a long descent and a climb repeated over the steep incline, but there were too many valuables, objects that might mean the difference between life and death, in the heavy sack. So, after one last check of the black woman's pulse and respiration, the elder druid started down the slope she had so laboriously climbed an hour earlier.

The descent, naturally, was a lot easier than the climb, and within ten minutes she had dropped so far that she couldn't even see the place where she had left Shandira.

Her legs were still cramping and sore, and she limped
with each jolting step. Still, she tried to ignore her dis-
comfort and despair, scanning the slope below her, looking for some indication of where her pack had ended up.

She spotted it shortly, saw that it had tumbled onto a
flat shoulder of the mountainside, halting its tumble a foot
short of the precipitous drop on the other side of the small,
flat space. Casting aside her caution, she hastened downward, sending a cascade of loose pebbles skidding into the
abyss. When she reached the backpack, she quickly saw
that it had remained closed and that, in fact, if it had rolled
a little farther it would have plummeted another five hundred feet.

Her first instinct was to thank the goddess for this
small bit of good fortune, but when she lowered her head
to murmur the small prayer, she found that the words
stuck in her throat. Instead, she lifted the heavy satchel,
balancing it on her hip as she pushed her arms through the
straps.

It felt like the heaviest thing she had ever carried, and
once again her despair seemed to double her burden. It
would have been easy to simply collapse, to cry to the
point of exhaustion, then to lie here until she died. Only
the memory of Shandira and the guilty knowledge that it
was Miradel who had brought her here forced her to turn
her attention upward again.

She looked at the sweeping slope, remembered the
pain of her initial ascent, and knew it would be doubled in
this next stage of her journey. Her vision extended beyond
the walled roadway that had been their goal, all the way to
the top of the vast citadel, where the gargoyle was now
visible on its lofty perch.

The sight of that beast sent a stab of fear through her,
for the stony guardian had changed. It remained in the
same place, the same pose as it had been before, but now

its eyes were opened, red and glowing like fire, and they seemed to be fixed intently upon the lone druid so far below.

"WAKE UP!" shrieked Roodcleaver, delivering a sharp kick to Awfulbark's belly.

"What you want?" growled the king of the forest trolls, instinctively squirming away to put the trunk of the oak tree between himself and his wife's next attack.

"The world!" she cried, her stark terror penetrating the fog of Awfulbark's ever-slow awakening.

"What about the world?" he grumbled, covering his own alarm with a veneer of irritation.

"It's breaking!" Roodcleaver declared. "Breaking right around us! Here, under my feet, under you fat butt and thick head! It's breaking!"

For the first time, the troll king realized that he was clutching the trunk of the oak tree simply to keep his balance. The ground heaved and pitched underfoot. Trees throughout the grove of oaks, which was just back from the Swansleep River, were whipping back and forth. Several venerable wooden giants cracked apart with lumber-ripping shrieks, massive trunks falling among trolls who were waking up to a world of chaos and panic.

"Go tell Natac!" Awfulbark blurted the first thought that came into his mind. Surely the general would know what to do!

Roodcleaver threw a chunk of wood at him, a near miss that bounced from the trunk a few inches from the king's eye. "You think he knows, maybe?" she screamed. "Do something! Save trolls! Save me!"

"Okay," Awfulbark agreed, groping for an idea, a plan. He seized upon the first thing that came to mind. "Everybody run!" he roared. "Get away from here!"

The river, with the numberless horde of the ghost warriors on the far side, formed a barrier in the direction of metal, but every other route seemed better to the terror-stricken trolls than staying where they were. Most of them instinctively started away from the river, from the enemy, from the war. Lurching and stumbling, Awfulbark let go of the tree, took Roodcleaver's hand, and tugged her along with the fleeing horde of trolls.

A huge tree smashed down nearby, trapping a young troll beneath a splintered limb. The king reached down, pulled the howling victim free, and left him on the ground. With luck, the wretch's shattered legs would knit before another oak came down on top of him. Awfulbark and his wife held each other up as the jolting ground pushed them this way and that. He was aware of other trolls all around—and in fact they frequently careened into him. But they were all moving in the same direction, and though many fell and others were trampled, the army of the forest trolls inevitably made a stumbling exodus from the position they had held for four days.

13

Fire in the Ghetto

Stinking smoke runs in your eyes
Babbled cursing outward flies
Deepest quicksand underfoot
Where the dead must needs take root

Traditional Goblin Chant

Borand came around the base of the hill with Aurand, both dwarves straining and sweating as they carried the large bundles formed by their saddles and gear. The brothers hauled the loads to the lakeshore, where Darann and Konnar had just finished pulling the boat onto a flat section of stony beach.

"What about the ferr'ells?" she asked.

"We turned them loose," Borand explained. "We'll whistle for them if we come back here; with any luck, they'll be within hearing range."

"Good. But we won't have room in the boat for the saddles," the dwarfmaid declared. "Can you find a place to hide them here?"

"Sure, and we probably don't need all of this food we have left. Dried trail bread and saltshrooms mostly. We can do better than that in the city, I'm thinkin'."

"Well, let's take what we can," Darann said. She looked across the water at the brightly lit sprawl that was Axial. The six great towers, outlined in coolfyre, rose to the very summit of the world, proud symbols of Seer might. One-quarter of the city, low against the water and to the far right from where they stood, was conspicuously dark. That was the goblin ghetto, she knew. "If we have extra food, I know there's one place in the city where it will be appreciated."

"Right, of course," Borand agreed.

She took her place in the stern, while the other three stowed their bundles in the center of the boat. The three males slid the boat into the shallows, hopping in one by one as the hull began to float. They took seats on the low benches. The brothers Houseguard each carried his weapon at the ready, while Konnor faced backward to man the oars. Darann held the tiller and tried to muster some sense of hopefulness.

In fact, she felt much better now that she had trusted companions. She allowed herself one moment of wistfulness—if Karkald was here, she would not have had even an iota of doubt—but then turned to the task before them.

"We can try to enter the city near the low quarter," she said. "I wouldn't be surprised if Nayfal is having our house watched. He knows I got away and that you will be returning here eventually. And once we get close to shore, we can decide if we want to come ashore in the ghetto or land in the Fishers' Quarter and come through the gates on foot. Then we have to find Hiyram and hope he can put us in touch with the pailslopper who has the proof about Lord Nayfal."

"Right. And in the meantime, I think we should not let anyone else know we're here," Aurand agreed.

For an hour Konnor rowed them in silence. Darann studied the lights of the city, the coolfyre beacons blazing from the six towers, the ring of watch stations glittering close to the shore around Axial's periphery. She remembered her first watch station, Karkald's post of some four centuries earlier. It lay far from the city, so far across the water that Axial had been merely a bright spot on the horizon. The station had been a lonely place but very peaceful as well, though at the time she thought she hated it. Now, she would have given anything to be stranded alone somewhere with Karkald again.

Those outer stations were abandoned now, cold and dark in the distant reaches of the Darksea. The dwarves were looking inward these days, and she grimaced at the awareness of the cowardice that seemed to have taken over her nation, her people. She made a silent vow, in her father's memory, to try and redeem that failing.

She wondered, then, about how she would find Hiyram. She had never approached the ghetto by water, though it seemed to her that this might be a safer route than trying to pass the guards posted at every gate into the rank goblin quarter. Looking at the beacons of the watchtowers, she saw the cones of white light play across the water, trying to pick a route that would take her up to the ghetto wharf without being detected.

As they made their way across the sea, the near shore vanished into the vast darkness of the First Circle, while the far shore gradually took on more detail, towers and streets and individual buildings outlined in eternal coolfyre. After another hour, Aurand took over the oars from Konnor, who moved to the seat just forward of Darann, as she steered them closer to the low, dark part of the city—the place the Seers had walled off to create the ghetto. It was eerily dark in there, though the wall itself and the offshore waters were constantly swept by those shifting beacons.

"Do you know where Hiyram lives?" asked the dwarven explorer, stretching his arms, rolling his shoulders to loosen the kinks brought on by his long stretch of rowing. She noticed for the first time that he was remarkably handsome, his eyes bright and cheery, his black beard neat and silky, even after several cycles in the wilderness. He had an easy smile, and she was glad that he was here.

"No, I don't. But everyone in there seems to know him. I've gone into the place a number of times, taking them the few necessities I can gather, and as soon as I pass the gates, someone always seems to send for him. I think that will happen again, that he will find *me* as soon as we get there."

Konnor was looking at her with a strangely emotional expression, his eyes wide and full of wonder. "You go in there by yourself? I mean, I had heard that you did, of course . . . but it seems . . . it seems so brave!"

"Brave?" She laughed, embarrassed. "Not compared to climbing around the edges of the world, going into Nightrock itself! No, I just do what small part I can to try to be useful, perhaps to resist the malady that seems to be dragging our whole people down."

"Well, I think it's really admirable. You know, you are quite a woman—I don't think I've ever met anyone quite like you."

She was suddenly uncomfortable with his words, his direct stare—even if it was affectionate and admiring. It had been long since a male had talked to her like this, and she couldn't help a sense of guilt, a feeling that to accept his affection would somehow be unfaithful to her long-dead husband.

"You miss him still," he said gently. "Don't you?"

She chuckled wryly, surprised—and not displeased—that he had perceived her care so readily. "I know that I will, always," she replied, remembering. Karkald could be gruff and impetuous, and his manners were poor at best.

But he was kind, and he had loved her very much. Darann felt a lump in her throat as she remembered his hands, so rough and callused, yet so perfectly gentle when they touched her.

Those thoughts, all of them, were instantly banished when she heard a stutter of sound borne through the still air: like distant screams. There was an unmistakeable crash, as of a steel blade coming into contact with something hard. The noise echoed, distant but sharp, lingering in her ears even after the sound itself had faded away. It was repeated, and again, quickly rising to a remote but ringing cacophony.

"What's that?" Darann asked in sudden fear.

They could all hear the sounds, which were too faint to fully discern. They could have been caused by either celebration or fear. Intuitively, she suspected a sinister explanation. She heard something else gradually emerging from the stillness: a rumbling beat coming from the city of Axial, from the lower flats along the null shore of the lake . . . from the goblin ghetto.

That was the measured cadence of armored troops on the march. Aurand rowed harder, pushing the boat through the water with palpable surges, leaving a visible wake behind them. Darann felt the lunge with each stroke, silently willing her brother to even greater speed.

"What do you think is happening?" Konnor asked as the boat cut swiftly through the eternally placid waters of the sea.

"It can only mean one thing," Darann said grimly. "Nayfal has given orders to the city guard, and they're moving against the goblins."

"Surely it hasn't come to that!" Borand protested.

"He's convinced lots of people, maybe even the king himself, that the goblins will rise up and attack as soon as the Delvers move against us," she replied. "I'm guessing that someone important—maybe just Nayfal, but who knows?—has decided to make a preemptive attack."

"But they'll be butchered!" Aurand protested. "The goblins won't have a chance!"

"All the more reason we need to get to our pailslopper and persuade her to tell the king what she knows," Darann said. She looked pointedly at her younger brother, who was straining at the oars. "Can't you row any faster?"

NAYFAL mounted his ferr'ell after the liveryman had saddled the beast and had carefully affixed the steel muzzle that prevented the partially savage creature from snapping back at its rider. The lord had learned through painful experience that no ferr'ell was to be trusted. Still, he was the only dwarven noble who had ever learned to ride one of the savage creatures, and at a time like this he was determined that his men would see him in the saddle, where he belonged.

He clutched the reins and spurred the animal forward, lurching in the saddle and wishing for at least the thousandth time that a ferr'ell had a more regular gait. Instead, the beast caused him to bob back and forth on the undulating back. Some of the most veteran Rockriders eventually learned to mimic this motion, growing naturally comfortable in the saddle, but such proficiency required many long miles of riding. As a powerful lord, he didn't have time for such diversions. Besides, he didn't trust the 'riders, most of whom had been recruited and trained by Karkald. Fortunately, the light cavalry and their savage steeds had become virtually obsolete in the days of goblin control.

Still, he relished the awe in the faces of Axial's dwarves as he trotted swiftly through the city streets. Youngsters gawked on the sidewalks, while women scurried out of his way and men stared admiringly at the dashing figure. The sleek animal held its head high, ears pricked upward and whiskers twitching, suitably impressive as it loped down the city street. Nayfal noted with pleasure that he still drew attention wherever he went.

He made his way down the Avenue of Metal, the wide boulevard leading toward the harbor. The ghetto lay before him to the right, and as he approached he was pleased to hear the clash of arms and the cries of frightened goblins rising from beyond the high wall. There was a company of city guardsmen standing at ease just outside the first gate, and these dwarves gathered around as he approached.

One brave sergeant even took the reins to keep the ferr'ell from bobbing restively. The toothy jaws snapped, and the dwarf clapped it across the snout with his gauntleted fist. Growling, the steed stood still.

"Lord Nayfal! The raid is progressing well," reported the leader, a gray-bearded veteran with a silver-lined helmet. "The goblins are running like sheep. We've already cleared out the blocks against the Metal Wall."

"Good. I expected nothing less, of course. But good."

"Only thing is, the gobs are getting kind of thick in the middle plazas now. We're getting 'em packed in tight, but we was wondering . . . what to do with 'em now."

"There's no choice. You'll have to kill them, especially the males—though if a wench raises a stick to you, well, cut her down as well."

The captain's eyes widened momentarily, but then he recovered and nodded tentatively. "You're wanting them butchered, then . . . *all* the males?" He shifted his balance from one foot to the other, an act of nervousness that annoyed the lord. "Can I be having that order in writing then, my lord?" the warrior had the temerity to ask.

"You have witnesses; the order comes from the king

himself," snapped Nayfal. "And he, as well as I, expect it to be carried out."

"Er, of course, my lord. Just that, well, that's a lot of killing . . . a lot of blood will run."

"Am I to assume that you don't have the stomach for this work, Captain? Because I assure you, I know plenty of officers who are more than willing to proceed."

"Please, lord, I meant no disrespect! I've always been one who follows his orders, to the letter; dots the i's and crosses the t's, I do. Just wanted clarification, which yer lordship was gracious enough to supply."

"Then get going!" demanded Nayfal. "There's a lot of work to do in there!"

He allowed himself a tight smile of satisfaction as the company of dwarves, swords drawn, tromped through the gate and started looking for goblins. The smile remained as he spurred the ferr'ell along, ready to pass the orders along to the armored companies waiting outside of each of the ghetto's gates.

"THIS one has a knife!" came the cry of the dwarven watch sergeant, ringing through the alley with a sound that, to Hiyram, sounded like a full bray of alarm. The goblin pulled back his weapon in horror, all but gagging as he saw the red smear on the keen blade. He wanted to stop, to explain that he was only defending himself, but that impulse was overwhelmed by the pressing urgency to escape, to survive.

Desperately Hiyram squirmed in the grip of the burly guard. Other dwarves closed in, for now they had him surrounded. The goblin hoped that Spadrool had made his escape and had led the females and youngsters to some semblance of safety. Perhaps the drainage tunnels, after all, might provide escape. At the same time he despaired:

safety? Where was that? What could they possibly do against these numbers, this brutal and organized intent?

For himself, he would fight. He had killed before, but never had he slain a Seer dwarf, and never had the sheen of blood on his blade looked so gruesome or caused him such anguish as it did now. Now the knowledge was heartbreaking, for he had killed one of Karkald's people, the dwarves who had been his friends for hundreds of years.

"Forgive me, Lady," he whispered again, closing his eyes against the force of his guilt.

But the guards were closing in, a ring tightening around him, menacing and cursing, weapons reaching out to do him harm. He had no choice: he stabbed again, slashing at the arm of the guard holding him. The keen steel sliced through gauntlet, skin, and tendon, drawing a scream of pain from the stricken dwarf.

"The bastard cut me! Kill him!"

In the next instant Hiyram felt the grip relax, and the goblin spun free. More dwarves lunged, but he threw himself flat on the ground, scuttling with two quick pounces between sturdy legs and iron-shod boots—though one kick thumped painfully into his knee.

But he was through the ring of guards! Bouncing to his feet, he sprinted away, ignoring the pain that jabbed through his thigh with each step on the bruised knee. He ran frantically but not blindly, heading down the twisting alley, his wide eyes perceiving the barrels stacked near the wall, the broken crate with the pieces scattered in his path. With a single leap he flew over the obstacle, his feet slapping against wet stone as he landed.

He heard the crashing of armor and tin as the pursuing dwarves tripped on the crumbled box. In the next instant he was around a corner—a dead end in the alley! But there was hope in that wall of loose masonry, and a second later he was leaping up the rickety framework on the side of an ancient building. His hand slipped on a slick stone, but he caught himself with two fingertips, holding himself long enough that his feet could find purchase and kick his body upward. In another second he was sprawled on the roof, lying flat, listening.

The first thing he heard was the pounding of his own heart. Quickly he discerned other sounds: the noises of fear and flight that were spreading through the terrorized goblin community, and the heavy march of the dwarven columns. They must have come through the wall in at least six or eight places, he estimated. How in the world could the goblins defend themselves when they had barely that many true weapons among them? Not to mention that malnutrition had been weakening his people for decades, leaving many of them barely strong enough to stand, much less fight! Why had the dwarves come now? What would his people do besides despair and then die?

"What would Karkald do?" the goblin muttered to himself soundlessly. He had campaigned with that venerable dwarf for centuries, and Karkald had always seemed to have—or be able to make—a plan.

The answer to his question came to Hiyram with surprising clarity. First Karkald would get organized, would try to learn what kind of assets he had, and what kind of challenges he faced. Of course!

Immediately the goblin felt better. He rose to a crouch and crept to the edge of the roof, looking down to where a dozen dwarves were poking through the rubble in the alley, still searching for the goblin fugitive. They turned over the barrels, kicking and cursing as they searched. Several chopped their blades downward, shattered the containers with a force that would certainly have killed him if Hiyram had been hiding within.

Now the goblin was not so much afraid as angry. He looked around, found a wall of loose masonry at the crest of the building, and took several heavy stones in his hands. Then he went back to the edge over the alley, took careful aim, and threw the first stone. In quick succession he tossed another and snatched up the rest, pitching five heavy missiles down onto the searching dwarves.

"Ouch! Hey, he's up there! Blind-blast it!" came the shouts as the rough-edged stones plunged downward. Hiyram wasn't worried about immediate pursuit—the dwarves would never make it up the wall he had climbed—and he would be long gone by the time they found another way onto the rooftop.

Organize, learn, prepare . . . all good plans, as though Karkald himself was here, making suggestions. They seemed to give Hiyram wings as he leapt across the rooftops, making his way toward the heart of the ghetto.

THE spotlights played across the water as the Seer dwarves in the watchtowers wielded their cooltyre beacons with unusual diligence. From the low, metal-hulled boat those washes of light seemed like sinister searchers, sweeping and probing across the surface of the Darksea. When another boat came into the glare of one beam it remained fixed on the watercraft for some time, and Darann could imagine the guards taking careful inventory of whoever was aboard that vessel.

The goblin ghetto opened only onto a small section of Axial's waterfront, a place crowded with piers and docks and fisheries and even a long-abandoned boatyard. The docks were strangely naked, Darann was not surprised to see, for she recalled that one of the first of King Lightbringer's goblin-control edicts was to ban them from owning boats. Not that goblins had ever been much for seafaring, but now they had no means of getting in and out of the ghetto by water. It seemed, judging from the vigorous sweeps of the beacons, that the dwarves intended to keep it that way. There seemed to be no gap, no way to slip between the diligent searchlights.

"We'll never get to the ghetto docks without being spotted. We'll have to land in the city and make our way there over land," Borand whispered from the bow, vocalizing the same conclusion Darann had reached on her own.

"Let's go to the ferry harbor," she suggested, veering the tiller to turn them in the direction of wood. "There's lots of activity there, and we'll be able to slip into the docks without attracting attention. And it's only a half mile down the waterfront from the ghetto wall."

"Good idea," Borand agreed.

For a while there was just the steady creaking of the oars and the solid rhythm of Aurand's deep, strong breathing as he pushed the boat along. The light grew stronger, not just the wash of the great beacon but the general spillage from a thousand household lamps, a hundred globular streetlights, and the torches that marked each of the hundred or so boats currently making their way along the waterfront. Darann could see their reflection in the water, knew that they would soon be spotted by dwarves in other boats, and on shore.

"Best we light our own wick," she said, nodding to the lamp dangling from a hook over the prow. "Nothing's as likely to arouse suspicion as the sight of us trying to sneak through the shadows."

"Another good idea," Borand agreed. "I'll get it." He pulled a bundle of matches from his shirt, torched one, and lit the lamp to bring their own little circle of light onto the dark coastal waters. Datann felt terribly exposed, wanted to hunker down below the gunwales. It took all of her willpower to avoid acting on her fear, but she managed to sit tall, just as if she absolutely belonged here.

Perhaps, she told herself, trying to inject a burst of confidence . . . perhaps she *did* belong here!

Soon they were approaching the vast, open harbor where the city's numerous ferries docked. Some of these were small boats, no different from the one Darann had commandeered, but a few were larger, raftlike craft that plied regular routes to some of the city's near environs. Each of these had many lamps, and when one glided past within two hundred yards, they could hear raucous laughter, the clink of toasting glasses as a large group of dwarves embarked on some jovial excursion.

Darann steered away from these big boats, making for a quiet section of the harbor. She had seen ports on Nayve, where breakwaters were regularly placed to block waves and, incidentally, channel boat traffic. She was grateful that no such barriers were necessary on the stormless Darksea. The entire anchorage faced open water. Several small boats glided nearby, but neither the rowers nor their passengers paid any attention to the four dwarves approaching the crowded waterfront. She steered them away from the traffic, and as they drew near to the shore they slipped between a couple of tall, empty docks. Feeling a little better now that they were concealed among the pilings, she had her brother paddle them in as close to shore as possible.

"Lash to the base of that ladder, there," she suggested, and soon the boat was made fast. Borand went up the ladder first, doing his best to look casual, though he checked to make sure his sword swung freely from his belt. Aurand went next. When Darann waited for Konnor, he gestured for her to precede him. In another minute all four of them had climbed to the dock and were ambling down the stone pier toward the waterfront.

They reached shore in front of a quiet inn, in the midst of a section of small warehouses. The ghetto lay to their right and, without speaking, they turned of one mind toward that direction. A few dwarves emerged from the inn, cast them uninterested glances, and turned to walk the other way.

They soon found themselves alone on a dark stretch of the wharf. The waters glimmered in the dark off to their right, and the buildings to their left—stone structures of one or two stories—were silent, projecting an air of dilapidation and abandonment.

"Business must be bad this close to the ghetto," remarked Borand. "I can remember when that place there was a dance hall as lively as any in the habor quarter—and you could buy and sell gold in the shop next door, trade it for anything in the whole First Circle and beyond."

"Not surprising they've all closed down now. Would you want to do business in the shadow of that?" asked Darann, nodding toward the dark wall that stood before them. It extended to the edge of the water, where it terminated in a watchtower capped by a platform and a swiveling beacon. They could see the silhouettes of three dwarves atop the tower, all facing the other direction; it seemed the trio were occupied with their bright light, casting a coolfyre beam back and forth through the ghetto and the water just offshore.

The foursome took shelter in a narrow alcove, the doorway to the last building in front of the wall, in order to discuss their options. "Sounds like the trouble is on the other side of the ghetto, at the Metal Gate," Darann said. "For now, anyway."

"Yep, seems pretty quiet over here," Aurand agreed. He looked at Darann. "You've been to visit the goblins before. How do you get in?"

"I just have to talk my way through one of the guard posts. They have 'em set up at every gate," she replied.

"But I don't think they'll be too likely to let anyone in now, not when there's some kind of raid going on."

"Well, let's have a look at the wall then," Aurand suggested. Moving to the end of the alcove, he leaned out to examine the barrier.

Darann heard something and pulled his collar, yanking her younger brother back in the split second before a troop of guards came into sight, emerging from a side street a stone's throw away. The soldiers turned toward them, marching along the waterfront.

The alcove was deep, and the four dwarves huddled soundlessly as the company—at least a hundred strong and fully girded for battle—hastened past at a double-time march.

"Heading for the ghetto," Konnor remarked.

"Looks like the Wood Gate will be the next to get it," Darann agreed. "I have the feeling we don't have much time."

14

Embattled Nayve

'e 'eld 'is 'ead
as 'e saw th' dead,
and 'e laid 'is blade
on the plain;

till 'e raised it again,
and 'e scoured the flame
and 'e led all o' trolldom
to fame!

From the *Saga of Awfulbark*
by Roodcleaver Kingwife

A volley of arrows arced through the sky, falling among the black-shirted Delvers as the dwarves sorted out their ranks. Again and again the Hyaccan elves launched their feathered, steel-tipped missiles, and many punctured enemy armor and flesh. But the steady barrage seemed to have no effect on the horde of attackers, as the dwarves formed their lines, lifted their shields, and started to advance.

"Mount up and fall back!" Janitha cried, furious at the necessity of retreat. For five decades her company had stood here, and she had allowed herself to believe that Riven Deep was a barrier that would stand forever. Now, in an explosion of dark magic, the Delvers had crossed that vast gulf in the space of a single hour.

The great slabs of stone had each borne a thousand or more Delvers. The air rafts, as she thought of them, had drifted across the chasm as gently as any lighter-than-air balloon. They had rumbled to the ground on the near rim, their edges cracking into rubble. The elves had ridden forward bravely, shooting hundreds of arrows, but the slabs were close together, and the attackers easily scrambled down these slopes of broken rock. Those who fell with broken legs or wrenched knees were abandoned as quickly as if they had been wounded on the battlefield, as the Delvers had quickly massed into their great, blocky battle formation. With shields raised over their heads to protect against the barrage of arrows, they had started forward at a fast march, forcing the mounted elves to withdraw.

That might have been the best—the only—time to have defeated the attack, Janitha quickly realized, but she lacked the warriors to make anything more than this token stand at resistence. Her elves were skilled riders and deadly archers, but they were outnumbered forty or fifty to one by the Delvers. The best they could do is shoot as many of them down as possible, then mount up and slowly withdraw.

Janitha gathered a hundred or so riders, led them in a sudden rush that broke through a Delver line. Slinging their bows for the moment, these elves chopped with swords, hacking back and forth as they left the rank of dark-armored dwarves scattered and bleeding. They gathered on the far side, and the khandaughter looked around, seeking another likely target.

Instead, a tall, faceless giant strode toward them—one

of the iron golems created in the Delver workshops of the First Circle. The monster moved quickly, but the mounted elves scattered, nimble ponies darting this way and that, eluding the giant's crushing blows. But that was no path to victory, Janitha knew. For how long could they run, if they didn't have any means of slowing the enemy's attack?

Yet for now, there was no other option.

"Rally at the Skull-Face Hill!" she cried, naming a landmark two miles back from the rim of the canyon. "Ride to the top where we can get a look at these bastards!"

The ponies and their elven riders streamed across the plateau, leaving the rim of Riven Deep behind. They raised a cloud of dust, but Janitha knew that they would need to send a better warning than that. Thankfully, she spotted a faerie buzzing along with the riders and waved him over with a gesture.

He flew beside her racing mount, gliding easily as her loyal stallion pounded at full speed. "Can you take a message to Natac?" she asked, shouting to be heard over the din of galloping ponies.

"Yes," he said. "I can tell him about—" He gestured vaguely in the direction the dwarves.

"Tell him we won't be able to stop them, even hold them up very much. If they start toward the Swansleep, he'll have to pull his army off the river, or he'll be taken by surprise."

"I will tell him," said the faerie with a bright salute. "Good luck to you, Lady Khandaughter!" he offered, then turned and flew away so fast that he seemed simply to disappear.

"Luck . . . that's the least of what we need," she muttered, casting a glance behind where the dwarves and iron golems were still forming ranks, taking time before they commenced the pursuit.

"We've got to have a miracle," Janitha concluded, with a grim and hopeless shake of her head.

For five days the druids maintained their vigil at the Swansleep River, backed up by the legions of elves from Argentian and Barantha, as well as by the trolls of King Awfulbark's tribe. There were a few gnomes there, too, by now, survivors of the disaster at the shore who had made their way inland. These Natac had armed with crossbows and held back from the river as a thus-far-unneeded reserve.

Countless times during that interval, during the days and during the nights, in misty darkness and searing sun, the ghost warriors had tried to force a crossing of the small stream. Each time the winds howled forth and the waters surged into the attackers' faces. Waves had overwhelmed them, and Nayvian weapons had cut them down, a crop of souls harvested in every onslaught.

Natac had not even tried to estimate the number of the enemy who had perished in these attacks, for the toll was really beyond comprehension. During the hour or two after each attack, the river channel would be choked with slowly decaying corpses, until the force of the current bore them on, pushed them along until they reached the fall plunging into Riven Deep. Not long after this natural cleansing, the enemy horde would come forward again, make another frenzied attempt to cross, and countless more of them would perish.

Despite the success of the defense, Natac had a number of worries. The defenders were growing fatigued, especially the druids, who were sleeping at their battle stations and inevitably roused several times a night to wage another furious fight. The elves and trolls were faring better, for the fury of the druid storm was such that they did not need all of their numbers to hold the line. As a result, they had taken to standing half of each force down for twelve-hour shifts.

But how long could this stalemate last?

Once each day Natac mounted Regillix Avatar and took to the air, scouting back and forth over the horde. He flew all the way to the canyon, watching with awe as the placid river abruptly plunged from the lip of the visible world, vanishing into the fog-shrouded depths of the canyon. The defenders seemed like a pathetically thin line on the center side of the river, while the horde of the Deathlord was a blanket of darkness across the water, spreading over the ground on the far side for as far as he could see. Every tree in the path of the advance had been hacked down, many of them burned while others were apparently just removed and cast aside. Each sward of green had been trampled into mud, with orchards ruined, sluice gates smashed, and terraces washed away.

The vast sweep of the army extended away from the canyon for a distance of more than twenty-five miles, as far as the Whitemarsh. There the Swansleep rose in a swamp of immense proportions, such that even the undead warriors of Karlath-Fayd could not pass. So it came down to this stretch of ground and this thin and desperate defense.

Throughout this time Natac was obsessed with worry about Miradel. He could spare no attention from his work with the army, yet he found himself fretting about her as he rode through the sky, or thinking of her during the last moments before he fell asleep and the first after he awakened. Where had she gone? Why? Was she hurt or—the unthinkable—had she perished? It was an agony of ignorance, and it allowed him not a moment's peace.

On the sixth day of the stand, he inspected the enemy front and saw no signs of any imminent change in tactics. The ghost warriors were still ranked across the river, Roman legionnaires together in their regiments here, the dead of the American Civil War over there. Some of the largest legions were the Tommies and Germans who had been harvested from the fields of France; they, too, waited patiently in formation, far enough back from the riverbank that the general would have plenty of warning of any impending attack.

Even so, he couldn't suppress his sense of nervousness. He talked to Gallupper and was assured that the batteries were all in place. Additional wagons of ammunition had arrived from the factories in the Ringhills, courtesy of the gnome King Fedlater of Dernwood Downs, so the centaurs were confident and ready. The Baranthian elves, too, were well rested and certain that, with the help of the druid windcasters, they could defend against anything the ghost warriors could send.

Next Natac sought out some of the druids, speaking to Cillia and Juliay. Both women were wan, even haggard. Cillia had begun to show streaks of gray in her long, ebony locks, and Juhiay had dark circles under her eyes.

"Maybe we should try resting some of the druids, like we are with the elves and trolls," the general suggested. "Do you think you could raise much of a storm with half your number?"

"I wouldn't like to try," Cilhia said with a firm shake of her head. "I think we have the upper hand, but it takes everything we can throw at them from all hundred—that is, ninety-eight—of us." She looked at him pointedly as she concluded.

"Has there been word of Miradel?" he asked quickly. "Do you know where they are?"

"Not exactly," replied the matriarch. "More, we have some evidence of where she is *not*."

"What do you mean? Tell me!"

"She is not in Circle at Center, nor is Shandira. But they did not come here. The sage-enchantress who was casting the spell didn't complete the last casting at her focal pool; she left, exhausted, and gave her position to another. But she didn't notice who replaced her."

"Could her spell have been sabotaged?" Natac asked in sudden panic.

"Unlikely. They would have had to talk to the sage-enchantress before the spell was cast, to confirm the details. I doubt they would have gone if they hadn't trusted the person doing the casting."

"The sage-enchantress . . . yes . . . but would it have to be an enchantress who cast the spell?"

"Well, yes," the druid answered. "At least, that's most likely. I suppose some of the elder sage-ambassadors might be able to muster the magic . . . at least, it's not inconceivable."

"It was Belynda Wysterian!" Natac said, anger and relief mingling in the realization. "She's been Miradel's friend for a thousand years or more. Perhaps they hatched some plan—but what?"

"That is impossible to tell, though perhaps Belynda could tell you," Cillia replied. "Or tell someone, since you are needed here, it seems to me."

"Yes . . . someone." Natac started thinking: could he entrust Horas of Gallowglen with such a mission? Perhaps—but first, there was the rest of his inspection to conduct. He thanked the druids for their information and continued along the riverbank until he found Tamarwind Trak at the command post of the Argentian elves.

"We're still driving them back every time they try to cross," the elf reported. "The wind and waves are getting most of them, and we pick off the stragglers before they can even crawl up the bank."

"Good. For the time being, we seem to be doing okay."

As if to mock his words, he heard a distant, deeply menacing rumble. The trembling of the ground underfoot was unmistakable: a quake. Though he had experienced plenty of them during his first life in Mexico, he knew they were extremely rare in Nayve and very upsetting to the residents of this once rock-solid world.

Tamarwind's face had gone pale, and his eyes were wide as he stared around wildly. "What's happening?" he asked. "The ground is moving!"

"It's a quake," Natac said. "Just ride it out—it won't last long."

Despite his confident words, the general was frightened by the intensity of the temblor. The ground heaved upward, and he staggered, dropping to his hands and knees to keep his balance. All around, Tam's elves were doing the same thing, many of them crying or shouting in fear.

Farther away Natac could see the oaks where Awfulbark had made his camp. Some of the largest trees were whipping back and forth, and several of them cracked and toppled before his eyes. Next the general looked across the stream, standing up and balancing on the lurching surface in order to get a look at the enemy troops. It was at least slightly reassuring to see that the formerly neat ranks were now disordered and confused as even the ghost warriors found it impossible to stand on the pulsing, rolling turf.

In another instant Natac went down, pitched by a casual shrug of the quake, and for several more minutes he concentrated on riding it out, trying not to get hurt or to tumble into anyone else. At last, after what seemed like a very long time, the rumbling faded away, and the ground settled back to a solid semblance of normalcy. The general pushed himself to his feet, staggering as if drunk from the memory of the shaking. All around him elves were sitting on the ground, stunned and frightened. One by one they tried to stand, weaving and bracing themselves on each other, looking around in awe.

Natac's next thought was of the trolls. He knew that, despite their size and toughness, they were easily spooked. He found a faerie settling down toward the ground—having taken the sensible precaution of hovering overhead during the quake—and quickly sent him to check on Awfulbark.

A few minutes later the faerie came back, reporting that the trolls had broken away from the riverbank and seemed to be streaming toward the plains beyond the Swansleep valley.

"Were the ghost warriors advancing yet?" asked the general.

"No." The faerie shook his head with certainty. "They still seem to be getting their bearings."

"Good, thanks. Tamarwind!" called Natac. The elf was there in an instant. "Can you send some of your warriors to cover the troll position? They got spooked by the quake. I'm going to get Regillix and go after them, hope-fully get them back on line."

"Sure," Tam said. "I have a thousand warriors just marching back from the bivuouac. I'll send them up the river right away."

Natac was encouraged by that prospect and guessed that the elves would be in position in time to prevent a sudden enemy move. His optimism was dashed almost immediately, as Karkald tromped up to him. "What is it?" asked Natac, alarmed by the dour look on the dwarfs face. Karkald was accompanied by another faerie, and he ges-tured for this flying messenger to speak.

"Bad news from nullward," replied the winged scout. "I've just gotten word from Janitha. . . . It seems the Delvers have crossed Riven Deep."

"How?" demanded Natac.

"I don't know," the faerie replied. "Some kind of magic, for sure. It happened at the same time as the quake, like the whole world was breaking up. And the Delver army came across, she said, and was marching this way."

Natac's heart sank at this disastrous development. Just when they had held so well, to get attacked by some impossible means. "What does it mean? How can they cross the canyon?" he demanded of no one in particular, though the dwarf took it upon himself to answer.

"I don't know," he replied laconically. "But it seems pretty clear that we've been outflanked. Where's the next place you want to try and fight 'em?"

MIRADEL'S first thought, when she spotted the gargoyle looking at her, had been no thought at all but merely instinct. She had thrown herself onto the ground and huddled between a pair of boulders, fearing at any instant that the grotesque creature would take to the air and swoop down upon her. Burying her head in her arms, she lay utterly still except for the trembling she could not control.

How long she stayed that way she couldn't remember. Eventually, however, she perceived that she had not yet been attacked. Hesitantly she raised her eyes, then lifted her head to look around the rock. She saw that the beast had made no move to leave its mountaintop aerie, though its eyes did remain open. They sparked brightly, crimson red in the distance, but no longer did they seem to be focused specifically on her. It was more as if the creature had gone from slumber to an air of general watchfulness.

Finally, she accepted that she would have to move.

Carefully she lifted herself to her feet, finding that the pack was not such a burden as she would have expected it to be. Trying to stay hidden as much as possible, she started climbing again, sticking to the low ripples in the terrain where for the most part she could remain out of view. Every time she came into view of the gargoyle she looked upward apprehensively, but still the beast had made no move.

The time was drawing close to the Hour of Darken when at last, exhausted, sore, and full of despair, she reached Shandira's position. Here she saw a sight more beautiful than anything she had beheld in days: her companion's eyes. The druid was awake!

"What happened?" asked the black woman, gingerly touching her blood-encrusted hair. "I fell, didn't I? How far? How long ago?"

"You took a bump on the head," Miradel said. "About midday, I would reckon. Now's it's almost Darken. Here, have a sip of water—and tell me how you feel."

"I have a headache," Shandira admitted. "But I think I'll be all right."

Miradel looked at the sun, so far away and so low in the sky. Soon it would start to climb away from them, and then in the skies there would be only the stars for light and nothing at all to keep them warm. "Belynda will be seeking us in a few minutes," she said tentatively. "I wonder if this, coming here, was a terrible mistake. Should I signal her to bring us home?"

"Well, no!" Shandira replied crossly, her spirited answer raising Miradel's morale considerably. "We have to do what we came here to do, or what's the point? And besides, I don't see a stream nearby, do you?"

"No. And yes, you're right. I mean, what's the point of stopping now?"

Miradel wasn't going to mention the gargoyle's minor

change, but her companion raised the issue as darkness closed around them. "Did you see it has its eyes open?" Shandira wondered.

"Yes . . . that happened after I climbed down to get my pack. I was afraid it saw me and was going to come after me, but it didn't move. It's still best to stay out of sight as much as possible," Miradel suggested.

The pair huddled together, using all four of their cloaks and their shared body warmth to survive the cold, cold night. They were both awake before Lighten and decided to get moving right away, reasoning that activity would be a better defense against cold than anything else within their power.

Once more they stuck to cover as much as possible, and as light returned to the worlds, they saw that the gargoyle remained fixed in place. Miradel couldn't escape the uncanny feeling that the great, stone eyes were seeking her, and once again they strove to stay out of sight throughout the long morning's climb.

It wasn't until late in the day that the incline began to level out, and they came into view of the great notch through the mountains, the pass that led into the shadowy maze of the Deathlord's citadel. The druids remained off the road, skulking along just below the roadside retaining wall, using that barrier as concealment from above. But now they had come to an open approach, and if they continued forward, it would be in full view of the stony sentry.

"I don't think we should go in there," Miradel said, abruptly halting.

"I don't like the looks of it either," Shandira said. "But what are the options? Should we wait here and see if the Deathlord comes strolling *out?*"

The elder druid chuckled in spite of her fatigue, her mood, their surroundings . . . everything. Then she laughed outright. "Well, that would serve us well. Might answer a lot of questions, in fact. But I was thinking more along the lines of us finding a different way to continue on."

Shandira nodded thoughtfully and looked skyward, toward the great summit rising on their right. "Such as . . . that ridge? The one that climbs around the far shoulder of the mountain?"

"That's what I had in mind. If we can stay on the right side of it until we're halfway up, it looks like the we could follow the crest the rest of the way and still be out of sight of the gargoyle."

"First light, then, let's give it a try."

They spent another cold night in the Fifth Circle, this time wedged into a crack between two rocks. It was cramped and rough-edged, but the close quarters seemed at least to help them conserve their body heat. Miradel found that she slept better than she had since their arrival. . . . How many days ago had it been? It was getting very hard to keep track of time.

Again they were up before the Lighten Hour, chilly and sore but anxious to get started. Their loads were noticeably lighter, Miradel thought—either that, or her muscles were getting so used to the strain that the backpack had seemed to become a part of her. She felt strangely invigorated, ready to continue the climb.

Shandira led the way around the base of the mountain until they were safely beyond the view of the gargoyle. Then they started to ascend in earnest. This slope was even steeper than the vast incline that had led them up to the pass. The ground was covered with loose rock that broke away without notice, and the going was very slow. They paused every two dozen steps for a quick breather, then resumed the ascent.

Miradel was amazed at the change in her condition: far

from the pain and exhaustion that had afflicted her during their first days, she now felt strong and invigorated, ready to continue each time she caught her breath. Even the shadowy twilight did not seem so oppressive. All this and more could be endured, she decided, with courage and the comfort of a good comrade.

By midday—during which it was no lighter than a cloudy twilight upon Nayve—they estimated that they had reached the point where they could climb to the ridge crest. They did so and were pleased to find out that they were now blocked from the gargoyle's view behind a shoulder of the mountain on the opposite side of the pass. Continuing on, they now followed the top of the ridge, which still rose steeply upward but seemed to offer better footing than the scree-dappled sides of the edifice.

By the Hour of Darken they felt as though they were nearing the top, though it remained impossible to see any great distance above them. But they resolved to continue on, slowed only slightly by the lack of light. An hour later, the two women made their way to the very top of the knife-edged ridge crest and collapsed there, finding a pair of boulders barely the size of narrow bunks. But each was solidly resting in the mountain rock and provided the first flat space they had encountered in the last six hours.

In the pale starlight they could see little of what lay beyond. Miradel perceived a maze of deep valleys and steep ridges, all leading toward a vast gulf of dark space some five or ten miles away.

Next the druid looked at the distant sun, now merely the brightest star high above Nayve, so far away across the Worldsea, and she shivered against the feeling of unnatural chill. Shandira, a short distance away, lowered her head and murmured an inaudible prayer.

The elder druid lay on her back and watched the stars,

full of fatigue but hopeful of their purpose. Then she sti-fled a gasp, clasping a hand to her mouth and staring.

"What is it? What did you see?" Shandira whispered, crouching at her side.

"Something was flying up there," Miradel said, still trembling. "It was huge, and its wings were so broad they seemed to blot out the stars. Look, there it is, flying around the side of the mountain."

"It is what we feared," Shandira said bluntly. "The gargoyle has taken wing."

THE trolls ran from their riverside camp, pushing through the thickets that grew in the lowlands, streaming among the oaks that had started to take root on the gentle hillsides rising a mile back from the Swansleep's banks. Awfulbark forgot about being king, abandoned any notion of trying to control anything but the direction of his own and Rood-cleaver's flight.

He did remember to hang on to his sword, however, and in fact the blade proved quite useful on those occa-sions when one of his countrymen was moving too slowly in his path. A swift stab proved remarkably persuasive, ei-ther convincing the laggard to hurry up or persuading him that he had better get out of the way or face an even more aggravating thrust.

They fled over the low elevation and across the smooth grassland beyond, running for hours, it seemed, until fi-nally fatigue began to take its toll. Trolls collapsed from exhaustion by the dozens, while many others staggered wearily along, losing any sense of direction and purpose.

"Gotta stop," Roodcleaver groaned, tugging on Awful-bark's hand. His first instinct was to yank her along for another dozen steps. He bulled forward until he heard an unfamiliar sound. When he stopped to look, he saw that his wife was sobbing and nearly exhausted. Her rough shoulders heaved, and she drew ragged, rasping breaths—breaths that emerged as great, grieving bleats of misery. When Awfulbark let go of her hand, she simply slumped to the ground and buried her face in her hands.

"Okay, we stop, rest for a bit," the king acknowledged. Looking around, he saw that the throng of trolls had thinned considerably. It occurred to him that many of them, weaker and lacking his own strong will, had probably already collapsed. Too bad for them . . . they were probably already caught by the . . .

Only then did he stop to consider what, in fact, had been the cause of their flight. With a sheepish look backward, he remembered the quake, the awful feeling that the world was lurching beneath him, actively seeking to do him, King Awfulbark, personal harm.

Of course, he had not been the only one to take off in flight, but he reflected that, perhaps, he could have set a better example. Natac had explained to him that it was important to keep the ghost warriors from crossing the river, and the trolls had really not done a very good job of that, not if the enemy had decided to advance some time in the last few hours.

Awfulbark had become a very chagrined troll by the time he saw the great, winged shape in the sky. Glumly he stood and waved, spotting Natac astride the great dragon's neck. Then the monarch of the forest trolls slumped in shame, looking at the ground as the serpent landed, and the general dismounted to speak to the troll.

"Greetings, King Awfulbark," Natac said politely. "I am relieved to find you well. I saw the damage wreaked in your grove by the quake."

The troll, expecting a rebuke for cowardice, was rather pleased by the general's words. He took a moment to ponder his answer. "Yes . . . some killed. But I lead trolls away from that place. We go back now?"

"I appreciate your courage, my loyal monarch," said Natac, reaching up to clap the lanky creature on his bark-rough shoulder. "But there has been a change in our battle plan. The quake we felt was caused by powerful magic—magic that brought the Delvers across Riven Deep. Now, we must fall back from the river."

"Fall back—you mean run away?" Awfulbark was stunned at first, and then indignant. "But we was winning fight!"

"I know. Your trolls did a magnificent job," the general declared, but he shook his head. "Even so, to stay here is to face ruin—so we must retreat."

"How far?" The king had only a vague idea of Nayve's geography, but he knew this was an important point.

"March toward the center," was the answer. "We will have to go as far as the Ringhills to make another stand."

"Okay," Awfulbark agreed. "You points us the way, and we goes there. And if the ghosts come, we fight!"

"Very good," Natac replied, seemingly sincere, though the troll king had never quite grown accustomed to sincerity. "The Fourth Circle is depending upon you, and you have answered the call, brave leader. Now, lead your warriors away from here, so that they may fight again tomorrow."

Awfulbark, feeling very pleased that he had not been rebuked for his impetuous flight, did just that, bellowing and cajoling even as the general and his mighty steed took to the air. His trolls gathered to him, and all within earshot echoed his orders to those who were too far away to hear the king directly. Gradually, the army of the forest trolls came together again.

————

MIRADEL no longer had a sense of daylight, even though she knew that the Lighten Hour, on Nayve, had passed several hours ago. As she and Shandira made their way up the narrow, black-walled gorge, however, they might have been climbing through thick twilight.

They had spent the cold night trembling on the mountaintop, scanning the skies for another sign of the gargoyle. But the massive creature, after flying past that one time, had not reappeared. The pale illumination of dawn had revealed it back in its position on the upper rampart.

The druids had proceeded over the ridge and pushed into the labyrinth of gorges and ravines on the far side, which is where they now found themselves in such stygian conditions. The rock walls seemed to be a mixture of dark gray and smooth, black stone that absorbed any trace of light that might have found its way here. In some odd way, however, the darkness was a comfort, for it seemed to lessen their chances of being discovered as they made their way closer to the great, dark vale they had seen from the crest.

"Are you sure that's the hall of the Deathlord?" Shandira asked once, whispering as the two women paused to drink some water and to rest.

"I have studied this place in the Tapestry, and yes, that high valley is the place where he sits on his great throne. It is the last place in this world or any other, as far as one can go in the direction that is neither metal nor wood. Beyond rises the great darkness, end of the cosmos. Every time I observed him, he has been as still and lifeless as a statue, but we will see if that is his true state or if he can be aroused by visitors."

"Visitors?" Shandira was looking at her intently. "Do you mean to pay a social call upon him?"

Miradel shook her head. "No . . . I wonder if we'll even find . . ." She didn't finish the thought.

"What? Find what?" Shandira demanded.

A shriek of uncanny power abruptly penetrated into the depths of the gorge. The sound echoed and rang, lingering for a long time after the original had faded.

"The gargoyle!" Miradel felt a stab of fear, sheer, unbridled terror gripping her entire body in a sweaty cocoon. Instinctively she was up, following the vague shape of Shandira, who was already sprinting along the winding floor. Glancing upward, she saw no sign of the monstrous pursuer, but that did nothing to hold up their pace as they raced, headlong toward the citadel of the Deathlord.

15

Blood Under Coolfyre

When twenty swords are ranged against you,
quick feet ever outweigh the strongest arm.

Goblin Proverb

"I can get this door open," Konnor whispered, as the three Houseguard siblings crouched in the alcove and waited. The company of dwarves had marched past just a few minutes before, and already they heard the smashing of at least one gate in the Wood Wall of the ghetto. "Maybe we can go through the warehouse and come at the wall farther from the waterfront."

"How can we be sure this place is abandoned?" Borand wondered.

"Look at it—dusty and dark, and quiet as a graveyard," Aurand replied. "No one's been in here for years!"

Darann readily agreed. "We don't have any choice. Let's go!" she urged, fearful that another company would be along at any moment. Next time, the shadows might not be enough to conceal them.

Quickly, Konnor eased the door open. The creak of rusty hinges seemed terribly loud to the four of them, but Darann hoped that beyond their hiding place the sound was buried in the greater tumult rising throughout the ghetto. Not daring to spark a light, they moved into the almost pitch darkness of what felt like a single, large room—at least, the little illumination spilling from the wharf side allowed them to see only empty space to either side. Dust kicked up by their feet hung in the stale air, tickling her nostrils, and Darann suspected that it was more than just a few years since this place had seen any activity.

When Konnor pushed the door shut, nearly soundlessly, there was no way to see anything at all. Borand risked lighting a match, the sulfurous flame shockingly bright, the smoke and scent pungent. In the flickering illumination they could see long, bare shelves extending into the distance on both sides. This certainly had been a warehouse, though it was now empty of goods.

Holding the match high, Borand led them forward, down a long aisle between the empty racks. Each step kicked up more dust, and there was a lingering smell of mold, slightly tainted by fish, in the air.

"An old fishery warehouse," Konnor guessed, whispering to Darann. "Probably abandoned not long after the king walled off the ghetto."

Darann was inclined to agree. She couldn't help reflecting that the cost of the goblin imprisonment had, in this case and many others, exacted a very real economic toll from the dwarves who had implemented that confinement. "What a waste," she breathed silently—at least, she thought she had spoken silently until Konnor turned to her and nodded in agreement.

Borand followed the aisle illuminated by his sputtering match all the way to the back of the warehouse, then turned and followed another wall toward the corner nearest to the ghetto wall. There was no sign of a door in this back wall, Darann saw in frustration. Her brother cursed and shook his hand as the flame flickered out. After a few seconds he lit another match and continued toward the side wall. Here they discovered a narrow corridor extending farther back into the warehouse. The building was huge, she realized, as they went another hundred paces away from the waterfront.

The corridor widened into another room, narrower than the large space fronting onto the wharf. This one had a tall ceiling invisible in the shadows overhead. Ladders placed at intervals along the floor led toward the lofty, unseen racks.

The third match revealed a pair of old cargo doors on the right side, secured against intruders with a heavy beam, in the terminus of the long corridor. Konnor and Aurand carefully lifted the beam out of the way, setting it gently on the ground to make a minimum of noise. Borand extinguished his match, and the dwarves gingerly pushed on the door.

They all cringed at the loud creak of hinges. A sliver of dim light, the faint background illumination of Axial's constant aura of coolfyre, outlined the entrance, and the older dwarf placed his eye to the gap. After what seemed like forever to Darann, he drew back and spoke.

"The next gate through the ghetto wall is a long ways away, but I could see a couple of guards on duty down there."

"Maybe we can try to bluff our way through," Darann said, "like we have a job with the guards?"

She was not surprised when all three of her companions shook their heads; the idea hadn't even sounded workable as she had voiced it. Every dwarf they had observed approaching the ghetto had been armored in breastplate and helm. Her brothers, in their leather riding shirts, and herself in the tattered tunic and leggings she had worn for the last five intervals, could not have looked more out of place.

"What about going *over* the wall?" Aurand suggested. "I saw some ladders back there leading to the warehouse loft. Maybe we can take one of them out this door and get into the ghetto that way?"

"Worth a try," Borand agreed. Ten minutes later they had muscled one of the heavy ladders down from its perch and carried it to the door. Darann went through first, pushing open the portal as quietly as possible, then standing aside as her three companions brought out their prize.

Fortunately, this section of the alley was buried in deep shadow, and the sounds of the door opening, the inevitable scuffing of the ladder, and the exertions of the dwarves were all swallowed by the larger chaos in the ghetto. The fighting and pillaging were still some distance away, Darann judged, but vigorous enough to raise quite a racket.

When the ladder was in place, Borand reached for it, but Aurand pushed past and scrambled quickly upward, his sword in his hand. He stepped off at the top and, crouching on the narrow perch, waved the others to follow. Her older brother went up, Darann went after Borand, and Konnor brought up the rear. She found that the top of the wall was flat and several feet wide, and she remembered that she had seen guards patrolling here on occasion. The four dwarves stayed low, pulling the ladder upward, then carefully lowering it down the far side.

It seemed to take forever to the dwarfmaid, but she judged it only to be a minute or so that they remained atop the wall. Even so, she was certain that a searching beacon would illuminate them or that some wandering guard would spot their silhouettes against the city's lights. As soon as the ladder was in place, they descended into a rank alley, with dark, shabby buildings pressing close, leaving a passage only five or six feet wide. Konnor suggested that they lower the ladder and hide it in the shadows at the base of the wall, which they quickly did.

"Which way?" Borand asked, keeping his voice hushed.

Darann had been looking around, wondering that herself. She saw a suggestion of movement, a flash of a bright eye, and bent over. There was something there, crouched in the shadows at the base of the wall, regarding them with wide-open eyes.

"Hi," she said, "I am the Lady Darann of clan Houseguard, goblin friend. Can you tell me where Hiyram is?"

"Hello, Lady," said a goblin, rising from his hiding place, squinting at the four dwarves. "I know of you—and trust you, for you sneak into ghetto, not smash gate."

"Good," she said. "And thank you. What do you know about Hiyram?"

"This way," said the goblin. "We see if he still lives, okay?"

LORD Nayfal was nervous. How could this be taking so long? The filthy goblins were unarmed, half-starved, and notoriously cowardly. How in the Underworld could they resist his elite companies? This should have been a simple matter of herding them into the plazas in the center of their ghetto, then wading in with unsheathed weapons, giving the wretches what they deserved.

"Captain Brackmark," he called. The lord's ferr'ell bucked under him, and he cursed, then slid down from the saddle to stand on the ground. He had been riding the beasts for fifty years, but this was one of those times when it seemed that he was simply unable to control his stubborn and willful mount.

The officer of the guard clomped up to him, saluting. "Yes, m'lord?" he asked.

"What's the problem? Why aren't your men pushing through to the central plaza yet?"

"Begging your lordship's pardon, but we're making good progress," Brackmark insisted. "We got 'em cleared out of the near buildings, and we're taking it street by street, pushing toward the center."

"That's not good enough. Send in the rest of the reserve battalion! I want this matter cleaned up by the end of the interval!"

"I will send them, sir, of course," replied the veteran footman, sidling away from the ferr'ell as the creature snapped and growled at Nayfal's liveryman when that dwarf took the trailing reins. "But it might still take another interval, maybe two, before we can round up all the males."

"Bah," snapped Nayfal. "What makes the pathetic wretches so hard to catch? If they're hiding behind the females, then catch—or kill—the wenches, too!"

"Not that we haven't tried, lord. But they seem to have a million hiding places in there. We chase 'em into what looks like a dead-end alley, and—poof—the whole bunch slips out through some narrow crack no dwarf could fit his head through. They got tunnels down under the streets, and they climb all over the roofs. I lost a good man, broken neck, 'cause he chased a gob onto some cursed trellis, couldn't nearly hold his weight!"

"Casualties are acceptable," retorted Nayfal pointedly. "The important thing is to round up all the goblins that might ever take up arms against us. I want to remove this threat from the city for once and for all!"

"Right, and we will, like I said, m'lord. It just might take a wee bit longer than we thought."

"Well, do as I command and send in the reserves!"

snapped the nobleman, angrily snatching the reins from his servant. "And I will personally lead them in the charge!"

He kicked his foot into the stirrup and hoisted himself up, praying that the beast would remain still long enough for him to get settled. Surprisingly enough, it did, and with another jerk on the reins, he turned the sleek head toward the ghetto gate. Prodded by a single kick, the animal bolted forward, carrying his rider toward the fight.

THE goblin dropped from sight before Darann, and she thought, for a moment, that he had run away. "Down here!" came the hissing instructions. "Safe way to Hiyram!"

"In that hole?" Borand demanded, skeptically eyeing the black circle in the ground. It yawned like a lightless well and seemed to emit many questionable odors. "I don't like the looks of it."

"You don't have to like it," the dwarfmaid retorted. "Just get going!"

Indeed, many fetid smells lingered in the air around them, and Darann felt grimly certain that most of that stink originated from within that pit. But she took a deep breath and knelt on the ground, reaching inside the dark circle until she felt a rung of metal placed in the wall. Leaning forward, she found another a foot below.

"There seems to be a ladder," she reported. "I'm going to follow him."

"Count me in." Aurand, not surprisingly, came right behind, then Konnor, and finally the still-grumbling Borand. Darann, grateful for the loyalty of her comrades, tried not to breathe through her nose as she groped her way down the slippery but solidly mounted rungs. Even so, the air actually *tasted* of foulness, coating her mouth with a residue that was cloying and choking at the same time. After eight or ten steps, she landed with a wet splash onto a slick floor and moved to the side so that her companions could join her.

Her brother struck another of his ubiquitous matches. They quickly saw that they were in a drainage pipe, brick-walled and tall enough for them to stand without stooping. The water was only a few inches deep, and the air was thick with those foul, albeit unidentifiable, odors. Here the smoke from the match was in fact a blessing, for it obscured those unknown smells. There was a stone arch twenty or thirty feet away, a support for the pipe apparently, and the cylindrical passage seemed to continue into the darkness beyond.

"This way," said the goblin, selecting one of their two options. In the light of the match his skin was a grayish green, and his mouth visible as a wide gash partially filled with crooked teeth, below those wide, brightly reflective eyes. His big feet slapped across the wet floor as he started off. After a moment's hesitation, the four dwarves came behind.

The match fizzled and went out, and for a time they slopped along in utter darkness, Borand not wanting to expend his complete supply in this featureless passageway. Once they passed under a shaft leading upward, hearing sounds of marching feet directly overhead. The goblin continued on, and the Seers followed.

Finally their guide stopped, a fact that Darann discovered when she walked into him in the inky darkness. "Go up here," the goblin declared. "Find Hiyram."

Now Borand struck another light, revealing a set of iron rungs similar to those they had descended. The goblin led the way, and again Darann was right behind him. At the top of the shaft they had to push a heavy iron cover out of the way, though as soon as they started it moving, willing helpers grabbed on from above and slid it off of the exit.

The goblin quickly popped up. "These good dwarves," he said. "Lady Darann comin' up!"

"The Lady!" Immediately hands were extended, and the dwarfmaid allowed them to hoist her onto the ground. Her three companions quickly followed, standing somewhat nervously in the midst of a throng of goblins. Some of this rabble was wounded, and many of them carried makeshift weapons, mostly clubs and stones. More than one cast a glowering look upon the intruders.

"Where's Hiyram?" she asked. "I need to talk to him!"

"Hiyram!" The shout was carried out from the group. "You waits here, stays quiet. Dwarves not happy in goblin-crowd, not now, not on this interval. Hiyram comes to find you."

"I understand—and thank you," Darann said.

A few minutes later, the crowd parted to let someone pass, and Darann practically sobbed with relief as she beheld the familiar, flop-eared visage. The goblin's face brightened momentarily, then darkened with sudden, intense concern.

"Lady—you get from here!" he urged, his eyes wide. "The ghetto bad place now! You gotta go away! Why you come here now? Why?"

"I know about the danger," she said. "And I'm sorry. I wish I could help you right away."

"Metal-shirt dwarves come. They say we kill dwarfmaid with hot oil! No gob do that—was more black ones, dwarves of the ferr'ell marshal! We saw 'em, chased 'em, but no catch. They kill maid, blame us!"

Nayfal! Darann was not surprised to hear that the corrupt lord was behind the current attack. "There's one thing I might be able to do. I have to talk to the king, to convince him that Nayfal has caused him to make a terrible decision. But I need help. You told me about a pailslopper . . . someone from the palace who heard of the plan to kill my father. I need to talk to her! Can you tell me how to find her?"

"She told me to tell none, but now . . ." Hiyram shrugged, gestured to their surroundings. "What choice do we have? Yes, I will say her name; she is called Greta Weaver, lives in room on top of Goat Hair Inn."

"The Goat Hair? I know that place. It's a soldiers' tavern, not far from ghetto, on the road to the royal tower," Konnor said. "I can find the place, once we get out of here."

"Yes, that Goat Hair tavern. Good luck," Hiyram said. "You can go from ghetto out pipe." He gestured to the goblin who had guided them here. "Red-Eye Fobber will take you."

"And you," Darann said. "Can't you get out of here, through the pipes underground?"

Hiyram shrugged again. "Lots of gobs go there, ladies and little ones. We fight here, till they can go. Send many away, but where to away? Get killed in ghetto, get killed in city, or drownded in lake? Find place to be safe—then we go, too."

"Good luck, my friend," Darann said, giving him an embrace. He hugged her back, then gestured. "Go, now!"

They started back toward the well they had emerged from, but they had taken only a dozen steps when a phalanx of dwarven guards came around the corner to block their path. The goblins and dwarves both froze for a second, until the sergeant of the Seers raised his axe and shouted a hoarse cry. Immediately, the dwarves charged forward.

"Run! Back there," Hiyram urged, tugging at Darann's hand. She hesitated, unwilling to flee in the face of her own countrymen, until Borand took her arm and pulled her along. She looked back, saw several goblins rush forward in attempt to slow up the attackers. A few sharp blows were enough to cut them down. The rest of the goblins turned and fled, carrying Darann and her companions with them.

"Here, another hole up there," Hiyram said as they approached another intersection. "Run up hill, look in alley at top, on sword-hand side of street."

"You come, too!" she urged.

"I come, but after you go—so run!"

Sensing that the stubborn goblin meant what he said, she cursed and started to run up a road that climbed the steep hill. Konnor fell in behind her, casting glances back at the pursuit, his sword ready in his hand. "Wait, here—take this!" said the dwarf. She saw that he had found a battered shield somewhere, now extended it toward her. Not sure what to do with it, she nevertheless took the buckler and held it awkwardly in her left hand.

Once more they looked down the street, toward Borand, Aurand, Hiyram, and the other goblins. They saw a wild melee at the intersection behind them, heard smacks of steel on steel and the surprised cursing of wounded dwarves. Somehow the motley group was buying them a little time.

"He said to look for an alley on the sword-side, on the right," the dwarfmaid gasped, running short of breath. She spotted a dark gap in the row of ramshackle buildings. "That must be it!"

A goblin was in front of her, and she recognized Red-Eye Fobber, their original guide. "Hole in there," he said. "Go down right away!"

She stopped at the entrance to the alley. A single glance showed her that the fighting down the hill was savage. Her brothers, side by side, were holding a half dozen dwarves at bay, but another big axeman was pressing against Hiyram, swinging his heavy weapon in round-house swipes that slashed over the goblin's head.

"This way!" Darann cried. "Hiyram—over here!"

She despaired as her voice seemed to vanish into the thunderous melee, then took heart as she saw the valiant goblin glance in her direction. He blinked once and turned his attention back to the dwarf, using the slender knife to somehow parry another slashing blow from the heavy axe.

But the power of the dwarf-at-arms was enough to send the goblin tumbling backward, and Darann could only watch as a dozen swordsmen spilled into the intersection, coming from the other direction. They met an equal number of goblins, but this rabble was unarmored, bearing but knives, sticks, and clubs as weapons. With a sharp rush, the disciplined dwarves scattered the goblins, killing four and routing the others back up the narrow, steeply climbing street.

A big goblin with a cleaver, one eye matted with a bloody smear, suddenly rushed from the depths of the alley, charging at Darann. She lifted the shield and grunted as the powerful blow knocked her against the wall. "No—I'm a friend!" she cried, but he didn't seem to hear or to care. Instead, he raised the cleaver and uttered a growl so piercing that it raised the hairs on the back of her neck. There was nowhere to go, so she used the shield as a weapon, charging against the goblin, pushing him away for a second.

Then Hiyram was there, rapping his fist sharply on the side of the big goblin's head. "This Lady dwarf, fool! She help gobs outta here!"

The bleeding attacker just scowled, but by then the tide of retreating goblins carried them along, away from the alley and the steep hill. "Gotta find you way outta here," gasped Hiyram. "Get you going now! This alley, around the corner then you go down hole!"

"Follow me!" Darann shouted, and Hiyram repeated the command. In another moment she was running along, followed by the sounds of broad, flat feet slapping against the bedrock. She raced as fast as she could, darting around the corner, then stopping as, finally, she saw the unguarded manhole cover.

Konnor was there, too, and several goblins came behind, though they initially shied away from the leather-clad Seer. Hiyram followed the dwarfmaid up to the narrow hatch.

"Through there," he explained breathlessly. "It goes into pipe, will lead you to the city outside ghetto, toward Royal Tower. Best escape for you."

"We'll go—but you come after, as soon as you can!" she cried.

"Bull-Hair, go with!" cried Hiyram, clapping the one-eyed warrior who had earlier attacked Darann. "Lead the gobs away from here. I come after the end!"

"You get started," Borand said. "Auri and I will help hold them up."

"No!" the dwarfmaid insisted. "You have to come, too!"

"We'll be right behind," her brother assured her. He turned to the big goblin. "Take her down there—now!"

Without hesitation the battle-scarred Bull-Hair dove through the hatch. Konnor and Darann started after, down the ladder and into the now-familiar dankness of the drainage sewer.

Her last sight was of Hiyram and her brothers as they gathered a dozen stalwart goblins and headed back down the street, determined to hold up the pursuing Seers.

"STOP them!" shrieked Nayfal, as his restive ferr'ell pranced beneath him. Of course, mounted as he was, he was in the best position to lead the pursuit of the fleeing goblins, but he was too reasonable to do that. Let the foot soldiers risk their lives. His role was here, in the saddle, and in command!

Two companies of dwarves charged forward, pitching in to the goblins who were battling with such unusual ferocity. Nayfal saw several of his men fall back, wounded and bleeding, but was pleased that others quickly stepped in. Axes and swords rose and fell, and he could only imagine—happily—the carnage that was being wrought.

But the number of goblins was shrinking faster than he could explain by death and wounding, and as the dwarves pushed forward, he got a glimpse from his saddle that confirmed his worst fears.

"They're getting away!" he cried. "Stop them!"

There could be no stopping the escape, however, not when the rear guard fought with such ferocity. It was only when the last of the refugees had vanished that the attackers overwhelmed the goblins, taking several prisoners.

It was then that Nayfal got his next surprise, one that brought a grim smile to his thin lips. For there, among the prisoners, were the two brothers of clan Houseguard. Somehow, fate had delivered them right into his hands.

"COME on—keep moving!" shouted Bull-Hair, the urgency of his voice amplified by the pitch darkness of the tunnel and the distant sounds of battle fading behind them.

Darann had held up, wanting to wait for her brothers, but Konnor took her arm and spoke to her softly, persuasively. "They'll meet us at the Goat Hair Inn if they can. Borand knows where it is; we've been there together, in happier times. But what they're doing, staying back there and fighting, that's for you. Don't waste it by staying behind."

"Dammit, you're right," she snapped, before turning and following the slapping footsteps of their goblin guide. Surely her brothers would find a way out—they *had* to! She wouldn't let herself believe that they could get snared in Nayfal's sweep.

They seemed to go for a long time, covering a greater distance than in their first subterranean trek, when they had been seeking Hiyram. Darann had no trouble believing that they had moved beyond the ghetto walls, but she found it impossible to get any sense of bearings, to have any idea where they were going. She simply followed along behind Bull-Hair, and when the sounds of his steps abruptly stopped, she halted, too.

"Here, go up," their guide said suddenly. "This quiet place; nobody see, if you careful. Be careful."

"We will—thank you," Darann said, squeezing the loyal guide on his shoulder. "You be careful, too."

She felt for the rungs, found that Konnor had already started up the metal ladder. She came along behind, silently climbing. A minute later the two dwarves emerged through a sewer drain on a quiet side street, several blocks away from the ghetto wall. Trying not to think about her brothers, Darann couldn't suppress a single, grieving sob as she looked down the hole they had emerged from. Were Borand and Aurand back there someplace? Or had, as she feared, they been snared by the attacking guards? Konnor put an arm around her shoulders, and she drew a breath, banishing her fears, angrily rubbing a hand across her moist eyes.

"The Goat Hair Inn is not far away," Konnor said, taking his bearings from the position of the city's great towers rising into view around them. "We can walk there in ten minutes. Let's hope Greta Weaver is at home."

"And that she's willing to tell us the truth," Darann agreed, drawing some comfort from her companion's calm awareness. He offered her his arm, and she took it, reasoning that their chances of being questioned by guards was lessened if they could be mistaken for a normal couple.

They found a main street and, though they wanted to run, walked along like a couple out for a stroll. True to his word, Konnor soon led her up to the door of a run-down inn. They heard sounds of raucous laughter within, while the not unappealing scent of coal smoke and grilled meat wafted into the street from the door. With an air of bravado that Darann hoped was real, Konnor swaggered forward, pushed open the entrance, and led her inside.

16

Broken Circles

Upon the foundation of worlds,
The First Circle stands,
Ultimate bedrock;

When Underworld trembles,
All skies can fall

From the Tapestry of the Worldweaver
Tales of a Time Before

The Worldfall tumbled from the zenith of all circles, carrying the stuff of creation into the mountainous Nullreach of Nayve. For decades it had pounded this ground, pulverizing the substance of the Fourth Circle in this region into a wasteland of chaos. Nothing could live there, nothing could so much as approach this shimmering vista of violence. The air churned with violent storms, and the ground was shattered and trembling, prone to quakes that dropped away great sections of terrain, sucking it right into the vortex of the great storm.

Yet for all that destruction, the storm had remained in this one location since its creation. The scope of the plunging debris, instead of expanding outward, remained localized, limited to that section of terrain that, in fact, no longer existed as anything resembling solid ground. Those bordering plains and hills that, one year, vanished into the chaotic tangle would re-form in another season; hill might be plain and flat might roll into lofty elevation, but the terrain would inevitably begin to re-form. It survived this perilous existence for an unknown time, before once again vanishing into the maw of destruction.

Across the world of Nayve, a far less violent phenomenon had been observed in the five decades since the discovery of the Worldfall. There, in an idyllic region of farmland and lakes, a land of gnomes and elves called Winecker, the ground had been subject to a series of upheavals. Hills had risen where gentle pastures once sprawled, and periodically, storms of wind would sweep the land, winds that swept away from Nayve, forming a vortex of upward-rising air. The scholarly druid Socrates had determined this to be a reaction to the Worldfall, an upward counter to that powerful and relentless downward force.

Despite the Worldfall's lethal power, many creatures had survived the plunge down the cataract of chaos, including the thousands of harpies who had swarmed into Nayve five decades ago and the massive dragon who had been sucked into the storm called the Hillswallower. That maelstrom had similarly wrought great destruction in the Sixth Circle as well, the overworld that was called Arcati by those who dwelled there. A whole province in the cloud world had vanished into the Hillswallower, leaving a region of chaos and destruction where once cumulous elevations had risen gently into the oversky.

So extensive was the storm, so vast its plunge, that it actually carried the stuff of the cosmos downward past the sun—for that orb was below Arcati and above Nayve. Rising and falling on a cycle of twenty-four hours, the sun at its loftiest height brought daylight to the Sixth Circle as the Fourth was plunged into night. Then it would descend, and the Lighten Hour would come to Nayve as the over-world was cloaked in cooling darkness.

The sun was oriented over the Center of Everything, the temple of the Goddess Worldweaver and her silver loom, the thousand-foot-tall spire of silver rising from her sacred precincts. Three directions marked the points from the Center: the direction of wood; the direction of metal; and the direction that was neither metal nor wood, some-times called the direction of null. Like the center of a web, the temple stood tall. Here the goddess performed her labors, while the druids studied the Tapestry, practiced their magic, and recorded their stories.

Nayve, the Fourth Circle, was surrounded by the Worldsea, beyond which lay the Second, Third, and Fifth Circles. The Fifth, in the direction of null, was the land of death and the end of all worlds. The First was below, the great city of Axial aligned directly underneath Circle at Center. Together with the Sixth, above, these worlds formed the core of the cosmos, the focus of all the worlds where magic dwelled.

Only the Seventh Circle, the world called Earth, lay be-yond the pale of the first six worlds. There were those druids who maintained that Earth, the Seventh Circle, is an imagined place, a dream woven by the goddess on her Tapestry for the edification of her druids. More rational minds discounted this argument, and indeed, since Earth was the birthplace of all humans who live upon Nayve, druids and warriors alike, there was a significant popula-tion on Nayve with very vivid memories of their world of origin.

The druids were summoned here by the blessing of the goddess, and each warrior was brought by the explicit act of a druid: the carnal Spell of Summoning, which brings a warrior from the place of his dying to the place of his eternal life. But all of them recalled past lives, lands, and peoples of Earth.

These spells were the final proof: the Seventh Circle was a real place, source of actual creatures, the humans who, increasingly, came to populate Nayve. Thanks to the water discovered by the druid Juliay, the Spell of Summoning could be cast without costing the druid her youth and her future. As a consequence, more and more members of the order had selected warriors from the battlefields of Earth, bringing each to Nayve at the moment of his death.

Still, there were not enough of them, as the ghost warriors teemed to the far horizons and beyond.

NATAC saw that the three great columns were marching onto the plains, with the Ringhills, some fifty miles away, as their goal. He sat astride the great dragon as Regillix Avatar flew three miles above the world's surface. From here they could see the valley of the Swansleep River, the vast plain, and the rugged horizon of the hills rising toward the Center.

Tamarwind's elves formed the rear guard as the army pulled away from the river, though the ghost warriors were not aggressive in their crossing of the Swansleep. The quake had proved very disruptive to them, even as it gave the means for the Delvers to cross Riven Deep. It was that dwarven crossing that had made Natac's position at the river untenable; if they had stayed in place, Zystyl's force would have attacked them from behind, and there would have been no survival. Instead, Natac had ordered the general withdrawal and now simply hoped to get his army away to fight on another day.

While the Argentian elves watched for pursuit, the

elves of Barantha and the forest trolls formed two vast formations, leaving behind the valley of the Swansleep as they started across the dry plains. From the back of the mighty dragon, Natac could see the plumes of dust raised by these marchers and knew that they would reach the hills within a few days. Each had a large contingent of centaurs towing their batteries, the silver metallic carriages mingled into the long files of warriors. It was encouraging to see that the troops, despite the orders to withdraw, were moving in good order and maintaining an impressive speed.

To the left Natac saw another column of dust, and they flew low to see the Hyaccan elves, the only mounted troops of his army. Beyond were the massive rock piles, where the slabs that had carried the Delvers across Riven Deep had come to rest. The Tlaxcalan had seen many examples of powerful magic since he had come to Nayve, but never had he witnessed anything comparable to this: the great uprooting of the very landscape, the use of that ground to carry troops onto an otherwise inaccessible battlefield. He didn't want to think about it too much, for when he did, it seemed impossible to comprehend any means whereby they could win this war, not against an enemy that could marshal such unspeakable power.

Yet still, they would try. Below him the riders of Janitha Khandaughter were already making the dwarves pay for their advance. The elves on their nimble ponies skirmished with the Delvers, riding close, showering the dwarves with arrows, then galloping away before the iron golems could come up. Like the elf and trollish infantry, the elven riders were fighting cautiously, giving ground instead of lives. Natac was confident they would reach the Ringhills with their numbers intact.

Swinging through a lofty circle, the dragon winged back across the plains. The ghost warriors were a teeming blot on the right, like a brown stain spreading across the ground. They had finally crossed the Swansleep, but they advanced on the plains as a great, broad front, not any formation of marching columns. Their numbers seemed infinite, extending far back to the river and beyond.

Far past that place, to the metalward of the enemy, there was one more group of warriors, out of sight even from this lofty altitude. Faerie messengers had brought word from Roland Boatwright, informing Natac that the druids and warriors whose boats had survived the battle with the armada had debarked onto shore and were marching toward the Ringhills. They would need to take an indirect route, crossing the Snakesea instead of the plains, since the enemy army was between them and their destination. That sea crossing was not difficult, not when powerful druids were involved, and Natac welcomed the thought of further help. Roland's force was not numerous but included many druids and the vast majority of the earth warriors that had been summoned to Nayve over the past fifty years. They would reach the Ringhills, and they would join his army.

But what would happen then?

Regillix Avatar seemed to be pondering the same question. He turned his great head, banking sideways to regard the general who was his passenger. "How do you intend to hold them at the hills?" he asked.

"We will need to dig a trench, erect an earthen wall," replied Natac, who had given the matter considerable thought. "As deep and as high as we can make them. Then we force them to a halt, and when they try to go around us, we simply dig a new ditch and raise a new wall."

"A wall around the Center, perhaps," said the dragon thoughtfully. "A great undertaking, to be sure."

"It's the only choice we have," Natac said, once more dejected about the prospects of the next battle. "But the pieces are set in motion now. We have to wait until Tamar-wind and Awfulbark reach the hills with their troops. For now, can you return us to the city?"

"Of course."

The dragon turned his bearing toward the Center of Everything, winging high over the plains. Regillix was exceptionally untalkative during the long flight back to Circle at Center, and this suited his passenger as well. Having seen to the deployment of his army, Natac's mind was focused on a single question. He only hoped he could find the answer when they got back to the temple of the Worldweaver.

The spire of the loom came into sight before them as the dragon glided over the Ringhills. The sun ascended toward Darken as they crossed the great lake. Knowing his rider's urgency, the wyrm flew low over the city, toward the center itself. People came into the streets as they passed, some of them cheering and waving, the vast majority, however, looking up in mute, prayerful hope. Natac barely noticed, so intense was the question burning in his mind.

Before full darkness, Regillix Avatar set down within the ring created by the Grove, the Senate, and the College, the sacred ground at the Center of Everything. Natac slid down the scaled flank, his own feet landing on the ground a split second after the dragon's. Druids were already coming toward them, but the general didn't want to wait around for greetings or other formalities.

"Thanks, old friend. Rest here as you need," Natac said. "I must go into the temple."

"Of course," said the dragon. "I grow hungry, but I know the druids will feed me well. Indeed, here come several with a small herd of beeves. A splendid appetizer, I can tell! Now go, learn what you must."

Immediately Natac was running toward the marble

temple at the base of the loom. He took note of the empty plazas, the gardens where the flowers bloomed in silent luster. Though Darken was an hour away, there were only a few druids present, a pair of stout, sturdy tillers working in a field, and a few carpenters hammering away in the boatyard.

"Where's Miradel?" he cried, bursting through the temple doors. There were a dozen acolytes within, spinning wool for the Loom of the Worldweaver. Several of them gasped, and one, an elder woman of Oriental origin, shook her head. "We know nothing of this matter—only the goddess sees all."

Natac looked at the golden doors leading to the inner sanctum. He had never passed through that portal, though he had come to this room with Miradel on numerous occasions, even going as far as the Rockshaft, the now-sealed chute that had once been open all the way down to the First Circle.

Passing the sealed iron portal of the shaft, he hesitated only for a moment, then strode forward, ignoring the entreaties of the druid wool spinners. "No—it is forbidden! You must not!"

He pushed the doors, which opened almost effortlessly despite their obviously massive weight. Stepping through, he swayed to a momentary sense of disorientation: it seemed that the room he entered was far larger than the exterior walls would allow. The opposite wall of the circular chamber was far away, and the whole periphery was a collage of brilliantly colored fabric. He could discern no details in those colors, but he knew at once that this was the Tapestry, the record of all histories on the Seven Circles, stories as woven by the goddess herself into the fabric of time.

The loom was a massive machine, as large as a cottage. Levers and wheels whirred, stroked, and turned. Six huge

spools were mounted at one end, feeding strands of thread
into the tablelike slab of the machine. Plates moved back
and forth, and these strands merged and mingled until the
finished Tapestry, a fabric no more than six feet across,
emerged from the end of the loom opposite the spools.
The Tapestry flowed toward the wall, where it formed the
terminus of the great coil of material, ever growing
longer.

"This is unusual."

The speaker was an elderly woman, a person Natac noticed for the first time. She sat at the loom, working the
pedals with her feet, moving strong fingers across the
threads, linking them and crossing them with dextrous
motions so nimble and quick that the man could not even
see the individual movements. This was the Goddess
Worldweaver, he knew, as he beheld the immortal being
for the first time.

"Explain yourself. Immediately," she demanded.

"Where is Miradel?" he asked bluntly.

He didn't know what to expect, but nevertheless, the
Worldweaver took him by surprise when she shrugged,
then curled her lip in scorn. "She is gone, dead. I care not,
and you should have more important concerns as well."

"What? No—impossible!" he shouted, though he knew
it was all too conceivable that his beloved had met some
dire fate. "Tell me—where did she go? How did she perish?"

"Go away. I have work to do, and so do you," snapped
the goddess.

Despite his determination, Natac found himself walking out of the sanctum, through the anteroom, onto the
lakeside plaza outside of the temple itself. He stared at the
swirling stars, the ghostly spire of the loom, and tried to
decide what to do. Why had he been dismissed so curtly?
Clearly, she was displeased—but with him or with Mi-

radel? And could he believe her words about his lover's fate?

"She lives!" he said with determination that might have been nothing more than his will. Even so, it was real belief, and it compelled him to continue his search for an answer. He left the temple to cross the gardens of the Center, coming quickly to the great ivory halls of the College. Here he made his way to the apartments of the elfwoman he had known for more than three hundred years. He paused for only a second, then pounded on the door, surprising himself by the volume raised by his blows.

"Natac!" Belynda said, paling as she opened her door in response to his insistent knock. "It has been long since we have seen you in the city! How fares the battle?"

"Where's Miradel?" he repeated, pushing through the door with an assertiveness that would not be denied. "Do you know what has happened to her?"

In the momentary guilt that flashed in her eye—elves were notoriously guileless—he knew that she did. But she quickly masked her expression and shook her head. "She is safe—for the time being, at least. But she has forbidden me to speak of this matter, especially to reveal her location."

"Thank all gods that she lives!" Natac cried, relief overcoming his frustration—at least initially. "The goddess herself claimed she was dead, but I did not believe."

"She told you that? I know that the Worldweaver does not approve of Miradel's quest, so she is cold. But I am surprised that she would lie," Belynda said. "You should know that Miradel strives for victory, serves bravely the cause of our war against the Deathlord."

"I had no doubt about that." He narrowed his eyes and confronted the sage-ambassador bluntly. "You *have* to tell me where she is, what she's doing," he urged. "Maybe I can help her. At least I deserve to know! She even deceived Cillia to go away, a fact I find hard to believe. Why?"

"She will tell you herself, when she returns," Belynda said. "Until then, I must keep the faith I have made with her."

Natac tried to change her mind, arguing, persuading, even threatening, but Belynda would not change her position. He was forced to leave her, eventually, when she pleaded that she would need to sleep before Lighten, and he realized that half the night had passed.

His mood was bleak as he made his way back to the gardens. He curled up under the great dragon's wing to snatch a few hours of sleep, disdaining any of the hundreds of fine rooms that would have been offered to him in the Center's environs.

He didn't know what to think or where to go.

THE call of the gargoyle echoed through the empty canyons, resonating until it seemed that the sound actively sought to drive Miradel mad. She clapped her hands to her ears, but even that did nothing to diminish the haunting refrain. Her stomach heaved, churning with raw fear, and for a second she had to clench her teeth against the urge to vomit.

"Are you all right?" Shandira asked, her dark brow furrowed with concern.

Miradel wanted to scream, *How could* anything *possibly be all right?* But she bit her tongue and forced herself to nod with some affectation of calm. "Yes—let's keep going," she urged.

After all, she reminded herself, the gargoyle had not yet discovered them. It had uttered its ghastly shriek several times during the night, but never had they so much as glimpsed it flying overhead. Instead, they had trekked for miles through the darkness, drawing—they hoped—ever closer to the vast throne of the Deathlord.

"Do you need to rest?" asked Miradel's companion.

It was with a sense of surprise that she was able to answer truthfully, "No." In fact, though they had carried their packs throughout the day and into the long night, she no longer felt the fatigue that had dragged her down upon her first tentative steps in this world of shadow and cold. Her shoulders were strong, her legs taut and supple, and even her lungs were in better shape; rarely during the last twenty hours had she even found herself out of breath.

"Let's keep going," she urged, and Shandira agreed.

"Just keep your eyes on the sky," counseled the African woman, and Miradel nodded seriously.

It seemed that they had been playing this cat-and-mouse game for many hours, ever since the beast had first cried out during the twilight that passed for the middle of the day. The druid had been very conscious of that illumination, and at the Lighten Hour had watched overhead as most of the stars faded. So dark was this distant corner of the Fifth Circle, however, that some of the twinkling specks remained visible even during the day. Viewed from such a deep hole, the sky was a thick, purpled cosmos that seemed to extend to infinity, even in the midst of what was full daylight upon Nayve.

Dark as was the sky, the inky rock walls of this gorge were even blacker. The slopes were irregular and jagged, far too steep to climb. Fortunately, the floor of the chasm was smooth and relatively free of debris. No more than twenty or thirty feet wide, it nevertheless made for a good pathway, and the two druids had been following it for two days, working their way deeper into the labyrinthine citadel of the Deathlord.

Just before Lighten, they had even speculated that they were within a few hours of the great throne room—that valley in the mountain's crest Miradel had observed through the Tapestry. That was before the gargoyle had screamed, however; since then, their efforts had been focused merely on survival.

"This way," she said, indicating a wide passage that descended toward the direction that was neither metal nor wood. "We need to get lower, I think."

The elder druid was in the lead, moving quickly, when Shandira screamed. The sound saved Miradel's life. She threw herself onto the ground and crawled behind a rock as the air whooshed around her and a cold, gray shape winged past just a dozen feet overhead. The gargoyle uttered a cold, grating shriek, straining to climb, and the two druids scrambled to their feet, reversed direction, and sprinted along the floor of the winding ravine, desperately seeking something, anything, that would offer a hope of shelter.

A backward glance showed the monster rising into the sky, laboring to lift the heavy body with those slender wings. Soon it vanished from view beyond one of the lofty ridges that closed their upward view into such a narrow groove. The greatest advantage they had, Miradel realized, was the narrowness of the gorge floor. The gargoyle was simply too huge to fly down this low. But how long would that protection last?

"Here it comes again!" Shandira warned.

Those vast wings spread out like sinister arms, scraping the cliffs to either side of the gorge as the monster plunged downward. The two eyes blazed red, as if some infernal fire burned within the hideous skull, and when it roared again, it was close enough to leave the stink of foul breath lingering in the air.

The two druids ducked behind a large boulder where the slope met the floor. Miradel cringed downward as the monster flew overhead, watched as the wings scraped rocks from the rock walls, sending trickles of debris spattering downward.

This time, however, the gargoyle did not climb away. Instead, it landed with a thud on the ground just after it flew past, furling its wings to stand on a strapping pair of legs. The creature stood three or four times taller than a man, though—aside from the broad wings—its appearance was startlingly humanoid. It pivoted to face the druids, and Miradel was stunned by the blazing force of its eyes: like twin orbs of fire set into a stone framework. She saw the broad, muscular chest, and a sinewy neck supported a head that was bestial in visage but manly in shape. The belly sagged downward, swaying grotesquely as the creature shifted its weight from foot to foot. When it growled, the gargoyle revealed a mouth full of long, sharp fangs, and the twin horns rising from its forehead looked sharp and lethal. It reached with a handlike forepaw, fingers studded with dagger-sized claws.

Shandira pitched a rock that, unnoticed by Miradel, she had taken up. The missile bounced off the snarling snout, shattering into shards. Immediately the beast drew itself to its full height, threw back that awful head, and roared.

"Drop your pack—run!" cried Miradel, knowing that was their only chance of survival.

The two women instantly shucked their loads, spun around, and sprinted away, Shandira halting just long enough to push Miradel before her. They ran around the S-shaped bends in the ravine floor, hearing the roars of the monster, the pounding cadence of its steps coming right behind.

After a hundred yards they met a crossing ravine, wider and straighter than this one as it extended to right and left. Miradel's first thought was that it was a likely route to the throne of the Deathlord; her second reminded her that their only chance was to find some narrow passage where the gargoyle could not pursue. She charged forward, crossing into the continuation of their original passage.

Here the narrow path started to descend, and this lent wings to their speed. At the same time, the walls grew steeper, closing in so that the gargoyle, even with wings tucked against its back, scraped roughly against the walls. The monster roared in rage as the route became more restricted, and from the fading sounds Miradel could tell that, at last, they were drawing away. The women sprinted so quickly that momentum carried Miradel right into the side when the corridor made a sharp turn. She simply pushed off and kept going, ignoring the pain in her scuffed palms, grateful that the sounds of pursuit grew farther and farther away.

"Here!" hissed Shandira, suddenly darting to the side. She grabbed Miradel's arm and pulled her after, drawing them both into a narrow niche beneath a flat, overhanging boulder. "Be quiet!" whispered the African woman.

They barely breathed as the gargoyle came loping after them. Miradel winced but made no sound as a taloned foot pounded the ground just a few inches from her own. In the next instant the creature was gone, growling and snapping as it hastened along the narrow track.

The druids waited for several minutes, until they were certain that the creature had continued on. Only then did they emerge, agreeing in a silent exchange of looks that they would return to the wide, crossing ravine and there seek a path to the throne of the Deathlord.

NATAC awakened to a gentle nudge. His reflexes, honed on the battlefield, caused him to sit upward and reach for his sword.

Then he recognized Belynda. She was kneeling beside

him. Dawn, the sun's initial descent toward Lighten, had just commenced, to judge from the pale violet of the sky.

"Come with me," whispered the sage-ambassador, "and I will show you Miradel."

Instantly he was up, following her through the garden until she came to a secluded glade. He wondered why she had changed her mind but didn't want to ask, not now. In the little clearing a small fountain spumed from a marble bowl, while an interlacing hedge of lilac screened them from observation in all directions. Natac's eyes fell upon the familiar shape of Belynda's Globe of Seeing, the crystal ball awaiting them on its velvet pillow, covered with a soft cloth.

The sage-ambassador sat on the stone bench and lifted the veil. Natac took a seat on the opposite side, his attention unwavering. He saw the darkness within the Globe slowly brighten until it was a pearly murk, still shadowy and indistinct but suggestive of someplace dark, dangerous, and forbidding.

"It is Lighten where Miradel is, just as it is Lighten here," Belynda explained. "But she sees precious little brightness from the sun."

Natac could make out the black gorge, the stone walls rising forbiddingly to both sides. Miradel was there, with Shandira, walking down the floor of this sheer-walled gorge. There was no sign of plant nor water on the barren ground.

"She has gone to Loamar, the land of death," Natac declared dully, certain in that instant of his identification. He looked at Belynda accusingly. "You sent her there. Why?"

"She insisted," Belynda said, not backing down from his gaze. "She thinks that the Deathlord may have a weakness, something that will allow us to battle him."

"She will die there," he replied, numb with despair.

"Perhaps," Belynda acknowledged unhelpfully. "But

there is a chance, a decent chance, that she will return. In any event, we have a plan, if she can find a swirl of water. And maybe she will learn something of great importance before she does."

"Why did the goddess deny her?" Natac wondered.

"I don't know. She told me that the Worldweaver did not want her to make this trip, said it was hopeless. But also, the goddess spoke in terms that made Miradel believe even she did not fully understand the nature of Karlath-Fayd. So she has gone to find out for herself. She has survived this far, and she draws closer to the Deathlord's citadel with every step."

"Strange . . . what can the Worldweaver fear?"

"I don't know, but that is why I decided I must show you and tell you. Since her goddess has apparently turned her back on her, you and I are all Miradel has."

"Indeed, she is not dead, not yet," said Natac, an agony of despair hushing his voice, "but she may as well be."

"Do not despair. I will watch her as much as I can. If there is something you can do, I will send for you. Beyond that, we can only try to do our jobs."

"I have been thinking," Regillix Avatar said, his voice sonorous and immensely dignified. He spoke to Natac and Belynda, to the sage-enchantress Quilene, and to Cillia and a score of fellow druids, including the ancient scholar Socrates who stood strangely intent, his wire-framed spectacles perched on his thin nose. To Natac, it seemed as though the elder druid was not really listening; nevertheless, his presence here indicated that the dragon had something rather thoughtful to say. The serpent cleared his throat and lowered his head so that he was looking at the humans and elves from very near their own level. "There is a place I could go for help in this war."

"Where?" asked Natac, more curious than hopeful. After all, he had spent the better part of five decades working on that very problem and had not been able to come up with any dramatic ideas.

Full daylight found this group arrayed near the lakeside, at the edge of one of the few fields large enough for the great serpent to land and, more important, take off again. The temple was nearby, the silver spire striving toward the fully bright sun. As if to punctuate the dragon's words, the goddess chose that moment to cast her threads. Humans, elves, and dragons waited patiently as the crackling ball of light slowly ascended the silver spire, finally exploding outward in a burst of lightning that blasted upward to vanish into the sky.

"A powerful storm of wild threads, today," Cillia said. "That bodes ill for Earth."

"These are days of ill tidings for many circles, including my homeland," the dragon continued. "But I intend to go there, to the Sixth Circle, Arcati. There are many dragons there, and some mighty angels. All of them, I am certain, would be willing to aid us in our cause."

"The Overworld?" Cillia sounded as surprised as Natac felt. "Even supposing you could get there, why would the dragons and angels go to war for Nayve?"

"The harpies have ever been the curse of our circle, hated by all creatures of knowledge and kindness. Dragons and angels both take a long view of existence and also of responsibility. When they learn that the harpies have come here, down the Worldfall, I believe they will want to pursue, to make war upon them in this place they do not belong. Furthermore, I understand more about the Deathlord than I ever knew before. As you druids have explained, this is a war not just to preserve Nayve, but to save all the cosmos. I believe this completely, and my fellow dragons will accept my word."

"I believe you completely, in turn," Natac said. "But that raises the far greater question: how can you return to a circle that lies on the other side of the sun?"

"That is the bigger problem, old friend of mine. I can only say what I am thinking about, not what I know."

Natac waited expectantly, and the dragon lowered his crocodilian head in an almost sheepish gesture. "I shall try to fly there," he explained.

"How? Fly past the *sun?* Impossible!" Voices murmured disbelief and outright shock, sounds that slowly faded as the dragon raised his head and, once again, looked lordly and imperial.

"I will make the attempt," he informed them. "And I shall have a little help. Perhaps my counselor would be good enough to explain?"

For the first time Natac saw that Socrates, far from daydreaming, was paying very close attention. The scholarly druid came forward and shrugged his shoulders tentatively. "There are forces hammering upon the Fourth Circle, as we all know. Most notably, the Worldfall.

"But less is understood of the counter to that force, in the region of Winecker. My analysis has shown that there are periods of great upheaval there, especially of wind. This, I believe, is air swelling upward in response to the power of the Worldfall. It is theoretically possible that someone—a flyer, of course—could exploit this upward current of air, riding it even beyond the Fourth Circle, perhaps all the way to the Overworld."

"Theoretically?" declared Natac. "But practically speaking, you'll burn up as you go past the sun!" Why did it seem as though all those he cherished were determined to throw their lives away on doomed, foolish quests?

"Not necessarily," Regillix Avatar demurred. "It will be hot, certainly, but I may survive. And in any event, I intend to try."

17

King of the Seer Dwarves

Monarch of sunless realm
Ruler of ever dark
'Neath the banner of coolfyre
Came the Lightbringer kings

From the Tapestry of the Worldweaver
Legions Under Coolfyre

The Goat Hair Inn was a worker's tavern, the kind of place Darann had rarely entered. She was grateful to have Konnor at her side as they passed through the door and seemed to draw every eye toward them. There were two or three dozen patrons, loosely assembled into groups at the low, stone tables; males outnumbered females by at least three to one.

She heard a low whistle of appreciation, but when Konnor took her arm, the other dwarves turned back to their conversation. The pair made their way between the tables to the bar, where the burly innkeeper was busy wiping out mugs with a somewhat grimy towel.

"What'll wet ye down today?" he asked.

Darann was about to ask about Greta Weaver, when Konnor pinched her arm and spoke. "We'll take a couple of ales from the cold cellar," he said pleasantly, dropping a gold coin onto the bar.

"Ah, the good stuff," replied the bartender.

As he went to draw the mugs, she leaned close to Konnor. "We're in a hurry, remember?"

"Yes," he replied calmly. "But we'll stand a much better chance of finding out what we need to know if we're happy customers, not strangers who come in asking a bunch of questions."

The wisdom of her companion's words was proven a short time later, when Darann found out that Greta Weaver had a room upstairs and that she had returned an hour ago from her job in the Royal Tower. "We don't rub elbows wi' the lordly types down here, not too much," the bartender explained. "But she's up there reg'lar, even sees the king now and then!"

They finished their drinks in a hurry and went up the stairs at the back of the common room, to the third door on the right, the room described by their host. Darann knocked quietly.

"Wh-who's there?"

"Greta? Greta Weaver?" asked Darann, responding to the tremulous voice. "Can you open up? I need to talk to you."

"No . . . go away," replied the pailslopper.

"Please . . . its important. It's a matter of life and death—not for you, but for a thousand, ten thousand, of our friends at the bottom of the hill!" She was pleading now, casting about for the right words, desperate to reach the frightened dwarfmaid. She didn't know what to say, and Darann was startled to see the door squeak open, a brown eye study her warily through the narrow crack.

"What friends?" asked Greta suspiciously.

Darann lowered her voice. "Hiyram told me that I

might find you here. I am the daughter of Rufus House-guard."

Finally the door opened all the way. Within was neither the scruffy serving wench nor the decrepit chamber that Darann had expected. Instead, Greta Weaver wore a brightly colored frock and maintained a very tidy room, brightly lit by a flamestone lamp. The pailslopper's face and hands were clean.

"How is Hiyram?" she asked, a tremor in her voice. "It's terrible, what they're doing . . . because they claim a gob killed a dwarfmaid!"

"But they didn't, did they?" Darann asked.

Greta shook her head. "It sounds like the kind of thing only Nayfal could do. But Hiyram—is he safe?"

"He's not safe, but he was alive when we left. Hiyram is doing the best he can to save his people. What we need to do is to help."

"But . . . how?" Greta asked. "What can we do? Your father tried to help, and Nayfal—"

"Yes, I know what Nayfal did to my father, and I thank you for trying to get word to me, to warn him." Darann reached into the pocket of her tunic and pulled out the golden letter tube. Quickly she opened it and pulled out the parchment. "Tell me, did you write this?"

Greta barely glanced at the page, then met Darann's eyes. "Yes."

"You say that Cubic Mandrill was Nayfal's toady. Do you mean the attempt on the king's life was a ploy, staged by Nayfal? In an attempt to turn the Seers against the goblins?"

"Yes, that's what the purpose was. And it worked perfectly. The king agreed to wall up the ghetto, to keep the goblins locked up. And they started to hate us, and this scourge happening right now—it was inevitable!"

"How do you know about Nayfal?" Konnor asked.

Greta Weaver sat straight and looked at them both, her expression defiant, even proud. "Cubic Mandrill was my father," she said. "He did not know that I knew what was happening, but I listened at the door. I was just a little girl. He and Nayfal paid me no attention, just sent me to bed. But I heard them make the plot."

"But your name is Weaver," Darann noted.

"I was married—to a soldier, who's dead, now. But I kept his name; I did not want the kind of attention the name Mandrill would have brought me."

"Will you tell the king what you just told me?" Darann asked, stunned.

Greta shook her head. "Nayfal would kill me!"

"Not if we can make the king believe you. Then you would have the protection of the crown and perhaps redeem the wrong done by your father," Konnor interrupted, "What we need is proof of this plot, proof that we can take to the king!"

"You told my father, in the letter, that you had proof. Do you?" pressed Darann.

"Yes, I have proof, here," Greta said. She went to a small chest at the foot of her bed, opened it, then took out a tiny strongbox, which she unlocked with a key she wore on a chain around her neck. She produced a small leather sack, and from that removed a very large golden circlet, a disk too large to be called a coin, though that is what it most resembled.

"My father insisted that Nayfal pay him with this. . . . I think he was worried about betrayal, later. But he never thought he'd be killed in the very act he was being paid to perform. He was just supposed to catch these goblins sneaking in to the throne room. They were going to be slaughtered by the Royal Guards. I think Nayfal made sure that Cubic was killed, too, because he was the only one who knew that the lord was behind the plot."

"Why didn't you tell someone about this years ago?" demanded Konnor, causing Greta to flinch as if she had been struck.

Darann placed a hand upon the warrior's shoulder. "Because she was a child," she said. "And who would have believed her? May I look at that?"

Greta gave her the golden disc, which was heavy enough to indicate that it was probably pure gold. It was crudely marked, as though it had been carved, not molded, but the dwarfmaid could clearly see the ornate "Nay" cut into one side, the payer's mark. The other side displayed a writing of "Cubic Mand," more legible than the lord's name; this was the receiver's mark.

"It's proof, some proof anyway, that Nayfal paid Cubic Mandrill for something," Darann agreed. "But we need more. Will you come with us to the Royal Tower? We're going to speak to the king!"

"I couldn't!" said Greta Weaver. "I'm only a pailslopper! He would never allow me—"

"It's no longer a question of what this city's masters will allow," retorted Darann. "It's a question of what we're willing to do."

"What would I have to do?" the pailslopper asked hesitantly.

"You have to avenge the loss of your father and give me a chance to avenge the murder of mine! Take us into the tower, and we'll make our way to the king somehow. Do you know the Royal Guard is in the ghetto right now, killing every goblin that comes within reach of a dwarven blade?"

Greta winced again, her eyes filling with tears. She shook her head, whether, in denial or pain Darann couldn't tell. "We *have* to stop them," the servant maid said at last. "I will come with you. But what do I tell the king?"

"Tell him what you know about Nayfal and your father!" Darann urged. "And we can only pray that's enough."

"I might have expected to find you two living among the goblins," Nayfal said with a sneer, strutting between the two prisoners—only after he had ordered that Borand and Aurand Houseguard be soundly trussed and forced to kneel on the cold, slimy paving stones of the ghetto street.

They glared at him soundlessly, though he could read the hate in their eyes. The intensity of their emotion gave him a little thrill, despite the fact that he found it somewhat frightening, as well. Walking this close to them, staring down into their faces, even touching the ropes that bound their arms so securely behind their backs . . . these things made him feel very brave.

"You just didn't ever learn your place or the goblins' place. In fact, that was your father's failure, as well. He was too soft on our enemies, too blind to see the threats dwelling right under his nose."

"Our father was ten times the Seer you will ever be," the younger one—his name was Aurand, the lord recalled—hissed. Despite his bonds and his helpless position, the dwarf did not seem frightened. "Know this, coward: he will be avenged!"

With a sudden lurch Aurand knocked a shoulder into Nayfal's hip, sending the dwarven nobleman staggering to the side. A guard stepped forward and cuffed the prisoner so hard that he toppled onto the flagstones. Nayfal, furious, gave him a sharp kick in the face. "Be careful about your talk of vengeance!" he snapped. "You are in no position to make threats!"

Spitting blood, the imprisoned Seer squirmed up from the ground, though the guards seized his shoulders to prevent him from rising off of his knees. Nayfal's hand closed around the hilt of his sword, the blade as yet unblooded in this night of pillage. He was tempted to draw, to stab this insolent dwarf right in the heart. Indeed, that would be the perfect complement to this raid that had turned out to be far more complicated than he had supposed it would be. He could slay the sons of Rufus Houseguard, gut them both, let each watch the other die. . . .

His sword was out, all but dancing in his grip. Which one first? That was easy: the young, impetuous one. Of course, he would need to make sure the other was securely bound. Who knew what efforts his grief might impel him toward?

But then a sense of caution held his blow. He considered: these two dwarves had been taken in the midst of the enemy camp, in fact as part of a group of goblins actively resisting the king's guards. What clearer proof of treachery could he hope to find? Indeed, this was a masterful stroke of luck, when he thought about it: the king was altogether too reluctant to see the danger right under his people's nose. Yet with this proof, dwarven captives—scions of an esteemed clan!—taken right out of the goblin mob, there could be no room for doubt, no mistaking the depths to which corruption had penetrated the Seer people.

Indeed, taking these two prisoners was about the luckiest thing that could have happened to him! Clearly, his best course of action was to take them to the monarch, and let King Lightbringer pass the only sentence that fit such a crime: execution for high treason.

There would be plenty of time, then, to watch them die.

"HERE, this is called the Pailslopper Gate," Greta Weaver said, holding her head high, as if challenging Darann to impugn her menial chore.

She had led them through quiet side streets over a distance of a mile or so, to bring them to the rear of the Royal Tower. This was a part of the king's palace that Darann had never seen. There were corrals for darkbulls nearby, the beasts snuffling and lowing and emanating their characteristic stink, and tiny shops where servants and other menial workers could purchase clothes and other items, including inexpensive food like pale fungus and blindfish that never would have found its way onto a table in one of the nicer quarters of Axial.

Finally she had brought them to this door, which was guarded by a lone, elderly palace guard. He had greeted Greta with a cheerful "Hello," then simply nodded to Darann and Konnor as they had accompanied her through.

"Thank you for getting us this far," said the lady of clan Houseguard. "You are giving us a chance to make a difference in the history of our people."

"Well, we'll have to do something," Greta said, shaking her head as if she still couldn't believe what she was involved in.

In another moment the trio had slipped through the anteroom and found the worker's lift that would lead to the many higher levels of the Royal Tower. This was a larger cage than Darann was used to; Greta explained that sometimes as many as a hundred workers were coming or going at one time, and the conveyance was needed to efficiently move these crowds. Now, fortunately, there were only a few dwarves—blacksmiths, to judge from their burly arms and leather aprons—waiting at the bottom. In a few minutes the cage arrived with a hiss of steam. The gate clanked open, and the trio entered behind the smiths.

"Level twelve," declared one of the workers, as the operator closed the mesh gate.

He looked toward Darann expectantly, but it was Greta who spoke. "Take us up to twenty-three."

The ride lasted for several minutes and passed in silence, except for some quiet banter among the metalworkers. The smiths departed at their destination, and the last eleven levels seemed to pass at a snail's pace. Finally the lift rattled to a halt at the twenty-third level, and they exited to find themselves in some sort of barracks room with several passages leading in different directions from this central chamber.

"The Royal Hall is two levels above here, but there is no lift station—not for the workers' lift—up there. This is where the maids get dressed for work. If we can find a friendly face, I think I can get us up to the throne. Of course, then we have to hope that we find the king there. If he's in his private quarters, there's no way we'll get past the guards."

She started down one of the corridors, and Darann immediately noticed a large iron door, secured with a massive lock. She heard sounds of steam and hammering coming from behind the portal and asked Greta about it.

"That's where that crazy engineer is working on his Worldlift," the pailslopper reported. "I don't know why they waste the time. But they say that shaft goes all the way through the Midrock, to Nayve if you can believe it, before the blue magic barrier closed it off."

"I've known Donnwell Earnwise all my life," Darann pointed out. "He's about the smartest dwarf I've ever met. If anyone can make a Worldlift work, I think it would be him!"

Greta merely shrugged. "I don't know why anyone would want to go to Nayve, anyway. We've got everything we need down here." She was only echoing a senti-

ment believed by many dwarves, Darann knew, choosing
not to argue the point. Even so, she recalled the warm sun,
the waves on seas and lakes, the green hills and vales with
suddenly poignant affection. She wished that, somehow,
she would be able to see those wonders again, just once
before she died.

"There he is!" Greta whispered excitedly, waving at a
man-at-arms who was just coming through a door at the
end of the corridor. "Larson! Hello!"

"Why, Greta!" declared the dwarf, beaming like a fellow who has just seen a woman toward whom he holds a
great deal of affection. "This *is* a pleasure; I thought they
had you on the first shift, these days. I miss our little—"
For the first time he apparently noticed the two other
dwarves accompanying his sweetheart. "Um, talks."

"Me, too," Greta said, her tone lighter than it had been
at any point since their meeting at the Goat Hair Inn. She
might have been a young maiden, stopping to flirt with
her handsome soldier; indeed, Darann thought, that was
exactly what she was.

Yet Greta showed that she was not lacking a certain capacity for guile. "This is my cousin Dari, from the Metalreach, and her husband. . . . She's in the city for a few
cycles and has never been up here. I told her there was a
chance we might be able to spot the king—you know,
from the wings of the throne room. Do you know, is he in
the hall?"

"You're in luck," Larson said, then lowered his voice
and looked around furtively. "Not too happy about it, he
ain't. Was all set for bed, when he got a message that Nayfal needed to see him. Something about the troubles in the
ghetto. Anyway, he's on his way up, and the king is waiting for him."

"Can you *please* be a dear and let us in the side door?"
Greta asked, giving the warrior's arm a squeeze.

"Why, I surely can," he replied, blushing. "But you'll have to promise to be quiet—*mouse* quiet! When he's in a mood like this, it won't do to be disturbing him."

"Oh, you know how quiet I can be," Greta said with a wink. "And Dari can do the same, right?"

"Mouse quiet," Darann assured him.

"All right—come this way, then."

The friendly guard turned around led them through the door he had just exited, taking Greta's hand as they started up a stairway. Darann's heart was pounding, and her stomach churned nervously as they climbed several flights and at last came to a door guarded by two Royal Guards.

"A little late work," Larson said, nudging one of the guards, who grinned in return. Darann was certain the thumping in her chest was loud enough to raise an alarm, but somehow she managed to smile charmingly. The guard smiled back, then opened the door to allow them to pass through.

"Thanks—you're a sweetheart," Greta said, giving Larson a quick kiss on the cheek. He quickly pulled her close and gave her a more intimate embrace, smacking her on the buttocks as she finally broke free.

"You know where to find me," he said, looking at her seriously. "And I meant it, Gret—I really *miss* you!"

"I'll find you soon!" she promised, then pulled away. "This way," she said to Darann and Konnor.

"Thanks, friend," Konnor said to the guard as the trio started down another hall.

This one opened into a wide chamber, lit by numerous coolfyre chandeliers, and Darann felt her nervousness rise again. This was the throne room! Greta led them forward, and they saw that they were on a side platform that was itself the size of a large banquet hall, raised twenty or thirty feet above the truly expansive hall of the Seer dwarf king.

They moved past a pile of folded linens, then around a

compartment where mops and buckets were stacked. Clearly this was some kind of housekeeping area, Darann deduced. Because it was raised so far above the main floor, they were able to advance almost to the edge without exposing themselves to view from the floor below.

There was a stone wall, about waist height, at the edge of the servants' balcony, and when they made their way to this, they were concealed by shadows and that wall but able to see some of what was happening in the great room below.

The first thing Darann thought was that this chamber was the last place her father had been before he died. So much history had been made here . . . and, lately, so much corruption had been worked, to steer that history. Would that ever change? She resolved that she would do everything in her power to see that it did.

She looked around. The arched ceiling was at least a hundred feet overhead. Stone columns stood out from the walls, twelve of them rising all the way to the top, merging into the arches that all melded together in the center of the high vault. At four places around the room, including where they stood right now, there were raised platforms, allowing for a good view of the wide hall. These upper alcoves were all cloaked in shadow, though the main floor of the chamber was bathed in cool, white light.

And it was that floor that drew their attention.

Darann could see King Lightbringer, seated upon his high throne. A half dozen royal guardsmen, dressed in the ceremonial golden helms denoting palace duty, were arrayed around his seat. Aside from a few servants standing close to the walls, there was no one else visible in the great room. Darann quickly noticed that the guards and the king seemed to be directing their attention to the main doors. As she looked that way herself, those lofty portals were opened, and a servant in red livery stepped forward to announce.

"Lord Nayfal comes from the battle—and he brings two prisoners!"

Darann stiffened as the hated nobleman strode arrogantly forth. It was all she could do to restrain a cry of shock when she saw the prisoners, as her brothers were prodded forward by four armored Seers. From their mud-caked uniforms, she guessed that all of this group had come here directly from the ghetto.

Konnor gasped beside her, and when his hand went to his sword, she laid restraining fingers gently upon his arm.

"Your brothers!" he whispered urgently. "They're captive!"

"I know," she replied. "And we'll get them free—but we need to wait until the time is right!"

Greta looked at them in alarm, raising her finger to her lips in a gesture for silence. Darann nodded and crouched down so that she could listen and see right over the rim of the wall.

"Your Majesty!" proclaimed Nayfal, sweeping into the room with a flourish. "I am grateful that you consented to see me at this late hour. I bring word from the ghetto—important word!"

"Very well, good lord," said the king with a sigh. "Tell me why you summon me here thus."

"I have here, sire, nothing less that a proof of the most base treachery—treachery lurking in an esteemed family, plainly writ for all of Axial to see."

Aurand started to say something and was silenced by a brutal cuff from one of the guards, a blow from the hilt of his sword to the young dwarf's skull that staggered him. With a groan, Aurand slumped to his knees, but not before

Darann could see that his face was bloody, with one eye swollen shut.

"Who are these dwarves?" demanded the king, this time speaking with a little determination in his voice.

"Brothers, sire . . . the two sons of Rufus Houseguard. They were captured in the midst of a mob of goblins, having taken up arms against your own Royal Guard. As I said, clear proof of treachery."

"Borand Houseguard, I know you—I thought—as a loyal soldier, one of my ferr'ell masters. Is this true?" asked King Lightbringer, fixing the elder brother with a stern glare. "Explain yourself."

"Sire, I am innocent of treason," Borand declared. "My brother and I were working to prevent treachery, to uncover truths that we might bring to your attention."

"Cease your impudence!" Nayfal snapped, taking a step toward the prisoner.

"Lord Nayfal!" the king barked. "Let him speak."

"Of course, sire," replied the nobleman with a deep bow. "But beware of his sweet words. All these men, here, will testify that he was taken in league with the goblins. There is blood on his blade—the blood of your own guardsmen!"

"What is the treachery of which you speak?" Lightbringer said, addressing Borand.

"There is a plot at work, sire . . . a plot to convince you that the goblins are our enemies. It began forty years ago, with the attempt on your life . . . the scheme that claimed the life of Cubic Mandrill. And it continues to this day, with the murder of the dwarfmaid beyond the ghetto wall. That was not the act of goblins, Your Majesty."

"I have heard these allegations before," said the king impatiently. "But no one has brought proof."

Darann stood and found herself speaking loudly, her

words carrying through the great hall. "I have proof, Your Majesty!"

The king looked up, shocked, while guards shouted in alarm and started running toward the balcony.

"Guards, to the stairs!" cried Nayfal, blanching. "Sieze her! Beware another attempt on the king's life!"

"Stay!" roared King Lightbringer, and the lord, the guards, the prisoners, Darann, and her companions all froze at the force of that one word. The monarch squinted up at the balcony as Darann stepped to the top of the stairway leading down to the floor. "I know you, too," Lightbringer said. "You are Darann of clan Houseguard, wife of the hero Karkald," he said. Then he frowned. "These would be your brothers."

His scowl deepened. "Your brothers are prisoners, and your family is accused of treachery. Strong proof is required against these charges."

"I bring proof and a witness, sire," she replied, as Greta and Konnor came up to stand beside her. As the king waved them forward, they descended toward the floor, and an escort of guards flanked them as they approached the throne.

"And who are these?" asked the king.

"Konnor is another of your loyal soldiers, sire, one of your Rockriders. He has seen to my safety, when there have been those who would have killed to prevent me coming here."

"I see. And the maid?"

"This is the daughter of Cubic Mandrill, Your Majesty. She knows the true story of how he died."

Darann addressed the king, but her eyes were on Nayfal as she spoke. The lord's face twisted in fury at her words, and he looked about frantically, no doubt seeking some escape from the net closing about him.

"Your father was a great hero," said the king to Greta.

"I did not know he left behind a child, else I would have taken care to see that your needs were met. I am sorry to learn this so late."

"I have done fine by myself," Greta replied calmly. "And I seek no bounty on the name of my father. I tell you truly: he was no hero—he was a traitor who schemed to fix our people's hatred against the goblins."

"Liar!" shouted Nayfal, growing pale. He drew his dagger and lunged forward with shocking speed. "I will silence your slanderous tongue."

Konnor reacted faster than Darann—or their guards— could see, stepping forward and knocking the lord's weapon hand to the side. Nayfal twisted away and raised the weapon for another strike when the king's words held him.

"Let her speak, my lord. And know that such impetuous displays do you no favors!"

Darann saw that Greta was shaking, and she stepped forward to put an arm around the younger dwarfmaid. "Show him the coin."

Still trembling, Greta drew the leather bag from her belt pouch and tugged at the drawstring, finally opening it. She stepped forward, Darann at her side and Konnor behind, while alert Royal Guards closed in from either side.

"It is a forgery, sire! An attempt to smear my name!" cried the nobleman, hurrying forward as well. Apparently sensing that the king was not listening, he lapsed into worried silence, his fingers caressing the hilt of his dagger.

"Your majesty, this was given to my father as payment for his part of the scheme. He was to discover the goblins in your palace. They were exactly where Lord Nayfal told him they would be, since the lord had paid them to be there. My father arrested them, but when Lord Nayfal came to claim the prisoners, a scuffle ensued. Cubic Mandrill *and* the goblins were killed. The lord was credited with saving our king, and my father was labeled a hero for uncovering a plot, when in fact he was paid for his presence at that exact time and place."

King Lightbringer took the golden disk and studied it for a long time. Lord Nayfal started to stammer something, but the monarch gestured him to silence. Finally, he raised his eyes, his gaze falling directly onto Nayfal.

"Why?" The word was short, as abrupt as the fall of an executioner's axe. "Why would you betray me, betray us all, thus? Do you know the evil that has been wrought in the last forty years, because I *trusted* you?"

Nayfal shook his head frantically. "That's just it, Your Majesty. There is no good reason for me to go to such lengths!" He stared pleadingly at the king, but for a second his eyes shifted to Darann—and in that second, she understood.

"He did it because he lied about the battle at Arkan Pass—and that means Karkald is alive. He must be in Nayve!" she declared suddenly. "The marshal must realize this; that's why he has turned the whole of your attention inward, sire! It is always the goblins that must be controlled, or defenses prepared against the Delvers massing just beyond the range of our light beacons! Who has fought your efforts to commission the Worldlift more urgently than Nayfal? It is because his secret will be revealed if ever we open up travel between our world and Nayve!"

"More lies!" shrieked Nayfal.

Once again the dagger was in his hand. In a bestial fury, he charged at Darann. This time Konnor met the blow with his own sword drawn—a quick slash that cut the lord's wrist to the bone. Nayfal screamed and stumbled back, and the infuriated Rockrider closed, knocking him to the ground with a punch. Shaking with rage, Konnor stood over the fallen lord and pressed the tip of his blade through the tangle of the noble dwarf's beard.

"Tell the truth!" he snarled. "Or by all the Seven Circles, I'll cut your heart out. What happened to Karkald?"

Nayfal started to blubber a denial, then screamed and gurgled as the sword sliced the skin of his throat. "No—I will tell!" he shrieked.

Konnor eased the pressure of his weapon enough to allow the dwarf to draw a gasping breath. Blubbering, Nayfal squirmed, finally speaking when the sword pressed down again. "Magic—he was taken by blue magic after Arkan Pass . . . the Delvers, too . . . all of them raised up . . . the blue magic came and surrounded them—and they were gone!"

"To Nayve!" Darann repeated with certainty, her hopes rising to heights they had not attained for decades. "That's where they were taken!"

"Yes—at least, it stands to reason. The barrier itself is blue magic," Borand declared. "It comes from the same source."

"Your Majesty!" Nayfal croaked. "Do not be misguided—the goblins—"

"The goblins have suffered and died to bring you this information, sire," Darann interrupted. "Make no mistake; hundreds of them have perished in the last few hours, and more are being killed every minute—in Your Majesty's name!"

"But they killed a dwarfmaid—poured hot oil over her!" the king protested. "A brutal murder!"

"Brutal indeed, but who committed that murder, sire?" Darann retorted. "Did you see the goblins do this—or did Nayfal tell you that's what happened?"

"Of course I didn't see," the king snapped. "But I had the report—from . . ." His glowering gaze fell upon the hapless lord, who had risen to his feet. "Another lie, my lord, isn't it?" Lightbringer drew a deep sigh. "A lie that has resulted in more innocent bloodshed."

He glowered, sitting straight in his throne, seeming to grow as they looked at him. "You, more than anyone else, has crusaded against the malignance of treason. Yet now it seems that you are treason's most able practitioner. To this end you have caused to be murdered an innocent dwarfmaid, a palace guard—if he was corrupt, he was corrupted by your hand—and countless goblins. You have much blood on your hands. There can be only one sentence for such treachery."

"No!" the lord screamed. He broke away, starting toward the back doors to the great hall.

"Stop him!" the king snapped, as some of his guards drew their swords and the archers, near the door, raised their crossbows. "Immediately!"

It was over in another instant, the twang of a crossbow spring shockingly loud in the lofty chamber. The echoes lingered even after Nayfal, shot through, fell to the floor and lay still.

18

Roads to High Circles

When the wyrm made his High Flight
All the cosmos held its breath

From *The Last Ascent of Regillix Avatar*
by Sirien Saramayd

The elves of Barantha reached the Ringhills first, but it was the trolls, arriving at that natural barrier a full day later, who made the real difference in preparing the defenses. Jubal spoke to Awfulbark even as the lanky forest dwellers were spreading wearily along the outer slope of the hills, and that worthy king responded with an energy that the Virginian found deeply gratifying.

"We can dig a ditch and pile up a dirt wall, sure," Awfulbark declared. "Where you want?"

"Up the slope a short distance," the man explained. "So that the ghost warriors have to start climbing the hill before they get to the ditch. But close enough to the bottom that archers on the wall will be able to shoot arrows into the enemy troops as they gather at the foot of the hill."

He showed the trolls where to collect picks and shovels, the tools that continued to arrive by the wagonload from King Fedlater's miners on Dernwood Downs. Im-

mediately Awfulbark's warriors set out along the line and
wasted no time in displaying their great capacity for dirt
moving. Natac had selected the forward slope of the first
ridge for the position, some hundred feet above the table-
top expanse of dry plains extending Nullward from this
section of the hills, and Jubal had the elves mark off the
proposed excavation with flags and pickets.

"Dig it deep enough so that the bastards will fall into
the ditch," he ordered, demonstrating at the barrier of the
sharp-walled trench. Then he marked out the sample of
the wall, the obstacle the enemy would have to attack as
soon as they crawled through the ditch. "And make this
high enough and steep enough that the bastards will roll
right back down into the ditch again!"

The Argentian elves arrived as the work was beginning, and both Tamarwind and Kelland set their warriors
to helping. For the most part the elves were mere by-
standers, however, as the trolls attacked the ground with
relentless chopping pickaxes, then scooped away the
loose rubble with a churning of shovels. Jubal watched as,
minute by minute, the long ditch grew deeper, the match-
ing wall climbing higher above the rugged slope.

Within another forty-eight hours, the fringe of the
rocky rise was scoured by a trench and adjacent breastwork some thirty miles in length. Each hilltop along that
winding path had been turned into a palisade in its own
right, surrounded by an earthen wall, with a flat platform
excavated as a mount for one of Gallupper's batteries. Un-
fortunately, the line was so long that not every hilltop
could be defended with one of the lethal guns, and even
those thus equipped had but one. That weapon would have
to be wheeled into position for shooting forward or toward either flank.

Jubal's troops were deployed thinly along that long
line, but he was pleased that so much of the approach

could be covered. As he strode along the crest of the wall he was reminded of a great fortification on Earth—he had learned about it, seen pictures in a book, when he had been a child in Virginia. It was a wall thousands of miles long, protecting the entire northern border of China; it was not hard to imagine that, given a little more time, Awful-bark's trolls would be able to create a barrier of similar extent.

This was a useful realization, for he knew that the hills presented a more than four-hundred-mile circumference around the entire span of Circle at Center and its great lake. If the ghost warriors moved to one side or the other, then the defenders would have to follow the same course. Fortunately, many parts of the range were precipitous and jagged, with lots of sheer cliffs and deep gorges. He knew that those were places no army would try to traverse.

Other places were more vulnerable, however, and if the enemy changed the direction of its advance, he and Natac would simply have to move their army to one side or the other to continue to block the approach to the city. It was a tactic eerily similar to that employed by Robert E. Lee in his defense of Richmond. Jubal tried not to dwell on the fact that, for the Army of Northern Virginia, these maneuvers had eventually, perhaps inevitably, resulted in defeat.

For the first day the scouts reported that the attackers were coming across the plain like a flood, a great dark stain across the ground. The ghost warriors were loosely formed into columns, but each of these was a mile or more across, composed of a seemingly endless number of plodding, purposeful killers. The dust raised by these massive formations formed a self-sustaining cloud in the sky, and by Lighten of the second day this murk was visibly approaching the Ringhills, an ominous storm.

As that day progressed and the trolls and elves and the few surviving gnomes labored to deepen the ditch and raise the dirt wall of their immense palisade, the columns themselves came into view. From his vantage on a high hilltop Jubal thought they looked like snakes, great black predators, reptilian in nature, slithering closer and closer to the Ringhills and the Center of Everything.

Gradually, toward sunset of that day, another force became visible, marching from the direction of Riven Deep. These were the Delvers, the general knew. As they came closer, he could begin to make out the gigantic iron golems striding among their number. If all remained as it was, the dwarves would fall upon the far right flank of his earthwork barrier, while the ghost warriors would come up against the center and the left.

Near the Hour of Darken the Hyaccan elves rode forward in a great raid, harassing one of the columns with a shower of lethal arrows. As dusk closed around the massive formation, the elves turned their nimble ponies and scampered away. None of the riders was wounded, but neither did their attack seem to inflict any perceptible delay upon the great column.

The night's approaching darkness seemed exceptionally complete. The ghost warriors built no campfires nor fires of any kind, so only the camp of the Delvers was visible from the heights. And even that small portion of the attacking army seemed to kindle a million fires, blazes winking like stars across a great swath of the plain.

Finally Jubal went to the high hill crest near the very center of the line, the elevation he had taken to calling Hill Number One. There was a pool of water there, and—as they did every Darken and Lighten—a trio of druids began to spin the water. This was to allow teleportation from Circle at Center or elsewhere. Idly the Virginian watched the scene, half expecting the twinkling lights to indicate that someone was arriving magically.

When nightfall passed with nothing happening, he

stepped to the edge of the parapet and looked out over the plain, trying to hide his concern. But he couldn't help wondering:

When would Natac return?

"I think this has a very good chance of working!" Donnwell Earnwise said. "Better than fifty percent, for sure."

"That's not good enough!" Borand said to the engineer before turning to his sister. "This is crazy; I forbid you to go!"

Aurand, standing beside his brother, simply laughed. "Haven't you learned anything about our sister?" he asked. "What makes you think you can forbid her to do *anything*, once she's made up her mind?"

Darann looked at her brothers with affection, then turned to King Lightbringer, who stood with Konnor almost diffidently, a little way back from the dwarves of clan Houseguard.

"Truly, my dear," said the monarch of the Seer dwarves, "If you wait a little while, we can run some additional tests, try to increase the chances of success. The Worldlift . . . well, it is a good idea in theory, and certainly it can be made to work— eventually. But we really don't know, not yet, anyway."

"I have faith in Uncle Donnwell," she said, winking at the engineer. "And I have waited fifty years to find out what happened to my husband. I don't plan to wait another interval longer, not one!"

"Very well," said the king. He turned to the engineer. "You have my permission."

"Splendid!" declared Donnwell, scratching his beard, then peering through his thick glasses at the blueprint spread out on the stone table. "Ah, yes—there is a blast radius—the rest of you had best withdraw behind the iron door."

"Blast?" Borand said. "What about my sister? You're going to blast her?"

"Yes, that's precisely the point," declared the engineer, blinking in confusion.

"Why doesn't *she* have to get behind the iron door?"

"Dear me, I thought you understood the point of the Worldlift. You see, the cage is powered by a rocket. When I ignite this fuse, the fuel explodes, coming out the bottom here in a great rush of heat and smoke. It is the inverse of that force, in fact, that propels the rocket, and the passenger, upward. By the time they reach the summit of the First Circle, they will be going so fast that, theoretically, they will penetrate the barrier of blue magic. Within a matter of hours she will find herself in the upper reaches of the Midrock, safely on her way to Nayve.

"You recall, of course, that this chute is a straight route all the way to the Fourth Circle, right to the Center of Everything, in fact. It was bored out two centuries ago and used for trade—cargo hauling up and down—until the barrier of blue magic put a stop to that."

"Theoretically? Upper reaches of the Midrock?" Borand was still fretful. "I just don't like the sound of this. I think I should go instead."

"In the future, good lad, we shall all go, but this prototype, I tried to explain, has but the capacity for a single passenger."

"And that passenger is me!" Darann said. "Now, will you all stand back and let Uncle Donnwell do his work?"

They did as she requested, her brothers reluctantly and Konnor, too, holding back. He took her hand and spoke seriously. "I . . . I hope you find him," he said. "And I hope he knows how much you care, how much he means to you."

"Thank you, my friend . . . for everything," she said.

Next she stepped through a low hatch into a circular metal room with a single chair—a chair with its back on the floor, oriented so that one who sat in it faced the ceiling. Donnwell fussed over an array of straps and buckles, taking care that she was properly fastened in.

"This shield over your head," he explained, "is solid steel, two inches thick. It should deflect any obstructions that have fallen into the Rockshaft over the last fifty years. And the rocket has enough fuel to carry you all the way to Nayve—so long as you penetrate the blue magic barrier."

It was as the iron door clanged shut that she became afraid and suddenly felt very, very lonely. She thought of Karkald, wondered if she was doing the right thing. If he was alive, in Nayve, then she *was* doing the right thing. And if he was dead, it really didn't matter. Once she reached that understanding, she felt better, more confident.

Until she heard the sputtering of the fuse, and all her misgivings returned tenfold. A few seconds later, there was a powerful rumble, as of something seizing her chair and shaking it violently back and forth. Smoke billowed around her, choking her nostrils, stinging her eyes. It was very hot, as if a furnace had ignited beneath her chair. Explosives roared with a sound like uncontained thunder.

And then, the violence really began.

"LET'S stay close to the wall; we'll be harder to spot that way," Miradel whispered. Shandira nodded and shrank against the dark stones where the cliff met the floor of the winding ravine.

They were following a passage that was considerably wider than the one where they had fled from the diving gargoyle. Another day had passed as they made their way deeper into the citadel, and still they had not encountered the vast hall of the Deathlord. But Miradel was confident that this major ravine, gently descending as it did, was taking them in the proper direction.

Their progress was slow because they advanced in short dashes, moving from one place of cover to the next. They hadn't seen the stony guardian for several hours, but neither of them was inclined to take any chances. Finding shelter in narrow cracks in the cliff wall, against the base of overhanging cliffs, even under flat boulders, they were scraped and sore, dirty and weary.

But they managed to keep moving.

How long they had been following this passage, Miradel couldn't begin to recall. It seemed like it was becoming a way of life, an eternal journey toward a place that didn't really exist, a survival of hiding, where life itself depended upon avoiding discovery.

Until they came around a final bend in the widening ravine, and the cliff walls terminated to either side. They were faced with a steep drop, perhaps a hundred feet down a slope of large, tumbled talus, that spill of stone spreading, fanlike, onto the floor of a vast basin. High, black mountains surrounded the depression, which was at least a mile in diameter. The feet of these summits were sheer blocks of stone, descending to the flat floor around the entire periphery, except for the six or eight places, like this ravine, where gaps in the surrounding mountains created passages into this place. The background sky, across the bowl, was an impermeable, lifeless black—the end of all worlds.

"This is the Throne of the Deathlord," Miradel breathed, staring through the shadows at the cliff on the far side of the basin. "You see the two eyes, glowing so high above."

"Yes," Shandira breathed, hushed and awestruck.

The glowing beacons of those fiery orbs burned in the air, suspended a hundred feet above the mountain shelf that served as a seat for that mighty throne. As the druids watched, the fire seemed to swell, an inferno of evil power growing as if in response to their intrusive presence.

It was difficult to discern much detail through the shadows—only as she tried did Miradel realize that night had fallen—but she was utterly certain this was the place. The images she had seen in the Tapestry were perfectly mirrored here, even to the extent of the vast blankness rising above the mountains on the far side of the valley. There, in the direction that was neither metal nor wood, she knew that she was looking at the very terminus of the cosmos.

"Let's start across now, while it's dark," Shandira whispered, her lips close to Miradel's ear. Soundlessly, the elder druid nodded.

They began to pick their way down the talus slope, feeling big rocks shift and wobble from the impact of their passage. The footing was irregular, with wide gaps to drop between or narrow crests to teeter along. Miradel went first, exerting great care to keep any of the stones from tumbling free. A rockslide that trapped them here might be deadly in its own right; in any event, it was certain to attract the attention of the one who was entrusted with guarding this place.

Without speaking they adopted the safest formation, each of them descending at the same elevation, side by side but some twenty feet apart. If one of them did start a slide, at least she minimized the chances of catching her companion, below, in the path of destruction. Miradel felt as though she was walking down a stairway of slippery bricks. She took care to test each foothold, very gradually, before putting all of her weight on it.

Several times they heard the rumble followed by a

clunk of a boulder shifting slightly, rebalancing in the loose pile. Once a small rattle of debris skittered downward, shockingly loud in the still night. Miradel gasped and froze, seeing the outline of a similarly motionless Shandira to her side. For several minutes they remained still, and as the soft echoes swiftly faded, there was no other sound that rose from the night in response.

Finally they continued, even more gingerly. How long it took to complete the descent was far beyond Miradel's awareness. By the time they reached the bottom, however, her shirt was soaked through with sweat, and in the chilly air this dampness seemed to penetrate right into her bones. They paused to rest for a few minutes and soon her teeth were chattering.

"We'd better get moving," she said. "I'd hate to get this close and then die of exposure!"

"I admit . . . I'd hate to die for just about any reason, if I didn't have to," Shandira said. "So, let's go."

They started across the flat floor of the bowl-shaped valley. In the sky were myriad shifting stars overhead, while the great throne of the Deathlord rose like a miniature mountain itself. The gray shape atop that throne was barely visible, utterly motionless, except for the crimson slits of its eyes.

They were perhaps halfway across when Miradel saw something fly across the vista of the stars. The two druids were far from any shelter, could do nothing but stand in fear and wait as the gargoyle glided to the ground and came to rest before them, sitting squarely astride their approach to the Deathlord's throne.

"I am ready."

With these words, the ancient serpent tried to convey a sense of farewell and love, sentiments he felt perhaps more deeply than any mere human could know. He saw that Natac was moved beyond his own ability to reply, the man reaching out to touch a hand to the smooth scales of the long, supple neck.

The night was dark around them, this pair who had come together on the lakeshore for a farewell that might be their last meeting. For fifty years they had flown and fought together, forming a partnership of leadership and power that had mustered one of the great armies in the history of the Seven Circles.

Regillix Avatar had, for all his life, been a solitary, remote, and aloof creature. He had lived for nearly ten thousand years, most of that time in the cloud world of Arcati, the Sixth Circle. Yet he was forced now to acknowledge that this most recent half century had been the most profoundly important part of his life. Now he was strangely reluctant to bid farewell to this place, these people . . . this man, in particular.

Yet Darken was progressing, nearly halfway along by now, and the serpent knew that he had a long way to fly before dawn. He had talked to Socrates and made the plan that seemed most likely to work, but this required him to be high over the region of Winecker at the Lighten Hour. The scholar had speculated that, in addition to the rising current opposite the Worldfall, the descent of the sun would create a reverse pressure away from the center of Nayve, and Regillix Avatar would try to ride that draft of air all the way through the region of intense heat. Then he would rely on his own strength to lift him to the Overworld.

"It is time to go," he said. "You will return to the army at Lighten, and I will try to return home."

"Good luck, old friend," said Natac.

"And to you, as well."

With that he was off, springing into the air, then wing-

ing low over the smooth lake, using leisurely strokes of
his wings to climb as he approached the far shore. He
passed over the Ringhills, almost directly opposite the
crest where the army of Nayve was preparing to stand,
and continued to climb as the ground below faded into a
patchwork of broad forests and wide lakes. Mist rose off
the water, obscuring much of the landscape, and the
dragon was strongly reminded of his own world.

Now he started to climb in earnest. He felt the draft rising around him, and as the Lighten Hour drew near he
rested, coasting on widespread wings, and even then he
continued to rise. He began to allow himself a measure of
hope.

The sun began to brighten, and he knew that it was descending toward Nayve. He spread his great pinions again
and began to stroke the air, heading away from the center,
the sun's rays warming his back as he flew. Regillix
worked easily to gain altitude, trying to conserve his
strength for when he would really need it.

Full Lighten drew near, and the wind against his belly
became a rush, air pushing upward with relentless force,
bearing him away from Nayve now with a hurricane
force. The sun was hot, hotter than he had ever imagined,
but still he kept his back to it, wings spread, riding the
powerful updraft. Wind blasted and buffeted his belly and
underwings, and he fought for control, trying to master
the air. He caught the power of the rising drafts, climbing,
soaring skyward, leaving Nayve an invisible distance
below.

Until the heat began to sear him. He squirmed and
twisted, desperate to escape the scalding fire that seemed
to rage across his back, as if it would melt his scales
and bake his flesh. But he kept his wings spread, and the
wind blew, and it seemed that his body was burning

away. Yet the mighty dragon could only drift upon the wind between worlds.

THE sage-ambassador teleported him at Lighten, and in an instant Natac arrived at the pool on Hill Number One. Jubal and Tamarwind were there, both greeting him with visible relief, supporting him as the disorientation from the magic spell sent him reeling away from the casting pool. "Thanks," he said after a moment, shaking his arms free, standing steadily again.

It did not surprise him to realize that, here among the troops of his army, he felt more at home than he did anywhere else in the cosmos. He clasped the hands of man and elf, then turned to inspect the scene of the imminent battle.

As Natac surveyed this scene from his hilltop, he found it hard to find any shred of hope. His memory of Miradel came back: the shape in the darkness, running for her life through the labyrinth of the Deathlord. A voice nagged at him: he should ignore this fight, turn his back on these armies, and go to the woman he loved.

To rescue her, or to die with her. It didn't matter, not really . . . nothing mattered. Why shouldn't they be together now, as they faced the end of all worlds?

But he could not do that, for he knew that, if he was gone, this army was doomed. Never before had he felt the weight of command as such an immense burden. Now it was a trap bearing him down, smothering, suffocating. In one way or another it would kill him, he knew.

It was well past midnight when he got the only dash of good news from this long, dark day. Horas of Gallowglen buzzed up to the hilltop and did an aerial bow before the general. The bounce in his flight suggested something other than disastrous tidings, Natac observed with interest.

"You have some more helpers," the faerie reported. "Roland Boatwright is here with the warriors and druids from his fleet. There are many of them, half a thousand druids and that many warriors, too. And Crazy Horse has come with them."

Reinforcements! And not just additional bodies; Natac knew that the each of the little boats had been crewed by a powerful, windcasting druid, accompanied by one of the veteran human warriors brought from Earth. These veterans would be immeasurably useful in the defense of the wall.

"Tell them I will be right there," said General Natac. He followed the direction of the faerie's flight as he started down the hill, toward the campfires of his own army. He knew that those blazes were warm and friendly, but they seemed paltry and feeble when contrasted to the vast darkness of the encompassing night.

19

Faces of the Deathlord

Shadows of silence,
Nightmares of death;
Mem'ries of violence,
Shortage of breath;

Shades shout "Hail!"
And pray
To the mistress of fate.

From the Tapestry of the Worldweaver
Bloom of Entropy

Regillix Avatar was past the sun now, barely conscious as he drifted upward on the blast of the hot, dry wind. His wings smoldered, seared by the intense heat. He closed the protective inner lids over his eyes, reducing his visibility to a cloudy murk, and even that wasn't enough to insulate him from the massive, fiery orb.

He lapsed into a kind of torpid agony, his body numbed to all sensation, reducing the awful pain to something he could at least tolerate. Water . . . he thirsted for the life-giving kiss of water, but there was none to be had, not even a cloud in these parched skies. There was just that air, as hot and dry and crushing as if it emerged from a blast furnace. It pushed him from below, rushing past in an explosion of wind, seemed to dry out every drop of moisture in his flesh.

Even in the depths of his groggy pain, however, the mighty dragon realized that it was the very force of this air that gave him a chance of surviving. He still rode his massive wings, extending those vast membranes to either side. No longer did he have the strength to stroke, to pull his way upward through the labor of his muscles. But still he continued to rise, because the air was bearing him upward with such force. The cosmic draft between the worlds was flowing fast, a strong current of air—Socrates had been right—countering the Worldfall, aided by the surge of Nayve's Lighten, it lifted him, bore him toward home.

Gradually a new awareness penetrated his mind; he knew that time was passing, that the day of Nayve would be approaching its end. At the Hour of Darken the sun would begin to rise, and the corresponding rush of air into the vacuum created by its departure would start to flow downward. If he had not reached his destination by then, he never would.

So once again he worked, driving his wings through the dry air, lifting, pulling, straining now as the image of the Overworld came into his mind. How far above? He couldn't know. When he looked upward, he saw that the sky was light around the edges, darkening to black in the middle, as if he looked into a hole stretching impossibly far into the distance. But the sun was far below now, and the air was not so lethally burning. That patch of darkness became his objective, and he strove mightily, thought of nothing else. . . . Reach that place, and his burning flesh would be cooled.

Still he labored, and at last he began to move beyond

the lethal fire, until finally the crushing heat was but a memory. Soothing coolness surrounded him, masking the rays of the now-distant sun. For a long time this was blessed relief, moisture caressing his burning scales, filling his nostrils with invigorating mist. The burned scales, the seared membranes of his wings were balmed by the moisture.

It was when that mist began to thicken that he began to understand where he was. He had to work to move, to fight through increasing resistance. More and more water surrounded him, dense and choking, until he was swimming, struggling upward through actual liquid. No longer could he breathe, for he was in the depths of the Cloudsea, had reached Arcati only to pass into his home world through the bottom of the ocean.

How ironic, he thought, as darkness closed in from the edges of his vision . . . how ironic that he would fly through the air, through lethal heat, to go home. . . .

Only to drown in the depths of the Overworld's largest sea.

NATAC told Crazy Horse where he would find the elves of Hyac. Together with about a hundred survivors from the fleet of druid boats—all of them human warriors with cavalry experience—the Sioux chief made his way along the base of the vast earthwork, marveling at the extent of the wall that had been raised in just a couple of days.

The barrier finally terminated at the base of one of the largest of the Ringhills, a craggy bluff that served to anchor the rampart, which abutted the base of the precipice in a very strong position. Walking around that elevation, the warrior found a shallow stream flowing out of the hills and followed it into the valley where he had been told the Hyac were encamped.

Crazy Horse found the elven warriors in their bivouac, which was nestled very much like a Sioux camp in the lightly wooded valley between a couple of rocky outcrops. The elven huts were rounded domes, not cone-shape tepees, but they were still formed of animal skins draped over wooden frames, close enough to the abodes he had known all of his earlier life to give him a pleasant sense of memory.

And these beautiful hills! It did not take a lot of imagination to be reminded of his beloved Black Hills. Even the pine trees scattered along the upper slopes and the crests would have been right at home in the lands of the Dakota. He looked along the rounded lower elevations, half expecting to see the hummocked, shaggy brown shapes of grazing buffalo.

"You men wait here," he suggested as they reached a flowered meadow beside the stream. "I will seek this Janitha, daughter of the khan."

The smell of the horse herd was a fine perfume in the still air, and he paused to admire the steeds grazing just a short distance downstream from the elven camp. There were thousands of them, sturdy and muscular, fattening up on the valley grass. Several of the animals were exceptional prizes, spotted pintos, golden mares, and a sleek, black stallion. "You are the chief's horse, are you not?" he murmured to this one.

He smiled, remembering countless thieving expeditions, when he set out with his friends to take ponies from the Shoshone, the Crow, or the Pawnee. Even as he enjoyed the memory he could not avoid a taint of regret in that smile, for he also recalled how much of his energy he had expended against those other tribes, and they against the Sioux. Since he had come to Nayve he had begun to imagine the power they would have had together, if they had united. Instead, they had allowed petty wars to drain their strength and their focus, all the while allowing the real enemy to encroach farther and farther onto their lands.

Idly, he picked out another fine stallion, a pinto, admiring the way the horse watched him alertly, even moved to interpose himself between the human and the mares when the warrior approached. A touch on the nostrils calmed the animal, and Crazy Horse whispered a greeting. "You are a warrior yourself, aren't you? I'll bet you fairly fly into the fight!"

Energized, he breathed the Ringhills air with new awareness, tasted the lush pines in every pore. This was a place worth fighting for, he knew. He had a sense, for the first time upon Nayve, that he might have found a home.

A few minutes later he came to the first picket, an elven archer who studied him carefully with an arrow nocked in his bow. "Natac sent me," the American warrior explained. "I am to seek Janitha Khandaughter."

The sentry gestured with his weapon. "There. Her hut is beside the third fire."

That elfwoman was eating a meal of beans and rice, using her fingers to scoop the mixture from a leafy plate into her mouth. She looked up as Crazy Horse came to her campfire, finished her last bite, then rose, wiping her hands on her leather pants.

"I would like to join your company. I bring a hundred men from the druid fleet," he said. "If you will have me."

"That depends," she said, looking at him critically. "Do you know how to ride a pony?"

"DON'T move!" Shandira said, standing rigidly still in the middle of the bowl-shaped valley.

Miradel didn't need any encouragement. In the first instant after the gargoyle landed she had been frozen by terror, transfixed by those hellish, glowing eyes. As soon as she stopped moving, however, the creature's focus shifted, and it seemed to be looking around as if it had lost sight of her.

The monster shifted position, taking a step forward with a sound like the scrape of stone grinding against stone. Those massive, bestial legs stretched and extended, bent as it crouched, the grotesque belly dangling, swinging loosely. Miradel could barely suppress her gasp of horror as the gargoyle peered around, blinking, uttering deep, bone-shivering growls. The two wings looked to be solid stone, but they spread wide easily, as if they were made of tanned leather. The beast fanned them convulsively, and the blast of cold air struck Miradel like a physical blow. She needed every bit of her strength and courage to keep from staggering backward; somehow, she continued to hold herself statue still.

Standing between the two druids and the lofty throne across the valley, the gargoyle seemed oddly hesitant. Miradel could see their objective, tantalizingly close now, on the mountainside rising before them. The shimmery substance was not a godly robe, she now perceived; it was water, spilling from a crack in the rock, flowing across the face of the mountain, then pouring into a stream that spilled from the front of the ledge forming the seat of the Deathlord's throne.

Karlath-Fayd's massive, burning eyes still glowed above, disembodied, floating against the darkness. How often had she looked at them in the Tapestry, seen and feared the power there. Yet now, in the hall of the god himself, it was the servant, the gargoyle, that truly inspired fear.

"We have to get closer!" Shandira said. "I have an idea—but you have to stay still, like a statue, until I say to move."

At the sound of the druid's voice, the gargoyle looked in her direction but did not step forward. Miradel, trembling, saw that the black woman stood rigidly still, a monolith of human pride before monstrous evil. Only her eyes moved, roving this way and that, seeking . . . what?

"When it comes after me, you go!" said the African woman. "You'll only have one chance. Run as fast as you can!"

At first Miradel did not fully grasp what her companion intended; perhaps her mind balked at the reality. When she did understand, she was numbed by horror and awed by the other druid's courage. Shandira was saying something quietly, praying, Miradel realized.

". . . walk through the valley of the shadow of death, I shall fear no evil . . ."

"Shandira—no!" cried the druid. She thought of a mad impulse herself: she should move, dance, run—anything to draw the monster's attention! But she remained frozen, only her mind in motion, bringing words to her mouth. "We'll get out of this together!" she shouted. "Don't!"

"For Thou art with me." On the last word, Shandira looked at Miradel and smiled. Her expression was calm, almost beatific. "Thank you for all you have shown me, taught me," she said. "I think on the world of our birth, you would be called a saint."

"Shandira!" Now Miradel moved, but it was too late. The tall druid was already sprinting to the side, away from her companion. The gargoyle again uttered that low, ground-shivering growl and pounced after her with catlike speed, landing with a crash of stone on the flat ground where Shandira had been standing.

But now she was running with exceptional speed, evading the savage grasp of those monstrous claws in her first burst of acceleration. She darted to the side as the beast pounced again, nimbly evading the lumbering charge.

"Miradel—go!" screamed the African woman, the word echoing like an immortal command in the vast emptiness of the mountain hall.

Miradel took off in that same breath of sound, racing unnoticed behind the gargoyle as it lunged after her companion. She ran with her eyes on that lofty throne, nothing else even existing in her mind. The sounds of pursuit, the roars of the monster, seemed to be coming from very far away . . . another place . . . even another life.

Her feet pounded across the ground, the rhythm of her flight the only sound she knew. Her momentum carried her up as she reached the foot of the slope, until massive rocks like steps for a giant blocked her ascent of the mountainside.

Here she pulled with her arms, kicked, crawled up one after the other. Higher and higher she climbed, hearing no sounds now except the rasping gasp of her own respiration. She didn't dare to look back. Instead, she only climbed, scrambling over another obstacle, ignoring the torn skin on her knees, the fingernail that ripped away during another frantic upward pull. Always she worked to climb, the great shelf of the throne drawing nearer with each second.

At last she stood on the seat of that lofty throne and stared upward in disbelief. The seat of Karlath-Fayd resembled nothing so much as a natural shelf in a steep mountainside. The spring on the far wall leaked a spray of water down the cliff, draining into a cut that had eroded across the rocky surface over countless centuries.

And those eyes? The immortal orbs of a lethal god, red fire that she had observed for centuries, had studied, and feared?

The two slits, the fiery eyes of the Deathlord, were

merely cracks in the rock. The heat of the infernal ground, bubbling lava and spuming fire, glowed through.

The throne of the Deathlord was . . . simply . . . empty.

The gargoyle roared, throwing its head back, bellowing the blast of sound toward the dark sky. Now Miradel looked across the basin, the valley floor. Shandira was gone, and the monster was enraged. It bellowed again, face turned toward the sky, until that bestial visage lowered, the glowing eyes coming to rest upon the lone druid on the mountain shelf.

"It's not real; there *is* no Karlath-Fayd!" Miradel gasped out the realization, then cried out in anguish. She understood everything in that instant—and chief among those realizations was the knowledge that she had gained enlightenment too late . . . too late to help Shandira, to help the people of Nayve . . . even too late to help herself.

The water spilled from the gash in the stone, pouring across the empty rock, trickling through its channel and spilling off the ledge. The gargoyle took a step forward, strangely silent now, and she was grateful for that, grateful that at least she could hear the deceptively peaceful noise of the stream now, in the last moments of her life.

The monster stared at her for what seemed like a long time, those red eyes flashing wickedly. Wings spread, it crouched, then sprang into the air, taking flight toward the druid on the lonely mountainside, alone at the end of the cosmos.

DARANN regained consciousness to a sensation that she was still in the middle of an explosion of uncontrolled violence. Her body was trembling, and noise roared in her ears. She was numb over most of her body, mostly deafened, and had been battered so much that her teeth hurt. In fact, she was rather surprised to find out that she was still alive.

The walls of the great chute were passing in a blur, masked by the reality of impossible speed. She felt strangely weightless, an effect that Donnwell Earnwise had warned her to expect. How long had she sat in this chair? How far had she traveled? It was quite impossible to tell.

Then—miracle! She felt her tremendous speed begin to slow, though the missle still rose through the long tunnel in the Midrock. There was nothing to see—the shield of heavy steel at the head of the rocket masked any forward observation—but she was sure that, by now, she had passed through the blue magic barrier.

Only one question remained: would she reach Nayve alive?

"Is he alive?"

"I don't think so. But let's fish him out anyway. From the look of that wing, he's a big one. Someone will want to know that he got drowned."

Regillix Avatar felt an annoying tug on his neck, claws digging into his chin and jowls. But he lacked the strength even to utter a growl of displeasure. Instead, he submitted to the indignity of being dragged from the Cloudsea onto the rainbow brightness of the shore.

At least, his head and neck were dragged out of the water. It turned out that his rescuers lacked the strength to pull his whole, massive body out. Even so, he drew a ragged, choking breath, then exhaled a cloud of steam in relief.

"He's alive, Daristal! Go tell your sire! We found a big dragon!"

"Don't you recognize him, silly Cantrix? This is

Regillix Avatar! He fell into the Hillswallower storm
when we were just newts, when he went to look for Plar-
inal!"

"Well, you're right, it is! You get your sire, and I will
tell the angel Gabriel. Regillix Avatar has returned!"

AWFULBARK stood at the crest of a hill, above a precipitous
drop to the plains of brown grass. Jagged, irregular clumps
of granite obstructed the smooth ground below, in the
shadow of the Ringhills, but he could see around those outcrops and far across the landscape beyond. That land was
covered, as far as he could see, by the creeping presence of
the Deathlord's horde.

The troll made his observations from the lip at the summit of a cliff, nearly a hundred feet above the great earthwork that his trolls had erected with such alacrity. From
here he could see for miles along the wall in both directions. This was the left end of the barrier. For this stand,
though—unlike at the Swansleep River—Natac had
mixed the elves and trolls together. Instead of protecting
one flank, Awfulbark's warriors were now stationed
across the whole length of the line, approximately one
troll with every band of twenty or thirty elves. The top of
the barrier was lined with these defenders, weapons ready,
troops silently watching the approach of their enemy.

Beside the king stood a grizzled dwarf, one of the Seer
veterans who had been brought to Nayve with Natac half
a century earlier. He was a gunner, manning a shiny steel
battery, and Awfulbark looked at the weapon with awe.
The troll king had seen the lethal silver spheres fly from
the powerful spring, exploding with white-hot fire among
the enemy; now, he was glad that it was up here, backing
up the defenders of the wall.

"Another half hour and they'll be in range," noted the

dwarf laconically. "Superlong range, to be sure . . . might not hit the exact fellas I'm aiming at. But once they get that close, can't hardly miss, y' know?"

"I know," Awfulbark observed solemnly. "I count . . ." he started to grunt a tally, concentrating, his gaze sweeping across the many ranks of dark warriors marching in a snake like column. "I count lots of 'em, with about a million spears in front."

"Well, we'll give 'em a good taste of fire and steel, eh?" The dwarf's tone grew more somber as, like the troll, he studied the mass of darkness, stretching as far as they could see across the plain. "A taste, for starters anyway."

"For start, and for finish," Awfulbark concurred. He suspected—seeing that horde, he *knew*—that the finish would be an unhappy one. He really, really wanted to go away. But if elves could stand here, and dwarves, and even those few gnomes who had escaped from the beach, it made him feel somehow that the trolls should stay here, too.

And really, he argued to himself, where could they go that these ghost warriors wouldn't follow?

"Good luck," said the dwarf.

"Yes. Good luck for you, too," the king replied, feeling somehow better to have shared the blessing. He turned to the more gentle rear slope of the hill, started to climb down. He would join his warriors on the wall, for, once more, it was time to fight.

The ghost warriors halted their advance and spent an entire day spreading out, forming a vast front more than five miles across, arrayed like a massive battering ram before the right center section of the wall. The huge phalanx of the Delver army and its iron golems were opposite the far right of the wall, but for now they held back, ten miles or more out on the plains.

Other formations of ghost warriors, each a massive

army in its own right, broke off from the rear of the horde, maneuvering to the right and the left of the barrier. These warriors were not visible from the ramparts, but their progress was marked by columns of dust rising skyward. Natac estimated that it would be several days before they came into the fray, but he started making plans for that dire contingency. In the meantime, his faerie scouts would keep him apprised of the enemy positions.

For an hour after Lighten the great army stood still. Gradually over that time a sound of wailing arose, a mournful sigh of noise that, at first, was just a rustle in the subconscious. Minute by minute it swelled until it was a cry louder than the wind, penetrating into the very bones of the defenders. Trolls muttered superstitiously, while the elves looked to their companions in dismay.

The sound remained shrill, greater than the keen of a million locusts, as the horde of the Deathlord began to advance. They swept forward like a fog rolling from the distant sea. At first, there was no perception of individual beings in the vast swarm of darkness, but gradually specific leaders—centurians, generals, chieftains, and captains—came into view. Spear tips waved like fields of grass in the wind, and the pace of the advance picked up, a perceptible rush now.

The batteries opened up first, at a range of more than five hundred yards, the silver spheres sparkling in the sunlight as they flew through the air. They landed amid the attacking army with specks of white light that flared like stars, then quickly vanished, leaving smoke to mingle with the churning dust cloud. Next the archers added their missiles to the effort, thousands of arrows in each volley, deadly darts arcing like clouds from the hillside behind the wall, flying over the palisade and then plunging down with lethal force into the blanket of attackers spread out below.

The elves were arrayed along the top of that rampart, a single line of now-veteran warriors, ready to fight with spears and swords. Here and there a gangly troll loomed head and shoulders above the elven helmets. There were gnomes among the defenders, too, the survivors of the defeat on the beach. These Natac had formed into companies of twenty, armed them with crossbows, and deployed them in many places just behind the wall, as defense against another breakthrough.

There were also humans here, druids and warriors from all corners of the Seventh Circle: powerful monks, acrobatic ninja warriors, archers and spellcasters from Asia, tall and muscular Africans, men and woman who came from Sweden and Germany, from Dakota and Tlaxcala, and all the other lands of their previous lives. They were all together here, all prepared to fight and, if necessary, to die.

Finally the attack smashed into the rampart like an angry storm tide striking a harbor breakwater. Thousands of ghost warriors skidded and fell into the ditch, tumbling onto their own weapons, churning up the loose dirt as more and more of their comrades fell on top of them. Many died, but some crawled out of the chaos and started scrambling up the front wall of the earthwork.

The palisade was steeply sloping, and many of the attackers slid in the loose dirt, skidding downward into the packed ranks of their fellows—and, in turn, impeding the advance of the following troops. But others pressed through, clambering and clawing up the wall, drawing ever closer to the defenders' thin line.

THE Hyaccan elves were mounted, thousands of riders milling about in the valley, waiting for word. The warriors who had come with Crazy Horse had all found steeds, for they would ride in this charge as well. The Sioux chief himself had claimed that same pinto stallion, leaping onto the sturdy back with a whoop. Janitha watched him, saw the way he seemed to merge with the horse into one unit, and she approved.

A faerie came buzzing up to her. "Natac says it's time!"

With that, she raised her lance and uttered her own yell. Shouting wildly, the riders spilled from their valley in a sweeping charge, ponies madly racing toward the flank of the invaders' army.

In the lead of the charge was the great Sioux war chief, shooting arrows with deadly accuracy as they raced close to the column of ghost warriors, guiding his nimble steed with his knees. Crazy Horse whooped and shouted, and the elves surged with him.

And the humans also: to his right was an English lord, on his left an Argentinian gaucho. A French chausseur and an American dragoon rode right behind, while the elves raced on all sides.

Janitha Khandaughter, mounted upon her stallion Khanwind, raced to catch up, and as she galloped beside this natural horseman she acknowledged with a certain amount of pleasure that she had at last encountered a mounted warrior who was her equal. She would have to learn more about him, if they could but live through this day.

TAMARWIND Trak stood atop the wall and heard himself shouting a long, ululating cry. The sound was bizarre enough that it startled him—and at the same time seemed to infuse the elves around him with renewed battle frenzy. A shower of arrows soared overhead, plunking among the tightly packed ghost warriors, and once again he raised his

sword and slashed, and stabbed, and parried against those
who had made it up to the top of the rampart.

The attackers churned through the ditch, clawing their
way up the sloping earthen wall, falling back as the elven
weapons chopped, and slashed, and slew. A troll roared,
seizing on a ghost warrior by the shoulder and knee, lifting the creature up in the air. Shaking the hapless attacker
like a rag doll, the troll cast the body into the faces of his
companions.

Druids stood among the many elves, casting winds that
sent dust clouds whirling into the faces of the attackers,
blinding and infuriating them. Cillia strode back and forth
on the wall, spinning a gale where it was needed, blasting
stinging debris across a blank section of the wall top, until
a dozen humans—warriors from Roland Boatwright's
fleet—charged into the gap and forced the attackers back
down.

The din of battle rose around Tamarwind, mingling the
screams of the wounded with the ghastly wail of the attackers. To the elf it was all a dirge, and his thoughts
turned, full of longing, to Belynda.

JUBAL strode back and forth along the line, exhorting his
fighters to renewed frenzy. He saw Juliay, her silver bowl
cradled against her belly, the casting spoon whirring, and
he felt a rush of love—love that turned to terror as three
ghost warriors pushed through the minicyclone to reach
the top of the rampart. They were dressed in tattered cloaks
and kepis, garments stained brown in color but still carrying a hint of Union blue.

In a flash the Virginian was there, his sword knocking
aside one bayonet, then striking forward to stab the second attacker through the throat. He had a bizarre sensation
of his final battle, a desperate fight on the breastwork

above Appomattox Creek. He had failed then, been pierced by the bayonet that had claimed his life and, unexpectedly, brought him to Juliay.

He would not let those same warriors, those same weapons, take her away from him. Jubal attacked like a madman, hacking his way through the company of ghost warriors. Bayonets jabbed at him but somehow he slapped them away, a lethal force of steel and determination. In seconds he drove them back, and Juliay spun hard, raising a stinging spray of dust that flew against the attackers, forced them off the summit of the earthwork.

But the tide of death began to press hard.

HOURS later the Hyaccan cavalry rode their weary ponies back into the valley, dismounting, turning the animals loose to drink and graze. The riders, however, simply selected fresh steeds and once more took to their saddles.

All except Janitha. Crazy Horse noticed that she still sat astride Khanwind, and that, furthermore, the black stallion showed no signs of fatigue.

"He and none other will carry me so long as he can stand," she explained, in answer to his questioning look.

Once more the throng was mounted, though they numbered many less than upon their first charge.

"Again! We will take them in the flank!" cried Crazy Horse, and Janitha whooped in agreement. Infused once more with the sheer thrill of war, they led another charge together, the riders of Hyac racing forward to attack.

But their numbers would only suffer more loss, as they rode so close in among the enemy that many of the brave riders were pulled from their saddles and torn to pieces. Others fell from stabs and slashes, and in many places the ghost warriors formed bristling walls of pikes and spears, deadly hedges the horses could not approach.

Yet there were always other enemies, and so they rode against the long flank, striking, killing, disrupting and, too often, dying . . . until their horses began to stagger from weariness, and once again the riders had to fall back.

AWFULBARK had lost his right hand, twice, and his limbs and chest were constantly scored by deep, raw wounds. But he roared, and bit, and continued to fight. He tore bodily into a trio of ghost warriors, ripping limbs, crushing a skull with one powerful bite. Staggering back, he saw the butt of a spear jutting from his belly. He tried to remove the weapon but howled in pain as it twisted even through his back.

"Comes out behind!" Roodcleaver shouted, gesturing with the gory arm of a ghost warrior, holding the limb in both hands.

Groaning, Awfulbark grabbed the weapon near his skin and snapped it off. His wife pulled it out from behind as he howled in agony. He was then forced to sit down to allow his innards to knit.

Five minutes later, when he stood and once more strode into the fray, he was a very angry troll.

CLEARLY, there would be no damming this tide.

Natac came to the grim truth as he fought with his own sword, personally leading a counterattacking force of elves as they rushed to reclaim a section of the wall. They drove the enemy off and then stopped, panting. Darken was approaching, all of his troops were growing weary, and there was no sign of any kind of cessation in the enemy's effort.

On the contrary, the general could see that the attack was spreading far to the flank, inevitably seeking a way around the edge of the great rampart. The cavalry was holding valiantly on the right, but to the left there was nothing to stem the tide. Faeries had brought word an hour before that the Delvers were advancing, their iron golems striding as a rank of steel in front of the dwarves. As soon as they drew near, the Hyac ponies would be forced off the plain.

He found Jubal below the position of the battery on Hill Number One. "Don't think we can hold for another day," the Virginian observed.

Natac shook his head. "They're swinging to the right and the left; we can't block both moves and still hold the wall."

"Seems odd for it to end like this, after what we went through, back home," Jubal noted.

"Yes. We must fight, but we cannot win," Natac conceded.

"General Natac!"

It was Horas of Gallowglen, buzzing at his elbow, speaking urgently.

"What?" he demanded.

"The sage-ambassador Belynda—she says she needs you in the city, now!"

"I can't leave!" was his first reaction, until fear jolted through him. "Miradel!"

"Yes, the lady druid is in dire trouble. The sage-ambassador only hopes that you might be able to help. But you must come at once."

All of his concern focused on that one woman, his lover, his partner. The battle . . . in his heart he knew that all the parts were in motion, and the bitter result had already been determined. "Jubal, you'll have to take over. I'm going to Miradel!" he said. "She needs me. I'm sorry to leave now—"

"Don't be," replied the other man firmly. Natac could

tell that Jubal, too, understood the inevitable collapse of their position, the fact that the battle was lost. "Go to her—and good luck. We'll hang on here as long as we can."

In two minutes Natac had raced to the top of the hill, where the druids maintained a teleport pool, a deep bowl of water on the rampart. Several warriors had already started the water spinning as Natac stepped up to the edge, and the sparks of teleportation magic quickly glowed around him.

A second later, Natac was at the edge of the lake, with the Worldweaver's Loom towering above him, rising into the same sky that had begun to Darken over the battlefield. But now he was in Circle at Center, staggering dizzily, suppressing the nausea that still afflicted him with teleport magic.

"Come here—look!" It was Belynda, a few steps away from the pool. She had her Globe of Seeing on the bench, and she gestured to him urgently.

"What can I do?" he cried, kneeling, peering into the sphere of cloudy glass.

He saw at once that Miradel was in a terrible place, alone on a shelf of rock, in a world of eternal darkness. "Can you send me to her?" pleaded the general.

"No . . . there is no swirl of water. In any event, I fear it is already too late. See!"

The image shifted, and the veteran warrior paled at the sight of a grotesque monster, gigantic and horned, with a bestial muzzle and wicked, talon-tipped fingers. "Is that the Deathlord?" he asked in horror.

"No . . . I cannot see the Deathlord. That is the gargoyle, the guardian of Karlath-Fayd's citadel. I watched it kill Shandira; she died to distract the monster from Miradel. Miradel climbed to this ledge, but I fear she is trapped."

"Look—there's water!" Natac indicated the stream flowing across the ledge. "Please—send me to her."

Belynda shook her head. "That is only a straight flow. You know that it must be swirled to allow the spell. Besides, I would not send you, merely to watch you both die. But watch—we will see if she gives us cause for hope."

At that moment the monster took to the air, launching itself with a powerful spring and flying with draconic grace, soaring directly toward the druid. Miradel stood as if transfixed, and the beast pulsed its wings, flying at tremendous speed. At the last instant she ducked away, rolling across the rocky ledge as the gargoyle crashed into the mountainside, just beside the waterfall, with enough force to break loose a cascade of rocks.

"She's doomed!" cried Natac, looking into the globe as Belynda maintained the spell of vision.

"No, wait—look!" whispered the elfwoman excitedly. "It is what she wanted to happen!"

Natac saw it, too: rubble, knocked down by the gargoyle's collision, now piled in the stream, damming the flow, instantly forming a small pool. Apparently Miradel saw it at the same time. She jumped into the water, which rose only to her knees, started to twirl madly, using her hands to scoop the liquid into a roundabout current.

"Now! Teleport!" Natac cried, as Belynda concentrated on the casting of the spell. The warrior groaned, willing Miradel to hear, to answer his summons. The monster turned, jaws gaping, talons reaching. The red eyes flashed, as if it was already savoring its prize.

And then there were sparks dancing in the air, right past Natac's face. In another second his black-haired druid was there, swaying weakly on her feet, taking a step forward before collapsing into her warrior's arms.

20

Tapestry

Picture painted,
Image stained,
Artist's likeness,
Goddess rained;

All lies are true
When sewn
From immortal thread

From the Tapestry of the Worldweaver
Bloom of Entropy

I n the end, the tide of ghost warriors proved to be unstoppable by even the most valiant efforts of the Nayvian Army. The fighting on the wall lasted for two days,
with a hundred or more ghost warriors slain for every elf
and each troll. But an endless supply of attackers insured
that there was no easing of the pressure and no hope of victory.

The ditch had long been full of corpses, and the foreslope of the rampart was likewise tangled with the dead.
The measured decay of the slain soldiers could not match
the rate at which fresh bodies were added to the pile. The

surviving ghost warriors merely climbed over their lifeless comrades, the attackers clawing and climbing upward
until they could hurl themselves against the weary defenders atop the wall. They fought well, those warriors of
Nayve, but they were mortal, and inevitably mortal limits
of pain, endurance, and strength began to impede their
courageous striving.

The warriors of humankind, the men summoned by the
druids over the last fifty years, were the bravest of all the
defenders. Each a hero of Earth, granted a second life on
Nayve, fought for that new world with a passion deeper
and more comprehensive than anything that had moti-
vated him upon the world of his birth. For a long time,
wherever one of these men went, the ghost warriors were
driven back, and the elves and trolls took heart.

A Zulu champion slew a thousand before clutching
ghost hands dragged him into the corpse-filled ditch. Even
in falling he killed, laying about with a short javelin and a
double-edged sword until he was buried by frenzied attackers. When the pile ceased twitching, not a bit of the
African's body could be seen through the heap of his vic-
tims.

A captain of artillery, raised on a Wisconsin farm and
schooled in the Iron Brigade at Gettysburg and beyond,
directed the fire of a lone battery from a strategic elevation. When all the elves on the wall below were slain, the
ghost warriors rushed the vacant rampart in the hundreds.
The brave gunner maintained a barrage of fire intense
enough to clear the platform until reinforcements could
arrive. Then, as a company of Argentian elves rushed to
fill the breach, he lifted the field of his fire, spraying explosives down the sloping wall, incinerating hundreds
more ghost warriors with each incendiary volley.

Bearing a sword in each hand, a stocky samurai warrior
whirled and stepped back and forth with lethal precision,

hacking and stabbing and laying waste to the enemy along a fifty-foot section of the rampart. When the teeming warriors showed a reluctance to press toward him, he shouted a battle cry and charged down the wall, into the enemy ranks. He cut his way through two lines, then fought his way back again, holding firm in the ditch as he stood on the shifting pile of bodies. Only when he tried to climb the wall back to the parapet did he fall, taken in the back by a spear. Three elves rushed down, trying to pull the stricken Japanese warrior up, but the ghost warriors pressed in with fury, surrounding the body, cutting the heroic fighter to pieces.

Yet there were too few of these heroes and too few of the elves and the trolls as well—though in many cases they displayed similar bravery, dedication, and sacrifice—to hold against a virtually infinite foe. Along one half-mile length of the wall all the defenders were slain, and the ghost warriors spilled across like water coming over a dam. In another section just a few wounded trolls tried to hold, and they inevitably succumbed to the hacking blades of a thousand attackers.

The gnomish companies that had formed the battle reserve also fought valiantly. At first they rushed forward to meet every breakthrough, firing lethal volleys of steel bolts from their crossbows. But it was the same story with them: there were too few reserves, too many breakthroughs. When the last of the gnomes had charged into position, the ghost warriors simply broke through in more places, breached the wall to the right and the left, poured onward with unstoppable pressure.

The breastwork still stood, but in many places the invaders began to force their way over the top. Tamarwind and Jubal tried to rally their elven troops along a section of the center, and Awfulbark pleaded with his trolls and elves on the left, but they were already too few for the task. The ghost warriors claimed the top of the wall in sections and spread out to the right and left, striking the defenders in the flank, clearing longer and longer stretches of the great rampart.

The defenders were forced into smaller pockets, finally defending only those sections of the wall where the batteries could cover them from above. In long stretches the warriors of Nayve were left with no choice but to flee the wall, breaking into small groups and scrambling up the rough slopes of the Ringhills.

ON the plain, Crazy Horse rode his fifth horse into the fray. The Hyaccan cavalry and their human allies attacked by the hundreds now, not the thousands, and each valiant charge left fewer of them to withdraw. But the leadership of their own khandaughter and the Sioux war chief, together with the plentiful supply of fresh mounts, allowed them to strike deep into the enemy ranks with each charge. Because of these attacks, the right flank of the wall was the one section that had held without wavering.

The battle had changed for them during the second day, however, when the Delver dwarves had advanced, taking over from the ghost warriors who had faced the riders earlier in the battle. These armored dwarves attacked with discipline and skill, and this forced the riders to increased desperation with each attack. The iron golems marched in front, gigantic and crushingly powerful, striding across the field with such force that nothing could stand in their path. The Sioux chief dodged around one of the massive giants—he had quickly learned to avoid these gargantuans, for no weapon he bore seemed to have any impact—and charged again into the ranks. His sword chopped down, again and again. Most of these creatures were faceless, and he killed them with dispassion.

Whirling through the melee, Crazy Horse spotted Khanwind, riderless, bucking in the midst of a horde of ghost warriors. Frantically he charged in, laying about with his sword until he drove back the ring of attackers and found Janitha, facedown in the dirt, surrounded by metal-clad dwarves. With a lean from his horse's back and a strong grasp of her arm, he lifted her over the pony's withers, spurring the steed away just a few feet in front of the furious attackers.

He checked for her pulse, and she opened her eyes, alive and feisty. He was surprised by how happy that made him.

"You ought to be more careful," said the Sioux.

"Put me back on my horse," she said, struggling to sit, facing him on the shoulders of the small pony. "And I'll show you careful!"

He laughed in warlike delight, guiding his pony toward Khanwind as he held a firm grasp around the elfwoman's slender waist. "What happened to put you on the ground?" he asked.

"I was hit by the ugliest bastard I have ever seen," she replied, rubbing her hip where a purple bruise showed between the links of her elven chain mail. "I'll remember his face until I die: a mass of red nostrils, and jaws of shiny silver, like teeth that had been welded over the scarred flesh of his face. He's a captain of those dwarves—and I wanted him!"

"I will find him, and kill him for you!" Crazy Horse pledged, as Janitha nimbly sprang across to Khanwind, who nickered in delight at the return of his rider. The ponies and their riders raced together, back into the fray.

————————

ZYSTYL cast a wary glance toward the great army marching on his right. The ghost warriors disturbed him, frightened him in some way that touched upon his arcane senses. He could smell their wrongness, and he feared that corrupt presence. He was determined to go none too close to the eerie horde.

Nevertheless, his dakali compelled him to attack, and so he had done, urging the army of Nightrock into an offensive against the far right end of the dirt wall. He understood that he was to interpose his dwarves and golems as a barrier between the ghost warriors and the elven cavalry that had vexed them so constantly during the fight.

He expected the charge, and when it came, his iron golems knocked many ponies and their riders to the ground, crushing both with stomping pressure and lethal smashes. But he did not expect so many of the accursed elves to ride right between the mechanical giants. Suddenly they were everywhere, chopping and kicking and charging through the neat Delver ranks. The little horses were shockingly fast and savagely warlike; they evaded the blows of the dwarven weapons even as they pressed home the charge, their riders striking down Delver after Delver. Even the mounts fought, kicking, biting, and trampling wherever they could. Zystyl's troops were veterans of centuries of campaigning, but never had they faced a persistent, mobile attack like this. They found it demoralizing and, for a long time, were unable to press the advance. Instead, the great regiments milled around like giants swatting at biting flies.

Still, they fought well, and neither did they retreat. Zystyl himself swung his mace when a rider came close. Once he took a blow at a beautiful elven female, squealing in pleasure as his blow knocked her from the saddle. He had moved forward, eager for the kill, but the swirl of battle carried him away.

The arcane did not see the new attacker coming for him, not until it was too late. This was a bronze-skinned man, not a fair elf, and he was nearly naked as he rode an unsaddled horse, his black hair trailing in a long plume. Despite his lack of armor, he somehow evaded all the cutting steel of the Delver foot soldiers, striking through the ranks as if he sought Zystyl on some personal mission of revenge. The arcane raised his sword to parry, but the weapon was bashed painfully against his own face by the force of the rider's blow.

Then he was on the ground, tasting blood—his own blood! "No!" he croaked. "This cannot be!" He barely felt the next blow as the human's sword stabbed through his throat, but he couldn't breathe nor even move; it was as if he was pinned to the ground.

His strength waned rapidly, flowing from his flesh as freely as the blood that drained from his body into the dirt. His last thought was stark, painful, and undeniable.

It was not *fair* that he should die like this!

THE trolls were handled more roughly even than the other defending forces. Many of Awfulbark's warriors had been permanently slain by the grisly attacks. The ghost warriors had learned from their past encounters: now when they pulled or knocked down a troll, they stood and hacked the creature until there was nothing left but a patch of gore. From such total brutality, even the regenerative forest trolls were unable to recover.

At last the king stood alone on a section of the wall, ghost warriors swarming over the rampart to either side. He roared and slew with his sword any attacker careless enough to come within range here. Awfulbark was ready to die here. And why not? Surely this was the end of the world!

It was Roodcleaver who grabbed him by the back of his neck and roughly pulled him away. The two trolls tumbled down the back of the wall together. The king stood at the bottom, angrily brushing himself off.

"Why I not fight?" he demanded. "Die like king!"

"Die like fool!" she retorted, further assailing his dignity. "You want to fight, come up hill with me. Stay here and we die. Go, and we fight some more. Maybe die up there, you want to die so bad! So go!"

It was hard to argue with that kind of logic, though the king made a valiant effort to come up with some devastating reply. But his mind was a blank, as usual. There was nothing left to do but follow his wife up the hill, and stay alive.

"WHERE'S Natac?" asked Tamarwind, as he found Jubal and Juliay on a low hill, overlooking the weary withdrawal of the once-mighty army. Everywhere troops were streaming off the wall, picking paths up the slopes of the Ringhills, in between the most rugged elevations, while the ghost warriors claimed the length of the parapet and, for now, seemed to be gathering their strength before they pursued.

"He had to go back to the city . . . an emergency, with Miradel. If he comes back, he'll teleport onto Hill Number One. They're still holding there, the last that I heard . . . but I don't know how long that can last," Jubal replied, putting his arm around Juliay. "I don't blame him. At a time like this, things coming to an end, a man should spend those minutes with the woman he loves, I reckon. Not much hope for tomorrow."

Tamarwind felt that remark with a stab of longing. "I've had a thousand years that I could have spent with that woman," he said, "and I wasted them all. Would that

I could have but one of them back again, I would go to Belynda and tell her what I know."

Roland Boatwright and Sirien joined them on the crest, another pair of lovers finding themselves on the field of the last battle. "What can we do now?" the druid and shipbuilder asked.

"Fall back, I guess," Tam said. "As far as Circle at Center if we have to. Until there's no place left to retreat."

"What's that in the sky?" asked Sirien, the keen-eyed elfmaid. She pointed past the ghost warriors, toward the murky horizon in the direction that was neither metal nor wood.

Winged shapes were visible there, tiny specks weaving through the columns of smoke and dust. There were lots of them, wings beating unmistakably, coming this way.

"Reckon it's more harpies, I suppose, Jubal said in resigned despair. "Spread the word. We're not even safe up here. We've got another attack coming in. And these look like big ones."

"Wait," said Sirien, holding up a slender hand.

"Why?" asked the Virginian impatiently. "They'll be here in a few minutes."

"I know," said the elfwoman, strangely unperturbed. "But look . . . look at them again."

KARKALD and Belynda hurried to keep up, Natac half carrying Miradel. At first, immediately following her teleport home, he had ordered her to lie down and rest, but she would have none of that. Instead, she had barked an order of her own.

"The temple—take me to the Goddess Worldweaver, now!"

So he offered her an arm and a shoulder, which she leaned upon gratefully. Weak as she was, she still managed to hurry them along, across the lakeside park to the marbled plaza and the great golden doors. She would not explain what she had learned on the Fifth Circle, but her lips were drawn in a tight line, and her face was ashen.

They burst through the door, scattering the acolytes in the outer chamber. Quickly they passed the exit to the old, unused Rockshaft, with its bolted iron door, pushing their way right into the sanctum with its massive loom and surrounding Tapestry.

Within, the goddess looked up from her weaving, then slowed the pace of her pedaling until the great machine came to a rest. With immense dignity she stood.

"I was not so certain that I would see you again," she declared coldly. Her eyes were like ice, glittering, cold.

"But you do see me, and you will hear what I have learned," Miradel declared. She had found her strength, stood without assistance, and glared icicles of her own.

"What is that?" The goddess stepped away from her loom.

"There is no Deathlord, is there? Karlath-Fayd does not exist, no more than the gods and goddesses of the Seventh Circle!" Miradel said quietly. "All of that is pretended. There is only you, and this game you have us play."

"Do not trifle with me. I have moved armies across chasms, even between worlds. I could crush you with a wave of my hand." She sneered contemptuously. "What might seem like a game to you is truth, reality, to me."

"Me, trifle with you? Don't be ridiculous—it is you who trifle with *us!*" snapped Miradel. She stood on her own, strong and steady now, and took a step forward, gesturing for Natac to come with her. She pointed to the threads, coming off the loom. "You think that is all fates, all futures, all pasts?" she asked him.

"It is the Tapestry of the Worldweaver," he said, puzzled.

"It is merely a vain woman's toy," retorted the druid. "I want you to cut it, cut it off right now!"

"REGILLIX Avatar must have made it home!" Tamarwind exclaimed. "Those aren't harpies—they're dragons!"

"I know," Juliay said in a strangely peaceful tone. "Aren't they the most beautiful things you've ever seen?"

The dragons filled the sky with wings and fire. They came from the direction that was neither metal nor wood. Diving with meteoric velocity, the wyrms swept across the top of the ghost warriors, belching massive clouds of flame, slaying with talon and fang. The serpents soared in their hundreds, maybe a thousand or more of them, spreading across the sky to span the whole of the ghost warriors' horde. They ranged in colors from indigo so deep it was almost black to pale pastels of peach and green, shades varying even upon the same dragon, underbellies always darker than backs.

They swooped and cavorted. The smaller serpents were nimble and quick, often circling and looping about the greater wyrms or racing low to puff orange fireballs, blossoms of flame that seared a dozen or a score of the attackers. They flew onward, driving their slender pinions, quickly soaring aloft again.

The greater wyrms were true lords of the battlefield. One dragon of emerald green, nearly as big as Regillix himself, landed in the midst of a throng of ghost warriors, incinerating a hundred with a massive exhalation of oily flame. The two broad wings came down, crushing more of the invaders, and as the serpent leaped into the air it raked another dozen with its trailing claws. More dragons swarmed along the length of the wall, and everywhere the attackers fell back, off the rampart and down through the gore-filled ditch.

The soldiers of Nayve emerged from their hiding places or ceased their panic-stricken flight. They whooped and cheered from the slopes and the crests of the Ringhills. Jubal and Juliay embraced, while Tamarwind shouted himself hoarse in exultation.

One giant serpent broke from the fight and winged closer. Tam quickly recognized Regillix Avatar as the lordly wyrm came to rest on the nearby hillside. He looked smug, curling up like a cat and grinning at Tamarwind and the others like a contented crocodile.

"I missed this place," he allowed. "Did you know that there is no beef in all of Arcati? And I learned that I have developed quite a taste for cattle flesh."

"Welcome back!" cried Tamarwind. "We're rather glad to see you."

"Everyone, except perhaps the cows," Jubal allowed. "But we're grateful for your epic flight, Lord Dragon, and for a very timely return."

"The climb almost killed me," Regillix admitted, scowling at the unpleasant memory. "But my people understood the danger. As you can see, they were more than willing to help. And we had no difficulty riding the Worldfall back to Nayve—the same route that carried me some fifty years ago."

"Our last line had broken," Tam acknowledged. "We faced certain defeat—until we saw you."

"Elves of Nayve! Trolls and gnomes—men and women of all peoples!" Jubal shouted, waving his sword over his head, calling the routed defenders down from the heights. They came from every gulley and rise on the foreslope of the hills, still whooping, newly energized by the appearance of the dragons. They swarmed in small groups at first, quickly assembled into companies and regiments, charging to reclaim the wall that the ghost warriors had already abandoned to the dragons.

Tamarwind, grinning, charged down the hill with his elves, but not before he made a silent pledge to return to Belynda as soon as he could get away from here.

"GET away from that!" snapped the Goddess Worldweaver, her face blanching. "You don't understand what you're doing!"

"Perhaps not, but at last I understand *you*," replied Miradel. She kept her eyes on the immortal woman as she gestured to Natac. "Cut it—cut the threads!"

"No!" The Worldweaver shrieked her command. She raised her hand, palm outward. "Impudent humans—I gave you life on Nayve, and I can take that life away!" Her face distorted into something unrecognizeable, an image of unrestrained fury and immortal power.

The ground heaved, and Miradel fell. A great section of arch swayed, granite cracking, loose rubble plummeting downward. Cracks rippled through the smooth marble floor, and more debris spattered from the damaged ceiling. Even amid the chaos Natac noticed that the surface under the loom and the walls where the Tapestry was strung remained intact. In that instant he knew that Miradel was right—and that her idea was their only chance.

Sword drawn, the Tlaxcalan lunged to obey the druid's command but was forced back from the Tapestry when a great slab of marble smashed onto the floor before him. Pieces flew through the air, scratching his face, sending him staggering to one knee. Resolutely he stood again, planting his feet and bending his knees, trying to keep his balance.

A storm of wind arose, sending stinging shards into their eyes, against their skin. Despite his exertion, the warrior was pushed farther back. Karkald made a rush for the loom, but a gale of air curled into a fist and smashed him all the way to the door of the chamber. Natac stumbled to his knees, then rose up again, lunging to take Miradel's arm as she nearly tumbled into a widening crack in the floor.

All of them were shoved inexorably toward the door, Belynda flying like a rag doll after Karkald, while Natac clutched Miradel's hand as they staggered along like tumbleweeds in a whirlwind. In another instant they, too, were bashed against the door, which flew open and sent them sprawling on the floor in the anteroom.

The acolytes had fled, but the goddess was not going to give those who had offended her that luxury. She stalked through the door after them, stood like an avenging beast over their sprawled bodies. She seemed to have grown—or else the humans were shrinking. Natac sensed that she had withheld her true power in the sanctum, undoubtedly because she did not want to risk her treasured fabric. Now she was outside of that room, with the iron doors of the Rockshaft forming a dark barrier behind her as she raised her hands for a final, lethal blast.

The explosion came in a cloud of dust and smoke. Natac choked, surprised that he was still alive—and astonished to see that the goddess had been smashed forward to lie on her face. The heavy iron door of the Rockshaft had been blasted from its hinges, falling forward to stun and trap her. She groaned, pushed upward, and a ton of metal wobbled on her back and shoulders.

"She's down—go—cut the threads!" cried Miradel, slapping Natac on the shoulder. "It's our only chance."

In that instant Natac sprinted forward, through the door into the inner sanctum, racing forward and chopping in the same motion. He brought his keen blade through the colorful fabric as it spun off the loom. The Tapestry sliced away with no more resistance than he might have gotten from a spiderweb.

"No!" screamed the goddess, pushing mightily, rising upward to shuck away the heavy iron slab. "You have doomed this perfect place!"

She groped her way back to the loom. The World-weaver sobbed as she clutched at the trailing threads, which already seemed to be evaporating. Natac stood behind her with his sword raised, but he held his blow, not yet ready to strike her with the weapon. No longer did she terrorize or awe him. Instead, he felt numb and strangely regretful.

But the damage had already been done. They felt the rumbling through the soles of their feet, saw it in the cracks that appeared in the marble floor, gaps that twisted and snaked up the walls. The goddess collapsed, sobbing, taking the broken strands in her fingers as if she would tie them all together again. The Tapestry whirled off the wall, torn like it had been blown apart by a cyclone, trailing threads lashing through the air with whipcrack force.

Karkald pushed through the wreckage of the mouth of the Rockshaft, where smoke billowed out the gaping doorway. Something was there, a blunt object emitting sulfurous smoke. It was that object, Natac realized, that had blasted off the long-sealed doors over the shaft.

A crack appeared in the shell of the mysterious missile, a door opening to reveal a small compartment. A figure moved there, a stout dwarfwoman struggling out of restraining straps. Coughing and limping, she lifted herself free and stumbled into the anteroom.

"Darann? Is that you?" Karkald stammered in disbelief.

"Karkald!" It was the dwarfmaid, shaken and covered

with soot, rushing toward her husband. With a sob he collected his wife in his arms. "I knew I would find you here! I *knew* it!" she cried.

"Run!" urged Miradel, standing over the loom and the Worldweaver, gesturing toward the door.

"Come with me!" Natac demanded. The druid looked at the Worldweaver, anguish etched upon her face, and then she turned and raced beside the warrior toward the lofty door leading to the exterior garden. They ran into sunlight and clean air, kept running until they had to pause and gasp for breath.

"Look," Miradel said, her voice hushed.

The Worldweaver's Loom glowed like a magical light. Sparks rained downward from the tall shape, and electrical bolts of power blasted into the sky like lightning generated from this massive metal pole. Thunder crackled, nearly crushing their eardrums, and the scent of ozone was acrid in the air. The ground heaved and buckled underfoot, while the waters in the lake and the lagoon churned and frothed. The air was strangely still in the midst of this chaos, as if the world of Nayve held its breath.

"It's going to fall," whispered Natac.

And then, slowly, the silver spire of the Goddess Worldweaver began to sway. All of them ran again, as fast as they could, panic lending wings until they were far away across the parkland. Here they turned to watch in horror and awe. The lofty tower toppled slowly at first, leaning, then plunging, breaking apart in the air to slam downward, splintering into an explosion of light, casting sparks toward the sky in an explosion of blue magic.

HE had fought from Flanders to the Metal Coast, battled across the Swansleep River and marched over the dusty

plains of Nayve. He had assaulted the palisade at the
Ringhills, wounded again, but he had prevailed as, once
more, the attack carried the enemy away before him.
He even survived the aerial onslaught of the dragons, like
his fellows feeling no fear as the monstrous serpents
soared overhead, spewing fire and rending with their
mighty claws.

He was grievously tired yet compelled to advance. He
knew that there was another battle before him, another
war after that. . . . He had to go on. For this was his existence, his life, his being.

Until there was an explosion, a wave of blue magic
that penetrated to his core. And in that instant he was re-
leased, became lighter than air, rising away from Nayve,
from everywhere. . . . He was by himself, and he was one
with everything.

He was free.

"How did you know . . . about the goddess, and the Tapestry?" Natac asked, surveying the damage wrought by
the falling spire. It had taken out much of the temple garden, with the top splashing down in the sacred lagoon.
Shards of metal jutted upward like silver eggshells, jar-
ringly delicate and fragile now that the power of the goddess had dissipated.

"When I saw that Karlath-Fayd was nothing at all, no
more than a pair of fiery slits in the bedrock of the Fifth
Circle, I saw the truth," Miradel replied. "There was no
deity but the Goddess Worldweaver, and so all of this—
the wars, the dying, the destruction—these were things
she spun on her loom, simply to keep herself amused. As
she grew more and more bored, her wars became more
and more violent and destructive."

"*She* caused the war?" Natac asked in astonishment.

"Mustered the ghost warriors, brought the Delvers from the First Circle, created the Worldfall? That was the Worldweaver's doing?"

"Yes. And with her passing, so go the ghost warriors . . . and the magic that fueled our power and theirs. I can sense it already. Nayve is mundane now, like the Earth."

"But why did she do this? Bring such pain and devastation?"

"I think . . . I think she was simply bored. And I see that we meant nothing to her, nothing at all. All of us—humans, elves, dwarves, trolls—we were simply game pieces that she moved about the Six Circles."

"And our world . . . the Seventh?" wondered Natac.

"Perhaps she was inspired by the wars of Earth; I don't know. I feel certain life will go on there, the normal cycle of birth and death. Our world was never magical, you remember, so it will not heed the passing of magic from Nayve or anywhere else. But outside of the Seventh Circle, the villainy in the cosmos was her own."

"But cutting the Tapestry . . . that broke her power? And you knew this?"

"Well," the druid admitted, "that was a lucky guess."

Darann and Karkald were nearby, probing through the wreckage of the loom. They hadn't ceased holding hands since they had emerged from the doomed temple. Stopping only for a long embrace, they ambled serenely on.

"There's a story," Natac said with a dry laugh, smiling at the dwarven couple. "I can't wait to talk to Darann."

He and Miradel, holding hands themselves, started over to their old friends.

"It'll take some digging," Karkald was explaining, "but we'll get the upper end of the Rockshaft opened again. This Worldlift that Donnwell Earnwise created—it really worked! Rocket power, traveling between worlds!

We'll get the bugs out, and then people can go back and forth between the First and Fourth Circles again!"

"More than that, we can do what we please on these and the other worlds," Miradel declared. "There will be no more barriers of magic, not blue nor any other color. Nothing beyond the constraints of our own hearts. . . ."

Epilogue

Threads unraveling,
Currents rise in gentle hands.
All souls are free now.

Epilogue to the Tapestry of the Worldweaver
History of Time

The passing of magic from Nayve and the rest of the Six Circles was lamented by some, unnoticed by most. The most dramatic effect was geographic: the Worldfall ceased its destructive spill, and normalcy was returned to the Fourth Circle in the direction that was neither metal nor wood. The Worldsea remained placid, rich with fish, swept by squalls known more for their exotic beauty than for the danger they presented. Rain nourished the fields, crops flourished, and the trees of the forests continued to grow tall and strong.

In Circle at Center and other cities the loss of arcane power had numerous effects on the populace, causing changes but not disasters. Wind and rain became functions of nature, not druidic will. Transportation became a matter of energy expended, assisted by technology, not teleportation. Druids and the elven sages, no longer spell casters, found other useful pursuits. Sailboats moved under the power of real wind, and artisans mimicked the skills they had learned in centuries past. Progress would continue, but it was progress born of Nayve, not copied from Earth.

Regillix Avatar elected to remain in Nayve, along with many of the dragons who had descended the Worldfall. They lived in the mountains and the Ringhills at first, but eventually most of the dragons settled into caves and niches in the walls of Riven Deep. The dark dwarves and their iron golems remained in the Fourth Circle as well, and they presented a danger. But they fell back from the Ringhills and, in the end, made homes for themselves in the limestone caves near the feet of the Lodespike Range. There, carefully watched by giants and gnomes, they withdrew from the hateful sun.

A delegation of Seer dwarves arrived in the capital city and set to work perfecting the Worldlift; soon travel and trade would again be commonplace between the First and Fourth Circles.

The newest residents of Circle at Center were the royal couple from the New Forest, King Awfulbark and his wife, Queen Roodcleaver. They settled into a great manor house and became legendary for their banquets and feasts, galas they would hold upon the slightest excuse. Natac, Tamarwind, and the other heroes of the wars were regular guests at these fetes, while Awfulbark became well-known for the generosity of his heart and the plentitude of his spirits.

Upon the home world of humans, the goddess passed without notice. Men would continue to destroy each other, with no influence from any god required. But the souls of those who died were, at least, liberated by that death, no longer subject to the whim of a bored and willfull goddess.

The humans who dwelled upon Nayve would stay there. Crazy Horse was delighted to discover that there were great herds of buffalo dwelling in the deeper valleys of the Ringhills. With Janitha at his side, he set about to explore this new world in peace. They hunted and slept and made love where they wanted to, under a sky of eternal summer. Jubal and Juliay settled upon the Metal Coast, where together they collaborated upon a series of histories, endeavoring to record the tales of the Goddess Wars.

If, with the passing of magic, natural death became more commonplace on the Fourth Circle, this new reality was balanced by another: a great increase in the children born to elves, trolls, and all the denizens of Nayve. For the first time on Nayve, the humans who had come here procreated. One of the first of these new lives was a daughter born to Miradel and Natac barely a year after the Loomfall.

Tamarwind and Belynda remained in Circle at Center long enough to hold the baby and to congratulate the two lovers and their child as they settled into their home on the villa above the lake. Then the two elves went away together, supposedly on a journey back home to Argentian—though, nearly ninety years later, they still have not arrived.

The Seven Circles trilogy by
Douglas Niles

CIRCLE AT CENTER
In the realm of the Seven Circles,
a peaceful era is about to end as members of
the various races ban together to incite war.
To protect the land, the Druids decide to recruit
warriors from a world where war is a way
of life—a world called Earth.

❏ 0-441-00960-3

WORLD FALL
All creatures in the realm of the Seven Circles have
always lived in harmony within their own
spheres—until the face of evil forces a
druid princess to defend the peace...with an army.

❏ 0-441-00998-0

Available wherever books are sold or
to order call 1-800-788-6262

B036

Hugo and Nebula Award-winning author of
The Left Hand of Darkness

Ursula K. Le Guin

THE TELLING

Once a culturally rich world, the planet Aka has been utterly
transformed by technology. But an official observer from
Earth named Sutty has learned of a group of outcasts who
live in the wilderness. They still believe in the ancient ways
and still practice its lost religion—The Telling.

0-441-00863-1

Also from Le Guin:

TALES OF EARTHSEA   0-441-01124-1

THE OTHER WIND   0-441-01125-X

THE LEFT HAND OF DARKNESS
                           0-441-47812-3

Available wherever books are sold or
to order call: 1-800-788-6262

B946

From national bestselling author

Patricia Briggs

DRAGON BONES

0-441-00916-6

Ward of Hurog has tried all his life to convince
people he is just a simple, harmless fool...And it's
worked. But now, to regain his kingdom, he must
ride into war—and convince them otherwise.

DRAGON BLOOD

0-441-01008-3

Ward, ruler of Hurog, joins the rebels against
the tyrannical High King Jakoven. But Jakoven
has a secret weapon. One that requires
dragon's blood—the very blood that courses
through Ward's veins.

Available wherever books are sold or
to order call 1-800-788-6262

B054

THE ULTIMATE IN
SCIENCE FICTION AND FANTASY!

From magical tales of distant worlds to stories of
technological advances beyond the grasp of man, Penguin has
everything you need to stretch your imagination to its limits.
Sign up for monthly in-box delivery of
one of three newsletters at

www.penguin.com
Ace

Get the latest information on favorites like
William Gibson, T.A. Barron, Brian Jacques,
Ursula Le Guin, Sharon Shinn, and
Charlaine Harris, as well as updates on the
best new authors.

Roc

Escape with Harry Turtledove, Anne Bishop, S.M.
Stirling, Simon Green, Chris Bunch, and many
others—plus news on the latest and hottest
in science fiction and fantasy.

DAW

Mercedes Lackey, Kristen Britain, Tanya Huff,
Tad Williams, C.J. Cherryh, and many more—
DAW has something to satisfy the cravings of any
science fiction and fantasy lover.
Also visit www.dawbooks.com

*Sign up, and have the best of science fiction and
fantasy at your fingertips!*

b133

Penguin Group (USA) Inc.
Online

Your Internet gateway to a virtual environment with
hundreds of entertaining and enlightening books
from Penguin Group (USA) Inc.

*While you're there, get the latest buzz on
the best authors and books around—*

Tom Clancy, Patricia Cornwell, W.E.B. Griffin,
Nora Roberts, William Gibson, Robin Cook,
Brian Jacques, Catherine Coulter, Stephen King,
Ken Follett, Terry McMillan, and many more!

**Penguin Group (USA) Inc. Online is located at
http://www.penguin.com**

PENGUIN GROUP (USA) Inc.
NEWS

Every month you'll get an inside look at our upcom-
ing books and new features on our site. This is an
ongoing effort to provide you with the most
up-to-date information about
our books and authors.

**Subscribe to Penguin Group (USA) Inc. News at
http://www.penguin.com/newsletters**